THE GOSSIP OF AN EARL

LINDA RAE SANDE

Twisted Teacup
PUBLISHING

The Gossip of an Earl

ISBN: 978-0-9964433-8-8

Library of Congress Control Number: 2016915984

Linda Rae Sande, Cody, WY

PRINTED IN THE UNITED STATES OF AMERICA

To my editor, Katrina Teele Fair, and my proofreader, Sarah Lipinski, for all the help and encouragement

ALSO BY LINDA RAE SANDE

The Daughters of the Aristocracy

The Kiss of a Viscount

The Grace of a Duke

The Seduction of an Earl

The Sons of the Aristocracy

Tuesday Nights

The Widowed Countess

My Fair Groom

The Sisters of the Aristocracy

The Story of a Baron

The Passion of a Marquess

The Desire of a Lady

The Brothers of the Aristocracy

The Love of a Rake

The Caress of a Commander

The Epiphany of an Explorer

The Widows of the Aristocracy

The Gossip of an Earl

The Enigma of a Widow

The Secrets of a Viscount

The Widowers of the Aristocracy

The Dream of a Duchess

The Vision of a Viscountess

The Conundrum of a Clerk

The Charity of a Viscount

The Cousins of the Aristocracy

PROLOGUE

*D*ear Readers, I hardly know where to start in this retrospective, the last issue of The Tattler under our editorship. Next week, you shall be learning the latest on-dit from someone else, although I assure you that you will be left in good hands (or good ears). You asked how it was possible a nearly thirty-year-old earl ended up betrothed to a younger daughter of the ton in the course of only two days. Truth be told, the courtship lasted two full months. Yes, dear readers, I am guilty of having withheld information from you. In the interest of full disclosure, here is where our tale begins. Do pay attention to the dates. ~ The lead story in the May 14, 1818 issue of The Tattler.

*F*riday, March 13, 1818 in Lord Weatherstone's gardens
A man's lips weren't so very different from a woman's, Lady Emelia Comber decided as she glanced in the direction of the nattily dressed gentleman having a word with her mother. Maybe not as pink, of course, but still much like a set of miniature pillows stacked atop one another. From beneath her parasol, she allowed her gaze to sweep over the crush of attendees lest the man take notice of her taking notice of him. And his lips.

Her mother's laughter had her attention returning to the man. He had obviously said something witty, for Patience Fitzsimmons Comber, Countess of Aimsley, rarely laughed.

Tittered sometimes. Giggled on occasion. But she rarely *laughed*.

Emelia was about to wander in the direction of the refreshment table—not a single footman had walked by whilst she stood waiting for her mother to finish her conversation with... she frowned. She didn't even recognize the man with the perfect pillowed lips. The dark blonde hair worn just a bit longer than her brother, Alistair, wore his. The eyes so blue, they seemed to pin her into place that one fraction of a second he caught her staring at him. A straight nose that had never been caught unawares by a fist or a feisty horse. A relaxed stance making him appear so at ease in this mass of aristocrats and their families, he may as well have been the host of the soirée.

As to how old he was, Emelia had no idea. From one perspective, he appeared about the same age as her brothers—mid-to-late twenties, perhaps—but when he laughed along with her mother, the creases on either side of eyes and mouth had her wondering if he were ten years older.

Who is he? she wondered at the very moment a footman stopped beside her carrying a tray of champagne in tall flutes.

"Pardon me," she whispered as she took a glass from his tray. "Would you know who the man is with Lady Aimsley?"

The footman surveyed the crowd, as if he were scoping out where he would next take his tray of bubbly. "Lord Fennington, my lady," he whispered hoarsely, his gaze continuing past the man in question.

Bless his heart, Emelia thought as she gave the footman a nod of thanks.

"An earl, if I remember correctly. Unmarried and quite vocal in this session of Parliament. Inherited the earldom from his father not quite five years ago. He will be thirty on his next birthday."

Emelia's eyes widened. Goodness! Were all the Weatherstone footmen this well-versed in the peerage? Before she could reply, the servant was off to offer champagne to a nearby couple.

Well, an earl minted in the last five years would certainly explain why she didn't recognize him. She had been in finishing school in Switzerland until just a few weeks ago. Given her travels back to England had included several stops along the way, she had only been back in Aimsley House a few days.

The Weatherstones' garden party, an early Season event designed to show off the lord's spring plants, was a favorite of the women who lived in London year-round. The fact that there were so many men in attendance was a reminder that, other than the theatre and Parliament, which had convened in late January, there were few diversions in London this time of the year.

In the middle of a sip of her champagne, Emelia blinked when her mother turned and waved in her direction, a gloved hand indicating she should join her and the man.

Almost unable to swallow, Emelia blinked. *The very worst thing a recent returnee to London can do is to attend a garden party*, she thought. She hardly recognized anyone. Despite having lived in Switzerland for the past four years—or perhaps because of it— she was shy. She wasn't about to simply introduce herself to the younger ladies she might have at one time played with in Grosvenor Square or Hyde Park, or even attended school with the one year she did so in London. And now her mother was insisting she be introduced to Lord Fennington and his gorgeous lips and blue, blue eyes and wavy blonde hair, and his straight, never-been-broken nose.

Taking a deep breath and then swallowing the rest of her champagne in a single gulp, she left the glass on the edge of a footman's tray and made her way to Lady Aimsley's side. She gave the man a deep curtsy. Now was not the time to wonder if her yellow sprigged muslin gown with its contrasting pelisse and parasol were appropriate for such an affair. The ensemble had been fashioned by a modiste in Geneva, but the pattern differed from most of the gowns on display on the bright green lawn behind Lord Weatherstone's mansion.

"Lord Fennington, I'd like you to meet my only daughter, Lady Emelia," the countess said by way of introduction. "She's been on the Continent for finishing school these last few years, and is most talented at drawing portraits," she added when her attention was caught by another woman. "Would you please excuse me? Lady Torrington has just arrived, and I haven't seen her in an age."

Felix Turnbridge, Earl of Fennington, gave a quick glance in the direction of the Countess of Torrington. "Of course. Do give her my regards, won't you?" he replied before turning his attention to Emelia. The way the countess rushed off only a moment after calling her daughter over to join them would have any witnesses to their conversation thinking she had engineered a meeting for her daughter with the unmarried earl.

Nothing could be further from the truth.

Felix had asked for the introduction. Indeed, he had nearly begged the Countess of Aimsley for an opportunity to meet her daughter. From the moment he had spotted the young lady emerge from the back door of Lord Weatherstone's ballroom at her mother's side, he had been intrigued.

The clothes she wore were different from those worn by the other young ladies in attendance, but they were perfect. Her tiny bonnet—almost a hat—allowed her entire face to show and displayed her blonde, coiffed hair to its best advantage. The manner in which she held herself had him realizing she hadn't been in London very long. Not with her shoulders pulled back as they were, making her appear confident despite her shorter stature—not all slouchy like so many of the other young women preferred to stand—and that erect posture permitted her perfect figure to show to his benefit.

She wasn't anything like the other young women who flitted about the grounds, garbed in white and wearing bonnets with brims so deep, their profiles were completely hidden. "Hullo. It's very good to meet you, my lady," he said with a deep bow. He took her gloved hand and kissed the back of it.

"And you, my lord," she replied with a deep curtsy. *Goodness!* If Emelia thought he was handsome from over ten feet away, she had no idea what word to use to describe just how gorgeous he was up close!

"Fennington, please," he stated. "I was good friends with your older brother, Adam, back when we were at Eton," he added, noting how her expression changed when he mentioned Viscount Breckinridge, the future Earl of Aimsley. *Probably figuring out how old I am*, he thought, hoping she wouldn't err on the high side. Most people thought him much older than he was, a situation he found he could do nothing about.

Emelia angled her head. "Would I have had the pleasure of meeting you in the past, then?" she asked, quite sure she didn't recognize the earl. No wonder the man had her mother laughing, though. He was probably regaling her with tales of Adam's antics whilst at school. Although, when she gave it more thought, her mother might have been left weeping at hearing some of the things her oldest brother had done whilst at Eton.

Adam hadn't been the best behaved son of an aristocrat.

Felix shook his head. "Unfortunately not. Breckinridge and I didn't become acquainted until we met at Eton," he replied.

"Oh, of course," Emelia managed, desperately wondering what to ask next. Given her shyness, keeping up her end of a conversation was a challenge. *Who. What. Where...* "Do you live in London year-round?"

Rather surprised at the unusual question—young ladies usually commented on the weather—Felix nodded. "I do. And will you be staying in London now that you've finished school?"

Angling her head to one side, Emelia regarded him as she felt a warmth creep up her neck. At any moment, her cheeks would bloom bright pink, but she couldn't help the excitement that seemed to skitter through her entire body at the thought the earl would be the least bit interested in where she ended up living. "I will, yes," she replied. And then she realized the conversation ball was back in her court. Well, horses were always a safe subject when it came to men, she thought. "Do you keep a favorite breed of horse here in town? Or perhaps I should ask if you even ride."

Felix knew at that moment Emelia Comber was special. Not just because she was pretty or had a pleasant figure or because she drew portraits or because she seemed interesting. Before this very moment, no other woman had ever asked if he preferred a specific breed of horse!

"I own a Percheron. She's not too large, and she handles well in the traffic," he replied before finishing off his champagne. "Would you care to join me on a stroll?" he asked as he held out an arm. "I am of a mind to walk for a bit."

Rather surprised at the invitation, Emelia allowed a nervous grin as she gave a quick glance in the direction of where her mother was engaged in conversation with a group of older matrons. "I would. It's very kind of you to offer, especially since I've never been in these gardens before." She placed her hand on his arm and set her pace to match his, hoping he didn't think she was babbling.

"Your mother tells me you've been on the Continent. Did I understand her correctly? Geneva?" Felix questioned as he waved to another man in the crowd.

"Indeed. I was there for four years," she managed, thinking her cheeks must have bloomed an even brighter pink when she realized her mother had been telling the man about her. "I was not the only Londoner, however. I lived in the home of Mr. Burroughs. He's an expatriate—a banker—and he was my protector during my stay. I shared a room with his daughter, you see." *Now, I'm babbling.*

"After Geneva, I do hope you're not finding London too boring."

Stunned at the comment, Emelia nearly stopped in her tracks, and then had to when the earl paused to capture two glasses of champagne from the same footman who had spoken with her just moments ago.

Struggling to avert her eyes from the footman's quick glance in her direction—she was sure his eyebrows were waggling—Emelia thanked Fennington. "I've always found London diverting," she replied before taking a sip of the champagne. Did the man know she had already downed a glass not five minutes ago? At any moment, her knees would begin buzzing. "And finishing school in Geneva is not nearly as diverting as it may sound."

Felix led her to the edge of one of the gardens, the new shoots of greenery already leafing out and budding to display an array of what would one day be daisies. "Pray tell, why there, and not finishing school in London?" he asked as they continued around a row of short shrubs that led to another garden behind a hedgerow.

"Oh, I was at Warwick's for a year," she countered with a nod. "But... I did not care for it."

Surprised by the comment, Felix paused and regarded her for a moment. "The school? Or a particular teacher?"

Emelia visibly stiffened. "I'd really rather not say. That is, if you don't mind terribly, my lord. My discomfort had nothing to do with the school. Many of my friends attended Warwick's, and they liked it just fine. It just wasn't right... for me." She sighed inwardly, wishing she had never put voice to her opinion.

One of Felix's brows furrowed as he realized he had touched on a rather touchy subject with the young lady. He had given her the perfect opportunity to put voice to her complaint, though, and yet she hadn't.

How refreshing, he thought.

Faith! Was he really so jaded as to expect every young woman capable of voicing displeasure or complaints or... *gossip* when invited to do so?

Well, yes, actually.

He supposed he had to suffer it, given his avocation. And

given his avocation, her comments now had his curiosity piqued. If it wasn't the school Lady Emelia found objectionable, then perhaps one of the instructors had been guilty of something that had her fleeing to Europe. Guilty of some wrong-doing.

Had there been inappropriate advances, perhaps?

The idea of a rake taking advantage of the young lady raised his hackles. He had been friends with the older Comber boy whilst they were at Eton. Given neither of Emelia's brothers would have been in London at the time she attended Warwick's —both Adam and Alistair were in university at the time—meant her father would have been the only one to defend her honor. Did Mark Comber learn of the issue, though? Or had his countess simply seen to moving her daughter out of London and to her favorite school in Switzerland? The woman had spent some of her own youth in Geneva, and had probably attended the same finishing school.

Felix made a mental note to look into who had been employed by Warwick's five years ago. An exposé on the school or one of its employees might have appeared in the paper.

In the meantime, Emelia had knelt down to cradle a daffodil in one gloved hand, her nose barely touching the white and yellow petals as her parasol listed off to the side. Felix didn't know if it was the way the sun lit her face just then, or the expression she displayed, or how her long lashes rested on the tops of her cheekbones, but he was transfixed.

Emelia Comber was truly pretty. Delicate, like the flower she held. A bit shy. Probably didn't have a mean bone in her body.

How positively refreshing.

"It's so lovely," she murmured.

"As are you," Felix responded, the words out of his mouth before he could censor them.

Her eyes widening at his compliment, Emelia slowly stood up. There was a moment where her eyes took in his lips and then had to be torn away to look into his eyes. "It's awfully kind of you to say, my..."

"Fennington," he murmured, interrupting her. Before she could respond, his lips lowered, their soft pillows searching to rest against hers. At the moment they touched, a most pleasant buzzing settled into his head and knees.

He wasn't about to blame it on the champagne. Nor give it any undue credit.

Emboldened when she didn't pull away, he dared to use the tip of his tongue to split her lips apart. When her mouth opened, he captured her lips with his own and continued the kiss.

Jesus! She should have slapped him. She should have pushed him away. She should have screamed bloody murder, but he was ever so thankful she did not.

How long had it been since he had tasted a woman's lips? How long since he had enjoyed the feel of a woman in his arms? For a moment, he couldn't recall ever having kissed a woman quite like this.

Certainly not the mistress he had employed before he realized he could no longer afford such a luxury. With her, kissing on the lips had been verboten.

Certainly not the barmaid in Oxford who offered herself every time he visited his favorite pub during his years at university. She had only wanted a quick tumble and the payment to go with it, though.

Emelia's sudden inhalation of breath brought him back to the present. He let go his hold on her lips, but just barely. Just enough to allow her a moment to put voice to a complaint, to a protest, or hopefully, to a plea for him to continue. When she made no sound at all—indeed, he felt her entire body nearly fall against the front of his—he resumed the kiss, his lips molding to her open mouth, suckling her lower lip before taking her mouth again and again in a kiss that was as tender as it was possessive.

He claimed her then. There could be no other word to describe how one hand moved to grip her shoulder while the other wrapped around the back of her waist, pulling her hard against him. His tongue delved into her mouth. She tasted of champagne and sweet berries. She smelled of honeysuckle. She felt luscious beneath his hands. She was everything he had ever wanted in a woman, and he could do nothing but imagine what life might be like with her at breakfast every morning, with her at tea and during dinner, with her in the library for walnuts and coffee. With her in his bed every night, round with his child...

Felix blinked, rather heartened to find Emelia's lashes still covering her eyes. When he finally pulled away, he left his forehead pressed against hers. "I know I should apologize, but I find I..."

"Do not," Emelia whispered quickly, her breathing labored, her eyes squeezed shut.

Felix stilled himself, reluctantly removing his hands from her body when he was sure she could stand of her own volition. "Please, do not think me a rake, for I have never done anything like this before," he murmured, his lips barely touching her forehead.

"Of course not," Emelia replied, her eyes still shut. "It was all my fault, of course."

Felix frowned, wondering at her words. He lifted her chin with one finger. "It is not, my lady. It simply... happened. I do not believe the heavens or the earth could have prevented it."

Nor will they in the future, if I have anything to say about it.

Emelia's eyes opened then, their irises blooming with bright green as her pupils became pinpoints. "I could have," she whispered. "I should have."

Giving his head a quick shake, Felix kissed her again, a soft, tender kiss that lasted but a moment. When he finally pulled away, he allowed an audible sigh. "If I do not return you to your mother this very moment, I shall have to take you to Scotland," he whispered hoarsely.

Not quite sure what he meant, Emelia nodded. Her mind was a swirl of thoughts, none of them coherent. "Of course," she managed to say, a wan smile finally appearing. "Lead the way."

Feeling a profound sense of disappointment, Felix Turnbridge finally offered his arm and led them around the end of the hedgerow and back to a cluster of women which included her mother. He kissed the back of her gloved hand and made sure to hold on just a second longer than was necessary.

"I look forward to when next we meet," he murmured, relieved when she finally made eye contact.

"As do I," she said as she curtsied.

Within moments, Emelia was in the company of the Countess of Aimsley, and Felix was on his horse in the drive in front of the mansion.

His mind a whirl of plots and plans, Felix considered what to do next. Had anyone seen them kissing in the gardens, Emelia would be ruined. He would be forced to offer for her hand, a situation he realized he wouldn't mind in the least.

He could only hope she would accept.

CHAPTER 1
ASKING PERMISSION TO
MARRY GOES AWRY

las, dear Reader, if you have ever found yourself in the throes of Cupid's cruel trick, you will know the agony that must be endured. But you must not feel the least bit of sympathy for us. We were foolish in love and worse for we had never learned not to mix business with pleasure. ~ The editor's final story in the May 14, 1818 issue of *The Tattler.*

arch 13, 1818, Aimsley House study in Park Lane
"You wish to *what?*"

Mark Comber, Earl of Aimsley, had barely leaned back in his dark leather chair when he pitched forward and regarded his visitor with surprise.

"I wish to marry your daughter."

The older earl waved the other earl into the chair across from his desk. "Since when?" The two words were filled with suspicion, as if Aimsley couldn't decide if Felix Turnbridge was playing a trick on him, or if the man was serious. He had been good friends with Aimsley's oldest son, and heaven knew Adam was a troublemaker if there ever was one.

Felix inhaled slowly and wondered how much to admit. He

pulled his chronometer from his waistcoat pocket and gave it a glance before replying, "Fifteen... make that sixteen minutes ago."

Aimsley House was only a few doors down from the Weatherstone mansion, after all.

Aimsley slowly leaned back in his chair, never allowing his stare to leave the Earl of Fennington. "And just what happened sixteen minutes ago?"

Exhaling the breath he'd been holding, Felix decided honesty was best. What's the worst that could happen? It's not as if Aimsley could deny him. "I kissed Lady Emelia. During the garden party at Lord Weatherstone's mansion."

Waving a dismissive hand, Aimsley made a dismissive sound. "Is that all? Jesus, Fenn, you had me thinking you claimed her virtue," he complained. "Don't be thinking you have to offer for her hand over a..." He paused as his eyes widened. "You haven't proposed to her already, have you?"

Felix frowned. "Of course not," he said. "I wanted your permission first."

Aimsley seemed to give off an air of relief. "Well, don't fash yourself. I'm not going to hold a peck against you, especially one that took place in Weatherstone's gardens."

Narrowing his eyes, Felix wondered at the man's unexpected response. In fact, Mark Comber's cavalier attitude about his daughter—his only daughter—being kissed—in public, no less— had Felix feeling a hint of anger just then. "It wasn't just a *peck*, Aimsley! I kissed her. Several times. *Thoroughly*," he added, rather proud of how he was owning up to his unexpected rakish behavior.

After all, he chided others for the very same. Publicly, although not in his own name. Wrote damning articles and published them on a weekly basis. The earnings from his avocation were the very reason he could now afford to take a wife.

Aimsley leaned back in his chair and lifted one booted foot

onto the edge of his desk and then crossed the other over it. His hands clasped in his lap, the earl appeared as relaxed as any wealthy man with nothing better to do. "Hmm," he murmured. "Just like that, you kissed her?"

Felix sighed. "Yes."

"Without provocation?"

"Well, none from her, of course." When Aimsley aimed a frown in his direction—*finally!*—Felix added, "She was... regarding a daffodil at the time, holding it in her gloved hand..." He pantomimed the gesture as he spoke. "And she sniffed it, and I was..." *Overcome*, he almost said. "Bewitched," he finished, one brow cocking up, as if he dared the other earl to counter his claim.

Rolling his eyes, Aimsley twiddled his thumbs for a moment. He glanced out the window behind his desk. He sighed. "All right. Here's what we're going to do. You're going to court my daughter. Properly. Take her for rides in the park— with a chaperone—have tea with her, take her to the museum. Dance with her at balls. All that rot."

"Agreed," Felix replied quickly, about to say more when one of Aimsley's hands lifted as if to cut him off.

"For eight weeks."

Felix blinked. "Eight weeks?" he repeated.

"Indeed. And you can only escort her once a week. If, at the end of that time, you're still enamored with her, you can ask for her hand. I'm not going to force her to marry you, though. If she turns you down, you're done."

Not having given thought to just how Emelia would feel about marrying him, Felix allowed the sudden sense of disappointment he felt to wash over him.

Once a week?

"Why?" he whispered. "Why are you... Why are you not *requiring* me to marry her like any decent, vengeful, angry father would do?" he asked as his voice took on a hint of impatience. "Your reaction is entirely at odds with how you're supposed to react to having learned your daughter—your only daughter—was kissed!"

The other earl displayed a grin Felix found rather evil just then. "You're completely forgetting there are others we must take into consideration here."

"*Others?*"

Well, there was Emelia, of course.

The Earl of Aimsley shook his head. "I have a countess. The mother of my daughter. The voice of reason in this household. The love of my life, I might add," he said in a quieter voice, remembering how bereft she had been at his reaction when he learned his second son had sold his commission in the army. He had disowned Alistair, refusing to honor a promise the young officer had made to provide fifteen pounds a month to a late soldier's widow.

All was well now, of course, for once Patience had made Aimsley see reason, he had made amends with their son and was seeing to the payment of the monthly pension for the widow. Meanwhile, Alistair had become a leading consultant for Tattersall's and the head groom of the Harrington House stables, a position he had agreed to in exchange for permission to marry Julia Harrington. His first and only granddaughter had just been born from that union. "If my countess learned I had given permission for some rake to marry Emelia..."

"I am not a rake!"

Aimsley gave Felix a quelling glance. "You just admitted to having kissed my daughter—*thoroughly*," he countered with a bushy brow arched up. "Anyway, I'll let Patience know what's happened..." He paused when he paid witness to Felix's sudden strained face, rather enjoying just how much discomfort he was causing the man. "And consider *her* thoughts on the matter."

It was at that moment that Aimsley remembered Felix wasn't as old as he looked. This was a young man who had been friends with Adam, his heir. They had gone to school together. Patience rather liked Felix, he remembered, for Felix had tried to keep

Adam out of trouble at least as much as the two were in trouble. "Take heart, Fenn. Emelia must be rather fond of you, or you would be displaying a shiner about now," he added with a teasing grin. Then he waved his hand as if to dismiss the earl.

Wondering at the reference to a shiner, Felix gave the other earl a bow and took his leave of Aimsley House.

He had some research to do and a courtship to arrange.

"*D*id you enjoy the party?" Patience asked from her side of the town coach, curious as to her daughter's silence since leaving the Weatherstone's gardens.

"Oh, very much," Emelia replied with a nod, her gaze darting to something outside the window. "I can certainly understand why their balls are so popular. The ballroom is beautiful, as are the gardens."

The countess allowed a grin. "I'm so glad Fenn was there. Why, I haven't seen him in an age."

Emelia was beginning to think her mother's reference to 'in an age' must have applied to any amount of time more than a few months. Then she realized just who her mother meant by the name 'Fenn'. "He seems... nice," she offered, not quite sure what to make of a man who would kiss her senseless and then claim he wasn't a rake.

On the one hand, she should have thought of him as a rake— she hadn't even been in his company for ten minutes when he was suddenly kissing her. She could feel the blush creeping up her neck and blooming on her cheeks at the thought of how he had been staring at her just before his lips pressed against hers.

On the other hand, he had seemed sincere with his words even as he realized she would be hard to convince.

What had he been thinking? They had been out in the open, in front of God and who knew-how-many garden party guests just on the other side of the hedgerow!

"Nice?" her mother repeated in disbelief. "My darling, if that man were ten years older, and if I were ten years younger..." Patience stopped speaking, and for the first time in Emelia's life, she paid witness to her mother blushing.

"He is handsome," Emelia agreed with a teasing grin. *And he kisses as if it were his sole purpose in life.* To bestow those gorgeous lips on poor, unsuspecting young women who knew better but couldn't help themselves. "By the way, what does it mean when a man says he might be forced to take a woman to Scotland?"

Patience Comber tore her gaze from a horse and rider outside the town coach window and stared at her daughter. "Did Fenn say that? To you?" The question was asked with so much hope and enthusiasm, a startled Emelia could only blink.

How should I reply? To answer in the affirmative would let her mother know Fenn had indeed said it and said it to her. Did she want her mother knowing such a thing? *Depends on what it means.* "I overheard it whilst I was waiting for you," she finally said with a shrug.

The disappointment her mother conveyed with how her shoulders sagged had Emelia wishing she had simply admitted Fennington had said it. "What does it mean?"

The countess scratched her eyebrow with her ring finger. "Elopement, my darling. It means that if a man cannot wait the three weeks for banns to be read, he'll take his betrothed to Scotland for a quick wedding," she explained. "Gretna Green is the closest village to the border, so it's the most popular place to get married. To elope."

I shall have to take you to Scotland. The words echoed in Emelia's head. Did Fennington really mean he wanted to marry her? Or that he would have to marry her because they were about to be caught kissing behind the hedgerow?

Well, no matter. It wasn't as if she would see the man again anytime soon. He had probably already forgotten about the kiss. Forgotten about her.

She couldn't forget about him, though. She would be reliving the sensation of those lips on hers when she climbed into bed and attempted to sleep. She would be reliving that moment when she looked up and saw how Fennington gazed down at her. Reliving that moment when his arms were suddenly steel bands around her shoulders and waist, pulling her hard against the front of his tall body, the evidence of his arousal pressed into her belly and sending shivers of excitement up and down her spine.

That moment when he kissed her one last time. So tender. So filled with promise.

Patience watched her daughter, realizing the girl was lost in thought. *Good thoughts,* she hoped, for Emelia deserved nothing less. And if those thoughts included the Earl of Fennington, then all the better.

CHAPTER 2
A GOSSIP MONGER PLOTS A COURTSHIP

Oh, dear Reader, it's at this point in our tale that we must admit to having made a grievous error. We were selfish, you see, and it cost us. Our goodwill coffers will be forever empty as a result of just one miscalculation. ~ Part of the editor's farewell article in the May 14, 1818 issue of *The Tattler*.

Late afternoon, March 13, 1818, in the editor's office of The Tattler

Donning a dark brown wig in front of the ornately framed looking glass in his office, Felix Turnbridge regarded his image and frowned. He looked awful. The hair color aged him at least ten years, and the style of the wig had him looking as if he were still living in the Georgian era. But when he added a matching mustache and a pair of wire spectacles that rested just beneath the bridge of his nose, his transformation into Mr. Frederick Pepperidge, editor of *The Tattler*, was nearly complete. Changing into a topcoat suitable for a clerk or solicitor ensured no one would suspect he was really a man of quality.

His office said otherwise, but then he had always thought it needed to project a certain *gravitas*. A hint of wealth rather than tawdriness prevailed. This was the office in which lives could be easily ruined with a pen and ink. When someone did pay a call, it was usually to provide news worthy of publication.

But there were also those who took exception to the articles that appeared in *The Tattler*. Once those visitors were shown to his office, they were usually too intimidated by the rich furnishings and carpet to put voice to their complaints about unfair treatment in his publication. He especially enjoyed watching the guilty realize they had been caught, fair and square. They needed to feel shame for their actions.

"Afternoon, Mr. Pepperidge," his front office clerk said from the threshold of the main door into the office. Another door, somewhat hidden at the back and side of the office, gave the earl the means to get in and out of the building without being seen by the young man who stood before him.

"Connors. Any news?"

The clerk nodded as he stepped into the office. "Had the usual weekly visit from Lady P, and some urchin dropped this inside the front door and ran away," he said as he placed a thick bundle of parchment and a scrap of paper displaying a scribble on one side.

Intrigued, the editor took the papers and set them on his desk. "I'll have today's garden party article finished in a few minutes, but in the meantime, here's the article from last night's visit to the theatre." He had attended a production at the Theatre-Royal in Covent Gardens in the hopes of overhearing gossip. He wasn't disappointed. The tidbits would fill an entire column.

"I'll get this typeset right away, sir," Connors said as he took the article.

Pepperidge watched as his clerk made his way past the iron press and back to the front office, rather glad the young man didn't seem suspicious as to the identity of the man for whom he had worked since the beginning of the gossip rag. *The Tattler* was nearly three years old, its start due to his extreme boredom and curious nature.

And dwindling bank accounts.

No matter where he went or what event he attended, gossip seemed to entertain more than the *musicales* or soirées or even the balls at which the gossip was exchanged.

Which begged the question—would the average Londoner, far removed from the *ton* in terms of lifestyle and entertainments, be interested in gossip that featured members of the aristocracy? Were Londoners really that interested in the lives of those who made up the *haute ton?*

Well, after circulation numbers increased ten-fold before the sixth issue rolled off the iron press at *Tattler Publishing,* he had his answer.

A resounding *Yes!*

What was it about gossip that had so many so eager to buy a weekly rag?

Curiosity, of course. And perhaps a bit of spite. For to read about the foibles and farces of aristocrats meant they were just people at heart, people who were no better than the common folk who populated most of England. An accident of birth determined whether or not someone was an aristocrat or a commoner, after all. The fact that they would pay to read such dreck was as much a surprise as it was a windfall for his bank account.

His coffers needed extra money to pay off his father's gambling debts, although if he cut back on his gambling and replaced his older tenant farmers with younger ones, he might do just fine on the earldom's income.

But, he rather liked a game of whist now and again. And he didn't wish to replace any of his tenant farmers. He had known some of them since he was a toddler.

Seating himself at his massive mahogany desk, Felix opened his ink pot and pulled a sheet of parchment onto the blotter. He quickly wrote a summary of that day's garden party, making sure to include notes about those in attendance, descriptions of the food on the refreshment table, and a compliment about the generous amount of champagne served by a phalanx of footmen. He mentioned the most welcome appearance of Lady Torrington, the garden party being her first *ton* event since giving birth to twins.

He lifted his quill from the paper. He rather wished he'd had an opportunity to speak with Adele Slater Worthington Grandby. The countess was always a joy and sometimes dropped tidbits of gossip without realizing she was doing so. At least she looked well. She looked happy. As had Grandby. In fact, the earl looked as if he had youthened ten years as the result of becoming a father.

Perhaps he had. Felix knew the man had been spotted in the company of his countess and an extra wide perambulator, proudly pushing the conveyance containing his twins whilst they took a walk in the park.

Would I look as if I had youthened ten years should I become a father? he wondered.

Trying to imagine himself in such a scenario, Felix found he could not. He could certainly imagine Emelia holding their babe, though.

He shook his head and returned his attention to the parchment, remembering he should include a note about her return to London after a lengthy absence, and then he added a mention of the stylish design of her gown and pelisse.

Here he paused and sighed. Even when he wasn't thinking about her, he was thinking about her, it seemed.

Aimsley's instructions had been clear. He could call on her once a week for eight weeks. Then he could ask for her hand.

Realizing he couldn't yet put her out of his mind, he decided an invitation was in order. Drawing a sheet of stationery embossed with the seal of his earldom, Felix quickly penned a note to the Earl of Aimsley's daughter.

Dear Lady Emelia, I hope this note finds you happy and in good health. I thoroughly enjoyed our walk earlier today and all that it entailed. I do believe daffodils are now my favorite flower.

It is my fondest desire to escort you (and your maid, of course) for a ride in the park during the fashionable hour. May I come by Aimsley House at four o' clock to collect you? I look forward to your favourable reply. Very sincerely yours, Fennington.

As he reread the missive, he realized he hadn't indicated a day, but decided he would simply plan to be at her house every day until she appeared ready to leave with him. Or perhaps she would dictate the day in her reply.

The thought of receiving a reply had a shiver running through his body. *Faith!* Is this why young couples were so ridiculous when they were in love? He felt almost giddy thinking about Emelia, his heart seemingly skipping a beat here and there.

Too bad Aimsley had decreed he could see her only one day a week, though. Given the restriction, he hoped the calendar wouldn't start its countdown until the following day. *Aimsley certainly wouldn't include today as one of the days, would he?*

Folding his note into a neat square, Felix dribbled some wax onto the seam where the four corners met at the back, and then stamped the Fennington seal into the hardening puddle.

Although a courier would be by to pick up his mail first thing in the morning—probably before he was even in the office—this particular missive would need to leave from his townhouse in Bruton Street. No use having a courier wonder why an earl's mail was included in letters from the publishing offices of *The Tattler*.

Since he had the time, he pulled another sheet of Tattler Publishing stationery onto the blotter. He penned a note to Moyer, his private investigator, with instructions to look into Emelia Comber's enrollment at Warwick's. Remembering she had been in Geneva for four years, he narrowed down the timeline for when she would have been at Warwick's Grammar and Finishing School to at least four years ago. He wondered who else had attended the school at the same time. Certainly Mayfield's daughter, Julia, and Chamberlain's niece, Samantha. Maybe Bostwick's wife. Would one of them know what had happened?

Then he recalled her father's comment about him not having a shiner.

Felix straightened in the leather chair.

Had Emelia punched someone?

A grin split his face as he tried to imagine the demure young lady balling up a fist and hurling it into a man's face. He frowned when he realized how much it had to have hurt her delicate hand. She might have broken a bone or two!

Discover whatever happened to necessitate Lady Emelia Comber leaving the school in favor of attending one in Geneva, he wrote. *A physical alteration may have been involved. ~ Pepperidge.*

Folding up the note, he made sure to use his other seal in the wax. The seal that displayed the name of his publication in an arc around the shapes of a quill and ink bottle.

The Tattler.

Once the wax was dry, he tossed it onto the salver for his courier.

The scrap of paper the clerk had delivered still rested where he left it. Lifting it between two fingers, he struggled to make out the feminine writing.

Lord M has made an offer to a courtesan for her services. Contract is said to be signed and a townhouse secured in Green Street.

Frederick Pepperidge frowned. *Lord M?*

Morganfield?

He couldn't imagine David Carlington arranging a mistress,

not with the woman he had married, but then, he couldn't think of another lord whose name began with an *M*, either. For tips such as this, he could simply print them as they were provided. In this case, he decided to do so. He risked an angry visit from the marquess, but he would simply explain it was a tip provided by someone else.

Lady P's thick bundle opened up once he had the yarn undone from around it. Three pages of gossip spilled forth, most of it notes from calls the old woman paid on other aristocrats' wives. A good deal of cattiness on the part of the viscountess, to be sure, but then Lady P lived for gossip. He skimmed the notes, not particularly surprised by anything he read but he had to tamp down the urge to laugh at some of what he read.

That is, until he reached the last page.

A certain name jumped out at him.

Lady Emelia has returned from her extended stay in Switzerland, presumedly because she has finally completed finishing school. Time will tell if four years away from her brothers has reformed the tomboy.

Pepperidge blinked. And blinked again as he reread the entry.

Lady Emelia, a *tomboy?*

He couldn't begin to imagine how the delicate woman he had escorted in the gardens—not two hours ago—and kissed with such abandon—could possibly have been a *tomboy.*

She did have two brothers, though.

Older brothers.

Adam and Alistair Comber.

Allowing a chuckle of mirth to burble forth, the editor took up his pen and inked through the comment about Emelia being a tomboy. Did he dare ask her about it when he took her for a ride in the park?

But another option seemed preferable. What if he asked her as Mr. Pepperidge? What if he arranged a meeting with her to allow her to comment on the news that she had been a tomboy?

Well, it would give him more time with the young woman.

Settling back in his deep leather chair, he considered how to write his next missive. Given Aimsley's dictate that he could only court Emelia one day a week, perhaps this was a way he could see her more often. In secret.

He had to.

He already knew he would spend the entire night tossing and turning with thoughts of Emelia. Perhaps he would even pull a pillow against his body and hold it as he hoped to one day hold her in his bed.

No wonder some of the men in the *ton* behaved as they did with their wives. They enjoyed kissing!

Kisses.

Emelia's kisses had been magical. He might have initiated them, but she had returned them measure for measure. With passion. With her body pressed entirely against his. Although he didn't expect he'd be able to kiss her again until the day of their betrothal, he could at least *imagine* kissing her again.

Just to be in her company would tide him over for a time. A half-hour. Just the two of them. Alone.

The idea that came to him was so brilliant, so unexpected, Felix blinked several times as he reconsidered it. A way to meet her in the park—just the two of them—alone.

Was it too cruel, though?

Possibly.

Would it work?

Well, of course, if the young lady was the least bit concerned over gossip about her appearing in *The Tattler*. She had just returned to London, after all. The very last thing she would welcome was gossip that had her kissing out in the open, in broad daylight, during a *ton* event.

Oh, and the reminder that she had at one time been a tomboy.

He pulled a sheet of *The Tattler* stationery onto the blotter. Changing his handwriting so the lettering was straighter than his normal slanted hand, he composed a letter proposing a bargain.

Dear Lady Emelia, As the editor of The Tattler, London's leading publication on gossip, I was most intrigued when I paid witness to your time spent with Lord Fennington in Lord Weatherstone's gardens yesterday. Would others be as surprised as I was when you kissed the earl? And not just a quick peck on the cheek, a la the French way of greeting a friend, but rather a series of passionate kisses that took my breath away?

He shook himself. *Careful*, he thought, aware of the growing bulge behind the placket of his doeskin breeches.

Imagine the feature article I could write about such an event! Lady E Plants a Kiss on the Earl of F in Lord W's Garden! Will Love Bloom? Or Wilt, Once the Ton Weeds Her Out of Their Garden?

What might have me reconsidering the publication of such an article?

You, my lady. Your presence in Hyde Park. Thursday mornings at eight o' clock for eight weeks. You bring the gossip you collect from the calls you pay on other ladies and the on-dit you hear during soirées and musicales. In return, I shall not print a word about your elicit kisses with Lord F.

If you agree, meet me this Thursday at the park bench located as per the map below.

Sincerely, Mr. Frederick Pepperidge, Editor

Sighing, Felix drew the map of where a particularly well-sheltered park bench was located not too far from the park's main carriageway. Hidden by a hedgerow and a series of bushes and other plantings, and given the early morning hour, the bench would afford them time away from prying eyes. It would also give him an opportunity to learn if Emelia was really as demure as he believed or if she were truly a tomboy as Lady P asserted.

Would she tattle on her fellow ladies? Share the latest *on-dit?* Revel in the foibles of others? Or instead behave as a perfect lady, insisting there wasn't any gossip of interest for his readers?

Although he could always use more fodder for the gossip rag, he rather hoped she would prove as demure and ladylike as he suspected she was.

Would she show up for their meetings, though? Would she take his letter seriously? He truly meant her no harm, but this kind of offer had to be too good for her to pass up.

Show up or risk the *ton's* censure.

Oh, call it what it is, he scolded himself.

Blackmail.

Sighing, he quickly folded the letter and applied *The Tattler's* seal to the wax. Carefully addressing it so his handwriting matched that of the note inside, he tossed it onto the salver and went about writing the other articles for the next edition of *The Tattler*.

CHAPTER 3
INVITATIONS AREN'T ALWAYS SO WELCOME

here was a moment after completing the invitation when we nearly tore it into tiny pieces. We probably should have done so, but can you really blame us for wanting to spend more time in a lady's company? ~ The final editor's article in the May 14, 1818 issue of *The Tattler*.

arch 14, 1818 in the Aimsley House salon

Patience Comber, Countess of Aimsley, watched her daughter as the young woman opened invitation after invitation. "Are there any you'd like to attend?" she asked as she poured tea into the dainty cups she had inherited from her grandmother.

"All of them," Emelia replied happily. "Although, I dare say we shall never spend a quiet evening at home if I do."

The countess added a lump of sugar to her cup of tea and gave the other to Emelia after adding a dollop of milk. "Every Season offers more events, it seems. Now that almost all the theatres have been rebuilt, or are in the process of being rebuilt —Little Drury Lane will be finished later this year—we could be entertained by opera or plays or a naval reenactment nearly every night."

Emelia grinned as she took a sip of her tea. When she opened the next note, she frowned at the odd seal on the back. Her brows furrowed as she began to read. They furrowed deeper as she finished reading, her head shaking from side to side. "No, no, no," she murmured, turning the missive over again so she could study the seal on the back again. *The Tattler*. A gossip newspaper, she realized.

"What is it, darling?" Patience asked as she quickly placed her cup in its saucer and moved to get up from the floral settee.

"Oh, it's just disappointing news, is all," Emelia replied quickly as she waved her mother to stay where she was. "The Burroughs' return to London has been delayed a few weeks. I was hoping Sophia would be able to join me at some of these entertainments, is all," she explained quickly. She had read Sophia's letter before all of the invitations, but the news of their delay in travel wasn't unexpected. Sophia's father, Lord Maximilian—better known as Andrew Burroughs these days—had warned her they might stop and play tourist in some of the cities along the way, not unlike what Emelia had done during her travels back to London.

"Oh," Patience managed as she helped herself to a lemon biscuit, still wondering at her daughter's odd reaction. Well, she supposed she could take a peek at the letter later. "You never did say how it went with Fenn yesterday."

Emelia blinked. "Fenn?" she repeated, her mind still on the fact that someone had paid witness to the kisses she had exchanged with the Earl of Fennington.

"Yes, Fennington." The countess rolled her eyes. "You wouldn't know him as 'Fenn', of course. He was Adam's very best friend in school. His mother—the dowager countess—is a gem. Too bad her husband was so bad at gambling. Left her practically penniless. Fenn has had to shore up the family accounts in order to keep the earldom from falling into ruin."

Emelia's eyes widened. She wondered how he'd been able to manage. "So, he's one who might pursue a young lady for her dowry?" she asked with a raised eyebrow.

Her mother seemed to shrink into the settee, as if she had never before considered Fennington's financial matters as they might relate to taking a wife. "I suppose it's possible," she murmured. "I so hoped you two would suit. I think he did, too."

Oh, if only I could tell her we did, Emelia thought with a sigh. But she had no idea if the earl would ever come near her after what had happened in the gardens. He probably thought her fast. Probably thought her a wanton.

Probably knew about her reputation. He was good friends with Adam, after all.

Had her brother told him why his little sister had to go to Switzerland for finishing school?

Despondent, she hung her head and stared at the last note, not actually seeing the seal that covered the space where the four corners met.

She blinked and flipped the note over. A bright white envelope sealed in red wax. An earldom's seal. Tearing it open, she read in haste, not believing the words that appeared before her.

A ride in the park? Today? With Fennington?

There was no date or day of the week in the invitation. "When did this arrive?" she asked as she held up the invitation to ride in the park.

Patience angled her head to one side. "Sometime this morning, I suppose."

"Oh! What time is it?" she asked in alarm as she stood up.

"Three o' clock. What is it?"

"I've an invitation to ride in the park. With Fennington." Although her heart raced at the thought of spending the afternoon in the company of the earl, she also experienced a moment of hesitation. What if the editor of *The Tattler* saw them together? Well, her maid would be with them, of course. And

Mr. Pepperidge had claimed he wouldn't divulge the news about the kissing if she met him in the park.

Thursday mornings at eight o' clock.

A brilliant smile appeared on Patience Comber's face. "Well, this is good news, I should think," she said, her voice quiet. After a moment, she sighed. "Well, then, I suppose you need to change clothes. He'll no doubt be here in an hour or so if it's to be a ride during the fashionable hour."

"Four o'clock, yes," Emelia agreed as she waved the invitation in the air. She curtsied and hurried up to her bedchamber, the note clutched in one hand. The other invitations and letters, forgotten, were left behind.

When she was sure Emelia wouldn't be returning to the salon, Patience plucked the last letter from the collection of unfolded missives and began to read.

Stilling herself whilst she read the odd script, Patience understood Emelia's earlier reaction. Her series of 'no's' had been because of this letter.

Dear Lady Emelia, As the editor of The Tattler, London's leading publication on gossip, I was most intrigued when I paid witness to your time spent with Lord Fennington in Lord Weatherstone's gardens yesterday. Would others be as surprised as I was when you kissed the earl? And not just a quick peck on the cheek, a la the French way of greeting a friend, but rather a series of passionate kisses that took my breath away?

Imagine the feature article I could write about such an event! Lady E Plants a Kiss on the Earl of F in Lord W's Garden! Will Love Bloom? Or Wilt, Once the Ton Weeds Her Out of Their Garden?

What might have me reconsidering the publication of such an article?

You, my lady. Your presence in Hyde Park. Thursday mornings at eight o'clock for eight weeks. You bring the gossip you collect from the calls you pay on other ladies and the on-dit you hear during soirées and musicales. In return, I shall not print a word about your elicit kisses with Lord F.

If you agree, meet me this Thursday at the park bench located as per the map below.

Sincerely, Mr. Frederick Pepperidge, Editor

Patience inhaled deeply and let the air out slowly as she returned the letter to the pile with the others, her fingers recoiling from the paper as if it were burning. Although she felt a great deal of anger at the editor of *The Tattler*—he was blackmailing her daughter!—she couldn't help but smile at learning just why he was doing so.

Fenn had kissed Emelia in the gardens whilst on their walk!

As for what to do about the gossip monger, Patience would have to enlist the help of her most trusted friends. Certainly there was something they could do to undermine his plan.

CHAPTER 4
THE GOSSIP GODDESS
IS BORN

Unbeknownst to us at the time, a group of ladies had been called together for tea and conversation by a rather well-regarded countess. Their mission? To plot against us. We say plot, dear readers, for there can be no other word to describe the almost sinister plan they devised to undermine the mission of The Tattler—to report the gossip of the ton. ~ Part of the final article by the editor for the May 14, 1818 issue of *The Tattler*.

March 15 1818, Aimsley House parlor

"I just received your note. What is it? What's happened?" Adele Grandby, Countess of Torrington, asked as she and another lady behind her stepped into the parlor at Aimsley House. The countess glanced around, startled to discover Clarinda Fitzwilliam, Countess of Norwick, and Adeline Carlington, Marchioness of Morganfield, were already present. On her heels was Jane Fitzpatrick, Countess of Stoneleigh, garbed in widow's weeds but obviously pleased at being in their company.

Patience Comber waved Adele and Jane into the parlor and quickly shut the door behind them. "Nothing life and death, I assure you, Adele." She turned to Jane and angled her head. "So good to see you, Jane. I feared you wouldn't join us."

The widow allowed a grin. "I so appreciate the invitation. I haven't been out of the house in an age, and I admit my curiosity is piqued."

A tea tray had already been delivered, and Adeline was serving. "As I said, it's not a matter of life or death, although a certain gossip rag's editor might have lost his head yesterday if I'd been able to remove the broadsword from above the fireplace," Patience said as she joined Adele on the settee. Jane took a chair next to Clarinda.

The other four women dared a glance at the fireplace, frowning when there was no evidence of a broadsword. A painting of a still life—a vase of flowers and some fruit—was the only item hung above the carved mantle.

"In the study," Patience added with a sigh. "The beast of a weapon is heavier than I am." She lifted a folded missive from the low table in front of the settee. "My daughter received this letter from Mr. Pepperidge, the editor of *The Tattler*, yesterday." She allowed everyone their moment of startled murmurs and gasps. "Emelia doesn't know I have it, nor is she to know we are meeting on her behalf." She paused again, giving everyone an opportunity to indicate their agreement.

"Where is Lady Emelia now?" Adele asked, thinking the young lady might overhear their conversation if she were somewhere nearby.

"She's gone to the Temple of the Muses with Lady Sommers," Patience replied, understanding the countess' concern. "Said something about looking for books on historical scandals. I don't expect her back until mid-afternoon." After another moment, she held out the letter and began to read. When she finished, she held her breath a moment.

The more times she read the letter, the angrier she seemed to get, and yet, her reaction the first time had been so different— she had been so pleased to learn the Earl of Fennington had kissed her daughter, she hardly gave a thought to the matter of the *blackmail*.

Before the others had time to respond, Patience said, "I've not yet made Aimsley aware of the matter." Truth be told, she wasn't sure how the earl would react. Outrage? Humor? Indifference? With Mark Comber, she just never knew.

Clarinda was the first to say anything. "The cur!"

Adele arched an eyebrow. "Are you referring to Lord Fennington or to Mr. Pepperidge?" she queried. "It's past time Fennington take a wife, so at least he's on the hunt."

The other countess angled her head and rolled her eyes. "Why, Mr. Pepperidge, of course. He's blackmailing Emelia!"

The marchioness sighed. "Emelia seems like a perfect fit for Fenn," Adeline murmured. She refilled several teacups. "As for Mr. Pepperidge, I am sure we're not the only ones at odds with the man's gossip rag."

Jane felt the color leave her face at the memory of what had been written about her when her husband had died. "I would have helped with brandishing the sword," she offered.

Feeling a bit of satisfaction that the women seemed to agree in their reaction—they were more appalled by the editor's attempt at blackmail than they were by the suggestion that Fennington had kissed Emelia—Patience knew she could rally them to her cause. "I have a plan for how we might undermine Mr. Pepperidge and *The Tattler*."

"Well, I'm all ears," the Countess of Torrington replied, taking a teacup from Adeline.

"I propose we let Emelia meet the rogue in the park..." Patience had to stop to allow the sudden sounds of shock to dissipate. "And send her there with the most outrageously boring gossip we can devise."

"What?"

The chorus of surprise had Patience grinning. "We make up stories. We make up names."

"Fake aristocrats?" Adele questioned, a gleam developing in her eyes as she considered the possibilities.

Jane giggled, the musical sound drawing the attention of the others. "And we back it up by sending it in written form as if it's come from someone else. That way, he won't suspect Emelia of trying to bamboozle him."

Patience's eyes widened. "Oh, that's good. That's very good."

"Which one of us should do the written version?" Adele asked.

"We could do it anonymously," Clarinda suggested.

"I'll do it," Patience said, her attention on the Aubusson carpet, the pattern of cherubs woven into the design giving her an idea. "As The Gossip Goddess," she murmured.

"Oh, that's good," Adeline gushed. "And write it on pink paper."

"Perfumed paper," Jane added with a teasing grin.

"I'll visit the stationer's this afternoon," Patience agreed, rather excited at how their plan was developing. "Now, we just have to come up with some good gossip."

"With believable names," Clarinda put in.

"Lord Beasley," Jane offered. "That was my dog's name when I was a child."

"Lady X," Adeline said with an arched brow. "Xenobia hasn't been in London in an age. Is there a Lord Reardon?"

The others shook their heads after a moment of thought.

"What if Pepperidge decides to add on to the number of meetings?" Adele asked. "What's to prevent him from continuing to blackmail your poor Emelia after the eight weeks are over?"

Patience angled her head to one side, realizing the countess had a point. What would prevent the editor of *The Tattler* from simply adding on to his demands?

She gasped. *I am married to an earl, for goodness sake!* Surely he could be compelled to act on his own daughter's behalf. *I probably should have told him already, but then, I wouldn't have had a reason to call this group of women together.* Hell hath no fury like ladies of the *ton* who were out for revenge, after all. "He will not," she stated finally. "For should Mr. Pepperidge attempt to meet with her more than the eight times he specified in his letter, I shall have my husband pay him a visit at his offices," she stated firmly. "With the broadsword."

"You're not worried that Mr. Pepperidge will tell your husband he saw Lady Emelia kiss Fennington?" Lady Torrington asked, her brows furrowed.

The Countess of Aimsley settled deeper into the settee and allowed a shrug. "I am not, for should it become public knowledge that my daughter was seen kissing the earl, I am quite sure he will make an offer of marriage."

"Marriage?" Clarinda repeated in shock. "Would *she* be agreeable to such an arrangement?"

Patience rolled her eyes. "Well, I should hope so," she replied. "She kissed him in the gardens. In broad daylight."

The others surreptitiously glanced at one another, realizing Patience Comber was rather pleased with the thought of Lord Fennington kissing her daughter.

"As for these meetings in the park... do you think this is wise?" Adele asked, concerned as to how she was going to keep the affairs of this meeting from her husband. Why, Milton Grandby, Earl of Torrington, would challenge Mr. Pepperidge to a duel at Wimbledon Common if he learned any of his goddaughters had been threatened in such a manner. "She'll have to meet with him—alone—in the park for eight weeks," she added in alarm. "Someone might see them. And what then? She might be forced to accept an offer of marriage from the editor of *The Tattler!*"

Patience shook her head. "No one will *be* in Hyde Park at eight o'clock in the morning on a Thursday," she countered. "Most of London is abed, and those who are up are not in the park."

"Still, Adele has a point," Clarinda stated. "What will we do if someone should see them in the park?"

Patience considered the query. "To whom will it matter?

Mr. Pepperidge is the editor of the very gossip rag that would print the story, and he won't print one in which he is the rake," she reasoned. "Remember, though, not a word of this to your husbands."

The other women nodded in agreement.

"Pink paper it is," Patience said before finishing off her tea.

"Perfumed pink paper," Jane added with an elegantly arched brow.

"From *The Gossip Goddess*," Adeline murmured. The marchioness grinned, her expression devious. "Mr. Pepperidge will regret the day he ever paid witness to a kiss in the gardens."

CHAPTER 5
A BIT OF GOSSIP PROVES RIDICULOUS

ow, dear readers, you are probably wondering how we vet the stories we're provided by some of our subscribers. Although most of the reports you read in The Tattler *are first-hand accounts, we occasionally receive tips that send us on a quest to learn the Truth of the matter. We must, for if we printed everything we receive, you would think us more ridiculous than you already do.* ~ An article in the March 26, 1818 issue of *The Tattler.*

arch 18, 1818
Opening the note that had been left with his clerk, Felix's first reaction was to lean back, as if the contents were about to jump out at him. His next was to lift the paper to his nose, for the most pleasant scent wafted across his nostrils.

Perfumed paper!

What glorious woman would waste her most expensive notepaper on a letter to Mr. Pepperidge?

His gaze darted to the bottom, where the flourish of a faux signature could be found. *The Gossip Goddess.*

Felix blinked. Well, this was certainly a first. Usually gossip was provided anonymously.

He perused the letter, his brows furrowing as he read a number of short articles written in the most beautiful script. Definitely feminine, but given the signature, it was to be expected.

> *Whilst attending the Theatre Royal last evening, Lord Beasley ducked into the box belonging to Lady L. He did not emerge for the rest of the evening.*

Mr. Pepperidge frowned. Beasley? *Who the hell is he?* And Lady L? He racked his brain in an effort to put the letter with some lady whose name started with an 'L' and who had her own box at the theatre, but found he could not.

> *Lady X was seen leaving the bachelor quarters of Lord Tattinger at six o' clock in the morning (yesterday).*

Tattinger? *Who the hell is he?* And Lady X? Wasn't she Lord M's courtesan? Felix shook his head and continued reading, wondering where these particular lords and ladies resided. On the other side of England?

> *The oldest son of Lady O was caught in bed with the wife of Lord Reardon last Monday afternoon. Reardon is said to be considering divorce or a ménage-a-trois.*

Rather sporting of him, except... *who the hell is Lord Reardon?*

> *Lord and Lady E have been engaged in a torrid affair with each other for nearly a year!*

At this last entry, Felix squeezed his eyes shut. *A married couple having a torrid affair with one another shouldn't be considered gossip,* he thought in dismay. He rather hoped he would have a torrid affair with Lady Emelia for the rest of his life once they were wed!

And the final line had him simply shaking his head.

Should you require assistance in putting together the content of The Tattler, say at such time you decide to resign or retire from your duties, do let me know. I feel I am most qualified to fill your shoes, Mr. Pepperidge. Yours very truly, The Gossip Goddess.

The pleasant perfume filled his nostrils as he waved the paper in front of his face, as if to fan himself. Glancing at his bookshelf, he realized he could determine the likelihood of the reports just by checking the names in his copy of *Debrett's Peerage and Baronetage.*

A half-hour later, Felix shook his head and wondered just what *The Gossip Goddess* had in mind when writing her false reports. They had to be false, for he could find no lords with those names!

What the hell?

Taking a whiff of the paper, he was about to toss it into the waste basket next to his desk when he paused and instead considered an alternative. What if *The Gossip Goddess* had a column? A ridiculous list of reports about non-existent members of the *ton?* He would have to preface the column with a disclaimer, of course. *The following reports are completely fictitious, the creation of our new contributor, The Gossip Goddess. Enjoy!*

Grinning, Felix settled into his large leather chair. If the woman calling herself *The Gossip Goddess* thought she would bamboozle him with false gossip, she would be most surprised to discover he was not so easily fooled.

CHAPTER 6
A MARQUESS GROUSES
ABOUT GOSSIP

e admit to knowing we made enemies during these past few years. What new business does not? But offending those in power is not recommended. We found out the hard way. We recommend you do not. ~ The final editor's article in the May 14, 1818 issue of *The Tattler*.

arch 26, 1818, Carlington House

David Carlington, Marquess of Morganfield, stared at the ceiling of his master bedchamber, silently wondering how he could personally see to the downfall of the gossip rag, *The Tattler*. Earlier that day, the news sheet inferred he had arranged for a townhouse, pin money, and a modiste for his latest mistress, some courtesan the rag referred to as 'Mrs. X'. The report was entirely false, of course, for why ever would he employ a mistress when he had an Italian seductress as a wife?

Adeline Carlington hadn't always been a seductress, though. David had married the daughter of an Italian count whilst on his Grand Tour of Europe, mostly because he would be spared another Season of meeting insipid chits and their mothers at a series of boring balls and soirées. Had Adeline been a seductress back then, as she was now, David never would have employed a mistress who would one day ruin him by passing his pillow talk to a French army officer. When the source of the exposed secrets had come back to haunt him, David had lost nearly everything—including Adeline.

His wife took to immersing herself in her charitable endeavors, spending time in the parlors of every woman of substance with whom she was acquainted, and taking frequent holidays to Bath and Brighton, separating herself from David in every way but divorce.

But with a bit of assistance from an unlikely source—the sister of the very mistress who had cost him so much—Morganfield had repaired his political ties and regained his status as one of the most powerful lords in Parliament. That same woman, Josephine Wentworth Theisen, had been responsible for teaching his wife a thing or two about the bedroom arts.

He would never forget the night Adeline had come to his bedchamber wearing a rather scandalous red gown, one that would have been considered inappropriate at any dinner or ball in that it was nearly translucent.

Dismissing his valet with a simple point of her finger toward the door, and without another word, she had slowly undressed David. She removed each piece of clothing with deliberate care, folding it and setting it aside so as not to upset his valet.

By the time he was completely naked, her torturous strokes and occasional feather kisses had him thoroughly aroused. She led him to the bed, pushed him onto it and crawled atop him, spreading open the lower half of the diaphanous gown to reveal her own nakedness. Impaling herself on his rigid manhood, David thought he would never forget the sight of her atop him, the gown's bodice still covering her generous breasts, their erect nipples leaving their silhouettes in the filmy fabric, her head thrown back so her entire torso was bowed back.

And then she had begun to move.

Sweet Jesus! He had made short work of the gown's bodice, popping the single fastening with his teeth and using the palms of his hands to push the offending garment off her breasts and shoulders, essentially trapping her arms at her sides. His mouth had claimed one of her breasts in the process, his tongue laving across her nipple until he had her murmuring in Italian. He made short work of the other breast before flipping her onto her back and finishing what she had started, his release so powerful, his euphoria left him unable to move for the rest of the night.

Adeline had been forced to sleep in his bed that night, a practice she had since adopted for several nights every week.

The nights he wasn't in her bed.

His thoughts back to the present, David stopped short of remembering that Josephine was also his current son-in-law's former mistress—a woman responsible for seeing to it Elizabeth and George ended up married to one another.

Now married to a respectable man engaged in trade, Josephine was still providing him with important information he could use in Parliament.

Better to remember her as my savior in more ways than one.

So, how could he take down a gossip rag like *The Tattler?*

David considered the two women he knew who had some influence on the legitimate presses in London. His own wife, Adeline, had some pull when it came to what was printed— and what wasn't. How else could he explain why it was that the most scandalous events at his own soirées and *musicales* were never mentioned in *The Times* or *The Morning Chronicle?* He certainly wasn't lunching with the editor the following day to discover what might or might not be printed.

The other woman just happened to be Josephine Theisen, the most politically astute woman in all of London. Hell, she was probably more politically astute than most of the Lords in Parliament. She was also rather influential when she plied her craft with the editors of the most popular newspapers in London. David wondered if she could be compelled to discover how—and why—damaging information about him would appear in *The Tattler*.

Who was the editor? 'Mr. Pepperidge' had to be a pen name.

A quiet knock sounded at his door. "Come," he called out, not sure if he welcomed the respite from his murderous thoughts. At the sound of silence once the door clicked shut, David dared a glance in that direction. He immediately got to his feet at the sight of his wife regarding him with her head angled to one side.

"May I ask as to why you're hiding in your bedchamber when your daughter and her husband are in our parlor?" Adeline asked, finally moving to join him next to the bed.

David lifted one of her hands to his lips and kissed the back of it, never once taking his eyes off of hers. "I'm afraid I would not be good company at the moment, as I am contemplating how to remove a certain gossip rag from the face of the earth," he murmured. "I cannot abide their lies," he added.

Adeline's eyes widened before she allowed a shake of her head. "Oh. *The Tattler*," she said, sounding relieved. "If it's any consolation, I don't believe a word they print," she claimed as she wrapped an arm around his neck. "Especially the past couple of weeks." Her lips captured his in a quick kiss. "Unless you think I should," she whispered when she pulled away and gave him an arched eyebrow.

Truth be told, she had read the short article about Lord M, grinning at the description of David with his new courtesan because *she* had been the one to provide the *on-dit* to Patience Comber, who then included it in her *Gossip Goddess* letter she mailed to the publisher. At the time and date of the supposed sighting, David had been with *her* at the theatre and then later in her bed, quite exhausted and partially covered with her diaphanous blue French negligée.

She couldn't recall where their giant ostrich feather had ended up in the fray. Or the tray of mint sweets. Or the bucket of ice.

Anyone who had been at the theatre that night knew David wasn't with a mistress, which made it look as if *The Tattler* was printing a false report.

Breathless, David stared at his seductress of a wife. He shook his head and then considered what he had read. "You can believe the rumors of my sexual prowess, that my appetites are insatiable, and that I am quite the lover when given the chance to prove myself. But only as it applies to *you,*" he responded, his expression daring her to counter his words.

Adeline regarded him with an arched brow. "I expect you to prove that again, my darling, but later this evening. In the meantime, I think it's time you came downstairs."

David allowed a sigh. "Am I suitably dressed?" he asked, not having checked his image in the cheval mirror.

His wife stepped back and gave him a quick glance. "Of course. You always look rather dashing," she said with a wink.

The marquess allowed a wan smile and pulled his wife into his arms. "Have I told you how much I adore you?" he whispered, placing a kiss on the side of her head and moving his lips so he could nibble on her ear.

"Why, yes, just this morning, in fact. And I would allow you to prove it to me again right this very minute, except that if we leave our daughter alone with George in the parlor for one minute more, they'll be doing the very same thing down there that we are doing up here." She gave David a peck. "If they aren't already," she added with an arched brow.

"Point taken," the marquess replied as he pulled away and offered his arm.

Giving him an arched eyebrow, Adeline placed her arm on his. "And hopefully redirected later this evening," she murmured suggestively. "Afterwards, we can devise a whole new salacious story to send to *The Tattler*."

David swallowed before allowing a nod. "Of course, my lady." His eyes widened. "Wait! That story wasn't about my mistress. It was about you!" he accused as he just then realized he had been with Adeline the night of the supposed meeting with a mistress. "Lady X, I presume?"

At least Adeline had the decency to blush. "Indeed. And I am not the only one providing fiction to Mr. Pepperidge," she said as she took his arm and led him down the stairs.

"Oh?"

"The editor has earned the wrath of a certain countess— one who is seeing to his eventual downfall over a matter of blackmail."

"Blackmail?" he repeated. "Christ, Adeline, the man needs to be arrested and transported!"

"No, no, no. At least, not yet. We're all having far too much fun making up stories with fictional characters."

David considered her words as he reached the bottom of the stairs.

"We?"

Adeline gave one shoulder a slight shrug. "Yes, darling. There are... a few of us," she hedged. "Better you not know the particulars."

The marquess couldn't help the bit of amusement he felt at learning some ladies of the *ton* were involved in bamboozling the editor of *The Tattler*. That is, until they reached the parlor. "*I am not a fictional character,*" he stated.

His marchioness allowed a teasing grin and leaned over to whisper in his ear, "No, but who would ever believe the things we do really happen?"

David held his breath a moment before frowning. "I see your point, my sweeting. Carry on."

The two entered the parlor and greeted their guests, interrupting Elizabeth and George's rather scandalous kiss. "I don't suppose you're including articles about them?" he asked under his breath.

Adeline shook her head. "With those two, it would only be gossip if they *weren't* always doing something scandalous," she replied with a sigh.

CHAPTER 7
A WIDOW AT A BALL

ow, I know what you must be thinking, dear readers, when you see the date of this entry. What happened during the intervening seven weeks? Well, we met with Lady E every Thursday morning in the park as per the plan. We just didn't realize our plan had been discovered. ~ The final article in the May 14, 1818 issue of *The Tattler.*

ay 6, 1818, Lord Weatherstone's ballroom
Although the heat in the ballroom was almost oppressive, Jane Fitzpatrick found she didn't mind in the least. Twelve months of mourning her late husband, a man she could consider no more than an acquaintance, was over, and she was finally able to attend a *ton* event again. Her gown, a confection of unadorned lavender watered silk, was more sedate than any other gown in the room, but given her situation, she felt it was a safe choice for Lord Weatherstone's ball. By the time the Little Season events started in the fall, she would feel comfortable wearing her favorite royal blue gowns.

If she was still living in London.

She had a luncheon to attend at Worthington House on the

morrow. If she determined she no longer had a place in Society, she thought to simply take her leave of London and start over somewhere else. Months of time to consider her options had her thinking Italy the most likely destination.

Away from Society too long to expect an offer of a dance, Jane experienced a pleasant surprise when David Carlington, Marquess of Morganfield, saw to it she had a partner for the cotillion. Breathless at the finish, she thanked him as she curtsied. A passing footman offered champagne, and she took the flute and nearly drained the contents in a single gulp.

When the supper dance, a waltz, was just about to begin, she thought to make a quiet exit from the festivities. Only a few other women her age seemed to recognize her, although she had been a frequent visitor in their parlors back in the day. Back in the day when she was the Countess of Stoneleigh, and not a widowed countess as she was now. Back in the day when her husband, Michael Fitzpatrick, Earl of Stoneleigh, was a proud member of Parliament and an even prouder property owner.

Jane couldn't fault him for his diligence. He merely insisted his earldom in Kent be run as efficiently as possible, which meant he spent a great deal of time in Milton. She was quite sure he didn't spend the time there alone, of course, since Stoneleigh had made it clear early in their arranged marriage that he had a mistress. A mistress whose company he apparently preferred over her own, for Jane was never invited to spend time with the earl in Milton.

Blinking back the tears that pricked the corners of her eyes, tears of regret more than of mourning, Jane decided it really was time to take her leave of the Weatherstone mansion. *From whence had the maudlin thoughts come?* She was enjoying the ball enormously, enjoying the swirl of glittering, bejeweled ladies and the elegantly garbed gentlemen, the music of the quintet that played in a raised box at one end of the ballroom, and the bits of conversation she overheard as she made her way around the potted palms lining the walls.

She was especially enjoying the spectacle of one particular gentleman as he escorted a series of young ladies into the gardens, only to have each one return without their escort, their bee-stung lips betraying the kisses they had no doubt enjoyed behind a hedgerow.

The young man had obviously been left to wait a few more minutes in the garden. Unless she had missed him during the cotillion, he was still out there!

Had she been twenty years younger, that same young man might have asked her to join him in the gardens. Had she become a widow a few years ago, the Earl of Torrington might have chosen to escort her to all the events of the Season. But, alas, he had finally married a different widow, Adele Slater Worthington, and was now the father of twins.

The opportunity to have an attentive man in her life had long since passed, she decided. It was time to turn her attention to a life away from London, away from paying calls on other ladies of the *ton* or to spending her afternoons window shopping or in the stacks at the lending library. Time to move to the Continent, perhaps. She had heard marvelous reports from Italy, although everyone complained of the heat in the summer. How could it be any worse than London, though?

Italy it is, she thought with a bit of excitement, deciding right then and there she would return to her townhouse in South Audley Street and see to the arrangements.

So it was a bit of a surprise when a rather tall gentleman stepped in front of her and gave a bow. "May I have this waltz, my lady?" he asked as he held out his hand.

Jane blinked, for she was quite sure she didn't know the identity of the man who stood before her. Had the marquess sent him to provide a poor widow with one last dance before she took her leave? Or had Lady Weatherstone taken it upon herself to see to a dance partner for her last-minute guest? How considerate of the woman to send an invitation the day before, claiming she had just learned that Jane had completed her twelve months of mourning, and would she be amenable to a night out?

Jane could have declined the invitation, of course, just as she could decline the offer of a dance, but the thought of a ball had her once again looking forward to life in the *ton*, and the thought of a waltz had her allowing a brilliant smile. "I would like that very much," she said as she gave a curtsy and offered the rather tall man her silk-gloved hand.

"Andrew Burroughs, at your service," he said before lowering his lips to her glove. One of his eyebrows had arched as if he half-expected her to recognize him.

"Jane Fitzpatrick," she replied, not bothering to add her title. *Countess of Stoneleigh.*

Not *Dowager Countess of Stoneleigh.* She couldn't claim her son had inherited the earldom, since she had never given birth to one. In fact, she hadn't given birth to any of Michael's children. His mistress had had that privilege, even though none of the three bastard sons could inherit. The Stoneleigh earldom was now in her brother-in-law's control, and his newly minted countess was half the age of Jane. "It's very good to meet you, Mr. Burroughs," she replied as she gave him a curtsy.

With the barest hint of a grin, the man led her to the edge of the dance floor and gave her a nod before sweeping her into the circle of couples who performed the elegant dance.

"I cannot begin to tell you just how good it is to see you tonight. I feared you would not come," Andrew said in a voice just loud enough for her to hear.

Jane blinked. His comment implied they knew one another, yet she couldn't place where she might have met the man before. He seemed familiar, though, now that they were under the hundreds of candles mounted in the chandeliers hanging from the ballroom ceiling. "I apologize, but I don't recognize you," she said. "And yet, I am sure we have met before." His voice was familiar, certainly. *Burroughs?* Why, there were dozens of them in the *ton.*

Rolling his eyes in a manner suggesting he didn't find her words a surprise, Andrew managed a shrug despite the moves of the dance. "I cannot blame you," he replied. "It has been a long time. Too long, in fact."

The way in which he said the words had Jane furrowing her brows.

Too long?

So, they had met before. But when? She struggled to remember how he had introduced himself.

Andrew Burroughs.

Burroughs? Why, the Ariley ducal line was made up of Burroughs. He was far too young to be the fifth duke, but he could be his son, or the son of William Burroughs, the former banker. *Goodness, Sir William must be in his seventies by now,* she considered as she thought of the man who was her father's banker. And would still be her own banker if the man hadn't retired the year before.

Or perhaps Andrew wasn't a member of that particular Burroughs family at all. She was about to consider other possibilities when Andrew leaned over and whispered in her ear, "You knew me as Max," he said, his lips so close Jane was sure they touched her ear. A shiver passed through her entire body, leaving behind a sensation of excitement.

How long had it been since a man whispered in her ear?

Too long.

When Andrew pulled away, there was a gleam in his eye.

Jane nearly lost her place in the steps of the waltz, relieved when Andrew's strong lead and firm hold on her waist kept her moving in the right direction.

Max? Lord Maximilian?

"Oh, faith!" she breathed. Of course it was him! The last man to have whispered in her ear!

The planes of his face were a bit thinner, his nose a bit longer, his hair a bit gray at the temples, but his green eyes were still those of the young man who had taken her for several rides in Hyde Park. The man who had kissed her so tentatively in the gardens behind the very ballroom in which they now danced. The man who had pledged his heart but warned her that he couldn't make an offer that night. *I must speak with your father*, he had said in a hoarse whisper, his lips brushing the whorls of her ear as he made the comment.

That had been the night before her father informed her she would be marrying the heir to the Stoneleigh earldom.

The feeling of disappointment had been crushing, the sense of loss profound. The title of viscountess didn't begin to make up for losing Maximilian Andrews Burroughs as a possible husband. Lord Maximilian. *I would have been Lady Maximilian*, she thought with a sigh.

Michael Fitzpatrick had been a viscount back then, prone to late nights at his club and even later nights at brothels, but a betrothal to him ensured she would be married to a titled gentleman and not to the youngest son of a duke as her father apparently feared.

The nephew of a banker.

She allowed a tentative grin to appear. "Max," she repeated in a breathy voice. His nickname had been short for Maximilian, a name far too large for a young man who could never hope to inherit a dukedom given he had two older brothers. "Where have you been?" she blurted, not having seen him since those days when she was quite sure he might offer for her hand given his words of eighteen years ago.

Eighteen years ago?

If only he had. How different her life might have been! Her father would not have allowed the match, though. Not when a potential earl had offered for her hand.

Andrew shrugged again. "Brighton, Bath, Rome, Athens, Prague, Geneva..." He allowed the list to trail off. "But now I am back in London, and I intend to stay."

Her eyes wide as she considered the cities in which he had apparently visited since she had last seen him, she angled her head. "Banking, perhaps?" she guessed, and then remembered that as the son of a duke, he probably wasn't allowed to work.

"Indeed," he confirmed with a nod. "Unlike my older brothers, I could not abide a life of leisure, nor the life of a military man," he explained. "My uncle came to my rescue, thank the gods, and I found some inspiration in the determination of another who wished to learn a trade in order to make a living."

Jane continued to stare at him, trusting he wasn't about to dance them into the path of another couple. "And how is my father's banker these days?" she asked, barely aware the waltz had ended. Andrew and taken her hand and placed it on his arm, leading her somewhere. She found she didn't care where.

"Cantankerous," Andrew replied with a wink. "Old. But he still has all his faculties. I expect he'll outlive all of us," he claimed with a grin. "I've been working with him on a special project in Chiswick. Keeps him young, and it will provide me with a place to call home when it is finally finished later this week."

Jane allowed another grin before she realized Andrew's manner had changed. "What is it?" she asked.

"Are you hungry? Supper is served, but..."

"Oh, no. I hadn't planned to stay this late. It's my first ball since..." She allowed the sentence to trail off.

"I know," he replied, steering them in a different direction.

Jane arched an eyebrow. "You know?" she repeated. Goodness. She sounded like a parrot!

"I figured tonight would be the soonest you would dare make an appearance at a Society event," he said as he led them into the vestibule, not bothering to add that he had mentioned her situation to Lord Weatherstone a few nights ago at Boodles. The older earl had promised he would inform his wife and see to it an invitation was sent.

The host obviously kept his promises.

A footman hurried to retrieve their coats.

The comment had Jane regarding the gentleman with widened eyes. "How... how would you know that?" she asked as she allowed him to help her with her wrap.

Andrew finished donning his cape coat and top hat. "I used a calendar, of course," he answered matter-of-factly. He led them through the front door, the butler giving them a nod as they took their leave. "Did you come in a carriage?" he asked, oblivious to the stare Jane aimed in his direction.

"I... I did," she replied, tearing her gaze from him to search for the Stoneleigh coach among the dozens that lined the street in front of the Weatherstone mansion in Park Lane. "I should have walked, though," she added, rather wishing she had. The townhouse she had let upon Michael's death was just a few streets down in South Audley Street. At least the cur had left her with enough funds to live out her life in familiar comfort. She rather doubted her brother-in-law would have been as generous if it had been left up to him.

There was a fortune in the accounts her father had left her, though, should she ever need to tap them. Should she make the move to Italy. At the moment, though, Italy was far from her thoughts.

"Should we send the coachman on his way then?" Andrew asked.

Jane wondered at his query. "Probably better that I go in the coach. It's my first time wearing these slippers in a very long time" she hedged, wincing when she realized how uncomfortable they were when she gave them half a mind.

"As you wish," he said as he stepped up and opened the door to the town coach bearing the Stoneleigh crest. He helped her in and then followed, taking the seat opposite.

Rather surprised he had followed her into the coach, Jane regarded him for a moment. "Pray tell, what are you doing?"

"Seeing you safely home, of course," Andrew replied as he removed his top hat so he could sit up straighter. His head nearly touched the ceiling! "You obviously don't have a companion nor an escort, so I shall do the honors." He held his beaver between his gloved hands for a moment before setting it aside on the upholstered bench.

"That's rather kind of you," Jane said, a heady mix of anticipation and dread settling over her. "I do hope your wife won't mind."

Andrew stifled a laugh. "There is no Mrs. Burroughs. At least, there hasn't been for some time. Bess died of pneumonia the year Prinny became Regent," he responded in a quiet voice, his kid-gloved hands clasping together just inches from her knees. "We were living in Prague at the time."

"I'm so sorry," Jane offered, remembering there had been an inordinate number of deaths that particular year.

"Thank you for saying so. I missed her at first, of course. We had become good friends. We'd been married... just over ten years, I suppose. Goodness, how time flies. She gave me two sons who are now at Cambridge and Eton, and a daughter who just begun finishing school," he explained with a shrug. "I hosted Lady Emelia Comber for the past few years in Geneva whilst she attended finishing school. I wanted to be sure Sophia, my daughter, had someone a bit older to help her along," he explained. He paused a moment. "Bess was a very agreeable wife," he added, as if he thought it important he mention his late wife again.

Jane nodded.

A very agreeable wife.

She supposed that's what she had been to Michael Fitzpatrick. Agreeable in that she didn't complain about the amount of time he spent in Kent, nor about the fact that he had a family with his mistress but never one with her. Although she had been tempted to take a lover—it would have been within her rights, she supposed—she had remained faithful to the earl until the day she received the missive from Kent with the news that he had died.

Twelve months of mourning commenced. Twelve months of loneliness. Twelve months of hell.

So tonight's ball had been a welcome end to her life as Michael Fitzpatrick's wife. As Michael Fitzpatrick's widow. She was done with mourning. Had she borne him any children, she might gave considered another six months, but the earl hadn't seen fit to bed her beyond their wedding night and a few nights when he happened to be in London for Parliament. The nights he wasn't so drunk he could actually find his way to her bedchamber.

"Even if she wasn't my first choice," Andrew added with an arched eyebrow.

Jane stared at the man who sat across from her, their knees so close they nearly touched, his head dipped low so their foreheads were within inches of one another.

Not his first choice?

She blinked. Did he mean that *she* had been his first choice? Her heart raced at the memory of his promise that night in the gardens. She had imagined herself in love with Lord Maximilian at that point, imagined what life might be like with him as her husband. But her father's words to her the day following the ball had changed everything. Changed her entire life.

"I have no intention of leaving you alone tonight."

Pulled from her reverie by the odd statement, Jane stared at Andrew. "Oh?" was all she could think to say.

Andrew allowed a chuckle. "I do hope I haven't scandalized you, my sweeting."

My sweeting.

Goodness, they had just become reacquainted after eighteen years, and he was already using an endearment only suitable for couples who were...

Lovers.

Jane inhaled sharply. Is that what Andrew Burroughs intended? To make her his mistress? To offer *carte blanche*?

"Oh, Christ, I *have* scandalized you," he said with a roll of his eyes. He straightened in the squabs and shook his head. "I apologize, my lady. It's not my intention to take liberties, nor to..."

"I am rather flattered, actually," Jane interrupted. "No one has ever called me 'sweeting'. Not even my husband, but then I suppose you already knew that." This last was said in a quieter voice, as if she realized her place in her husband's life was well known to others.

How many women in the *ton* knew of her despair at being left alone for months at a time as her husband spent all his time away from London? He was only ever at their mansion in Westminster when Parliament was in session, and even then, he spent most of the time when he wasn't in the House of Lords at his club, Boodles.

"I did not," Andrew said. He sighed and was about to say something else when the coach suddenly halted.

"We're here," Jane said with a quick look at the ceiling, wondering if the driver would get down from the box and open the coach door. There were no footmen to do so, of course, although sometimes the butler would come from the townhouse to see to opening the door and setting down the steps. She had decided to employ a rather limited staff given she was the only one in residence.

Claiming she wouldn't require his services, she had given her butler, Simonton, the night off to spend it with his wife, a housekeeper in the Norwick household. She wasn't expecting to be gone from the house for a ball, after all.

Andrew was up from his seat and opening the door before she could give it another thought, though. He offered his hand and she took it, noting that at some point that evening, he had donned a pair of kid gloves. Given the lack of stairs, he merely lifted her from the carriage and lowered her to the pavement once he had turned toward the townhouse.

"Thank you," she managed, well aware of how close he stood once she was safely on her two slippered feet. She didn't even wince at how the footwear pinched her toes but merely stared up at Andrew in wonder.

He offered his arm and led the way to the house, frowning when the front door didn't open upon their arrival. Reaching out, he turned the handle and opened the door, peeking around the edge to ensure no butler stood there with a weapon.

Or to greet them.

"My butler has the night off," Jane said. "I didn't know until this morning that I would be attending the ball. This is my first night out in a very long time, and..."

"It's fine," Andrew remarked as he led her over the threshold and took her wrap from her shoulders. "A blessing, really, given how servants can sometimes gossip when they shouldn't." He double-checked the front door to be sure it was locked once he had it shut.

Jane realized he spoke the truth—how else would *The Tattler* know of some of the gossip it reported unless it learned it from the servants of aristocrats?

She watched as he hung her shawl on a hook on the wall and then removed his cape coat. Instead of hanging it on the adjoining hook, though, he draped it over an arm, retrieved his hat from where he had set it down, and offered her the other. "As I said in the coach, I have no intention of leaving you alone tonight."

Her breath catching at his words, Jane swallowed. "Out of concern for my safety?" she asked with an arched brow.

Andrew angled his head first to one side and then the other. "That, and the fact that we have much to discuss. I do hope you'll afford me the time for such a discussion."

Jane considered his carefully chosen words. *So he's not out to seduce me,* she reasoned after a moment, rather surprised at the sense of disappointment settling over her just then. *But what did he intend?* "So, the parlor, or...?"

"The study, I should think. Is there brandy in there, perhaps?"

Blinking, Jane wondered at just what he intended to discuss. She had to admit to feeling a bit of relief that he didn't suggest they hold their discussion in her bedchamber. She had a thought he merely intended to bed her, a situation she thought she couldn't abide just then. But another part of her had hoped his discussion would be one of a carnal nature. Ever since she had learned his identity, she had felt excitement at having him so close.

Good grief, what is wrong with me?

She was playing coy at the same time she was hoping to be tumbled! Being in Andrew Burroughs' company was certainly a conundrum.

"I believe there is a decanter of brandy in there," Jane finally replied.

Andrew nodded as he held out his arm. "Lead the way, my lady," he replied.

Jane held her head high as they made their way from the vestibule past the great hall's round table. The huge vase of hot house flowers gave off a heady scent that filled the front half of the house. Another day, and they would be resigned to the refuse heap in the alley behind the house. She would need to see to a new arrangement from the back gardens or allow the vase to remain empty until such time as the gardens produced suitable blooms.

Just past the dimly lit hall, the first door to the left led to the study. Although she had been good about keeping up the household accounts, she hadn't spent all that much time in the room. Her prized collection of books filled the mahogany bookcases, and her quill and ink pot were evident on the blotter in the middle of the small mahogany desk. The ledger for the household accounts lay open but set off to the side.

Jane hurried to the lamp on the edge of the desk, turning the key to bring up the flame so its light filled the room.

Behind the desk, a credenza between the bookshelves sported a silver salver upon which were bottles of various liqueurs.

Although she usually only helped herself to a glass of claret on occasion, Jane had seen to keeping brandy and scotch in the event someone of importance ever paid a call. Now she felt satisfaction at having insisted the liquors be included in the study when she and her housekeeper were setting up the household.

Andrew did the honors, pouring brandy into two of the brandy balloons set up on the adjacent salvers. He turned and offered her one.

Her eyes widened before she accepted the brandy. He hadn't even asked if she would join him but rather assumed she would, it seemed. "Thank you," she murmured as she took the glass of amber-colored liquor.

Without another word, they moved to the upholstered chairs set up near the fireplace. Although several lumps of coal were set up in the firebox along with kindling, the fire hadn't been lit. Andrew helped himself to a flint and crouched to light the kindling. Within a minute, he had a bright fire lighting that end of the dim study.

Jane settled into one of the chairs, rather liking how Andrew took the one adjacent but angled so they could converse over the side table in between.

"I cannot help but wish we could have done this twenty years ago," Andrew said before holding out his brandy balloon. *And every day since.*

Angling her head, Jane touched the edge of her glass to his "To regrets," she murmured, wondering if her words were appropriate. Of course she regretted marrying Michael Fitzpatrick. How could she not? Eighteen years wasted as a countess without a husband in residence. Eighteen years as a neglected wife, hosting others for tea on the occasions she wasn't in their parlors.

Eighteen years of desperation.

Andrew took a sip and gave an expression of approval. "French, no doubt," he said quietly.

"I've really no idea," Jane countered. "I merely asked that some be included in the household stores."

He smiled. "You were an excellent countess, no doubt," he said before taking another sip.

"I hardly know if I was or I wasn't, given Stoneleigh was rarely in residence," she replied with an arched brow. Although she might have at one time said the words with a hint of melancholy, she no longer felt sorry for her situation nor resented Michael for having left her alone in London all those years.

As a result of his extended absences, she had learned to live alone, learned to attend the theatre with a friend. Learned to spend her days shopping or visiting museums. Learned to appreciate an entire day spent reading a book in the gardens or part of a day walking in Hyde Park or riding her horse during the fashionable hour with a footman in tow.

Sleeping alone every night.

The life of an independent woman wasn't so very bad, she had decided. She had already made plans to continue it, although on a far more enjoyable level by including travel and a fatter purse. As for continuing to sleep alone, she really hadn't given that matter any thought.

That she might not be sleeping alone tonight had her breath catching, had her heart racing in anticipation.

"He was a fool," Andrew stated as he leaned forward.

Jane blinked at his accusation. "Sometimes," she agreed, uncertain as to what he meant.

Andrew shook his head. "I was a fool."

At this, Jane frowned. "What... What are you talking about?"

Angling his head to one side, Andrew set his glass on the table between them. "I asked for your father's permission to marry you, only to learn that you were already betrothed to Stoneleigh. Since it sounded as if you had been betrothed for some time, I wondered how it was you would seem amenable to an offer from me—"

"But I wasn't," Jane interrupted, her head shaking from side to side, remembering that back then, she didn't know she had signed a document to the contrary. "Or, at least, I had no idea my father had made an arrangement on my behalf until the following afternoon. I was quite surprised—disappointed, rather —I assure you."

"I know that now," he acknowledged with a nod. "But I admit, I was... incensed thinking you would lead me on." He ignored her gasp of surprise. "So, when I was approached by Lord Craven regarding his daughter, Elizabeth, that very same day, I..." Here, Andrew stopped, his brows furrowing with a combination of anger and remorse.

Jane set down her glass of brandy next to his, absently noting how his was nearly empty while hers had barely been touched. "You what?" she prompted, alarm bells going off in her head.

Andrew sighed. "I accepted his offer of a rather generous dowry in exchange for marrying her."

Stilling herself, Jane waited a moment before saying, "Go on." She could hardly fault him, she supposed. Especially if her father had made it clear she had been promised to another.

Her guest stared at her a moment. "My eldest is not my own," he whispered, the words coming out as if he had never put voice to them before. "I knew it before we married, of course," he added, his eyes darting to the side.

Jane closed her eyes. "You married a ruined woman," she stated quietly, the words not meant to sound like an accusation.

Andrew nodded. "Bess had been attacked one night, shortly after leaving the theatre. Although she had an escort that evening, Lord Brougham was waiting for her in her coach. He threatened the escort, who ran off. Bess was left alone with the devil. She told no one, of course, but..."

"She was left with child," Jane said in a whisper, her breaths coming in short bursts as she felt a combination of remorse and anger for what had happened to one of her peers. Bess Smith-Jones had probably done nothing to encourage Lord Brougham to do what he had done. He was a known rake of the worst kind, though, a despicable man who took what he wanted and could because, as an aristocrat, he was practically above the law.

"She had the baby?" Jane half-asked, realizing just then that Bess had delivered a healthy baby boy.

The son that now attended Cambridge.

"I raised him as my own," Andrew acknowledged with a nod. "Him as well as two other children who are mine. James is at Eton, and Sophia has just enrolled at Warwick's Grammar and Finishing School."

Jane held her breath, wondering what his next words might be.

"Had I any idea marriage to Michael Fitzpatrick wasn't your first choice, I would have stolen you away in the night and taken you to Gretna Green," Andrew stated firmly.

Gasping, Jane regarded him for a moment. She blinked as she considered his claim. "And I would have gone with you," she murmured. "Willingly."

Andrew was out of his seat in a second, his arms out to lift her from her chair at the same time.

His lips were on hers in an instant, the firm pillows as possessive as they had been their first night in the gardens behind Lord Weatherstone's mansion. His arms were as unyielding, the steel bands wrapped around her waist and shoulders in an embrace that crushed the front of her body against his.

She knew not how long he held her there, how long his lips kept her captive. She found she didn't care. Her entire world centered around this man and everything he had meant to her eighteen years ago.

"I will not object should you decide to spend the night in my bedchamber," she heard herself murmuring when he finally allowed her to take a breath.

Goodness! Had she really just invited him to spend the night?

"And as I promised, I shall not be leaving you alone this evening," he countered, easily lifting her into his arms and carrying her out of the study and up the stairs.

About to protest—she could walk up the stairs on her own—Jane decided instead to simply let him have his way. When he paused at the top of the stairs, she motioned to the door of her bedchamber.

Had Michael done this on their wedding night? At the residence in Westminster? She couldn't remember him doing so. But then, she could hardly remember Michael at all. She couldn't even conjure an image of him in her mind's eye at the moment. Her entire world was just Andrew Burroughs.

Max!

"Then I shall not be asking you to leave," she finally murmured when he opened her bedchamber door and crossed the threshold.

CHAPTER 8

A BALL OFFERS GOSSIP GALORE

Everyone who is anyone in the ton has received their invitation to the one ball that has everyone returning to London for the Season. Be sure to read the May 7, 1818 issue for the special coverage of the Weatherstone Ball! ~ An advertisement in London's premiere gossip rag, *The Tattler*.

May 6,1818, earlier that night at Lord Weatherstone's annual ball

Felix Turnbridge, Earl of Fennington, did his best not to scowl as he surveyed the assembly before him. As was the case every year, Lord Weatherstone's spring ball was proving to be a crush. Every candle in the five crystal chandeliers was lit, and every jewel glittered, whether it be on the wrist of some aristocrat's wife or in the pin securing a gentleman's cravat about his wretched neck.

And then there were the debutantes.

He sighed as his gaze swept the white-clad young ladies. He should be dancing with them, he considered. It was past time he at least look as if he planned to take a wife, even if he didn't plan to consider any of them. The idea of being wed to a woman almost half his age held little appeal, and even less when he heard several tittering at some comment one of them made.

Well, except for one of them.

He allowed his gaze to sweep the room in search of her, a sense of disappointment settling over him when he didn't immediately spot Emelia Comber among the younger ladies present.

Was she hiding for fear Mr. Pepperidge was present? Felix felt regret just then. With each time he collected her for their weekly rides in the park, he was more aware of her apparent hesitance at being seen with him.

Did she think Mr. Pepperidge would up the ante on the terms of his blackmail? *God, I hope not.*

At least he would see her in the morning, the thought bringing a slight grin to his otherwise grim face. See her. Spend nearly thirty minutes in her company.

Alone.

Thursday mornings with her had him imagining an entire lifetime of mornings with her. Waking up next to her in bed, eating with her in the breakfast parlor, walking with her on his arm in the park.

Ah, mornings with Emelia.

He only wished he wouldn't have to spend the entire night at the office prior to seeing her on the morrow, though. It was doubtful he would get any sleep tonight, what with having to finish the front page of *The Tattler* and seeing to it the pressman completed the typesetting and printing before the news sheet was set to hit the streets at seven o' clock.

The rest of this week's gossip rag would feature quite an array of stories. A more-than-usual number of subscriber-supplied *on-dit* had either been sent in or dropped off at the offices over the past few weeks, almost as if there was a contest to determine just who could send in the most gossip and see it in print. Letters included news of people whose names he didn't recognize and obscure aristocrats he hadn't yet looked up in his tattered copy of *Debrett's Peerage and Baronetage*.

The most unusual news had been an ongoing exposé of the sexual exploits of some heretofore unknown Spanish Lothario who was making his way through London bedchambers, leaving a number of unnamed women rather happy in his wake.

Everyone loved reading about rakes, but this particular libertine was proving far too popular with his readers. Their interest would wane if he didn't divulge more information about him, though. If he didn't learn the man's name, he wouldn't be including further mention of him in *The Tattler*, no matter how many satisfied females he apparently left in his wake. He was also beginning to wonder about the identity of Lord M. Everyone knew Lord M was the Marquess of Morganfield, but the most recent reports he was receiving had Lord M attending a number of clandestine meetings with Lady X at the same time Felix knew David Carlington, Marquess of Morganfield, was in the company of his wife or in the card room at White's.

So, who was this other Lord M?

A quick glance at one of the side walls of the ballroom had him doing a double-take. A row of young ladies in the guise of wallflowers looked as if they were holding up the wall. Most kept company with the potted palms that lined the ballroom. Shy or forced to keep close to their chaperones, they appeared as miserable as he felt. *Too bad they're not being visited by a Spanish Lothario*, he thought. *Or Lord M.*

One matron stood alone, though, her expression suggesting she was rather enjoying the entertainment as she watched the couples dance. *Lady Stoneleigh*, he realized, rather surprised the widow would be attending a ball so soon after her husband's death.

And then he realized it had already been a year since Michael Fitzpatrick had died. *Whilst riding his horse at night in Kent*, they said, although Felix was quite sure he had been riding something entirely different that night.

His mistress.

Served him right, Felix thought as he dared another glance in the direction of the widowed countess. The Earl of Stoneleigh had married one of the sweetest women in the *ton* and then left her in London so he could live with his mistress at his earldom's seat in Milton. *The fool.*

The story of the earl's death had filled only one column in the paper. Not particularly salacious—everyone knew the earl lived with his mistress and even had a family with her—the news had been met with yawns by those who bothered to read that section of the paper.

Felix sighed, half-tempted to ask the widow to dance. He wasn't really there to dance, although he had done so with Lady Emelia just the once. He was there to gather information. To listen in on conversations. To learn the latest gossip.

Everyone knew balls were a good source of the latest *on-dit,* and he needed as much as he could get. The next issue of *The Tattler* was due out the following day, and the front page was completely blank. He needed some gossip to go with the headline, *Weatherstone's Ball Best of the Season!*

"Have you danced even *once* this evening?"

Felix nearly gave a start at hearing the sultry voice of Adeline Carlington, Marchioness of Morganfield, as she looped an arm into his. Dressed in a red satin gown and adorned with an assortment of diamonds at her ears and neck, the daughter of an Italian count looked positively regal. Her dark hair, swept up into a smooth chignon, was pinned with a comb that probably cost more than his entailed properties earned him in a year. "Why, Lady Morganfield, are you asking me to dance?" Felix countered, deciding a bit of levity was in order. If left to his thoughts a moment longer, they would turn maudlin.

Adeline beamed. "Why, yes, I suppose I am. Shall we?" she agreed as she offered her other hand.

Felix was quick to escort her to the edge of the dancing where couples were whirling about in the first waltz of the evening. "How is it I have the honor to dance a waltz with you this evening?" he asked, his gaze darting between her and the other couples who made up the circle.

Well, almost a circle.

Several couples were somewhat out of formation with the rest, which meant he would need to keep an eye out to prevent any collisions. "Isn't Morganfield with you this evening?" he asked, quite sure he had seen the marquess about earlier in the evening.

Adeline gave a nod toward a couple opposite them on the floor. "He's dancing with our daughter," she said with a proud grin.

Glancing to his right, Felix quickly caught sight of the tall, lean marquess leading his daughter, Elizabeth, in the waltz. From his angle directly across from them, he was reminded that Elizabeth Carlington Bennett-Jones was in the later stages of breeding. "Am I correct in assuming she is about to bestow you with another grandchild?" he queried, thinking he could include a notice about the viscountess in the next issue of *The Tattler*. Her pregnancy wasn't really news—her condition had been reported by several news sources—but the *ton* always appreciated a reminder if they missed the entertainments where they could have seen it for themselves.

"Probably not even a month from now," Adeline responded lightly. "George is over the moon, of course."

Felix had to suppress a wince. Everyone seemed to refer to George Bennett-Jones, Viscount Bostwick, by his given name, which seemed a bit too familiar for his tastes. George had inherited the Bostwick viscountcy from an uncle—a miser of an uncle—and had never been much for formality, but he was a lord now. The least everyone could do was refer to him as *Bostwick*, Felix thought.

Another glance in the direction of Viscountess Bostwick, and Felix was stunned to see the Marquess of Morganfield hand off his daughter into the arms of her husband, the very man he had just been thinking about! George Bennett-Jones and his wife continued in the dance as if nothing untoward had happened. David Carlington, suddenly without a partner, simply stepped out of the circle and disappeared into the crowd that stood watching the dancers.

Felix blinked. It was as if the father and the viscount had planned the hand-off. One minute, Elizabeth was waltzing with her father, and in the next step, she was waltzing with her husband!

"I'll be damned," Felix murmured, realizing he had better pay attention to his own steps or they would collide with Lord Sinclair, who seemed intent on stepping on more toes than those belonging to his poor third-season partner.

Felix made a mental note to determine who she was so he could mention her and whoever made her slippers. *Poor dear.*

"It isn't the first time those two have made that move," Adeline said, realizing what had the earl cursing. "It is how my son-in-law was able to secure a dance with my daughter the very first time they danced. In this very ballroom, in fact, although it was back when Lord Weatherstone hosted the first ball of the Little Season."

Frowning, Felix wondered at her words. "Your husband handed her off to him like that?" he questioned, wondering if he could make mention of it in *The Tattler*. A story in retrospect, so to speak. How the unlikely pairing of a marquess' daughter to a viscount got its start. If he had space to fill, he could print the story, he decided.

Adeline rolled her eyes. "Actually, the Duke of Somerset handed her off that very first time," she said with a rather satisfied sigh. "Morganfield just likes to reenact it on occasion."

Felix nodded his understanding, wondering how he was going to describe the scene in the article he would have to write about the ball.

He was about to ask how the marquess was faring when a new couple appeared in the circle of dancers. A couple that included a young lady dressed in a white gown. "What's this now?" he murmured, not intending for the marchioness to overhear his comment.

Everyone knew a young lady couldn't simply dance the waltz —unless she had a voucher from one of the patronesses of Almack's. It was far too early for a debutante to have been granted such a voucher! Why, the Wednesday night subscription dances wouldn't start for another two weeks!

Adeline tried to follow his line of sight, her gaze settling on a rather tall gentleman dancing with Jane Fitzpatrick, Countess of Stoneleigh. "Andrew Burroughs!" she claimed with a good deal of excitement. "You must give him some leeway, I should think," she remarked, thinking perhaps the banker had drawn the earl's attention because he had erred in some steps in the waltz. "He's only just returned to London," she explained quickly, her attention on the middle-aged gentleman who seemed to be enjoying his first ball since moving back to England.

Following in his uncle's footsteps, Andrew had worked for over twenty years as a banker on the Continent. His uncle, Sir William Burroughs, had finally retired from the Bank of England just the year before, and Andrew was back to fill the void.

Unaware Lady Morganfield spoke of a different man than the one he had caught dancing the waltz with a debutante, Felix made a mental note to find out more about Andrew Burroughs just as the waltz ended. "Thank you, Lady Morganfield," Felix said as he raised her gloved hand to his lips and kissed her knuckles. "It's so good of you to afford me a dance," he added.

Giving the marchioness a bow, he stepped back and immediately turned to search for the man Adeline had identified as Andrew Burroughs. He found him in the crowd, although the young man was rushing from the ballroom with the white-gowned debutante in tow.

Felix couldn't believe his lucky stars.

The two were obviously heading out to the gardens, where

Andrew Burroughs would no doubt find a hedgerow behind which he could kiss the young lady he was leading.

Intent on paying witness so that he might identify the lady and be able report the incident as a witness rather than as overheard gossip, Felix followed at a discreet distance. Pretending to merely be taking the air, he sauntered on the flags. When he realized which set of hedgerows the banker had decided to use for cover, Felix ducked into the one just beyond, glad for his dark formal attire. The light from the paper lanterns that bobbed over part of the gardens was far too dim to give him away, though.

Finding an opening in the shrubs that offered a clearer view of the couple, Felix watched as the young lady stood on tip-toes. She was far shorter than the rather tall—what name had Lady Morganfield said? *Andrew Burroughs*—and seemed to be the one who initiated a rather long and passionate kiss with the banker.

A feeling of jealousy had Felix holding his breath. And wondering at his reaction. He didn't even know who the man was kissing, yet he couldn't help the odd sensation of envy he felt. That a young lady would simply encourage such a kiss was, well, it was scandalous! It was absurd. It was... well, it was rather sweet, he thought just then. The way the young lady seemed to lead on the young man. It was apparent the two had just met, and yet the banker had been able to lure the young lady into the gardens for what had to be her first kiss!

Or perhaps it was *his* first kiss! The young lady seemed to be the one making all the important moves!

Felix was still watching the two kiss when he heard the unmistakable voice of Lady Pettigrew calling for someone named Jane. The young woman he watched stepped away from the banker. Smiling, she thanked him, curtsied, and hurried off.

It was when she turned to go that Felix realized she was Lady Jane Browning, youngest niece of Lady Pettigrew.

He also realized that Andrew Burroughs bore a remarkable

resemblance to another young man in attendance that night. Why, he looked just like the Earl of Bellingham!

Well, I'll be damned, Felix thought as he wondered what might happen next. Lady Jane made some comment about coming out for air before she and her aunt disappeared into the ballroom. Had Lady Pettigrew even noticed how bee-stung her niece's lips had to have looked just then?

He was still deep in thought over Lady Jane's enthusiastic behavior when he realized the young man was straightening his coat. Felix watched as the banker strode from his hiding place and made his way back to the ballroom, acting as if nothing had happened.

The earl allowed a grin and decided he would keep his eyes on the banker—and the Earl of Bellingham—for the rest of the ball.

The night was still young.

Who knew if the young man had plans for any other young ladies in Lord Weatherstone's gardens?

CHAPTER 9
A BANKER BEGINS A
NEW LIFE

'*is the season for elicit affaires in the ton. Who will be visiting whose bedchambers this spring? To find out, be sure to subscribe or pick up your own copy every Thursday!* ~ An advertisement in the April 16, 1818 issue of *The Tattler*.

ay 7, 1818, very early in the morning
As Andrew Burroughs made his way from his uncle's mansion to Threadneedle Street, he couldn't help but replay the events of the night before in his mind's eye.

What a brilliant way to end a day! Although he had barely slept, his entire body seemed to thrum with excitement, a renewed vigor making his blood course through his veins as his horse negotiated the cobblestone streets along the way.

After all these years, she still feels affection for me, he thought with a grin he could barely contain. With any luck, they could be married before the end of the Season. Be on their wedding trip shortly thereafter. And he could be back at the bank when the rest of the aristocracy returned to London for the fall sessions of Parliament.

He thought of where he had found Jane that morning. With her head resting in the small of his shoulder, her entire body pressed against the side of his. One of her legs lay draped over one of his, the top of her thigh providing a perfect resting place for his manhood. Within seconds, the damned thing had sprung up as if it knew a better resting place was positioned only inches away.

Well, it did, and yet it was Jane who made the next move, lifting herself first on one elbow and then moving that luscious leg over both of his so that she straddled him. The next move had been his—or rather his manhood's, since he wasn't conscious of just how he was suddenly inside her. Warm and wet and so tight he'd had to think of King and country for a moment to keep from allowing his release, Andrew had held onto her hips and enjoyed the rather slow and provocative moves Jane made as she rode him to completion.

He hadn't expected the demure widow to do such a thing, especially in the gray light of early morning. Especially given her queries voiced in the middle of the night. Queries that had him feeling a bit relieved if also a bit nervous. Her late husband had obviously not been a frequent visitor to her bed, nor had he expected her to practice anything out of the usual with respect to sexual congress.

Andrew hadn't expected anything from his late wife, either. He had never proposed they do anything out of the ordinary, not that he knew much given his limited experience. Bess had never offered or requested something different. But then, he hadn't married her for the same reasons he wanted to marry Jane. The few times he had been welcomed into Bess' bed had been for simple acts of intercourse. Marital duty. His attempts to pleasure Bess had been met with polite declinations, and so he had simply ceased to try.

His decision to seduce Jane—he hated thinking of it in those terms, but no other word would suffice in explaining just what he had done—had come from a need for expediency and out of selfishness.

He wanted Jane. Had always wanted her. And given her year of mourning ended the day of the Weatherstone ball, he had the perfect venue in which to reintroduce himself.

As for how he had gone about it, even he was a bit shocked at himself. A rake, he was not, but now he wondered what Jane would think of him as this day went on.

He rather hoped she wouldn't think too much.

Should she come to believe he had done wrong, she might never agree to see him again. He couldn't abide life without her, though. He knew that now. Last night had confirmed what he suspected. He had loved Jane Vandermeer in the past, and he still loved her now.

Perhaps she would wonder what he thought of her, though, given what she had done whilst sitting atop him. Her moves had been tentative at first. Curious. Cautious. But once she gave into his hold on her, accepted his touch and his help in learning what to do, she took over and rode him to completion.

Perhaps she had surprised herself, for her cry of his name had filled the bedchamber as her torso had lifted from his, her neck arching back and her chin thrusting up at the same time her body seemed to quake atop him. Then she had tumbled down onto the front of his body, quickly covering herself with the little bit of a quilt still left on the bed. She burrowed her face into the space next to his ribs as if to hide.

"Good morning, beautiful," he had said while trying to fight the bubble of a chuckle that threatened to spoil the moment.

What else could he say?

She was the most welcome sight he had beheld at that time of the morning in probably his entire life.

Her first response was unintelligible, the words muffled and her lips tickling his ribs until he could reposition an arm and pull her back atop him. "I didn't quite catch that, my lady."

A lock of hair covered part of her face but still allowed one eye and most of her bee-stung lips to show. "You must think me the most wanton woman..."

"And if I did?" he whispered, his grin widening. "Would you find me despicable?" He felt her relax as she allowed a sigh.

"Of course not."

"Good. Because I rather adore you as a wanton." At her sudden gasp of shock and widened eyes, he added, "It's our secret, for I shall tell no one of your delectable body, or of how beautiful you are when you're making love, or how delightful it is to kiss you."

Jane swallowed before moving one hand to push away the hair in front of her face. Her lips sought his, the hand moving from her hair to cup the side of his face as she did so. "What happens now?" she whispered, her eyes wide.

Her query had been made with a hint of terror, as if she were truly frightened. It was at that moment that Andrew realized three things about Jane Vandermeer Fitzpatrick.

Before today, she had probably never awakened to find a man in her bed. If he'd had any concerns about her having become a Merry Widow since Stoneleigh's death, he needn't have worried.

She had probably never been pleasured by the earl. Although he didn't have a great deal of experience himself— his father had died before Andrew's sixteenth birthday, the occasion upon which his older brothers had been treated to entire nights in the company of a courtesan—he had been married for nearly ten years before Bess' untimely death. And there were books on the topic of sexual congress in the duke's library, each one having paid a visit to his bedchamber for late nights spent studying.

And finally, before this morning, Jane had never before initiated any kind of intimacy. The fact that she did so apparently had her feeling a bit embarrassed, perhaps even a bit surprised at her actions.

Andrew kissed her then, a slow, sweet kiss he intended to bestow on her every morning for the rest of their lives. "I regret that I must take my leave of you for now. I have meetings at the bank this morning, and I have a dinner party with one of my cousins in Chiswick this evening. I'll be spending the night at the old family house." His face screwed up as if he wasn't exactly looking forward to staying at a Georgian estate that had paid witness to at least five generations of Merriweathers and Grandbys and, for a few years since 1804, a family of Burroughs. Or perhaps at Woodscastle, if Gregory Grandby or the Wellinghams offer hospitality. "But I shall return on the morrow. May I pay a call on you in the afternoon? Take you for a ride in the park, perhaps?"

Although his initial words obviously caused disappointment—Jane apparently would have preferred to stay in bed the entire day, and truth be told, he would as well—she brightened at the suggestion of riding in the park. "Sounds lovely," she murmured.

Kissing her once more, Andrew pulled away and sighed. "I know one shouldn't have regrets, but I really wish I had pressed my case with your father all those years ago," he whispered as he removed himself from the bed. "Or just taken you to Gretna Green."

He could feel her eyes on him as he gathered his clothes, as she watched him dress. He supposed he should wonder at her curiosity—she was a widow, after all, and had probably seen her husband naked...

He blinked, realizing one more thing about Jane Vandermeer Fitzpatrick. She had probably never seen a naked man in the light of day before this morning.

Lord Stoneleigh had spent more time with his mistress in Milton in Kent rather than with Jane in London. He probably bed his wife while wearing a nightshirt that reached his ankles.

"Should I be concerned by your perusal of me in my current state of undress?" he asked with an arched brow, his voice giving away his teasing manner.

Jane shook her head. "No," she managed to get out, although

her voice sounded strangled, as if she were embarrassed at being caught staring.

Andrew had to suppress a chuckle "I don't suppose your butler is still abed?" he half-asked as he tucked in his shirt and buttoned his breeches.

Her eyes widening at the realization that the servants would know—probably already knew—what she had been doing for the entire night, Jane swallowed and glanced toward the mantle clock. "Simonton is probably still at Norwick House with his wife," she replied hopefully. "But there is a set of stairs to the left that leads down to the back door and to the gardens behind the house."

Andrew grinned as he buttoned his waistcoat. "Despite what you may be imagining, I have *never* been in this situation before," he claimed with an arched brow. "Having to sneak off in the morning fog from a dalliance with a beautiful woman."

Jane colored up at the comment. "If it's any consolation, neither have I."

Bending over the bed, Andrew kissed her once more. Twice more. When he finally pulled away, he allowed a sigh of disappointment. "I'll come for you at four o'clock tomorrow. We still have much to discuss," he murmured as he straightened the bedclothes and covered her with the bed linens and quilt.

After that, he had taken his leave of her bedchamber, made his way to the back of the house and crept down the back stairs. He might have made it out of the house without being seen except for the scullery maid who nearly collided with him at the back door.

"Pardon me, my lady," he said as he tipped his hat and traded places with her in the small entry. "I've just now realized I've got the wrong house!"

The maid's round eyes seemed to go from fright to delight at his words, but she didn't have a chance to respond as he hurried out the door. Giving a quick glance around the gardens, he followed the flagstone path to the gate and the alley beyond it.

How fortuitous, he thought as he realized the alley connected with the one behind his uncle's house four streets away.

He was home by seven o' clock in the morning, shaved and changed by eight, and on a horse to Threadneedle Street by half-past, his only thoughts of Jane Vandermeer Fitzpatrick.

CHAPTER 10
TATTLING TO THE TATTLER

Clandestine meetings are so much more enjoyable when the parties involved are warm and dry and comfortable. Should you ever plan one, do not follow our lead and meet in the park at eight o' clock in the morning. ~ Part of the editor's last article in the May 14, 1818 issue of *The Tattler*.

May 7, 1818, Hyde Park
Emelia Comber, the only daughter of the Earl of Aimsley, approached the bench in Hyde Park with more than a bit of trepidation. Backed by a hedgerow and fairly well hidden from all but the crushed granite path that passed in front of it, the bench was positioned among several tall bushes and a few trees that seemed to have been planted with the deliberate intention of affording the spot a fair bit of privacy. Anyone could happen upon her whilst she sat waiting for Mr. Pepperidge, though. Anyone could pass by whilst she sat with Mr. Pepperidge.

Heaven forbid.

Given the early morning hour, though, and the low fog

blanketing this part of the park, she hoped no one else would even be *in* the park, let alone in this part of the park.

She could only hope.

After all, she had visited this same bench six times before over the course of the last six weeks. How long could her luck hold out?

Gingerly, she took a seat at one end of the bench and inhaled a steadying breath, remembering just then to lower the veil on her hat so the top half of her face would be obscured from anyone who might give her a second glance. Without a maid or a chaperone, she was a sitting duck for any unscrupulous member of the opposite sex who might happenstance upon her.

Such as Mr. Pepperidge.

Well, he hadn't made any advances towards her in their prior meetings, so she rather doubted he would do so today. But that didn't mean he wouldn't *try*. The way the man gazed at her had her thinking he was undressing her with his eyes. Contemplating a stolen kiss, perhaps. Assessing her with the intention of... *something*.

She shivered, and not just from the early morning cold.

He couldn't. He simply couldn't. He knew quite enough— he knew she had been a tomboy in her younger days! He knew she had kissed Lord Fennington in the Weatherstone gar-dens!—and he certainly didn't need more damning information to put into his damnable publication.

Damn him, anyway.

Thank the gods her mother had been providing news she could pass along, almost as if she knew Emelia needed fodder for her meetings on Thursday mornings. The comments she made about others in the *ton* tended to be about people Emelia had never heard of, but then she had only been back in London for a couple of months. Mr. Pepperidge seemed to write down everything she told him as if her words were gold.

Emelia took a steadying breath, realizing she would require a vinaigrette should she continue her line of thinking. She was on the verge of fainting due to hyperventilation!

And I never faint!

Her gloved hands held in her lap, Emelia did her best to keep them still. Despite having spent time in the company of Mr. Pepperidge—six times, so far—she was always nervous with him. Nervous because he knew far too much about her. Nervous because he could use what he knew to ruin her standing in polite society. Nervous because if she should be seen in his company, word would get around that she was providing him with gossip.

Over the short amount of time Emelia had been back in London, she had learned that, as the publisher of *The Tattler*, the most popular gossip rag in all of London, Mr. Pepperidge was the bane of the *ton*. And apparently a star in the publishing world and to anyone who bought copies of his weekly news sheet.

Damn them, too, Emelia thought with a sigh, her breathing once again too fast.

The damning thought of Mr. Pepperidge seemed to conjure him into being, for the tall man with a funny bump of a belly, clothing better suited to a clerk than a supposedly rich publisher, and a rather tall beaver, appeared from the other side of the nearest bush and afforded her a deep bow.

Had he been hiding back there? Or had he followed a different path to get to the bench?

Emelia gave him a nod but did not stand up, nor did she offer her hand. "Good morning, Mr. Pepperidge," she said in a quiet voice.

"It will be, I promise," the publisher stated as he took a seat at the other end of the bench. A grin graced his face, making him appear genuinely happy.

Turning to stare at him, Emelia's eyes widened. Could it be he was planning to end their weekly liaisons? Could it be he felt he had extracted enough information from her that he would allow her to return to her somewhat staid and boring life as a daughter of the *ton*? "Does that mean I will have fulfilled my obligation to you after this meeting?" she asked with a bit too much enthusiasm.

Why, oh why, had she allowed the Earl of Fennington to kiss her? She had only agreed to a walk in the gardens with the man —in broad daylight, no less—during an afternoon soirée at Lord Weatherstone's gardens last March because, well, she was *attracted* to the man. But back then, she had thought his invitation was offered because her mother had suggested it. Emelia had accepted thinking the man's intentions were *honorable.*

Since then, the earl hadn't dared to steal a kiss whilst they were in one another's company. They had certainly been in one another's company. though. Besides his insistence on driving her in the park once a week for the past six weeks, Lord Fennington seemed to make an appearance at every garden party, every soirée, every ball, the theatre, *musicales...*

It was almost as if the man were stalking her. And yet, he hadn't made mention of the word 'marriage' nor asked her if she was considering matrimony.

Emelia shook her head. Perhaps she only noticed his presence because she had caught him staring at her when he thought she wasn't looking.

Several times.

His usual expression was rather glum, but when he was staring at her, his expression made him appear so much younger. Hopeful, perhaps. Thoughtful.

Happy.

She wondered how old he was. Certainly not as old as her father, but certainly not as young as any of the bucks who behaved badly at their men's clubs and made fools of themselves whilst racing phaetons in the dark. Emelia remembered him saying he had attended Eton with her older brother, so he would have to be close to thirty, she reasoned. *I should look him up in the copy of Debrett's in father's library,* she thought.

Emelia shook her head at the thought. *His kiss is what had her in this mess.* Just because she had agreed to walk with him in the gardens didn't give the earl the right to steal a kiss!

But then, she hadn't exactly pushed him away, either. She hadn't put voice to a complaint. She hadn't dissuaded him in the least.

In fact, she had returned the kiss.

Kisses.

Welcomed it.

Them.

Reveled in it.

All of them.

Her entire body shivered at the memory of that kiss.

Those kisses.

Thrilled at the thought that a man as handsome as Felix Turnbridge, Earl of Fennington, might be auditioning her for the role of his countess, Emelia hadn't even considered the two of them might be discovered behind a hedgerow in the middle of a simple kiss.

Apparently Mr. Pepperidge was good at hiding behind the other side of the hedgerow, for his note threatening to expose her kiss with the earl arrived at Aimsley House the following morning. At the bottom, a crude map showing the position of the park bench was drawn in ink.

Emelia would never forget that letter. Never forget that first meeting with the despicable man who introduced himself as Mr. Frederick Pepperidge, editor of *The Tattler*.

Never forget the terms of his blackmail.

His requirement for withholding the damning information about her? Meet with him every Thursday morning at eight o'clock in the park. Meet with him and provide the tidbits of gossip that she had been privy to whilst paying calls on the ladies of the *ton* during the week prior. The news she might have overheard whilst attending a ball or soirée. It was enough to have her thinking of staying at home, but she knew that would only delay the inevitable. Better to do as the rogue required and get it over with as quickly as possible.

Mr. Pepperidge shook his head at hearing her query about having completed her obligation to meet with him. "Not quite, my lady," he replied with a slight grin. "I was merely referring to the promise of better weather." He paused a moment, pulling a pad and a charcoal pencil from his greatcoat in order to record her words—or, at least, the gist of them.

He never actually used her *exact* words when writing his gossip column on Mayfair parlor talk, she noted. Emelia only knew this because she had been surreptitiously purchasing copies of *The Tattler* in order to discover how he was printing the news she provided. "One more time we shall meet, Lady Emelia. That will be the eighth time, and then we shall be done with one another," he added, managing to keep the sound of melancholy from touching his voice.

Emelia sighed and nodded her head. *One more time.*

CHAPTER 11
THE MORNING AFTER

Rumor has it widows are enjoying an especially busy Season this year! Between balls, soirées, and the theatre, many a widow has been spotted on the arms of some of our most eligible—and not-so-eligible—gentleman. They're no doubt spending time between the sheets, as well. Naughty, naughty! ~ An article in the April 9, 1818 issue of *The Tattler*.

May 7, 1818, very early in the morning

Jane watched Andrew as he moved to retrieve his clothing, inhaling sharply when she saw how the muscles of his back rippled beneath his skin. When he straightened, she sighed as he turned to her and gave her a wink. Perhaps he thought she would turn away as he pulled on his smalls, but she merely captured her lower lip with a tooth and stared in wonder.

She had never seen her late husband like this, completely naked in the dim light of morning. He had come to her bed on only a few occasions very early in their marriage, and then only a few times during the subsequent years, always wearing a nightshirt that covered him to his knees, his breath sour from too much alcohol. When he was done, he returned to his bedchamber on the other side of the dressing room. He never slept in her bed but for those few minutes after he had completed his business. She rather doubted Stoneleigh's body was anything like Andrew's, though. Despite his age, Andrew was still trim, still possessed a physique that defied his position as a banker.

Their brief conversation was as unexpected as it was reassuring. *Such a gentleman,* she thought as she watched him pull on his breeches. A sense of disappointment settled over her when a shirt suddenly covered his torso, hiding the sprinkling of graying crisp curls and sculpted muscles she had felt beneath her fingertips the night before.

She hadn't even expected to wake up to find him still in her bed—didn't all men leave their lovers' beds whilst it was still dark?

Apparently not.

Which had to explain what possessed her to do what she did. There had been that moment right after she had awakened, when she had climbed atop him. Before she quite realized what she was doing. Before reason had a chance to still her attempt at seduction.

What must he have thought to awaken with me atop him like that? she wondered.

Well, he did seem rather pleased, actually. Even assured her he rather liked her as wanton.

A wanton.

Never in her life could she have been accused of being a wanton!

When Andrew bid her a good day and promised to take her for a ride the following afternoon, Jane could hardly believe the sense of excitement she felt. She watched as he made his way to the door, watched with a wan smile as he opened it a crack to dare a glance into the hall, and then sighed when he hurried out. She waited for the latch to click before settling back into the mattress, a huge smile spreading over her face. She had half a mind to put on a dressing gown and hurry to one of the back windows to watch as Andrew made his way out of the gardens and into the alley behind the townhouse.

That is, until she realized how chilly the bedchamber was just then. Odd, given how warm she had felt only moments ago. Her maid would come in and build a fire in an hour or two, though. Until then, she would simply stay in bed and replay the events of the night over and over in her head, her lips displaying a smile she couldn't possibly hide.

Four hours later, she awoke with a start.

"What a relief, milady," Nicole, her lady's maid, said brightly when Jane sat up straight and stared around the room. "I don't recall you ever sleeping in this late, but then, I suppose you were at the ball until nearly sunrise. I didn't even hear you come in." This last was said with a hint of a question, suggesting Nicole didn't know what time her mistress had returned to the townhouse. It was also confirmation that Jane's arrival with Andrew Burroughs hadn't caused a stir amongst the servants upstairs.

"I had a wonderful time and simply couldn't go to sleep until nearly dawn," Jane admitted as she dared a glance at the mantle clock. *Eleven o'clock?* Faith! It was a wonder Nicole hadn't summoned a physician!

"Oh, I'm so happy to hear you say it, the ball being your first in so long, milady," Nicole said as she gathered up the ball gown and petticoats Jane had worn the night before. "I see you were able to undress yourself without any help."

Jane wasn't about to admit she'd had plenty of help. Why, Andrew's deft fingers had undone the buttons down the back of her gown while he kissed her senseless. The ties of her corset were no match for those same fingers, although how he had managed to get his lips between her breasts while doing so was a testament to the man's skills as a lady's maid. The ties holding up her petticoats had been undone at some point when his lips were trailing along one of her ribs, and, well, since she wouldn't be caught dead wearing drawers —even if Queen Charlotte had apparently taken to wearing them—she had been left barely able to stand on her own in her chemise, stockings and dance slippers.

She hadn't allowed him to remove the chemise. At least, not at first—not until she had been allowed to undo the buttons of his topcoat and waistcoat. While he removed the garments, she struggled with the fastenings of his breeches, well aware of his hardening manhood behind the placket. She had just about succeeded in her task when his hands had gently taken hers and moved them to his chest.

"Not just yet," Andrew had whispered as he lifted her into his arms and placed her on the bed. The linens had been turned down, the crisp white fabric a sharp contrast to the deep blue velvet counterpane folded down at the foot of the mattress. Once Andrew had her settled and her shoes removed, he turned and sat on the edge to remove his own dance shoes and stockings. "I have been wishing for this night for a very long time," he murmured quietly.

The words had made her heart soar just then. Soar and ache and beat so fast she thought she might faint. "It is good of you to say so, but certainly not necessary. I've been long out of the school room," she hedged, moving her hands to barely touch the fine lawn of his shirt. When he stilled his movements, she drew back, thinking she shouldn't have touched him. But one of his hands captured hers and brought it to his lips.

"They are not just words, Jane. I have wanted you ever since those afternoons I took you for rides in Hyde Park," he whispered, his lips covering hers. "And every day since," he murmured when he finished the kiss.

The admission had her breath catching, a tear threatening to spill from the corner of one eye. "I wish you could have had me," she whispered when he finally pulled away to remove his shirt.

Blinking when she realized Nicole was staring at her, Jane turned her attention to the maid. "I can undo my own buttons when the situation requires it. I certainly wasn't going to awaken you given how late I arrived," she added. She allowed a sigh when she realized Nicole must have been regarding her for some time.

"It was awfully considerate of you, milady."

Jane allowed a shrug, her mind once again remembering her words to Andrew, remembering how they had been tentative and yet sure. Their behavior with one another had been the same, as if they were poised on the brink of something important and weren't quite sure whether to take the plunge.

It was then Jane realized just how aroused her body had become. How ripe and ready she was for whatever Andrew had in mind for them that night. Part of her thought he would merely play lady's maid and then take his leave once she was sleeping—he had initially said he wanted to see her safely home. The other part thrilled at the idea that he had far more in mind. Kissing and touching and lovemaking, the likes of which she had never before experienced.

He had already accomplished the kissing.

His initial touches had been cautious, careful and light, his fingertips sending skitters of pleasure darting beneath her skin. Her light gasps and frequent sighs spurred him on until she was aware he was completely naked, naked and pressed against the side of her entire body, one elbow supporting him as he gently pulled the bow of one garter tie and then slowly pushed the silk stocking down her leg. When it was just about beyond his reach, Jane had bent her knee and watched as he pulled it completely from her foot. He had done the same with her other stocking, the light touch of his finger between her stocking and leg sending skitters of pleasure up and down her thigh.

"Oh, here they are!" Nicole announced with what sounded like a good deal of relief, briefly disappearing from Jane's view as she leaned down.

Pulled from her reverie, Jane frowned. "What are you talking about?" she asked in confusion.

When Nicole reappeared, the silk stockings dribbling from her fingers, one of Jane's legs jerked with the memory of how they had been removed.

"Your stockings, milady." She blinked and then angled her head. "Why, you must have had a wonderful time at the ball."

Jane stared at the maid, wondering what had her maid coming to that conclusion. "It was rather enjoyable," she hedged, now wondering at the maid's odd expression.

Truth be told, the ball had been a glittering but rather dull affair. Up until Andrew Burroughs had appeared and asked for a dance, the highlights of the evening had been the three instances that she witnessed the same young man take his leave of the ballroom in favor of the gardens with three different young ladies on his arm.

Then Andrew Burroughs had appeared and swept her into the waltz, and then into her carriage, and then into her bed. She could feel her face flush with the memory of the evening's events. She almost forgot they had spent a few minutes in the study, as well.

"Well, it's certainly brought color to your cheeks again, milady," Nicole commented. "Now, I'll just put these away and draw your bath," she added as she made her way into the dressing room.

Jane swallowed, wondering how long she would be able to keep the evidence of her carnal activities from her maid.

The thought of carnal activities had her remembering the moment when she realized Andrew had every intention of spending the entire night with her.

Once he had divested her of her stockings, his large hands had moved beneath her bottom and lifted it slightly. The palms of his hands slid along her thighs, lifting and spreading them wide and then pulling her knees to the sides of his torso.

When the length of his velvet-on-steel shaft pressed against her quim, she understood the meaning of his words about wishing to have her. It was quite apparent he was about to get his wish. *And I, mine,* she remembered thinking as her arms moved to wrap around his neck.

He barely moved his hips as his lips came down onto hers, his manhood sliding along her honeyed folds, his taut sac following to press harder. The sensation was so unexpected, she had to inhale and break the kiss, which only sent his lips trailing down her cheek to her jaw and then to her neck and collarbones.

When his tongue dipped into the hollow of her throat, she was aware of how his hips had lifted, and the tip of his manhood delved an inch or two inside her. The slow movement of his hips had him retreating and advancing just a bit deeper each time until he was finally buried as far as he could be.

The exquisite torture had her writhing beneath him, her chest rising with his slow thrusts until she whimpered for something more. Relations with her husband had never been like this, never been slow and sensuous, warm and wet, intimate and exciting.

She would have been quite satisfied had he simply allowed his release and left her body—who was she to expect there could be more? So much more?

So when his lips moved to one of her nipples, she gasped as a sharp shiver of pleasure had her arching her back. His lips on her other nipple had her reacting the same. But it was when one of his hands slid down the front of her body that she realized he was quite skilled in the art of lovemaking.

One of his fingers—or perhaps it was his thumb—pressed against the aching bud between her swollen folds and set off a series of sharp but pleasurable waves in her lower body. At the same time, he drove himself into her several times, his thrusts seemingly tied to the waves of pleasure she was experiencing so that when one crested and stayed suspended, she held her breath and reveled as he once again drew his thumb over her womanhood and sent the wave of pure pleasure crashing, the sensation so powerful, she was quite sure she saw stars and bright lights and flashes of lightening behind her eyelids. The sound of his gentle curse filled the room as her lower body seemed suddenly awash in warmth.

Her hands, until then simply hanging onto the sides of his body for dear life, slid down the length of his torso, rounding his buttocks before coming to rest on the back of his thighs. His seemed to shudder at her touch, his breaths hard and sounding loud in her ear. His body slackened over hers, and his head fell onto the pillow next to her head.

"I love you, Jane," he whispered, his breaths sending a wash of warmth across her shoulder.

Jane stilled herself, stunned at the simple words she had never before heard from a man's lips.

It had been nearly eighteen years since Andrew Burroughs had courted her! How could he admit such a thing now? Hadn't she changed since those days they spent riding in the park? Hadn't *he* changed since those days? Or had their time in bed sent his brain spinning, forcing him to say words he couldn't possibly mean?

"Do not think too much just now, my love," he murmured, as if he could read her thoughts.

She stilled herself and turned her head slightly. The simple movement sent a wave of pleasure through her body again, as if the first wave had been too much and some pleasure had been left in reserve.

"I don't know that I am capable of rational thought at the moment," she murmured with a sudden grin.

He returned the grin before moving to kiss her earlobe. "It's the irrational thoughts you should avoid right now,' he countered, the words sounding loud and breathy in her ear. "I want you, Jane. I always have," he whispered. With that, his body seemed to relax onto hers, his breathing finally evening out after a moment or two.

Although he was a tall man, Jane found Andrew wasn't particularly heavy, at least not so heavy the mattress couldn't support the both of them. She could breathe just fine, and she rather liked how his body seemed much like a heavy quilt in winter, draped over her body and acting as a cocoon of comfort. His even breathing told her he had fallen asleep, a situation she found rather endearing just then.

I want you. I always have.

Such welcome words! she thought in her drowsy stupor.

In moments, Jane, too was asleep.

They hadn't stayed asleep for long, though. It was as if their bodies were well aware of one another, their arousals timed so they awoke and made quiet love several more times throughout the night. One time had been almost frantic, as if they both craved a quick and intense release, while another was achingly slow and yet so satisfying, they had sighed in unison after the pleasure subsided.

The last time had been rather funny, as if the two realized what they had done and were inexplicably embarrassed at their behavior. His teasing touches had tickled and led to her titters and giggles. But his manner had soon sobered when he kissed her at the end. "I do love you," he claimed again just before his movements ceased and his body went rigid with his release.

Jane had kissed him then, kissed him with the same fervor he had shown the night before and then pulled his head down to her breast when she could tell he no longer had the strength to hold himself up.

She allowed a sigh of contentment at the memory before she realized Nicole was back from the bath and regarding her expectantly.

"Is there anything special happening in the household today?" Jane asked, about to get out of bed when she realized she wasn't wearing her nightrail. In fact, she wasn't wearing anything at all! The simple movement had also sent the scents of amber and citrus wafting from the pillow next to hers, which had her inhaling deeply.

Max!

She dared another sniff before realizing the side of the bed on which Andrew had slept was made up as if no one had slept there. *Such a considerate man,* she thought before she realized her maid was still staring at her. "What is it?" Jane asked as she pulled on her dressing gown. At least that garment had been within reach, probably because Andrew had seen to putting it there. She certainly couldn't remember having left it out on the bed.

"Elsie said she came upon a man at the back door of the house this morning."

Jane blinked, her breath gone from her body. "A man?"

Nicole nodded. "She was on her way to the coal bin. Said the gent was very well-dressed, as if for an evening at the theatre, and that he was quite polite. Said he had come in the back door, and realized he was in the wrong house and simply made to leave before anyone could discover him," she explained quickly. "Called her 'my lady', too. She'll not be forgettin' that for some time," she added with an arched eyebrow.

Not sure what to say—Nicole's manner didn't suggest she suspected anything—Jane thought it better to be safe than sorry. She allowed a look of worry to cross her face. "Should I call for a Runner, do you suppose?" she asked as she feigned panic.

Her maid seemed to think on the question for a time before finally shaking her head. "Probably not, my lady. From Elsie's words, the man seemed like a perfect gentleman. And it's not as if *The Tattler* will print a story about it."

At the mention of London's most notoricus gossip rag, Jane gave a start. "Why ever would *The Tattler* wish to print anything about a drunk man making his way into the wrong house?" she asked, her question meant to be rhetorical.

Nicole answered it, though.

"Why, you're a widow, milady. Some might think he was here to ravish you." Her eyes widened. "Or that he was here for a liaison!"

Jane blinked, her alarm not the least bit feigned. She was

about to murmur something like, *I could only hope*, but thought better of it.

What if Nicole reported her words to one of the writers for the gossip rag?

Andrew Burroughs *had* been there for a liaison, although certainly not one she had arranged in advance. Given how wonderful her entire body felt just then, she found she looked forward to future encounters with the banker. "Well, no harm done, I suppose," she finally replied, deciding a change of subject was in order. "I've been invited to Lady Torrington's luncheon today. As of today, no more widow's weeds."

Nicole nodded. "The lavender lawn then?"

Jane considered the question and realized she would have to pay a call on a modiste in the next day or so. She hadn't a single gown in the current style. Although she had several mourning gowns that weren't black, the thought of wearing lavender every day wasn't particularly appealing. "That will have to do," she sighed.

Although her expression suggested she wasn't looking forward to her day, the rest of her body certainly was. Especially to the following day. Andrew would be taking her for a ride in the park. And perhaps for a different sort of ride after that.

A smile finally appeared on Jane's face as she headed into the bath.

CHAPTER 12
LADY JANE GOSSIP

es, we were selfish. Yes, we did wrong. Yes, we justified it in the name of affection. But if we had the chance to do it over again and do it differently, would we have? No, dear reader, for we were a fool in love. ~ The editor's final article in the May 14 issue of *The Tattler*.

ay 7 1818, back in Hyde Park at eight o' clock in the morning

Mr. Pepperidge dared a glance in Emelia's direction, noting her nervousness, noting how the veil from her hat hid her beautiful green eyes from being seen by him or anyone else who might pass by. Not that anyone would be out in this fog at this ungodly hour of the morning, especially the morning after a ball that hadn't ended until the wee hours of the morning.

Christ! Just over ninety minutes ago, he had nearly decided to send his valet away, roll over, and return to the sweet dreams he had been enjoying just the moment before his valet opened the dark velvet drapes and woke him with the reminder that he had a meeting that morning. At eight o' clock.

He had only been in bed an hour! After leaving the

Weatherstone mansion just after the midnight supper—a rather dull affair except that he had learned a thing or two he could use —he'd had to head straight for the offices of *The Tattler* to finish the paper. There he found a letter listing various tidbits of gossip from an unknown subscriber, and the pressman, who was waiting for the type for the front page so he could finish printing the rag. He had set aside the letter and concentrated on getting the articles finished for the front page.

The letter! He slapped his forehead, disappointed he hadn't stuck it in his hat or waistcoat pocket. Left on his desk back at the office, it was unfolded and probably on the stack of other subscriber-supplied gossip. He hoped the pressman hadn't simply helped himself to it as a means to fill space.

He would pay a visit to the office in Sackville Street after the day's session of Parliament ended and determine if it included any news he could use in the next issue.

The thought of being able to see Lady Emelia had him nearly bouncing out of his bed, anxious to dress and help himself to a bit of breakfast and a cup of coffee before he hurried from his townhouse in Bruton Street and made his way to their assignation in Hyde Park.

Assignation.

He rather liked the word. It portended naughtiness. Intrigue. Danger.

Oh, who the hell am I trying to bamboozle? Meeting with Lady Emelia was more milquetoast than anything else. The poor girl didn't have a scandalous bone in her body! He always hoped there would be a bit of naughtiness in what Lady Emelia shared. A bit of a blush on her rather beautiful complexion. A bit of gossip that would put all the other gossip to shame. Instead, the news she shared always seemed familiar, as if he had already read it in the missives he was receiving from some reader who identified herself as *The Gossip Goddess*. The letters from that particular woman were always pink and scented with a delightful perfume. He had thought he might be able to figure out just who had sent the letters if he caught the same scent on a woman at a ball, or a dinner party, or during a soirée, but he hadn't had any luck. Yet.

As far as truly salacious, scandalous gossip was concerned, he had come to realize Lady Emelia apparently wasn't privy to it. She was the epitome of staid. Reserved. Behaved.

The perfect lady.

And he wouldn't be nearly as attracted to her if she were a gossip monger. He would probably despise her if she were.

He had certainly come to despise himself over the past few years of publishing the gossip rag. *Devil's work,* he thought as he considered how he was going to bedevil Lady Emelia today.

"Now then, what can you tell me about last night's ball?" Mr. Pepperidge began, his speech tinged with a hint of Cockney, hoping she could provide more tidbits than what he had already included in that day's issue of *The Tattler*. After all, Lord Weatherstone's ball was always the source of so much gossip, it took at least *two* issues to cover it all. "Everyone knows his gardens and library are the stuff of legend when it comes to assignations and dalliances. Why, you know it first hand," he claimed as his eyebrows waggled. "You must have been privy to a few... inappropriate couplings," he hinted, wondering whom she might mention.

Only one more week of this, and he would no longer be meeting Lady Emelia in the park. Only one more week and he could finally offer for her hand. His eight weeks of once-a-week rides in the park would be complete, although he hoped they could continue them on a more frequent schedule once they were married.

He would miss these quiet assignations with the young lady, though. Well, *young* was probably pushing it a bit, he considered, but she wasn't quite on the shelf. *Three-and-twenty,* he thought she might be.

He had a mind to ask Milton Grandby, Earl of Torrington, when he met him for drinks later that night at White's. He was quite sure Grandby was the girl's godfather—nearly every daughter of the *ton* of about that age was, after all. But to ask directly about Lady Emelia might have the earl thinking Felix was interested in her in that way. Grandby didn't need to know of his interest.

At least, not yet.

"Not particularly," Emelia replied, the disappointment in her voice quite evident. "I spent the entire time I was there in the ballroom. I was never near the library nor out in the gardens," she claimed with wide eyes. "And, no, Lord Fennington did not ask me to join him in the gardens."

She had been almost disappointed when he merely danced with her the one time. A cotillion. He danced the waltz with Lady Morganfield and looked ever so elegant doing it. Emelia hadn't stayed late enough for the second waltz to discover if he would have danced it with her.

"Did you dance the waltz with him?"

He instantly regretted the question. The way Emelia's shoulders slumped and her face fell had him realizing the young woman expected to do so. And had she still been in the ballroom when the second waltz was played, he would have been dancing with her.

I almost feel sorry for her, the editor of *The Tattler* thought for a moment.

He did feel sorry for her, although not because of what he knew would have the *ton's* tongues wagging if they knew. Kissing in broad daylight at a *ton* event was damning, and maybe quite surprising given her reputation as a perfect daughter of the *ton*, but Emelia seemed to think it would be the end of her life if others knew.

Didn't she realize it would be the end of *his* life as he knew it? His life as a single man? For if others knew what she had done—what they had done—Society would force them to marry, despite the Earl of Aimsley's odd response to the matter.

Gave me an 'out', I suppose, he thought. *Rather sporting of him.*

No, he felt sorry for her because she seemed lonely. Lost, almost. As if she didn't quite know what was next in life. At her age, unmarried and with all her friends already married— some with a babe or two—Emelia Comber, youngest child of the Earl of Aimsley, was headed for spinsterhood.

Or not, if his alter ego had any say in the matter. If she accepted his offer of marriage.

He still didn't have a feel for if she felt any affection for him. If she was even considering matrimony. Never having courted a woman before, he really had no sense of how it was progressing. There was even a Monday when she implied he was only taking her for rides because her father had asked him to escort her!

Obviously, Mark Comber hadn't shared what he knew with his daughter, which meant Felix had an opportunity to set her straight. To make his intentions crystal clear. And yet he had bungled that by simply claiming he enjoyed her company and needed to get some air.

Fool! Why was courting so... confusing?

He wasn't sure if he believed any of the rare gossip he had collected from others about Lady Emelia during his tenure as publisher of *The Tattler*. The report that she was sent to Switzerland because she had bloodied a man's nose turned out to be partially true. Moyer's report the week before confirmed she had punched a man, although she had done so because the man was attempting to ruin one of her classmates. By kissing her in front of several other classmates.

It's a wonder I still have a straight nose, he thought just then, about to lift a finger to stroke it when he remembered it was covered with a prosthetic and appeared rather bulbous just then. Besides, he might accidentally knock his fake mustache out of place.

Now he simply had to make sure nothing of note was ever written about Emelia. As the publisher, and for all intents and purposes, the writer and editor of London's premier gossip rag, he could ensure news of her never made its way onto the printed page.

The power of the press was only as powerful as its owner, after all. As for the gossip rag, well, he knew there were worse ways in which to make a living.

"So, tell me, Lady Emelia, if not news of last night's ball, then what other news do you have for me this fine morning?" he encouraged as his pencil pressed against the thick pad of paper he held.

Emelia allowed a sigh of resignation and began reciting her list of the *on-dit* to which she had been subjected whilst paying calls during the past week. "Lady Pettigrew is willing to add a sum to Lady Jane's dowry as an incentive to marry off her youngest niece," she began, deciding the tidbit wasn't particularly juicy. Everyone in the *ton* knew Eugenia Pettigrew, Viscountess Pettigrew, had been saddled with the responsibility of seeing to it her four nieces were married off. Three were either married or betrothed, which just left the youngest, Lady Jane, available.

"I hardly think that counts as gossip, my lady," Mr. Pepperidge replied, remembering he had seen the young woman in question dancing a waltz at Lord Weatherstone's ball with a young man who looked exactly like the Earl of Bellingham. He remembered Lady Morganfield had identified the gentleman as Andrew Burroughs. He had already confirmed with Lord Devonville that the man's oldest son, Will Slater, Earl of Bellingham, wasn't in attendance at the ball, but that his other son—his bastard son, Stephen Slater—was.

Pepperidge had watched as Lady Jane danced with either Andrew Burroughs or Lord Bellingham's brother—he was now beginning to wonder which was which—but most in the *ton* simply thought she had been dancing with Will Slater. The story in that morning's edition would have been made better if only all the players were actually at the ball. Apparently, Will Slater wasn't even *in* London, and if rumors were to be believed, he wouldn't return to town until either his father died or he found his long-lost love.

That wouldn't be anytime soon, he knew. Bellingham's father, the Marquess of Devonville, was a rather hale and hearty sort who was enjoying marriage to a younger widow, which had Pepperidge thinking word of another heir could be announced at any time. Although the legitimate brothers would be more than twenty-seven years apart in age, it wouldn't be the first time heirs were nearly a generation apart in age.

Emelia sighed again, deciding her knowledge of Lady Jane wasn't meant to be kept quiet. "Except that Lady Jane doesn't wish to be married," she countered with an arched eyebrow, hoping the editor of *The Tattler* would understand her meaning.

Despite the veil covering the top half of her face, the editor of *The Tattler* found the arch of Emelia's eyebrow especially fetching just then. The way it made her seem in control, confident, and just a bit naughty. He could imagine her making such an expression in his bedchamber, when he informed her she would be spending the entire night in his bed that night— or any night.

Every night for the rest of his life.

He could only hope.

But he had a news sheet to write. He couldn't be thinking of Lady Emelia as his wife just yet. He simply couldn't. If he wasn't careful, the evidence of his arousal would become, well *evident*, and he couldn't afford to have Lady Emelia notice how attracted he was to her just then. How he had spent the past six weeks thinking of her in those terms. Thinking of her naked and lying in his bed, her blonde hair splayed out on his pillows like some kind of angelic halo, her luscious body, warm and wet and willing, waiting for him to mount her, to impale her with his manhood, to make love to her until she fractured and cried out his name as ecstasy took her—and him—to oblivion.

Such an exquisite union they could have in his bedchamber.

Or hers.

He rather doubted he would even hear anything she said, for

he was quite sure ecstasy would have him deaf and dumb to anything else but the extreme pleasure he would experience as he spilled his seed into her, as his body would shake and shiver and collapse onto hers.

Mr. Pepperidge blinked, realizing he had missed the key words Emelia had just spoken regarding Lady Jane.

"Could you repeat that please?" he managed to get out without his voice sounding too terribly high-pitched.

Lady Emelia frowned. "Lady Jane doesn't wish to be married," she repeated, her look of confusion making him realize he had better concentrate on the matter at hand.

Gossip.

"Am I to find her wish of not finding a husband... scandalous?" the editor asked, his brows furrowed in question.

Emelia held her breath a moment. Well, she had found the claim rather surprising when she had overheard the young woman make it whilst out in the gardens behind Carlington House.

Oh, I'm not looking to marry, she remembered hearing the girl say when a cluster of young ladies were gathered around the refreshment table during Lady Morganfield's garden party last month.

Emelia thought Lady Jane to be about eighteen then, but as the youngest of several sisters, she hadn't yet attended a ball.

I find I would prefer the life of an independent woman, Jane added when a chorus of disbelief erupted from those around her.

Emelia rather hoped Lady Jane hadn't said anything to her aunt about her intentions. Word had it that Lady Pettigrew wanted to be rid of her charge as soon as possible.

"Perhaps not her desire to remain unmarried as much as her behavior to suggest otherwise, Mr. Pepperidge," Emelia finally said with a sigh.

The editor straightened on the bench, rather liking how Emelia presented her information. She seemed to dole it out in little tidbits, just enough to keep him interested whilst his mind was off creating naughty thoughts. Given how the lady provided information, he was almost inclined to offer her a position at the newspaper.

If she could write like she spoke, he thought *The Tattler* might gain some more subscribers.

"And what behavior might that be, Miss Comber?" he asked carefully. *Or Lady Emelia, rather.* For some reason, she had insisted on introducing herself as if she were a commoner. He had gone along with the ruse in the hopes it might gain him more information he could use in the weekly rag. Never mind that he had addressed her as 'Lady Emelia' when he first contacted her via the written missive that had her visiting him in the park every Thursday morning these past six weeks.

"Kissing, Mr. Pepperidge," Emelia replied, in a rather breathy voice that had the editor wishing he could be engaging in just such an activity with the comely Miss Comber right that very moment.

Didn't she realize he knew exactly who she was?

"She rather enjoys the sport," Emelia added, turning her head so she could regard the man through her veil.

She had to suppress the urge to blink, for she was quite sure one side of Mr. Pepperidge's mustache had come loose from above his lip and was listing to one side.

Could mustaches *do* such a thing?

Goodness, if the man wasn't careful, he could lose the despicable thing!

The man shook his head in an effort to clear it of his carnal thoughts. "Enjoying the sport of kissing isn't so unusual, Miss Comber," he countered, suddenly aware that his fake mustache might have come loose from his lip. Surreptitiously, he moved a gloved hand to his face in attempt to straighten and reattach it, trying to make it appear as if he was merely scratching the side of his nose.

When Emelia arched an elegant eyebrow, the editor found he rather liked the expression that came with it. He could imagine her using it on him when he suggested a more erotic position in bed. Perhaps one that had her atop him. With him at her mercy.

He swallowed in the hopes she hadn't overheard his strangled curse.

"May I remind you, sir, that Lady Jane shouldn't even be *engaging* in kissing at all?" she countered, sounding ever so much like a proper school teacher during the first year of finishing school classes.

Mr. Pepperidge blinked. "Oh, of course she shouldn't."

What was I thinking?

Carnal thoughts, of course, which merely reinforced his need for a mistress—or a wife. Perhaps he could offer Emelia Comber *carte blanche* in return for his promise of remaining mum on the subject that had her at his mercy.

Well, he could offer, but he was quite sure the chit would punch him in the jaw and storm off and never see him again, even if he did have damning information about her. Even if that damning information was merely about a stolen kiss in Lord Weatherstone's garden. With him.

He had to scold himself just then. The young woman was the daughter of an earl, for goodness sake! He couldn't be thinking about her in *those* terms.

Well, he could. He just couldn't act on them. At least, not for another two weeks. Her father, Mark Comber, Earl of Aimsley, had seen to that requirement.

What harm was there in imagining such a scenario, though? In imagining coming home to her, kissing her...

He blinked, realizing she was waiting for him to reply on that very topic.

Kissing.

"So, if she was seen kissing, she must have been kissing *someone*," he prompted, his charcoal once again poised over his pad of parchment.

Wait. Lady Jane *had* been kissing someone, he remembered. Andrew Burroughs. He had seen that for himself, although now that he knew just how much the man resembled the Earl of Bellingham, who bore an uncanny resemblance to his bastard brother, Stephen, he was no longer so sure about which one had actually been kissing Lady Jane.

Well, no harm. He hadn't used any full names in the report of the dalliance in the gardens. Just *Lady J and A. Burroughs*. Well, he had mentioned Mr. Burroughs' occupation as a banker, but who cared about bankers? They were often in trouble of their own making.

Emelia shifted her eyes to her gloved hands for a moment, realizing just then that she had no name for the man who had been kissing Lady Jane in the gardens last night. "Oh, I don't know his *name*," she hedged, her brows furrowing. "I was not introduced to the man. But he was quite handsome, and many others in attendance seemed to recognize him," she added, turning her attention back to the editor. "I remember thinking that if Lady Jane wasn't careful, she would be forced into a marriage with the man who had kissed her."

"I was told the identity of the man is Mr. Andrew Burroughs," Mr. Pepperidge stated, thinking the name might be familiar to her.

He blinked when he remembered something Emelia had said in Lord Weatherstone's garden on occasion of their first meeting. "You know him..." he started to say and then stopped.

Mr. Pepperidge wouldn't know about that conversation in the garden. Felix Turnbridge knew.

"Do you know him?" he quickly amended.

Emelia's eyes widened. "That cannot be!" she replied with a shake of her head. Why, the banker had spent most of the night in the card room and then been in the company of Lady Stoneleigh for the supper waltz. "Of course, I know Mr. Burroughs. He was my host in Geneva. And he's old enough to be Lady Jane's father. I assure you, *he* was not kissing Lady Jane last evening."

The editor's eyes widened, although he quickly recovered

enough to ask, "Then, if not Mr. Burroughs, who was the man kissing Lady Jane?"

Although Emelia truly hadn't recognized the rather handsome young man who had been engaged in the rather passionate kissing only the moment before, she could certainly understand why Lady Jane wished to be kissed by him. "I truly do not know, but I suppose Lady Jane does. She certainly seemed to enjoy his company."

She remembered feeling rather jealous of Lady Jane. And then feeling that same jealousy again not thirty minutes later when the man was back out in the gardens with a different young lady—Lady Lucida, in fact—bestowing a kiss on her that was also apparently her first. And then, even later in the evening, the man had been in the gardens with yet another young lady, although not one Emelia recognized.

Emelia blinked. She needed to be careful with how much information she shared with Mr. Pepperidge. If the news about Lady Jane was enough, she could use the information about Lady Lucida in their next meeting!

"Do I detect a hint of jealousy in your voice, Miss Comber?" Mr. Pepperidge murmured just then, his body leaning in her direction as if he meant to keep the query as quiet as possible. As he did so, he was aware of his Breguet, the timepiece reflecting a glint of the barest sunshine breaking through the fog. *Damn! It's nearly time to leave for the morning session of Parliament!*

"I was not jealous, I assure you," Emelia insisted, rather uncomfortable with just how close the editor was leaning in her direction. So close, in fact, she caught a whiff of his cologne. Not a scent she expected of the editor—eau du spicy awful—but rather a pleasant scent of sandalwood with hints of musk and amber.

A rather familiar scent.

And she realized his mustache was back to its original location above his lip. The detachable mustache had reattached itself!

She realized she had to say something or risk looking like a ninny. "He was a bit too … *large*, for my tastes," she complained, remembering the man's arms—*they were larger than my waist!*—and his height. He positively towered over Lady Jane.

"Large? As in… tall?" Mr. Pepperidge asked, realizing she probably referred to Stephen Slater. The bastard son of Lord Devonville was back from his tour of duty to his Majesty's Navy and was apparently on the hunt for a wife. And he had been at the ball last night.

"Very," Emelia agreed.

Mr. Pepperidge swallowed, rather disturbed to hear Emelia wasn't attracted to Stephen Slater due to his height. Indeed, she seemed rather horrified by his size. *This doesn't bode well for me given my height*, he thought in despair.

"I don't think I could abide a man who could crush me…" Emelia paused, inhaling sharply when she realized what she was saying and to whom she was admitting it—a gossip monger!

His brows furrowing just a fraction, Mr. Pepperidge regarded the young woman next to him for a long time before he inhaled and glanced at his chronometer. "I apologize. I must take my leave of you, my lady. Same time next week?" he asked as he stood up and leaned over to take her hand.

Startled at how quickly he lifted her gloved hand and kissed the back of it, Emelia had to suppress a gasp. "Yes, of course," she managed to get out as the man suddenly turned away and took his leave of her and of the park.

What a strange man! she found herself thinking only a moment later. And not just because of his behavior. Why, it was as if he regretted having checked the time, even as he knew he had to be somewhere else!

For just the briefest moment when he had bent to kiss her hand, she was quite sure he had done it before.

But the only time she had ever spent with the rogue was here in the park. She was sure of it. He had never lifted her hand to his lips before. Never looked at her as if... he *wanted* her.

Frowning, Emelia reached down and plucked his mustache from the crushed granite path at her feet.

"Eeewww," she murmured, wondering if she should keep it so that she might present it to him on their next visit. She could just imagine how to do it, too. "Is this yours, perhaps? I think you lost it last week while you were blackmailing me." Given the man's behavior, she rather doubted he would be the least bit embarrassed at having his missing facial hair returned to him.

She wondered if he would show up with a different one upon their next meeting and quickly shook her head, wanting instead to remember what he had looked like without it. She had a brief but clear view of Mr. Pepperidge right before he turned away to head off down the path toward the road. A view that had her wondering why the man would even sport such a disgusting facial ornament. For Mr. Pepperidge was a much more handsome man without it.

A rather aristocratic looking man, except for the nose. And the spectacles. And the awful brown wig.

A familiar man, although somehow not.

Pulling her small sketch pad from her reticule, Emelia began drawing what she could remember of Mr. Pepperidge— without the mustache, of course—and decided that, yes, he was a more handsome man without it.

Which had her wondering why he sported one at all.

A disguise? *But why would the editor of* The Tattler *require the use of a disguise?* she wondered.

What is he hiding?

Emelia straightened on the bench, determined to discover just what it was Mr. Pepperidge was hiding.

His true identity, she thought with some excitement.

For the first time in several weeks, Emelia left Hyde Park feeling light on her feet. Feeling a bit of hope for her future. Why, if Lord Bellingham asked her to waltz, she would agree without hesitation. Hell, if anyone invited her to waltz, she would do so, she decided, hang the need for a voucher from one of the patronesses of Almack's.

Well, maybe not with Mr. Pepperidge.

Mr. Pepperidge was despicable. He was oily. He was an awful man.

But underneath the disguise he wore, Mr. Pepperidge was a rather handsome man.

Perhaps he was also a better man.

Emelia rolled her eyes.

If he were a better man, he would never have blackmailed me in the first place.

CHAPTER 13
OFF TO WORTHINGTON
HOUSE FOR A LUNCHEON
WITH THE LADIES

our complete coverage of the Season's best balls continues in next week's issue with reports from the Weatherstone Ball. Don't miss it! ~ An advertisement for the May 7, 1818 issue of *The Tattler.*

ay 7, 1818, noon in South Audley Street

Jane pulled on a deep purple pelisse, rather sad the day wasn't expected to remain sunny. With the threat of rain— storm clouds were brewing on the horizon—she would have to travel in the town coach the few streets to the London residence of Lord and Lady Torrington in Park Lane. With her body still thrumming from the events of the night before, she would have preferred to walk.

Worthington House, the mansion Adele Slater Worthington Grandby had inherited upon her first husband's death, was one of the grander homes along the edge of the park. Having been married to Samuel Worthington, a wealthy man involved in the building of the early steamships, Adele had thought to simply live the rest of her life as a widow.

Milton Grandby, Earl of Torrington, had other plans, however.

After a Season spent squiring Adele to various *ton* events—balls, soirées, and garden parties as well as to the theatre—the earl had surprised her with a rather large sapphire and diamond ring and an offer of marriage. The following year, she had surprised him with a set of twins.

Adele had prayed for a boy, intent on giving her husband the heir the earldom required for a smooth succession, while her husband told everyone he wanted a daughter.

Both were rather pleased when they were blessed with one of each.

Grandby (the earl preferred being called 'Grandby' over his title, 'Torrington') enjoyed entertaining his daughter, Angelica, in the second-floor nursery almost as much as he enjoyed showing off his angel to any visitors to Worthington House. Meanwhile, Adele doted on their son, George, in the hopes the boy wouldn't feel ignored. Now that the babies were six months old and the nurses had a handle on their daily schedules, Adele had decided it was time to resume hosting events at Worthington House.

This small luncheon party was her first in nearly a year. *Mine, as well,* Jane thought with a wan smile as she made her way to the town coach at the curb, her parasol overhead and Nicole trailing behind. The time spent in the coach afforded her the opportunity to remember her evening spent with Andrew Burroughs.

How circumstances could change! Her outlook on life had been rather gloomy of late when those closest to her claimed she was finally free of a man who never loved her. She had plans to leave London. To leave the *ton* behind and see some other parts of the world. To live in Italy.

"You can be a Merry Widow," Adele had said in a whisper when they last walked in the park with Clarinda Fitzwilliam, Countess of Norwick, and Patience Comber, Countess of Aimsley. Although some might have thought that's what Adele had done to capture the heart and hand of Milton Grandby,

Adele had actually been living a rather sedate life after Worthington's death. There were the few months when she thought she would marry, but when she discovered her betrothed was deep in debt due to gambling and needed her fortune to pay his debtors, she had broken off the betrothal. Another month or so of independent life followed. She was more surprised than any of her peers when Grandby offered to escort her to an entire Season of events. A Season of merry widowhood followed.

Jane now understood first-hand the meaning of the term. *Merry, indeed.* She had to suppress a huge smile as she stepped down from the coach and approached the double-doors of Worthington House, sure if anyone saw her grinning like an idiot, they would think her a candidate for Bedlam.

One of the front doors opened before she could use the lion-head knocker. Bernard, the butler, gave her a deep bow as he waved her into the house. Instead of following on her heels, Nicole took the walkway around the side of the house to the servants' entrance at the back. While her lady was lunching with other aristocrats' wives upstairs, Nicole would be having tea with some of the servants of Worthington House, exchanging gossip and news below stairs.

Adele appeared in the great hall beyond the vestibule, angling her head to one side as the butler helped Jane remove her pelisse. "I am so happy to see you. Had you not come, I would have sent a footman to escort you," she warned as she moved to give Jane a hug. "Mourning or not."

Jane couldn't help the grin that appeared—she was happy for the first time in... she didn't know how long. "I do believe I am done with mourning," she replied with an arched brow, wondering if anyone would notice she had been tumbled the night before.

And that morning.

Adele noticed. "Why, you're glowing as if..." She lowered her voice. "You've been tumbled every which way but up," she teased in a whisper, an eyebrow arching up.

Her own eyebrows rising in alarm, Jane replied, "Oh, my. Is it that obvious?"

Adele blinked and then hooked her arm into Jane's to pull her aside just as several ladies appeared in the vestibule. "I thought I was teasing, but apparently I wasn't wrong?" she asked in a hoarse whisper.

Jane angled her head to one side, wanting desperately to confide in her friend. "When everyone has gone, and we're in the nursery, I'll tell you everything," she promised.

"I don't know that I can wait that long," Adele claimed as she turned her attention to her newest guests. Constance Roderick, Marchioness of Reading, Clarinda and Patience stepped up to greet their hostess.

"Lady Reading, Lady Norwick, and Lady Aimsley, so good of you to join me today," Adele said, her voice back to normal. "Lady Reading, I'd like you to meet Jane Fitzpatrick, Countess of Stoneleigh."

Jane curtsied. "It's very good to meet you, Lady Reading...'

"Oh, call me Connie, please," the marchioness insisted. "This is all so very new to me," she added. "I've just yesterday returned from the wedding trip, and I'm apparently about to be swept off to Reading for another.'

So, this is the Rake of Reading's wife, Jane thought with a mix of happiness and concern. Happiness, for the woman was a bit older than a typical bride and seemed rather satisfied with married life. Her concern had to do with the groom. Certainly the woman already knew of the marquess' reputation as a rake.

Before she could ask as to how the two had met, Clarinda said, "Connie is my husband's cousin. She and Reading share a love of race horses."

"Any kind of horses, actually," Connie interjected. "I've been living in a Norwick property in Sussex almost my entire life, raising and training horses." She didn't add that the property adjoined that of George Bennett-Jones, Viscount Bostwick. It was one of the viscount's horses that had sired a race horse that would be making its debut in this year's races.

"She is the only one who could tame Lord Reading," Patience said with an arched brow, her comment obviously meant for Jane.

Clarinda chimed in. "He is a new man since meeting Connie. I do not believe I have seen such devotion in any other man before."

Jane was sure she saw a flush of pink color Connie's face, as if the woman knew full well of her husband's reputation. An entire issue of *The Tattler* had been dedicated to the many dalliances of the marquess, the gossip rag deeming him *The Rake of Reading*. The moniker stuck, which may have served the marquess well during his days as a rake, but which proved a difficult reputation to overcome when, at the age of five-and-thirty, he was finally on the hunt for a wife. He had pursued Constance relentlessly, insisting she was the woman for him. After a time, Connie found she couldn't say 'no' to the man.

She had fallen in love with him.

And his horses.

"Except in your own husband," Adele put in, an arched eyebrow aimed in Clarinda's direction.

It was the other countess' turn to blush. "True. But Daniel has loved me since well before his twin brother married me," Clarinda claimed, a reference to her late husband, David, and the father of their twin girls. Any mention of the man had Clarinda glancing about, as if she expected the man's ghost to appear.

At the sound of a new arrival, the five turned toward the vestibule. Lady Eugenia Pettigrew appeared in the archway before the butler had a chance to take her parasol and the pelisse. "I've got it!" she claimed happily, waving something from one hand. "The first copy off the presses!" the older woman cried out.

Stunned at Lady Pettigrew's claim, Jane's eyes widened.

Whatever was the woman crowing about?

Then her gaze moved to take in the object of the viscountess' claim.

In her gloved hand, the widow held up the newest edition of *The Tattler*.

CHAPTER 14
PONDERING A WOMAN

ear Reader, please believe us when we say it was never our intention to cause undo hardship or to incite a member of the peerage into retribution. We were simply doing our job as reporters. ~ The editor's final article in the May 14, 1818 issue of *The Tattler.*

ay 7, 1818 in Hyde Park
Felix Turnbridge, Earl of Fennington, silently cursed himself as he quickly made his way to his phaeton. How could he have bungled the news about Lady Jane's kiss so badly? He was sure Adeline Carlington had been pointing to the man who eventually kissed Lady Jane in the gardens when he asked as to his identity. She had said he was Andrew Burroughs, but clearly, Mr. Burroughs was too old to be the man kissing Lady Jane.

So Lady Jane had to have been kissing the Earl of Bellingham's look-a-like bastard brother. That could be the only explanation.

Well, that week's issue of *The Tattler* was printed and already on its way to being distributed all over London. He might have to include an updated article in the next issue to clarify the news. Mr. Burroughs was probably too new to London to even know anything about his publication, so he rather doubted any harm would come out of the mistaken report.

He tossed a coin to the young boy who stood holding the reins of his gray mare. Juno could be quite high-strung if she thought she was being ignored or taken for granted. At the moment, she seemed rather content as the boy fed her a carrot

"Did she give you any trouble?" Felix asked as he made sure to give the spoiled horse a slight bow. Although she tossed her head, her attention was back on the boy, as if she thought he might have another treat for her.

"Not a bit, guv'nor. Think she's lonely, though, if you take my meaning."

Felix blinked as he regarded the boy, at first thinking him a bit cheeky. "And if I do not?" he countered, deciding he wanted to hear the boy's opinion.

"Time to have her bred, guv'nor. She's in season," the boy claimed with an arched eyebrow.

Jesus. The signs had been there all morning. Thank goodness he had come straight to the park from the mews behind his townhouse in Bruton Street. There hadn't been many horses in the streets that led to Rotten Row, but some of those that were around them made more noise than usual, and Juno seemed, well, more high-strung than usual.

"I suppose you have a stud in mind?" Felix asked as he took the seat on the high perch phaeton. Bright red but otherwise devoid of any crests that might identify him as the Earl of Fennington, the phaeton suited his needs for quick transportation about London. And right now, he needed to get to Westminster.

"You'll want to ask for Mr. Comber at Harrington House in Park Lane," the boy said with a nod, removing his cap as he did so. "He'll know what she needs, milord."

Grinning, Felix gave the boy a nod and tossed him another penny. *Mr. Comber?* The boy was no doubt referring to Emelia's brother, Alistair. The former Army officer had been allowed to marry Julia Harrington on the condition he remain in charge of the Harrington House stables. He was also responsible for beginning a breeding program to see to it the Earl of Aimsley had a race horse for every season.

Felix hadn't given any consideration to having his prized Percheron bred, but he supposed it would be one way of assuring he had a horse to replace her when it was time for her to be put out to pasture. In the meantime, he could imagine her and her colt pulling a barouche, or perhaps a small town coach. Not that he had any need of such equipage now, but at some point he would have to think about life with a wife. Siring an heir. Perhaps a spare.

A high-perch phaeton would hardly be suitable for transport about London when he had a wife. He could imagine Lady Emelia attempting to hold on as he negotiated the streets of London as they made their way to...

Felix furrowed his brows. To... *where?*

His office?

He certainly wouldn't be taking his wife to the publishing house, nor would she go with him to Parliament.

When he realized why he would require a larger carriage, he nearly slapped himself upside the head.

Shopping, he realized as he passed under the gate post of Hyde Park. *The theatre. Balls. Soirées.* They couldn't be expected to ride in a phaeton or a hackney when it was raining or cold, which meant they wouldn't be going out very often.

Cursing the traffic and the attention Juno seemed to be garnering from even the oldest horses along Victoria Street, Felix realized he had better ensure the stable hands knew to keep her sequestered from her barn mates in the mews.

When he finally pulled up to the curb in front of Parliament —a quick glance at his Breguet assured him he had a few moments—he spotted a groom heading in his direction.

"I say, can you keep her away from trouble? I'm afraid I didn't realize she was in heat," he said when the groom took Juno's reins.

"Of course, my lord," the man said with a bow. "I'll put her with the others."

Felix was about to hurry off—he needed to change into his robes—when he suddenly stopped and regarded the groom with an arched brow. "Others?" he repeated in alarm.

The groom paused a moment. "The other mares, my lord. There are a number in season this week." He gave a short bow and hurried off.

Felix sighed, wondering if he was the last to know.

How had he missed the signs?

Well, he had been a bit preoccupied with his own sexual discomfort. Preoccupied with the thought of seeing Lady Emelia. Despite the ridiculous hat with the veil that did little to hide her rather pretty face, Emelia appeared luminescent in the early morning light.

He was about to resume imagining what she would look like if she were his wife, if he returned home to find her waiting for him, but found he had to squelch the thought.

He needed to remove his spectacles, peel off his fake nose, and get out of the ridiculous wig he wore, and into his robes and periwig and the Chamber of Lords.

Duty called.

CHAPTER 15
A GOSSIP RAG LEAVES
LITTLE TO THE
IMAGINATION

Complete coverage of the Weatherstone Ball is here! We were in attendance and can honestly report we were not disappointed in the least. Although the lobster patties and champagne were divine (Ed. They really were! Lady Weatherstone's cook knows how to make these much maligned finger foods), we know you're far more interested in what happened in the gardens behind the ballroom. Or in the library. Or on the dance floor. Here, dear reader, is a recap of the evening's events. What we don't have space to include here will appear in the May 14, 1818 issue. Be sure to pick up yours at your favorite newsstand! ~ The lead article in the May 7, 1818 issue of *The Tattler.*

May 7, 1818, Worthington House

Adele stiffened at the viscountess' appearance. Although she had invited Lady Pettigrew, she had rather hoped the woman might have another engagement to attend. If the viscountess discovered Adele had hosted a luncheon and not included her on the guest list, Adele would suffer the woman's wrath in the form of pointed jabs during other *ton* events. And Eugenia Pettigrew was a gossip of the worst kind. There were some who secretly thought she was the editor and head writer for *The Tattler*.

"Lady Pettigrew, so good of you to join us," Adele offered as she moved to take one of the woman's gloved hands in her own. The other held the gossip rag, the main headline including the words 'Weatherstone Ball'. "I would have thought you would be exhausted after last night's ball, given you had to chaperone your niece," she added as she turned to indicate her other guests. "You know Lady Norwick, Lady Aimsley, and Lady Stoneleigh, of course," she said, waving a hand in the direction of the three countesses. "But I don't know if you've had the pleasure of meeting Lady Reading." She pulled Lady Pettigrew closer to the marchioness —Connie actually outranked all the ladies in attendance—and said, "Lady Reading, may I introduce you to Lady Pettigrew?"

Connie waited for the viscountess to curtsy and then gave one of her own. "It's very good to meet you. I do hope you enjoyed last night's ball as much as I did." The newly minted marchioness—she had only just married Randall Roderick, Marquess of Reading, last September—hadn't been back in London for a fortnight given the length of her wedding trip.

The viscountess straightened before angling her head. "I would have enjoyed it far more if my niece had secured an offer of marriage," she replied with an arched brow, the comment not including any hint of humor. "And you?"

Connie was left dumbstruck by the odd comment, but finally allowed a nod. "I did, indeed. I can certainly understand why the Weatherstone ball is so well attended." Why, she'd had no idea how many of the *ton* lived in London!

"Come, let's move to the conservatory and be seated," Adele offered as she led the ladies down the wide hall to the last room at the back of the house. Although the conservatory was warm, the air was filled with the heady scents of flowers and tropical plants. One of the walls was made up entirely of glass windows, allowing that day's sunshine to light the room. In the middle, a table set for six was the current favorite place for a white flutterby that seemed to be doing an intricate dance with a yellow one. The place settings—china decorated with floral motifs and crystal goblets from Waterford's studio—gave the tableau a formal feel despite the informal surroundings.

"It's beautiful," Connie breathed as she entered the conservatory. "I've been told there's one at Reading's summer house…"

"Oh, there is, and it's beautiful," Adele offered. "Far larger than this one, of course."

The comment had Connie's jaw dropping. "Larger?"

The other ladies tittered, the sound sending the flutterbies off into the tropical plants. "I was only there because the marquess invited Grandby to his stables. You'll see when you finally get there this summer."

Several footmen stepped up to pull out the chairs. Place cards in the shape of flutterby wings indicated where each guest would sit. Jane felt a combination of relief and terror at being seated between Adele and Lady Pettigrew. She moved to her spot and allowed the footman to push in her chair once she was sure Connie was seated across from her. The others took their seats and seemed to spend an inordinate amount of time placing their napkins on their laps before Jane finally turned to Lady Pettigrew.

"Have you had a chance to read *The Tattler*? I couldn't help but notice the headline," she added, deciding the level of stress in the room was because everyone else feared being mentioned in the gossip rag. Thank goodness she had spent the entire night playing a wallflower. That is, until Andrew Burroughs had stepped up and insisted she dance the waltz with him.

Had anyone seen them leave, though? They had done so together.

The thought had her heart racing again.

The viscountess beamed at being asked about the news sheet. "I have not. I discovered the majority of it was finished and printed so the editor had only the front page to finish in the middle of the night. Otherwise it would be *next week* before we would have the news of last night's ball," she claimed in a voice that suggested another week waiting for the news sheet would be intolerable. "I thought I would share a few tidbits before luncheon was served," Lady Pettigrew said hopefully.

"Goodness, I do hope they didn't pay witness to Grandby taking me behind a potted palm," Adele teased with an arched brow.

Clarinda tried but failed to stifle a giggle. "Or Norwick and me as we introduced ourselves to the statue of Cupid."

"Or Aimsley and me as we slipped into the library to read one of Homer's epics," Patience chimed in with a huge grin.

Jane allowed a tentative grin, delighting in how these ladies of the *ton* seemed to discount the validity of the news presented in *The Tattler*. "So, what is the featured story from the ball?" she asked, thinking perhaps it had something to do with the young man who had nearly every young lady swooning for him. Why, she had watched the handsome man escort three young women through the doors at the back of the ballroom and onto the flags leading to the gardens, each one different in hair coloring, complexion and height. Apparently he hadn't yet decided what type of woman he was attracted to, or else he merely favored them all.

Ah, young men, she thought wistfully, a fleeting image of Maximilian Andrew Burroughs coming to mind. She was sure a flush of color stained her cheeks just then.

Lady Pettigrew beamed as she opened the news sheet and quickly read the lead story. "Mayfair was awash in color and glitter and gold as Lord and Lady Weatherstone hosted their annual spring ball," she read aloud, lowering her spectacles to the end of her nose as she did so. "This year's feast for female eyes had to be the son of Lord D. The marquess' progeny not only danced with several young ladies in the ballroom, he also did so in the gardens. We either paid witness to or were informed of liaisons with Lady J,

Lady L and Lady V as they were each showered with kisses under the paper lanterns that barely lit the scene. Cupid, of course, paid witness as well. As to which one he shot, we don't yet know." She looked up and frowned briefly before turning her attention back on the news sheet. "Why, Adele, I wasn't aware your nephew was back in London," she commented lightly, concluding 'Lord D' referred to William Slater, Marquess of Devonville.

The Countess of Torrington angled her head, rather surprised the gossip rag would report Will Slater's presence at the ball when he was no where near London. Only a few days ago, the naval commander had returned to English shores after resigning his commission. His intention was to marry the earl's daughter he had fallen in love with prior to his service. "Oh, he was back in London for only two nights, but he has already gone off to Oxfordshire," Adele replied with a shrug. "He actually left London yesterday morning. I'm sure he's anxious to see his sister, Hannah, and to meet his brother-in-law, the Earl of Gisborn," she added, realizing Connie would be unfamiliar with her niece and nephew.

Lord D is the Marquess of Devonville, then, Jane surmised, realizing the young man she had spied with three different women was supposed to be his son. But wasn't, apparently. At least, not the son who had already taken his leave of London to find his long-lost love.

The color seemed to drain from Lady Pettigrew's face as she quickly reread the article to herself. "Well, if not Commander Slater, then who was the young man at the ball last night? The one who apparently looks *exactly* like him? Exactly like the Earl of Bellingham?"

A couple of the women shifted uncomfortably, as if they knew the answer but didn't wish to share the information. Speaking of bastard sons, or in this case, a bastard nephew, wasn't something any of them thought appropriate just then.

"The writer is no doubt referring to Stephen Slater, the

younger son of Lord Devonville," Patience explained lightly. "He was quite popular, and quite handsome," she added in a tone that suggested she could have been his mother. "Why, he looks *exactly* like his brother, Will."

"Who are Lady J, L and V, I wonder?"

Everyone at the table turned to stare at Lady Pettigrew, whose eyebrows were furrowed as she seemed to study the article in more detail.

"Young, unmarried ladies, no doubt," Clarinda replied with a wave of her hand. "What else did the editor write about? He can be so catty."

"Who said it was a *he*?" Lady Pettigrew asked as she lifted her head, her brows still furrowed in obvious worry.

The other women dared a glance at each other in turn. "Because no self-respecting woman would write such dreck?" Patience offered with a roll of her eyes. All the ladies at the table laughed except Lady Pettigrew, who seemed intent on reading the next article.

Since Jane had watched each young unmarried lady take their turns leaving the ballroom with the handsome bastard, she said, "Lady J is Lady Jane, Lady L is Lady Lucida, and Lady V is Lady Victoria."

There was a sharp inhalation of breath as Lady Pettigrew pinned her with a glare. "*My* Lady Jane?" she repeated.

Jane stilled herself, realizing the old biddy apparently knew nothing of Jane Browning's elicit activity in the gardens behind Lord Weatherstone's mansion. "Just a guess," she responded quickly, not adding that there were probably no other Lady J's in attendance of an age to be kissing Lord Devonville's bastard son. *I am certainly too old!* She didn't dare allow a thought of what it might be like to be escorted into the gardens and kissed in the presence of Cupid by that young man.

Now, if that man had been Maximilian Andrew Burroughs...

A shiver of pleasure seemed to pass through her entire body, forcing her to still herself as she regarded the old biddy who held the news sheet as if it were a piece of gold leaf.

Lady Pettigrew held up the sheet and began to recite the next paragraph just as a footman poured the first course of wine. "Meanwhile, another new man to London (*Ed.* or a returnee, I've just been informed), A. Burroughs, made his debut in the gardens, kissing a young lady senseless—or was she kissing him senseless? A banker is sworn to secrecy."

Jane straightened, her head turning so quickly it caught the attention of Adele. "May I see that?" she asked as she reached for the news sheet.

Lady Pettigrew regarded her with an arched brow. "Do you know this... *A. Burroughs?* I can't say I've ever heard of him, unless he's one of Ariley's brood."

Jane didn't answer as she reread the article, her heart racing at the news that Andrew Burroughs had been spied kissing a young woman in the gardens at Lord Weatherstone's ball. There might have been another 'A. Burroughs' at the ball— the Burroughs family was rather large and well-established in London Society—but an *A. Burroughs* who was also a banker?

That was too much of a coincidence.

Which meant the man with whom she had spent the entire night in bed had also been spied kissing a much younger woman in the gardens during Lord Weatherstone's ball.

A giant rock seemed to drop into her stomach just then, removing her appetite for luncheon as well as her appetite for life. Why, just that morning, she had awakened with a smile on her face. Her entire body had thrummed with the memory of what Andrew Burroughs had done with her, not once, not twice, but many times over the course of their night together in her bed.

"Do you know this 'A. Burroughs'?" Lady Pettigrew asked again, a look that could be considered almost predatory gracing her face.

Jane shook her head. "I just wondered who he was seen

kissing, is all," she answered in a small voice. It was the only response she could manage at that point.

"Lady J," Lady Pettigrew stated after she had taken back the news sheet and finished reading the rest of the short article to herself.

"Your niece?" Jane queried in confusion, her arched eyebrow daring the viscountess to deny the accusation.

At least, she hoped the older woman would do so.

The idea that Lady Jane had been spotted kissing not just one man, but two in the gardens, would lead to certain ruination for the young woman.

Lady Pettigrew turned to regard Jane with a look that could have only been anger. She obviously thought the widowed countess was inferring her niece was either fast or behaving inappropriately in the gardens. The viscountess' expression softened after a moment, though. "Yes. Yes, Lady J is my niece. I suppose," she murmured. "I hadn't thought of a banker as a prospective husband, but if he is of *those* Burroughs, I certainly wouldn't object to a match should he and my youngest niece decide to marry. As a banker, he is part of the *ton*, after all."

For a moment, Jane thought she might faint. The idea of Lady Jane—the young, impetuous chit who had apparently had several dalliances in the gardens last night—married to Andrew Burroughs had her green with envy.

After another moment, she found herself doubting the report.

Why the hell would Andrew kiss a girl half his age?

Why, he was old enough to be Jane Browning's father!

But what if he had?

What if Andrew really *had* been kissing Lady Jane Browning in the gardens, just moments before he found Jane Fitzpatrick keeping company with the potted palms and asked her to dance the waltz?

Warring emotions had Jane fearing she might cast up her accounts, although she hadn't yet eaten anything. Aware the others at the table were glancing at each other—the discussion had obviously made them uncomfortable—she stilled herself. "I do hope they'll be happy," she said as brightly as she could.

At that moment, a series of footmen entered the conservatory, bowls of soup perched on silver salvers. "Ah, luncheon is served, ladies," Adele announced, the sound of relief in her words barely masked. The announcement was meant to force Lady Pettigrew to set aside the gossip rag. Relieved when she did so, Adele gave a nod and the ladies began eating, and the topic of conversation changed to ball gowns and babies and children.

Anything but the gossip in *The Tattler*.

CHAPTER 16
A DRAWING REVEALS ANOTHER IDENTITY

he moment the use of a disguise is discovered, its effectiveness is rendered moot. Remember this, dear reader, for we all wear them on occasion. ~ The editor's final article in the May 14, 1818 issue of *The Tattler*.

ay 7, 1818, back in Hyde Park

Emelia Comber regarded the drawing she had just completed of the despicable Mr. Pepperidge. Despite how much better looking he appeared in her drawing than he did in real life—debonaire almost, with his bulbous nose, high cheekbones, square jaw, perfect pillowed lips, piercing eyes and gold-rimmed spectacles—she couldn't help but feel evulsion at seeing the man—with or without his mustache.

She gave a glance at the fake bit of hair that lay on the bench next to her and wondered if the man even realized he had lost it. He had left in such a hurry. What could have him taking his leave in such a rush?

She picked up the mustache in her gloved fingers and dropped it atop her drawing, arranging it so it rested above his pillowed lips. Pulling it away again, she frowned as she confirmed he was far more handsome without it. Especially given those lips!

Why would he sport such a disguise, though? Had he grown a mustache and then had it accidentally shaved off by his valet? If so, it must have only happened that morning, because he appeared clean-shaven that brief moment when he had taken his leave of her. And if that were the case, then where would he have acquired a replacement in such a short time?

Was there a shop that carried such mustaches? And was it open this early in the morning?

She supposed such a thing happened on occasion. A valet acted a bit too hastily, taking away a day's growth of beard along with a six-month growth of mustache.

Had the valet had been fired on the spot?

If she showed the drawing to her mother—Patience Comber was always asking to see her latest work of art—Emelia wondered if her mother would recognize the man. She tried to imagine how she would broach the subject, though.

"Mother, could you take a look at this gentleman and tell me if you recognize him? I saw him in the park this morning."

Her query would no doubt have her mother wondering what she was doing in the park at the ungodly early hour of eight o' clock in the morning. Well, she wouldn't have a suitable response, even though she had needed to take a walk. She was a victim of blackmail, after all, and an occasional walk was necessary to soothe the soul.

Deciding to keep the mustache with her sketch pad, she moved it back into place beneath Mr. Pepperidge's nose and folded the top cover of the sketch pad over the drawing.

Should Mr. Pepperidge ask as to the whereabouts of his mustache when next they met, then she would admit she was in possession of it. Otherwise, it would remain safely tucked away.

Finally rising from the bench, Emelia allowed a sigh and took her leave of the park, heading for Aimsley House at the south end of Park Lane.

CHAPTER 17
AFTERMATH OF A LUNCHEON

lthough we didn't spend the entire ball in the gardens, we rather wish we had! Oh, there were the usual couples paying their respect to the statue of Cupid—Lord and Lady B, Lord and Lady M, Lord and Lady D—there were some newcomers to this annual sojourn. We were told one particular gentleman, the Earl of B, made an appearance no less than three times—with three different young ladies! ~ An article on the front page of the May 7, 1818 issue of *The Tattler*.

ay 7, 1818, back at Worthington House

"As God is my witness, I am never again inviting that woman to luncheon on a Thursday," Adele murmured when she was sure the front door was closed and Lady Pettigrew was out of earshot. She turned to find her other guests giving one another nervous glances.

"What is it about Thursdays?" Connie asked as she pulled on her pelisse with the butler's assistance, her gaze darting nervously between the other ladies.

"*The Tattler* is published on Thursdays," Clarinda replied with a roll of her eyes. "Eugenia always manages to get one of the first copies."

"Probably because she helps write them," Patience added with a roll of her eyes. She gave a quick glance in Connie's direction. "She doesn't *really*, but she seems to know more of the *on-dit* than anyone else in Mayfair."

Jane pulled on her pelisse, her manner far more reserved than it had been when she first arrived. "Thank you for having us over today," she managed, not making eye contact with their hostess. She was afraid if she stayed another moment, she would become a watering pot.

"Oh, Jane, I have something for you in the parlor," Adele said. She turned to her other guests, noting that they were all ready to take their leave. "Thank you three for coming today. I'm sure I'll see you again tomorrow. It's your turn to host tea in the afternoon, is it not?" she asked, her attention directed to Clarinda.

The countess gave a nod. "It is. Thank you again for having us. Good day, Jane. Adele." She gave a curtsy, as did Connie and Patience, and the two cousins-by-marriage and the other countess took their leave of Worthington House.

Adele turned to Jane and hooked an arm into hers.

"What's in the parlor?" Jane asked, curious as to what the countess could possibly have for her.

Lady Torrington allowed a sigh but said nothing until the two were safely ensconced in the parlor with the door shut behind them. "A shoulder to cry on," she finally said with a sigh. "You looked as if you were going to burst into tears halfway through luncheon," she accused. "Pray tell, what has happened? You looked positively glorious when you arrived, and now..."

Jane rolled her eyes and slumped into the upholstered chair behind her. "Oh, Adele, I can hardly believe it, but..." Despite her best efforts, a tear dripped from the corner of one eye. "I woke up this morning—several times this morning, in fact—with a man who told me he *loved* me," she blurted. Tears continued to fall, which had Adele pulling a hanky from a pocket in her gown.

"Oh, my!" she replied in surprise, handing over the square of linen. Her expression changed to one of consternation. "Oh. I shouldn't think that would cause tears, though. Unless they are tears of happiness, but... yours are most certainly not."

Jane shook her head. "Is it true, do you suppose?"

Frowning, Adele took the chair opposite of Jane and leaned forward. "Is what true?"

Sniffling, Jane wiped her face with the hanky. "*The Tattler*. The mention of Andrew Burroughs kissing Lady Jane in the gardens during the ball." She barely got the sentence out before a sob robbed her of breath.

The countess let out the breath she'd been holding. "Andrew Burroughs?" she repeated. "The banker? Why, he's one of Grandby's cousins," she remarked as she settled back in her chair.

Jane nodded, tears once again pouring down her face. "Him."

"Was he kissing *you* in the gardens during the ball last night?" Adele asked carefully. It stood to reason someone might refer to Lady Stoneleigh as 'Lady J' since her given name was Jane, but it certainly wasn't proper form. But then, this was *The Tattler* they were discussing. The gossip rag wasn't exactly known to be respectful of aristocrats and their titles.

Shaking her head, Jane said, "We weren't kissing in the gardens because we weren't *in* the gardens last night," she whispered between sobs. She swallowed. "Just in... my bed."

Despite her best efforts to remain serious, Adele found she couldn't help but allow a grin. "Oh, Jane, this is *such* good news!" she replied happily, scootching forward so she sat on the front edge of her chair. "I've been so concerned you wouldn't take a lover after Stoneleigh's death. Goodness knows, you deserve all the attention you can get from a doting man," she added with an arched eyebrow. "Andrew is a widower, and such a nice man," she added with a nod.

Jane blinked. And blinked again, obviously shocked by Adele's response. "But don't you see? He was seen *kissing* someone else in the gardens last night. He's obviously a... *a rake!*"

Adele sobered, immediately understanding Jane's point. She took a deep breath and exhaled. "Tell me everything," she ordered, resisting the urge to ring for tea. Tea made everything better, but a servant might overhear part of their conversation whilst delivering the tea cart.

Once again rolling her eyes, Jane considered where to start. "He just appeared in front of me last night. I was standing at the back of the ballroom, keeping company with the palm trees, and he asked me to waltz. I didn't even recognize him at first."

"If it's any consolation, I didn't either," Adele admitted. "Grandby had to tell me who he was during the supper. He hasn't been in London for years, and he does look quite different than he did as a lad. Why, I remember when we used to call him 'Max'."

Jane sighed, not about to admit that she remembered his nickname all too well. "We waltzed, and he offered to take me into supper, but I said I was going home—I was just about to leave when he asked me to dance. He escorted me to the vestibule, and then to my town coach, and the next thing I knew, he was *in* the coach telling me he wasn't going to leave me alone." She paused, rather annoyed at how Adele sighed, as if her story was some sort of fairy tale with a happy ending.

"And?" Adele prompted in anticipation, still perched on the front edge of her chair.

"He kept his word," Jane acknowledged with a nod. "Didn't take his leave of my bed until just after dawn. Sneaked out the back door, although the scullery maid discovered him. Apparently he said something about being in the wrong house, so she merely thought he was drunk and disorientated and about to come *into* the house, thank goodness."

Adele blinked, not about to ask if the scullery maid was a simpleton.

"So, your lady's maid doesn't know?" Adele asked, her brows

furrowed. Maids seemed to know *everything* about their mistresses. "What about your butler?"

Jane shook her head. "My butler spent the night with his wife at Norwick House. I don't think Nicole knows anything. I certainly didn't admit anything to her. The man had the decency to straighten the bed linens, and he left things quite neat before he kissed me, and told me he loved me, and said we would go riding in the park tomorrow when he returns from Chiswick." Tears once again streamed down her face, the hanky barely able to keep up with the flow. "I was so... *happy* before... before Lady Pettigrew read that damned gossip sheet," she wailed.

Sighing, Adele shook her head. "I'm so sorry, Jane." She allowed another sigh. "I can have Grandby challenge him to a duel, if you'd like," she suggested, her words more teasing than they should have been. "I suppose he could overlook the fact that Mr. Burroughs is one of his younger cousins."

"Oh, would you?" Jane countered, her manner still rather serious. "Grandby's not my godfather, of course, but I wouldn't mind him adopting me for the purpose of seeing to Mr. Burroughs' immediate demise." After a moment, she sighed. 'I had no idea he kissed Lady Jane before he asked me to dance," she whispered between sobs. Her eyes widened. "*Damnation.* He's old enough to be her *father*," she added, which brought forth even more tears.

Angry tears.

Sad tears.

Adele stood up and moved to the sideboard. Pouring a generous dollop of brandy into a tumbler, she took it to Jane and held it out. "Drink it," she ordered, her manner most sober.

Jane did as she was told, wincing as the amber liquid burned her throat. "Oh, that's disgusting," she complained after a couple of sputtering coughs. Indeed, it wasn't nearly as good as the brandy in her study, the brandy that she and Andrew had shared last night. She had a brief moment of wondering if her half-empty glass was still in the study. If so, she would empty it completely when she got home. And maybe have another.

She remembered there would be a second glass in the study. The one Andrew had used. She nearly burst into tears again at the thought.

Adele took back the tumbler, frowning at the glass. "Don't ever let Grandby hear you say that," she warned. "That's his very best brandy." The countess paused a moment before sitting down again, a sigh escaping as she did so. "I cannot tell you what to do, Jane," she finally said in a quiet voice. "But I can tell you that you have a decision to make."

"I do?" Jane sniffled, eager to hear Adele's words.

The Countess of Torrington nodded. "You either forget you ever heard anything about the kiss in the gardens and go with Mr. Burroughs on a ride in the park tomorrow afternoon, or..." Here, she paused and took a deep breath.

Jane gave her an expectant look, waiting for her friend to state the alternative. "Or?" she prompted.

"You don't."

Jane blinked. All the air seemed to go out of her in a 'whoosh'.

Adele was right, of course. She could either forgive the man his indiscretion—he had apparently kissed Lady J well before he danced with her and escorted her home—or she could give him the cut direct when next she saw him.

Tomorrow.

When he came to take her for a ride in the park.

"You're absolutely right, of course," Jane replied as she stood up and pulled her shoulders back as far as her pelisse would allow. "Thank you for a lovely luncheon," she managed as she made her way to the vestibule. "Your flutterbies were so adorable."

Fortified by the brandy—a pleasant buzz permeated her entire body—Jane Vandermeer Fitzpatrick took her leave of Worthington House and marched back to her townhouse in

South Audley Street, entirely unaware her driver and town coach were following at a discreet distance.

The envy she had felt when hearing about Andrew's kiss with Lady Jane soon turned to anger—anger directed at the banker. *How dare he kiss Lady Jane and then turn around and spend the night in my bed only an hour later?* Anger turned to a rage that fueled her quick steps and saw her home only minutes after leaving Worthington House.

Her town coach, stuck in Park Lane traffic, arrived at the mews behind her townhouse a half-hour later.

Jane was in her vestibule and removing her pelisse before she realized that in her haste and blind fury, she had not only left without the coach, she had also left her maid behind at Worthington House.

Mortified, she ducked into the study and replayed Adele's last words in her mind. Relieved to discover her glass of brandy was still right where she had left it—the downstairs maid hadn't yet made it to this room—she downed the contents. Placing the empty balloon on the desk, she wondered about the glass Andrew had used. She found it on the side table. Glancing about the room, she decided she would simply return it to the tray next to the liquor decanters.

No need for the maid to think she had been imbibing too much.

Or entertaining male callers.

CHAPTER 18
AN EARL GETS AN EARFUL

Having delivered a set of twins to the T earldom hasn't seemed to diminish the beauty of Lady T. She was in high spirits and looking ever so lovely in a gold glitter gown accessorized with a gold tiara. Is it any wonder the Earl of T finds her wherever he can? In the library. In the alcoves. In the retiring room. On the dance floor. It's a wonder we didn't pay witness to them in the gardens last night! ~ An article in the May 7 issue of *The Tattler.*

May 7, 1818, Worthington House nursery

Milton Grandby, Earl of Torrington, sat cross-legged on the floor of the nursery in Worthington House. One knee held his daughter, Angelica, while the other provided a perch for his son, George. Dressed in the long gowns most babes wore before they could walk, the twins were indistinguishable from one another. They even had the same number of teeth, although those were only apparent when they grinned, as Angelica was doing in response to her father's entertaining faces.

Keeping quiet in the threshold of the nursery, Adele proudly watched her husband dote on their children for several minutes until George noticed her and cried out, "Muma," his chubby arms raised up in anticipation of being hoisted into the air. Her back to the door, Angelica had to turn around on her father's knee in order to see Adele, her foot intersecting Grandby's crotch as she did so.

"Watch it, Angel, or you shall render me unable to service your mother," the earl complained as he struggled to reposition the children onto the floor so that he could stand up to properly greet his countess.

"Milton!" Adele scolded as she moved to pick up George. "I rather doubt there's anyone who can accomplish such a task," she added in a teasing whisper, one eyebrow arching up as she remembered just how service-minded he had been the night before.

And that morning.

What was it about balls that had him so randy when they finally made it home at three o'clock in the morning?

"True, but leave it to a little lady to try," he countered with a mischievous grin. He bussed Adele on the cheek and then bent to pick up Angelica, the girl cooing in delight as she settled into his bent arm. "I take it your luncheon is finished?" he half-asked.

"Yes. But aren't you supposed to be in Parliament today?"

The earl angled his head first one direction and then the other. "I am, but I decided I preferred spending time with the twins over time with twats."

Adele gasped. "Milton!" she admonished him again, realizing it was too late to cover the twins' ears. "It's safe to come downstairs," she added, turning to lead them out of the nursery and down the steps. "But before you sequester yourself in the study..."

"I'm going to sequester myself in the breakfast parlor," he interrupted. "I haven't yet had any luncheon, and I'm starving," he complained.

"I'll join you then. Something's come up, and I wonder if you might know anything."

Intrigued by her words, Grandby handed off his daughter to one of the nurses while Adele gave up her hold on George to the other. Grandby watched with pride as she kissed both babies on their cheeks before giving a nod to the nurses.

Having given birth to the twins—her first babies—at an age when most women were having their last baby or none at all, Adele was proving to be a rather loving mother.

"From the tone of your voice, it doesn't sound good," he hedged, once they were out of earshot of the servants.

In the breakfast parlor, Adele gave quick instructions to the footman on duty. Knowing she and the earl would be alone for only a few minutes, Adele filled him in on what had happened with Lady Stoneleigh during the luncheon. "I'm angry Eugenia would bring that rag with her today, but in the end, she was merely the messenger. Jane would have discovered the news from someone else, no doubt, or read it for herself in the paper," she explained.

The earl regarded his wife for a moment. "Short of challenging the publisher of *The Tattler* to a duel, what would you have me do?" he asked with an arched eyebrow. "As much as I despise gossip, it's a fact of life amongst our kind. What would you ladies talk about if you didn't have gossip to share in your parlors?"

Adele rolled her eyes, knowing her husband spoke the truth. "How well do you know Andrew Burroughs?" she asked, keeping her voice low. "Didn't you two both live at Merriweather Manor when you were boys?"

Grandby shrugged. "Of course. He's much younger than me, though. We all just knew him as 'Max' back in the day." At his wife's nod and expectant look, he explained how the Burroughs boy had been saddled with the name Maximilian. "His uncle..." At Adele's furrowed brow, he added, "William Burroughs the Third, my original banker at the Bank of England." When she nodded her understanding, he continued. "He taught him the business of banking, and after Max worked at the Bank of England for a few years, off he went to the Continent. Always wondered why he left England so soon after he married Craven's daughter," he murmured. "Other than I heard he worked in banking all that time. Heard his sons are at Cambridge and Eton, and his daughter is in finishing school." He paused a moment, realizing his wife was waiting for more information. "Truth be told, I heard he was back in London, but I didn't see him until I spoke with him at the ball last night."

Adele nodded her understanding. "Did you see him... *canoodling* with Lady Jane?" she asked carefully. "In the gardens?"

Grandby blinked, wondering why she would think he would be in the gardens without her. "No, but I saw him waltzing with Lady Stoneleigh. Does that count?" he asked. At Adele's quelling glance, he sighed. "He spent most of the night in the card room renewing old acquaintances," he explained with a shrug. "I don't see how he would have had time to canoodle with Lady Jane in the gardens, or anywhere else, for that matter. I can ask him, though," he added with a shrug, despite not knowing exactly where he might find Andrew Burroughs at the moment. He knew the man had been seeing to a special project, although doing so from across the Channel. Now that he was back on British shores, Grandby figured he would be spending his days overseeing the final details. As for if he could find him that night, he didn't know if the man would be joining White's or had another men's club in mind for his evening pursuits. Given his father's politics, Grandby thought perhaps he might be a member of Boodles.

It was Adele's turn to blink. "You would do that?"

The earl shrugged. "Of course. It sounds as if a budding romance has been derailed because of that damned *Tattler*," he stated in disgust. "If the account about Mr. Burroughs is a lie, or perhaps simply a case of mistaken identity, as I suspect it is, then it's about time something is done to put that rag out of business." Even though he didn't really believe it was possible to put *The Tattler* out of business, he thought putting voice to the possibility would appease his wife.

Adele inhaled as if to argue, but she thought better of it. *The Tattler* provided the fodder for most of the gossip exchanged in Mayfair parlors. If her guests didn't have information from a printed source, the *on-dit* would come from suppositions and suspicion. The paper's approach wasn't mean-spirited—at least, not usually. The same couldn't be said for some of the gossip espoused by ladies of the *ton*, though.

Even if her husband could see to the demise of *The Tattler*, another gossip news sheet would simply pop up in its place. Rumor had it the publication was quite profitable for its owner.

"Mr. Burroughs will apparently be in Chiswick until tomorrow afternoon," Adele offered with an elegantly arched brow.

Grandby allowed a grin. "Visiting the old family estate, no doubt."

Adele angled her head, surprised at his comment. "What makes you say that?" she asked as a footman entered and poured wine.

Grandby shrugged. "Back in the day, Merriweather Manor housed generations of Grandbys and Merriweathers, including me. And Gregory. Aunt Sophia was a Burroughs, you see."

Adele frowned. "Sophia?" she repeated.

"Cousin Gregory's mother. She was the one who married the butler and disappeared with her inheritance," he explained as he leaned toward his wife and lowered his voice. He enjoyed telling a tale of how the butler did it. "Spent a fortune on property and made four fortunes within a few years. I always figured it was Uncle William who helped her hide the money."

While she listened to his explanation, Adele continued to frown. "But I thought Merriweather Manor was abandoned," she murmured, helping herself to some bread and cheese from the platter a footman had placed on the table. She put together a sandwich and gave it to Grandby.

"Indeed. It was for several years," her husband agreed with a nod as he took the sandwich. "But Uncle William decided it was worthy of restoration. He sold some of the unentailed land to an adjacent landowner, and he and Max added some of their own funds to pay for the restoration. Soon it will probably fill up with another generation of..." He stopped, frowning when he realized he didn't know who was going to live in the manor house. "*Us,*" he finally added.

Adele offered him a slice of cheese on an apple wedge and then set about making another sandwich. "Unentailed land implies part of the estate is entailed. To whom does it belong?" she asked, rather enjoying the opportunity to serve her husband his luncheon.

The earl frowned a moment before allowing a shrug. "Me, I think. But if not, it may be one of Ariley's," he replied, referring to the Duke of Ariley.

His countess stared at him in shock. "How can you not know who owns Merriweather Manor?" she asked in surprise.

He blinked. "As old as that place is, I have a feeling no one wants to claim ownership because it means taking responsibility for the bills. Grandma's family built it—the Merriweathers— generations ago, but then she married my grandfather. It might have been her dowry."

Adele shook her head. "Then why would Ariley have any claim to it?"

Angling his head to one side as he took the slice of bread with jam she offered, he replied, "The Merriweathers and Burroughs go way back. Wouldn't be surprised if it was part of the arrangement to marry off our youngest uncle, Roger—God rest his soul—to Sophia Burroughs. Quite a coup that was at the time."

"Because?"

Grandby took a bite of his bread, chewing as he gave her

question some thought. "Sophia Burroughs was quite a beauty—still is, given she's nearly... *sixty*," he murmured in disbelief. *Goodness! Where had the years gone?* "Had a line of suitors attending her at every ball. But Grandma saw to it she chose Uncle Roger." He took in a deep breath and let it out slowly. "I figure she must have bribed the Burroughs—perhaps with the house—or else she turned down a traditional dowry. Grandma—that would be Mary Margaret Merriweather Grandby—was rich, you see," he explained as he turned his attention back to his bread. "And she wanted Roger to have a Burroughs girl for a bride. Got a grandson in Gregory out of the deal before Roger succumbed to pneumonia. Gregory inherited twenty-thousand pounds when he reached his majority..."

"I thought he earned his wealth from investments," Adele interrupted, surprise evident in her voice.

"He did. Had to start with something, though," Grandby replied with a nod. "Once he proved he could make money, I had him do the same for me."

"Which explains why you're rich," Adele commented in awe, not having known from where her husband had obtained his wealth. He had always implied the Torrington earldom was a poor one. "So, I suppose it's not important who actually owns the manor."

He screwed up his face at her words. "As long as I'm not being billed for all the work that's being done to the place," he countered. "I heard it's being plumbed for toilets." He finished his bread and sat back. "I do believe it's time for me to pay a call on the old stomping grounds," he spoke as one of his bushy eyebrows waggled.

"Oh?"

"Aye. Give me an opportunity to say 'hullo' to a long lost relative, and to determine if I need to be bloodying his nose."

About to argue with the last part of his comment, Adele remembered she had promised Jane she would speak with Grandby about Andrew. She certainly hadn't agreed to ask for a duel, though. If her husband decided a duel of sorts was called for when it came to Andrew Burroughs, then it was best it happened in the country and not in London proper.

She could only imagine the *on-dit* should *The Tattler* print the story of cousins fighting over an incident originally reported in the gossip rag.

"But first, I'll need to read the article for myself," the earl stated, accepting the slice of tart and cheese his wife offered him. "I want to be sure I have the story straight," he explained at Adele's questioning glance.

"I'll have Bernard send one of the footmen for a copy right away," she replied, her displeasure at the idea apparent in her frown.

Grandby shook his head. "Och. That won't be necessary. There's a copy on my desk in the study." At Adele's widened eyes, he allowed a shrug. "I have a copy of *The Tattler* delivered every Thursday." Before Adele could respond—he could see she wasn't pleased by this bit of news— Grandby leaned over and kissed her on the cheek. "I have to keep up on the news of my goddaughters *somehow*," he whispered. "Do have a good day, my sweeting."

When he turned back to regard his plate, both of his eyebrows shot up. "Good God, sweeting. I thought I had eaten everything you offered me. Are you of the opinion I need to be putting on some weight?"

Rather startled by his question, Adele turned her own attention to the earl's plate and broke out in giggles. Several sandwiches, tarts, and slices of fruit covered the bone china plate from rim to rim. Her eyes darkened as she turned to regard him. "Perhaps I'll just have this saved and brought up to your bedchamber. You know how hungry you can get late at night," she hinted with an elegantly arched brow.

Milton Grandby, Earl of Torrington, stared at his wife for several seconds before a huge grin appeared. "Why, be still my beating heart. My wanton wife hath returned," he whispered. "Might have to let *The Tattler* know about this," he teased.

"You wouldn't dare!" Adele breathed in shock.

He angled his head a moment before he shook it. "I suppose not." With that, the earl was off to his study to learn what he could about the gossip from Lord Weatherstone's ball.

CHAPTER 19
AN EARL AT PARLIAMENT

Yes, dear reader, we admit to having donned fake noses and mustaches and to wear spectacles in order to maintain anonymity. However, it was necessary. How else is gossip to be acquired when we are so recognizable in our natural state? ~ The editor's final article in the May 14, 1818 issue of *The Tattler*.

May 7, 1818 at Parliament

"Good God, Fennington, you look as if you ran the entire way here," David Carlington, Marquess of Morganfield, remarked as the two donned their periwigs and robes. "Mistress keep you abed too long?" he added in a teasing voice.

The earl gave the marquess a quelling glance. "I rather wish I could claim that as my excuse," Felix replied as he straightened the black robe and took a quick glance at his reflection in a looking glass. *Although I was in the company of a young woman,* he nearly added with a wan smile.

Morganfield was right, of course. He did appear winded, his cheeks reddened from his race to Westminster, his spiked hair now safely ensconced in a periwig. Juno had done herself proud by simply barreling down the streets, around carts and horses and all manner of conveyances that could have hindered his on-time arrival.

A groomsman had seen to his phaeton and to Juno the moment he stepped down and onto the pavement. It was then he realized he had lost his mustache.

Damn!

Well, he had another in his box of disguises. He rather liked the one he wore today, though. Its color suited his face perfectly, and it was trimmed so it appeared as natural as a real one. Where could he have lost it?

In the park? In Piccadilly? Or was it on the seat of his phaeton?

He could only hope it might be found there. He would search for it later. Right now, he needed to concentrate on Lord Morganfield.

"You don't appear as if you rushed here, but aren't you here a bit later than normal?" Felix queried with an arched eyebrow. "Stay too late at the ball last night?" He knew the marquess was his party's leader, both in and out of Chambers. Morganfield was usually surrounded by his political peers, reviewing what topics they should and shouldn't agree upon when they came up for a vote.

The marquess allowed a nod. "My wife kept me abed a bit longer than normal this morning, I'll happily admit. She's rather talented when it comes to the use of feathers," he replied with a grin.

Felix was quite sure he saw the man blush!

Feathers?

"Feathers?" he repeated, resisting the urge to swallow. *In bed? And how?* He felt his own color rising and turned away, pretending to straighten his folded topcoat on the bench where he had left it a moment ago.

David regarded him with a grin before saying, "You'll have to tell your mistress to give them a try. Ostrich feathers are ever so... exotic." He turned his attention to one of the other lords who had just arrived. "I never took you for one to end up in the pages of *The Tattler*," he said to the newcomer.

William Slater, Marquess of Devonville, smiled broadly at the comment as he donned his robe. "Me neither, but apparently giving your wife a peck on the cheek at the theatre is considered scandalous. Who knew?"

The other marquess quirked a lip. "Well, if you had pecked my wife on the cheek, you would have had a shiner to show for it," he responded with a grin.

Rather protective of his marchioness, David barely tolerated another man kissing the back of her hand. At least he allowed her to dance at *ton* balls. The daughter of an Italian count was still a stunner despite her age.

"Och! You're certainly no fun," Devonville replied. "But I'm not the least bit embarrassed by the mention in that rag," he added. "I do feel for that poor girl who suffered at Lord Brougham's attention, however. Miss Grandby doesn't deserve such a mention."

David gave a nod. "And I'm sure Brougham has suffered for having bestowed Miss Grandby with any attention at all. I heard Gregory Grandby pummeled the rake at Gentleman Jackson's saloon, and the man isn't even a member there."

The other marquess straightened. "I would have paid money to see that mill," he said with awe.

"We all would have," David Carlington agreed. "Perhaps a rematch can be arranged. I rather doubt Brougham will return, though. At least until his nose has had a chance to heal."

Felix listened intently as the two marquesses exchanged comments about last week's issue of *The Tattler*. To learn that both read his publication was both a surprise and a compliment. He figured mostly women read the news sheet and then shared the information with others during their morning and afternoon teas. The articles were rarely mean-spirited, although a few members of the *ton* suffered more than others simply because he didn't like them.

Or their ways.

Lord Brougham was one of them. The fact that the woman he had been seen fondling during Huntington's soirée two weeks ago was now made famous by his gossip news sheet was probably a blessing as much as a curse. Most would give the young woman a bit—no, make that a good deal—of leeway, for everyone knew the lecherous viscount for what he was—a rake and a libertine. He couldn't even be expected to have to offer for her hand since he was already married.

Thank the gods. Ariel Grandby was the apple of her father's eye. Gregory Grandby would never insist on marriage. Especially after pummeling the man.

Would he?

I will simply invent a story to save her from such a travesty if it ever came to that, Felix thought quickly. The oldest daughter of Gregory Grandby deserved the very best in terms of a match, and he couldn't imagine any rake on the planet as her husband. The girl was far too young to marry anyway. *What was Ariel now?* he wondered. *Fourteen? Fifteen?*

Poor child.

Even her mother, Christiana, had been at least sixteen before her brother, Thomas Wellingham, finally allowed her to wed his best friend. And Gregory Grandby was one of the wealthiest men in all of England!

But hearing that Brougham was probably beaten to a pulp by the Earl of Torrington's cousin had him thinking up a headline for the next issue of *The Tattler*.

Incensed Father Defends His Daughter's Honor! Rake Pummeled, Nose Broken! See page 6.

He'd have to learn more about what happened after the Duke of Huntington's soirée before he sat down to write the article, though. The more details he could include, the more compelling the article would be to his readers. At least he knew the man's nose was broken. That would be a bonus in the telling. Everyone knew broken noses spewed blood all about.

Spewing blood sold newspapers!

And if Emelia Comber didn't agree to be his wife, he might have to see about acquiring a mistress. Lord Morganfield obviously thought he employed one, although he hadn't been able to afford one since he learned the earldom was so deep in debt from his father's gambling. He remembered the thought of offering *carte blanche* to Emelia Comber and wondered once again what her reaction might be should he do so.

Anger?

Contempt?

Interest?

Acceptance?

That last was rather unlikely, but he could always hope. Actually, it was far better when he thought of her as his wife. The thought of her body beneath his had his cock hardening, his heart racing, and his mind imagining all the ways he could pleasure her. All the ways he could have her saying his name as ecstasy took her and her lush body, how his own would seize up and send his mind into oblivion, into an existence so intense and pleasurable, his seed would spill into her and be on its way to create the next generation of Fenningtons.

Felix swallowed just then.

Mistresses couldn't give birth to heirs. Only wives could do that.

Emelia Comber had to agree to be his wife.

Why think of her in any other capacity but that of his countess?

She was the younger daughter of an earl. Not his favorite member of the *ton*, certainly, but Mark Comber, Earl of Aimsley, wasn't so bad compared to some of the others. His countess, Patience Waterford Comber, was rather a good woman, a compassionate woman, a good mother, and a devoted patron to her charities. A woman who had given birth to one of the most troublesome and yet friendly of men in Adam and one of the most compelling women he had ever had the pleasure of knowing.

He dared a glance down the front of his body.

Thank goodness he wore a robe just then!

The gong sounded, and those still in the robing room quickly departed for the Chamber of Lords.

Felix followed at a discreet distance.

CHAPTER 20
A VISIT TO MERRIWEATHER MANOR

Rumor has it that Merriweather Manor in Chiswick is undergoing massive renovations. While we haven't yet learned who is footing the bill, we do have to wonder—why? No one has lived there in the brick monstrosity for over ten years! Is someone expecting? ~ A snippet of an article in the January 29, 1818 issue of *The Tattler*.

Meanwhile, in Chiswick

Seven miles west of London, Andrew Burroughs pulled back on the reins of his borrowed horse and stared in wonder at the sprawling brick manor just off the Great West Road. Although Merriweather Manor had at one time fronted twelve-thousand acres, the grounds were considerably smaller now—six-thousand acres, according to the deed. Behind the huge, multi-winged structure stood a matching brick carriage house and stables. Three gardens covered part of the grounds, and somewhere in the back—behind the kitchen gardens and the formal garden—there was a pond suitable for fishing.

It seems smaller now because it is, he thought with a grin, rather happy to know that just selling off the back six-thousand acres to an adjacent landowner had raised enough funds to pay for nearly half the manual labor to restore the estate to its former glory.

Sir William Burroughs III had seen to that transaction as well as hiring the workmen required for the restoration of the house and remaining grounds. Exchanging correspondence with his uncle for nearly five years had kept Andrew current on the project, and the project ensured his uncle had something to keep him busy once he retired from his position at the Bank of England. At seventy years of age, William may have complained of aches and pains, but he wasn't a frail old man.

Although he had spent his youth at Merriweather Manor, Andrew hadn't been back to the house for nearly twenty years. Now that he and his uncle's plans to revive the old estate were nearly complete, he could hardly wait to see the results.

He allowed the trotter to set the pace as they made their way up the crushed granite drive. He half-expected a stableboy to see to the horse but had to remind himself that the household and stables staff had not yet been hired. With luck, a butler would be on site within the next few weeks as well as a housekeeper and cook. By the following month, if all followed the plan he had been considering since leaving Jane's bed that morning, they would take up residence as husband and wife at Merriweather Manor in time for the Little Season.

Several gardeners were raking the newly clipped lawn adjacent to the house, and a team of laborers were unloading furnishings from several dray carts.

When one tipped his hat, Andrew headed in his direction. "Hullo. I wonder if you might know where I can find the foreman?"

The workman jerked a thumb toward the house. "He's with the colorman in the main floor parlor."

Andrew acknowledged the man with a nod and hobbled the horse near the marble fountain in the center of the drive. Although no water sprouted from the figurines, the base contained what looked like fresh rainwater. He watched to be sure the horse could help himself to a drink before heading through the double-doors and into the house.

Stopping short, he was struck by the sense of déja vu he experienced. Although the large vestibule was newly painted, and the marble floor had been restored to a gleaming shine, it was still familiar. Some of the furnishings were missing, although he realized the workmen out front were still in the process of bringing in the household items that had been stored at a nearby estate during the renovations.

"May I be of assistance?"

Andrew turned at the sound of the query, removing his hat as he did so. "Yes, sir. I'm looking for Mr. Turner," he answered.

"Found him, you did," the man replied as he moved in Andrew's direction.

"Andrew Burroughs," he replied, holding out his hand.

The foreman shook it and gave him a nod. "You're the partner on this project, then," he said, his eyes widening.

"Aye. My uncle said it's my turn to check on your progress," Andrew said with a grin. "I do hope the old man has been reasonable to work with."

Mr. Turner gave a shrug. 'Haven't seen much of him, actually."

Andrew furrowed his brows, wondering if someone else had been touring the house and grounds in place of his uncle and providing him with updates. "The exterior appears to be nearly complete. It looks rather fine."

The foreman nodded and moved farther into the house. "Should be done today, if this weather holds. Just some chinking on the back side of the main house and on the carriage house. I'm having a bit of an issue inside, however."

Andrew paused mid-step. "Oh?" His cautious reply had the foreman sighing.

"Other than some minor carpentry issues in some of the bedchambers upstairs, the last room left to complete is the parlor. The men are here with the furniture, but the colorman has yet to mix the paint. He's arguing about the color."

Andrew frowned, attempting to remember the color scheme he and his uncle had come up with for the ground floor parlor. "Doesn't like green, then?" he half-asked, remembering the choice of a dark verde seemed fashionable for rooms with a few windows.

"Says it's poisonous. Says the ladies will be fainting whilst they have their tea," Mr. Turner said with an arched brow, as if he didn't know whether or not to believe the man's claim.

Alarmed by the comment, Andrew made his way to the parlor. "Poisonous?" he spoke to the only man in the room. "How so?"

The colorman regarded him for only a moment before he gave a bow. "Aye. To achieve that deep green shade, I have to use arsenic with the copper. Makes for a nasty mix, sir, even after it dries. Don't want to be leaving any windows closed for too long, especially in the winter."

Andrew nodded, realizing that if the paint included arsenic, the man spoke the truth. Not everyone knew arsenic was poisonous, of course, considering some were still using it to quell their coughs.

But arsenic in paint?

"No doubt. I suppose that's what makes the color on the wallpaper then?"

"Aye. No way around it if you're wanting those deep green walls."

Truth be told, Andrew didn't particularly care what color the parlor walls were. He had merely agreed with his uncle to use whatever was currently fashionable.

He remembered the cream-colored walls of Jane's bedchamber and had to suppress the sudden grin he felt touching his lips. He had spent the entire ride to Chiswick thinking of their night spent together. With any luck, there would be a lifetime of nights like that one in his immediate future.

He absently felt for the tiny velvet-covered box in his waistcoat pocket. Although he had an early start that morning by leaving Jane's townhouse at dawn, he had elected to walk to his uncle's house to wash and change clothes. He then borrowed his uncle's horse from the mews in the alley.

Instead of making his way directly to the Bank of England as he had originally planned, he directed the horse to Ludgate Hill. The doors to Rundell, Bridge & Rundell had barely opened when he arrived in search of an appropriate bauble for Jane. He had thought to simply find a bracelet or necklace when he realized he could buy her a wedding ring. She would no doubt accept his offer of marriage whilst on their ride in the park on the morrow.

He had declared his love for her—several times—and was sure the feeling was mutual even if she hadn't put voice to the same sentiment. Their time together after the ball had convinced him it didn't matter that nearly eighteen years had passed without the two seeing one another. They could simply pick up where they had left off all those years ago, before Jane's father had informed him she was betrothed to the Earl of Stoneleigh.

How different their lives would have been if her father hadn't insisted on her marriage to the despicable aristocrat! Andrew might never have left the Bank of England. Might never have left London to work on the Continent.

Would never have married Bess.

He shook his head. He couldn't think like that. If he hadn't married Bess, he wouldn't have his children. Wouldn't have had the opportunity to amass a personal fortune that allowed him to restore Merriweather Manor to its former glory.

It was the reminder of his bank account that had him perusing the trays and trays of rings the goldsmith held out for him to study.

What would my cousin choose? he wondered, thinking of Milton Grandby, Earl of Torrington. His uncle claimed the oldest

Grandby cousin patronized the goldsmith on a frequent basis, his countess the beneficiary of his purchases. *The bastard bought her three necklaces the night he discovered she was with child because he didn't know what color gown she would be wearing for dinner,* Sir William had said as he shook his head in disbelief.

When Andrew put voice to the query as to which ring the earl would choose, Mr. Rundell's eyes widened, and the trays disappeared to be replaced with another displaying rings with far larger gemstones and more decorative settings.

And higher prices, of course.

Ten minutes later, a sapphire-topped gold ring was stuffed into his pocket. A pair of earbobs and a necklace would be completed in a fortnight by the goldsmith, the jewelry intended as wedding gifts.

When Andrew was just a mile short of Merriweather Manor, he noticed a collection of greenhouses off the Great West Road. Locating the proprietor had been easy. Convincing her to deliver a large bouquet of daisies to Jane's townhouse in Mayfair had taken a bit of cajoling and an extra sovereign, but he was assured the flowers would be delivered later that day.

Satisfied he had done what he could to ensure he stayed in Jane's thoughts, Andrew completed his trip to Merriweather Manor.

"What about scarlet?" he asked the colorman, his attention on the one solid wall in the parlor that didn't include a door or a window.

"Aye. I can do scarlet."

Andrew nodded. "Then do so, and I'll let Sir William know about the change in plans."

"Very good, sir," the colorman acknowledged with a nod.

Taking his leave of the parlor, Andrew made his way up the stairs and through the long hallway to the west wing. Starting at one end, he walked into each and every room along the hall, examining the workmanship to ensure all the finishing work had been done by the carpenters.

When he was done in the west wing, he moved to the east wing and did the same, finding only two rooms that lacked part of their mouldings. Making a note of their location, he moved to the servant's floor and did the same with the rooms there. Although the third-floor rooms were simpler in design and smaller in size, he found several were still in need of a carpenter. He would have a word with the foreman before he took his leave of the house. A household staff would have to begin living in the house weeks before anyone else moved in, after all.

Andrew was about to descend the curved stairs to the main floor when he remembered the house included an attic above the servants' floor. A popular place to play hide-and-seek when he was a boy, the top floor featured slanted ceilings barely high enough for the tallest children to walk under without having to bend over. The back stairs at the end of the east wing were barely wide enough to allow him access, which had him wondering how all manner of trunks and old furnishings could have been stored up there.

When he reached the top of the stairs, he expected to find an expanse filled with the castoffs from the various families that had occupied the house over the years. Instead, he found it empty but for a few trunks and valises. Instead of a ceiling and corners decorated with cobwebs and the wood planks making up the floor covered in dust, he found the space swept and tidy.

Moving to one of the trunks, he reached down and opened it, surprised to find it empty. The valise next to it was empty as well. *Now it's just storage for luggage*, he realized when a large Louis Vuitton trunk proved to be empty as well.

"Most of what was up here was ruined when the roof leaked," a deep voice said from behind him.

Andrew turned to find one of his cousins regarding him with an expression that suggested he wasn't quite sure who he was addressing. "Gregory? Gregory Grandby?" he replied in disbelief.

"Aye. And you must be... *Max?* Oh, my God, it *is* you," the rather tall man said as he finished climbing the stairs and moved to grab Andrew's hand. "The foreman said Uncle's agent was up here. I had no idea he meant *you*, but I suppose I shouldn't be so surprised since you are expected for dinner at Woodscastle tonight. You are still coming for dinner, I hope?"

Andrew smiled and nodded. "I wouldn't miss it. So good of your wife to send the invitation. She learned of my return from Uncle, of course. How many bairns can you two claim now?"

Gregory straightened as much as he could given the limited headspace in the attic. "There are ten of the hellions," he admitted with a roll of his eyes. He motioned for them to move to the stairwell. "But they're all healthy and happy. The oldest, Ariel, is fifteen now, and I expect I'll be challenging suitors to duels in the next year or so."

Andrew regarded his much older cousin as they made their way to the stairs. "You haven't changed a bit!" he complained. "Although you look as if you've had a bit too much sun."

The older cousin nodded. "Indeed. I just returned from Dorset yesterday. Took the oldest children down to the southern coast for a fossil hunting foray. And to meet Mary Anning in Lyme Regis."

"Who?"

"Mary Anning. The fossil collector. She and her brother were the ones who discovered the first complete ichthyosaur skeleton." At Andrew's continued look of confusion, Gregory sighed. "The fish lizard? The dinosaur? Anyway, she has quite the collection of fossils. Been pulling them out of the cliff-side since she was a few years old. Seashells, mostly, but all cataloged and organized quite scientifically. She sells them to make a living. I was able to add to my collection, and I would have purchased everything she had, but I didn't have room in the coach to get it all home."

The younger cousin gave a sound of understanding. "You're the cousin who is the *naturalist*," Andrew remarked.

"Aye. Well, when I'm not having to help aristocrats earn money with their investments," Gregory replied as he stepped out of the stairwell and into the second floor hallway. "It's lucrative, of course, but certainly not as interesting as studying science." He turned his attention to Andrew and regarded him for a moment in the brighter lighting. "Perhaps now that you're back on these shores, you can take over that business," he suggested. "Still in banking, aren't you?"

Andrew allowed a chuckle. "I suppose that's part of what I'll be expected to do. And, yes, I'm back at the Bank of England."

"You haven't changed much in... what has it been? Nearly twenty years?"

The younger cousin nodded. "Hard to believe it's been that long."

"When I saw a mention of an 'A. Burroughs' in *The Tattler* this morning, I wondered who it might be. Now I realize it had to be you." Gregory continued down the hallway, stopping only once to peek into one of the rooms to announce it had been his when he was a boy.

"*The Tattler?*" Andrew repeated. Goodness, he had only been back from the Continent for a fortnight! *What could I have done to earn a mention in a news sheet?*

"Congratulations. You made the front page," Gregory said when he reached the mezzanine overlooking the grand hall. Instead of continuing down the main stairs, he headed for the west hallway.

Andrew gave him a look of confusion. "But, why would I be mentioned on the front page of... what is *The Tattler?*"

"London's premiere gossip newspaper," Gregory replied with a roll of his eyes. "Whoever publishes it must be making a fortune," he added with a quirked lip. "Rather wish I had been asked to be an investor back when it was first started."

Gregory was well known for the money he had made over the years with his lucrative investments, his initial inheritance having provided the seed money necessary to build his personal income so he was now one of the wealthiest men in all of England. His manner lightened. "So, Lady J, huh? I do hope you weren't robbing the cradle," he remarked with an arched brow.

Pausing halfway down the hallway, Andrew frowned and shook his head. "I was hardly robbing the cradle. Lady Stoneleigh and I are only a few years apart in age," he replied defensively, before he had a chance to consider he had only just renewed his acquaintance with the lady the night before. "And just what did this newspaper claim I was *doing* with Jane?" he asked in alarm.

Jesus. He had thought they had left Lord Weatherstone's house without being spied by anyone other than the two footmen who had seen to their coats. The butler who had nodded as they made their way out of the front door. Her town coach driver knew, of course, and there was the scullery maid he had surprised at the back door of Jane's townhouse this morning, but he was quite sure no one else had seen the two of them together.

Gregory angled his head. "Kissing in the gardens, I believe was the crime," he hesitantly answered. "But I do not think they were referring to Jane Fitzpatrick. A recent widow, isn't she?" They had reached the end of the hallway and Gregory turned back toward the front of the house, ducking his head into several of the bedchambers as they walked.

Andrew nodded. "And my future wife, I hope," he replied in a hushed voice, absently patting his waistcoat to ensure the ring box was still secure in his pocket.

The older cousin appeared impressed. "You've been back on British shores for how many days...?"

"Ten or twelve."

"And widowed for, what? Eleven years?"

"Not quite, but..."

"And you're looking to be leg-shackled again?"

"Yes, but I wasn't kissing *anyone* in the gardens last night," Andrew argued, ignoring the question about being leg-shackled. He was looking forward to marriage, actually. Looking forward to a life with Jane Vandermeer Fitzpatrick. *Good God!* If only a few nights a week were like last night, he might never get out of bed!

Gregory gave him a quelling glance. "Well, *someone* thinks you were." He reached the curved stairs and made his way down, Andrew almost alongside him, but he paused on the landing to the first floor. "Does Todd Vandermeer know you're after his cousin?"

Andrew blinked. "Who?"

The older cousin angled his head before rolling his eyes. "You were probably gone from London by the time Todd learned who his parents were," he murmured absently.

"And, once again, I ask, who is Todd Vandermeer?"

Gregory continued descending the rest of the stairs. "I cannot believe you don't remember him, but mayhap he was already a caddy for East India when you were in short pants," he replied, realizing that had to be the case. Perhaps Andrew hadn't even been born when Todd Vandermeer, Gregory, and their friend, Thomas Wellingham, played together as children.

"So?" Andrew prompted.

Gregory allowed a grin. "He's an import broker now. Taller than me, I kid you not. Works at my brother-in-law's import company. Has a mansion in Cavendish Square. His father, God rest his soul, and Lady Stoneleigh's father were brothers," he explained, finally establishing the connection between Jane Fitzpatrick and his friend Todd. "He's rather protective of what family he has left since his father died in service to the British Army, just before his mother died.

"For an orphan, he's done very well for himself."

Andrew considered the information. "Thank you for warning me. I think," he added uncertainly. He was still perturbed at learning someone thought he had been kissing Jane in the gardens, though. He rather hoped Jane didn't mind the mention in the news sheet. Perhaps she was reading about it right now and finding it more humorous than he did.

He could only hope.

As for kissing in the gardens, he could hardly believe anyone would mistake the potted palms along the sides and back of the ballroom to be part of the gardens. Even then, he hadn't kissed Jane beneath a palm frond, or even behind one. He'd been tempted, of course, but discretion was paramount right now.

It was then he and his cousin noticed that someone else had come into Merriweather Manor. Giving each other a lifted brow, they turned their attention to their visitor and both bowed.

"So good of you to join us," Gregory said as he straightened.

CHAPTER 21
UNWELCOME FLOWERS

Rumor has it Lady W ordered over a dozen potted palms from a Chiswick greenhouse for the back of her ballroom. The palms are a favorite of the wallflowers—far better to keep company with a potted palm tree than with the wallpaper—as well as some couples who just can't seem to wait until they're back in their bedchambers to steal a kiss or two! Lord and Lady M have their favorite tree, it seems, as do Lord and Lady B. ~ An article in the May 7, 1818 issue of *The Tattler*.

May 7, 1818, Lady Stoneleigh's townhouse

As her butler nearly collided with her at the door to the study, Jane worked hard to rein in her anger. She feared snapping at the older man should he put voice to any kind of pleasantry. Perhaps he sensed her distress, for he didn't say anything when he held out the salver containing that day's mail.

Jane gave him a quick nod as she took the missives. She rifled through the envelopes as she made her way into the hall and past the round table at its center, a part of her heartened at the number of invitations. Goodness! It was as if everyone in the *ton* knew she was done with mourning. Maybe it would be best to put off her move to the Continent until after the Season's events, she considered, remembering that today was the day she was to make the necessary arrangements to escape London.

Reviewing the wax seals on the backs of the envelopes, she recognized the Morganfield, Aimsley, and Torrington crests as well as several others. Pausing to open one of the envelopes, she dropped the others on the table.

Although the crystal vase in the middle had been empty since this morning—none of the summer flowers in the back garden were in bloom quite yet—a giant bouquet of white daisies now filled the vase.

Staring at the flowers, Jane angled her head to one side.

"Aren't they beautiful, my lady?" her housekeeper, Mrs. Adams, asked as she joined Jane at the table. "They arrived only a few minutes ago."

"Arrived?" Jane repeated before she noticed a card tucked into the top of the vase. She plucked it from its wooden holder and unfolded the missive. *I hope you're having a brilliant day. See you at four o'clock tomorrow afternoon. Love, A.*

Jane sighed, a small smile touching her lips. *How lovely of him,* she thought for a fraction of the second before she remembered just how angry she was at the banker.

How duplicitous! What a rake!

The rogue had probably sent the same bouquet to Lady Jane! Or one twice as large and made up of roses. The thought had her anger boiling again, and she struggled to bring it back down to a simmer lest she burn someone who didn't deserve it.

Turning to the housekeeper, Jane was of a mind to order her to destroy the flowers. At the woman's expression of adoration over the flowers, though, Jane took a deep breath and let it out slowly. "Could you see to it these flowers are moved to the servants' table below stairs? I'm sure they'll be enjoyed far more during your supper this evening than they will be here where no one can see them," she added after seeing the look of disbelief on the housekeeper's face.

"As you wish, my lady," Mrs. Adams finally replied with a

nod, her expression having changed to one of puzzlement. The older woman leaned over and carefully lifted the heavy vase from the table. Once she had it cradled against the front of her body she managed a curtsy and took her leave of the hall.

Aware she was once again about to cry, Jane gathered the envelopes from the table and hurried up the stairs to her room. *Damn him!* she nearly cried out loud as her body hit the bed. Her head and one fist landed on the very pillow Andrew had used when he hadn't been using her as one the night before, sending the scents of amber and citrus wafting past her nose and bringing back the memories of their exquisite evening together.

"Damn him," she murmured as the tears once again flowed down her cheeks. She fell asleep, the note from the flowers still clutched in her fist and the invitations scattered about the counterpane.

CHAPTER 22
ANOTHER COUSIN VISITS MERRIWEATHER MANOR

Rumor has it Merriweather Manor will be ready for occupancy in June. But who will live there? A search of public records hasn't yet determined just who owns the pile, nor who is writing the cheques for all the renovations. Our money is on someone at the Bank of England. Who else can afford twenty toilets and all that marble? ~ An article in the March 19, 1818 issue of *The Tattler.*

Meanwhile, back in Chiswick

As Milton Grandby, Earl of Torrington, stepped down from his phaeton, he regarded the brick structure before him and allowed a long whistle. Merriweather Manor had never looked this good. Not during any of the years he had been in residence—and probably not when it was first built the century or so prior.

A sense of melancholy settled over him just then. He hadn't paid more than a visit or two to his childhood home since he inherited the Torrington earldom, and that had been a very long time ago. *Thirty years?* No, not quite that long, he considered.

He dared a glance at the other phaeton parked nearby, a sportier version than the one he drove. Although he didn't recognize the equipage, he was fairly sure the horses belonged to his cousin, Gregory.

He turned his attention to the fountain in the center of the drive, wondering at the trotter that stood waiting there. Not recognizing the horse, he wondered who else might be in the house. *Lord Maximilian? Sir William?*

Several drays were parked off to one side, furnishings piled up on the carts much like large puzzle pieces interlocked together. A series of laborers were in the process of carrying in the loads, intent on their work and ignoring him as they did so.

Stepping down from the phaeton, Grandby made his way to the double-doors and paused before entering. The familiar odor of *home* didn't waft past his nostrils as he half-expected. Instead the vestibule smelled of fresh wax and polish and paint and sawdust.

New! he thought in surprise. *Uncle William has certainly outdone himself,* he realized as he entered the vestibule and took in the finishing details—mouldings, wallpaper, marble and brass—and let out another low whistle. The great hall beyond was much larger than he remembered, one of the straight staircases having been removed in favor of a single curved one off to the right. It should have made the symmetry of the hall seem off, but it did not, seeing as how a series of tall alcoves were tucked into the wall to the left. In each one, a pedestal supported a marble statue of a character from mythology.

Three stories above him, the painted ceiling featured a scene out of one of the tales of mythology. *Cupid,* Grandby thought, noting the quiver and arrow and depictions of the cherub's parents, Venus and Mars.

The mezzanine above, lined with carved wooden doors and fronted by a continuous balustrade, suggested the second story was nothing but bedchambers. *No upstairs parlor?* he wondered, pausing in the middle of the hall when he heard voices from above.

He watched as his cousins appeared from the western side of

the manor house. About to announce his presence, he instead listened when he realized they were discussing the very woman he was here to defend. The very woman who was apparently rather hurt by the thought that one of his youngest cousins had been kissing an even younger woman in the gardens during Lord Weatherstone's ball the night before.

Crossing his arms, Grandby watched as the two men descended the stairs, their conversation having turned to the Vandermeers. He screwed up his face in concentration, trying to sort how the Vandermeers figured into the equation when he remembered that Jane Fitzpatrick, Countess of Stoneleigh, was a Vandermeer. He wouldn't even know of the Vandermeers except that Todd Vandermeer was in business with Gregory's brother-in-law, Thomas Wellingham, who was a cousin to the current Earl of Trenton.

Milton Grandby rolled his eyes. It was a wonder he could remember how so many in the *ton* were related to one another, but if he didn't stop making the connections in his head, he would have a pounding headache. *As long as none of my goddaughters marry their first cousins—or bastard brothers, for that matter—all will be well,* he figured. He could just imagine how *The Tattler* might latch onto such a story. *Long lost daughter marries her step-brother from another mother! See page six.*

He rolled his eyes again, amazed that his cousins seemed completely oblivious to his presence in the middle of the hall.

Well, it was a rather large hall, he admitted as he glanced around again and realized there was a man in the parlor painting. *Pretty color,* he thought, watching the colorman as he brushed a dark red onto the walls. *At least it's not green.*

He returned his attention to his cousins, who had just then realized he was in the house.

"Grandby?" Andrew spoke in surprise from where he stood at the bottom of the stairs.

"Aye, 'tis me," he replied, giving a nod to his cousins.

Gregory hurried over, an arm outstretched. "I certainly wasn't expecting to see you out here in Chiswick," he said in awe. "What brings you?"

The earl shook Gregory's hand and then Andrew's. "Two reasons," he replied with an arched eyebrow, one hand waving to indicate the renovated house. "A visit to the old house, of course. My grandmother—and yours—would be thrilled to see what's been done in here," he commented, his gaze sweeping up and around the grand hall. He turned his full attention onto Andrew. "And the need to challenge Cousin Max here to a duel."

The silence that followed his proclamation was broken only by the sound of painting in the parlor, and even then, the sound ceased after a moment. A pin dropped onto the polished marble floor would have reverberated through the entire house.

"A *duel?*" Gregory finally replied, frowning as he turned to stare at Andrew. Although his feet didn't move, it certainly seemed as if he had taken an entire step away from his younger cousin.

Andrew paled, the look of confusion on his face almost comical. "A duel?" he repeated, sounding ever so much like a parrot just then. "But, what is it you think I have *done?*" he added in disbelief.

Grandby scratched his neck just above the mail coach knot in his cravat, wondering if the study had been stocked with liquor yet. He waved the two over to where the old study had been located during his youth. He opened the door to find it not much different from when his father had used the room as his basis of operations for an earldom located in Northumberland. Dutch cloths covered the desk as well as the furnishings near the fireplace.

Moving to the built-in cupboards behind the massive mahogany desk in the middle, he grinned when he realized none of the liquor had been touched. Indeed, the room seemed to have been spared from any renovation.

Setting out several tumblers, he poured a finger's worth into each and offered them to Gregory and Andrew.

"To family," he said with a nod as he lifted his glass.

"To family," Gregory and Andrew repeated before they all took a sip of the amber liquid.

"To widows," Grandby said, holding up his glass in salute.

Gregory frowned, but Andrew raised his glass. "To widows," he repeated with a grin. When both cousins turned to stare at him, he slowly lowered his tumbler as his grin disappeared. "What's wrong?" he asked in a quiet voice.

"I married one because I love her, madly," Grandby replied with a bushy eyebrow. "Truly."

When the two turned to stare at Gregory, he merely shook his head. "Don't look at me. My mother was a widow a long time ago, but her second husband is still alive. My wife may end up a widow, but I certainly don't have any widows in my life at the moment," he claimed in confusion.

Grandby and Gregory each turned in unison to stare at Andrew.

Andrew swallowed and finally angled his head to one side. "I admit it. I am in love with Lady Stoneleigh. Madly," he added, remembering Grandby's words. "Truly. Have been since we were... " His words trailed off as the other two cousins regarded him with a good deal of interest. "I plan to marry her. If she'll have me, of course. I have the ring here..." he said as he used his free hand to extract the ring box from his waistcoat pocket. "Bought it this morning from Mr. Rundell in Ludgate Hill."

The earl frowned even as he allowed an expression of appreciation. He had spent a good deal of blunt at Rundell, Bridge and Rundell over the past year or so, happily spending the earldom's funds on jewelry for his countess. "If you planned to marry her, then why the *hell* were you kissing Lady J in the gardens last night?" Grandby countered, his voice tinged with a hint of annoyance.

Andrew's eyebrows furrowed, his gaze darting to Gregory for a moment. Goodness, but *The Tattler* certainly had readership. "But, I wasn't kissing *anyone* in the gardens last night. I wasn't even in the gardens last night," he replied. "What makes you think I was? And who is this Lady J?"

Grandby leaned against the desk and angled his head, sighing as he did so. From the man's stunned reaction, Grandby realized Andrew spoke the truth. "A certain gossip rag claims you were," he said with an arched eyebrow. "And I believe the Lady J they are referring to is Lady Jane Browning, the youngest niece of Lady Pettigrew. Not *your* Jane Fitzpatrick, Lady Stoneleigh."

Andrew's eyes widened. "No!" he whispered as he shook his head. *God, no!*

"Yes," Gregory countered with a sad nod. Turning his attention to the earl, he added, "I read the same article, which means so did half of London. The other half will read it later tonight after their dinners."

The Burroughs cousin appeared defeated as his shoulders slumped and his glass of scotch ended up on the sideboard behind him. "Jesus," Andrew murmured in despair. "I don't look anything like the Earl of Bellingham," he added.

Grandby and Gregory both raised their eyebrows in unison. "Bellingham?" Grandby repeated. "What has Will Slater got to do with this?" he asked in confusion.

Andrew gave a shrug. "*He* was the one kissing Lady Jane in the gardens last night," he claimed. He paused a moment, his brows furrowing in confusion. "At least, I heard him addressed as 'Bellingham'," he added, not bothering to add how it was he knew the young man was in the gardens kissing a young woman. The Earl of Bellingham had done so with at least three that he knew of during last night's ball!

Gregory frowned, but looked to his older cousin for confirmation. "Is Bellingham back on these shores?" he asked, knowing the oldest son of the Marquess of Devonville had been in the British Navy since graduating from the naval academy.

Hadn't that been eight years ago?

Grandby nodded. "Just arrived a few days ago, in fact, but Devonville said he left for Oxfordshire yesterday morning." He straightened, realizing where some of the confusion had come in. "The man everyone thinks is Bellingham is actually his younger brother, Stephen Slater." Knowing the other two cousins were probably unaware of the bastard son of Devonfield, he added, "Bastard brother," before they could ask. "The resemblance between the two is uncanny, though."

Gregory and Andrew shared a look. "Max has a good point when he wonders how he was mistaken for Will Slater, though," Gregory said, an arched brow accompanying his comment. "They look nothing alike, and Max is probably old enough to be Stephen's father."

"Hey," Andrew started to protest and then closed his mouth when he realized he could possibly be old enough to have a son Stephen's age.

If I was thirteen when I sired him.

The earl allowed a shrug. "Sounds as if it's just a case of mistaken identity."

"*Just?*" Andrew countered in alarm, his brows furrowing. "Should Lady Stoneleigh see the account in the paper, why, she'll think... she'll think I'm a *rake!*"

Grandby and Gregory shared a knowing look and both nodded in unison. "Even if she doesn't see the account first hand, she'll no doubt learn of it in a Mayfair parlor," Gregory claimed.

The earl allowed a long, audible sigh. "She already *has*, in fact. At my countess' luncheon today," he said sadly.

A rock seemed to fall into Andrew's stomach, the weight causing him to exhale sharply. For a moment, he thought he would be sick. "*Dammit!*" He gave the two men a quelling glance. "Through no fault of my own, it seems I need to make amends. Immediately."

The other two cousins furrowed their brows in unison, the synchronized action so comical, Andrew would have laughed had he not felt so awful just then.

"What are you going to do?"

Andrew passed them on his way out the study door. "Order more flowers," he said over his shoulder. "And write a very long letter and beg forgiveness," he added, mostly to himself.

Damn Bellingham. And damn Lady J, the little tart, he thought as he mounted his borrowed horse and made his way back to the greenhouse in Chiswick.

He hoped the proprietor had more daisies.

Dozens and dozens of them.

CHAPTER 23
AN ANGRY WIDOW

umor has it a greenhouse in Chiswick has become the de facto floral delivery service for the ton in London. The proprietor reports an unusual increase in the number of orders as well as an increase in the frequency of orders from a certain gentleman. Everyone knows flowers are only in order when someone has either decided they are in love or have been caught doing something naughty! Which is it, we wonder? ~ An article in the May 14, 1818 issue of *The Tattler.*

ay 7, 1818, back at Lady Stoneleigh's townhouse

"My lady, there's been a delivery for you," Nicole said as she moved into Jane's bedchamber, her voice instantly quieting when she realized Jane was motionless on her bed.

Her mistress hadn't been downstairs since her return from Lady Torrington's luncheon, but the lady's maid was quite sure something had happened.

Something bad.

When had her ladyship ever left her behind when she returned home from having paid a call on another lady?

Jane lifted herself onto one elbow, her red-rimmed eyes a

testament to her recent cry. "What is it?" she asked, touching a sopping wet hanky to her cheek and sniffling as she did so.

"Daisies, my lady."

Sitting up straight, Jane stared at her maid. "Daisies?" she repeated. *My favorite flower*. But who knew...?

Max!

Andrew, she quickly amended to herself, a feeling of disappointment keeping any further tears at bay when she remembered the vase of flowers on the hall table and her subsequent discussion with the housekeeper.

Had that just been earlier that afternoon?

Goodness.

Will this day never end?

"Dozens of them, my lady. They barely fit in all the vases I could find. I've put them on the hall table for now."

"Toss them out," Jane ordered. "Or move them to the servant's table below stairs. That's what I told Mrs. Adams to do with them." It had probably been hours since she gave the order. Why would the flowers still be in the hall?

Nicole frowned. "She did, my lady," she said in a quiet voice. "This bouquet just arrived a few moments ago."

Jane blinked, her anger abating. "*More* daisies?"

"Aye, my lady," the maid acknowledged with a nod.

Sighing, Jane straightened on the bed. "Was there a card?"

Nicole held out the folded missive that had been tucked into the pasteboard box containing the massive order of flowers. "What's wrong, my lady? I have never seen you like this."

Jane regarded the maid for a moment, her expression at once one of despair and then one of anger. She turned her attention to the note and thought about simply ripping it up into tiny shreds.

But what if these flowers were from someone else? *Adele perhaps*. She would look awfully foolish treating this gift with wanton disregard if they were from the countess.

Breaking the blank wax seal on the back, she opened the four corners of the envelope and read the words scribbled on the other side.

It has come to my attention that someone thought we were kissing in the gardens behind Lord Weatherstone's house last night. Although I rather wish we had been kissing in the gardens, I wanted you to know that I was not the one doing the kissing. I couldn't, you see, since I was never actually in Lord Weatherstone's gardens last night.

From the number of articles in The Tattler regarding those seen kissing in the gardens last night, it seems you and I are the only ones who were not, however. At least, I hope you were not, for that would mean you were kissing someone other than me.

Are you Lady J, perhaps?

In the event you thought I was kissing someone and that someone was not you, please believe me when I reiterate that I was not. Kissing someone, that is.

And let us hope you are not Lady J, for she was apparently quite popular. In the gardens. Being kissed.

Please enjoy the daisies. I hope they are still your favorite flower.

With all my love and affection, Andrew.

P.S. I look forward with all my heart to our ride in the park tomorrow afternoon.

Jane stared at the missive and read it two more times before she let out a huff. She couldn't decide if she should be happy to read that Andrew hadn't kissed anyone in the gardens or incensed that he would think she would kiss someone other than him in the gardens!

Who is Lady J if not Lady Jane Browning?

What a conundrum!

"My lady?"

Her maid's quiet voice had her allowing a sigh. "Leave the flowers where they are," she whispered, deciding that, for now, she would give Andrew the benefit of a doubt. "And tell the cook

I won't be down for dinner. I've absolutely no appetite," she said sadly. "I think I will just go to bed early tonight."

Nicole nodded her understanding. "Then I'll be right back up to help you undress, my lady," she said as she hurried out of the room to let the cook know about dinner.

At some point, Nicole figured she might have the opportunity to look at the note her ladyship still held clutched in her hands. Although she could only read a few words, Nicole figured she could find someone else in the household who could help her read the rest.

Someone had sent flowers to her ladyship. Someone who had obviously hurt her enough to make her cry. Enough to make her grieve. Enough to make her so angry, she had left her maid and town coach and driver behind at Worthington House.

That someone would have to pay for his misdeed.

Although dozens of daisies did go a long way when it came to redemption, Nicole had to admit.

But was it enough?

CHAPTER 24
SEARCHING FOR A GOSSIP

The Mayfair Parlor Report has Lady M agreeing to chair another charity, Lady D off to Brighton to visit her mother, Lady T fending off a randy Lord T with a fire poker, and Lady J flirting with every gentleman in attendance at Lady P's garden party. Has anyone offered for her hand yet? Rumor has it Lady P is upping the ante with additional funds for the dowry. ~ An article in the February 19, 1818 issue of *The Tattler*.

ay 8, 1818, Norwick House

"Who is the most notorious gossip you know in all of London?" Jane Fitzpatrick asked when Clarinda Fitzwilliam appeared in the vestibule of Norwick House, one of her baby daughters perched on her hip.

Rather surprised the windowed countess had paid a call but insisted on remaining in the vestibule, Countess Norwick regarded her visitor with an elegantly arched eyebrow. "Lady Pettigrew, of course," Clarinda replied with a shrug of her available shoulder. "What's this about?"

Jane moved to stand before Clarinda, one gloved finger moving to caress the cheek of the cherub who was regarding her with round, blue eyes and the barest hint of a grin. "I need to know if I have made an awful mistake."

Clarinda stared at Jane, her brows furrowing. "Jane," she murmured quietly. "I rather doubt you would be capable of making a mistake..."

"I allowed Mr. *A. Burroughs* to spend the night at my townhouse night 'fore last," she spoke in hushed tones, appreciating that the butler hadn't returned to the vestibule when Clarinda appeared. "He wishes to take me on a ride in the park during the fashionable hour. Today."

Her eyes widening, more in a pleasant surprise than in shock, Clarinda allowed a brilliant smile. "Why, that's *wonderful!*" she exclaimed, her sudden happiness causing her daughter, Diana, to display a huge grin as well. A few teeth appeared between the chubby cheeks. Clarinda sobered. "Oh," she managed. Her daughter's expression sobered as well, her teeth disappearing just as quickly as they had appeared. When Clarinda's eyes widened again, and the smile returned, Diana merely blinked. "Are *you* Lady J?" Clarinda asked in a hoarse whisper.

Jane's shoulders slumped. "No," she replied with a shake of her head. "Lady Jane Browning has that distinction, it seems."

Clarinda sighed. "Do come in for tea," she encouraged, stepping aside.

The widowed countess shook her head. "I am off to pay a call on Lady Pettigrew," she replied, deciding it was best she confront the woman with her questions. "But I do appreciate the offer," she added as she turned her attention back to the baby "I would so love to hold a baby for a time. As you know, I never had one of my own."

When Clarinda moved to allow her to do just that, Jane shook her head. "Not right now, I'm afraid, or I shall lose my resolve."

Straightening, Clarinda regarded her visitor for a moment. "Just what is it you intend to do?"

Jane sighed. "Discover the truth. I wish to learn who her niece was kissing in the gardens during Lord Weatherstone's ball," she replied simply. "Thank you for seeing me." She turned her attention to the baby and gave a little curtsy. "Do be careful when you decide to kiss a boy, won't you? Don't let anyone see you."

Diana's eyes widened until they were round and her head bobbed up and down.

"Good day." With that, Jane gave Clarinda a curtsy and took her leave of Norwick House, seeing herself to the front door since the butler was still nowhere to be found.

Clarinda regarded her daughter for a time before allowing a sigh. "You and your sister may end up in a nunnery," she warned with an arched eyebrow. At Diana's sudden change of expression, one that made her appear as if she were about to cry, Clarinda shook her head. "Then just be sure you're not caught kissing a rake in Lord Weatherstone's garden," she whispered.

Diana seemed to nod her agreement as her grin returned.

"Hopeless flirt," her mother whispered as she turned and headed for the nursery.

Nicole paused in her effort to finish making her mistress' bed. The note Lady Stoneleigh had received the day before rested on the nightstand, refolded and looking as if it had never been opened. Making a mental note of just how it was positioned on the marble surface, she lifted it and regarded the script. Carefully pulling the edges apart, she held the missive to the light from the window and attempted to make out the words. The scrawl was nearly impossible to read, however, and Nicole sighed when she couldn't make it past the words, *It has come to my attention that.* She directed her gaze to the next words she could make out. *We had been kissing in the gardens, I wanted you to know.*

Nicole blinked before she scanned to the end of the writing, finally making out the word 'love' and 'Andrew.'

Well, no wonder her ladyship is upset if a man has let her know he was kissing someone in the gardens, she thought in dismay. Returning her attention to the script, she struggled to make out the rest of the words, finally sighing when she simply couldn't figure out whatever it was this Andrew was trying to say about a 'Lady J' and kissing and...

Perhaps that's what had her mistress so upset. She couldn't read the note!

Or perhaps she could, and she was upset at his having kissed someone in the gardens.

As to which gardens were involved, she once again wondered what the slanted words spelled out. She couldn't imagine anyone would be kissing in the garden behind the townhouse. It was just a kitchen garden, not at all hidden by a hedgerows or other impediments to being spied by prying eyes. Certainly no one would dare kiss there.

Well, Elsie would, but then, the scullery maid had a tendré for the footman and would allow him to kiss her wherever he wanted. Truth be told, Nicole decided she would let the same footman kiss her wherever he wanted to should he be so inclined.

She shook her head as if to clear it.

No, this had nothing to do with the gardens out back. Who could help her with the rest of the letter, though? She couldn't ask the butler—Simonton would be mortified to learn she was attempting to read her ladyship's correspondence. Elsie couldn't read. Mrs. Adams could read, but she rather doubted the housekeeper would agree to help her decipher the words.

Giving it one more go, Nicole started at the beginning of the letter and began to read. Once she had the words 'kissing' and 'last night' and some other simple words figured out, she was sure she had the gist of the letter. Andrew was denying having kissed Lady J despite having been seen doing so.

That was the reason for the daisies!

Dozens of them.

Who is Andrew? He had to be someone close to her mistress, for he had signed something having to do with 'love'.

When she made out the words, *The Tattler*, Nicole inhaled sharply.

The Tattler was a gossip rag!

Oh, dear, she thought in dismay. Was her mistress mentioned in the news sheet? Was Lady Stoneleigh the Lady J mentioned in the letter? Well, there was only one way to find out.

I have to get my hands on the latest issue of The Tattler, Nicole realized.

She knew exactly where she could find one. In the kitchens, probably in the hands of the cook.

Reading the very last line of the letter, Nicole allowed a grin as she realized she could make out all the words.

P.S. I look forward with all my heart to our ride in the park tomorrow afternoon.

Well, now all she had to do was have a look at whoever came for Lady Stoneleigh, and she would know who had sent the daisies.

Carefully folding up the note and placing it back where she found it on the nightstand, Nicole continued making the bed.

CHAPTER 25
PAYING A CALL ON A GOSSIP

umor has it Lady J has kissed three gentlemen in the past week! She's leading the charge in puckered lips for this Season's kissing contest! Does anyone else look as if their lips have been stung by a bee? Drop off your tales of kissing tarts at our offices! ~ An article in the April 2, 1818 issue of *The Tattler.*

ay 8, 1818, Viscountess Pettigrew's residence
Jane Fitzpatrick glanced around the parlor in the Pettigrew manor house, not particularly surprised at how dated the room appeared. Not only had it been decorated in the prior century, she wondered if some of the furnishings were leftovers from the Elizabethan era. The knickknacks scattered about the tables were charming, though, some made of metal while others were obviously carved from marble or wood.

"My husband's hobby," Eugenia Pettigrew said from the threshold.

Although the words had broken the welcome silence, Jane didn't jump at the sound of them. "He is a very accomplished sculptor," she commented, turning to regard the viscountess with a wan smile. She curtsied. "Please forgive my calling on you outside of the usual times."

Lady Pettigrew curtsied as quickly as she could, remembering that Lady Stoneleigh was a widowed countess. "Oh, it's no imposition at all," Eugenia claimed as she waved Jane to a chair. "Please do have a seat whilst I ring for tea."

"Would Lady Jane be available to join us?" Jane asked as she took a seat in the one chair she was fairly certain was from this century. She feared breaking any of the older chairs.

The viscountess allowed a nod. "I don't know why not." She moved and lifted a porcelain bell from a table near the double doors. The butler appeared as if he'd been hovering on the other side of the wall.

"Do bring tea, and let Lady Jane know we have a caller," she murmured.

The butler gave a deep bow and disappeared, leaving Eugenia to wring her hands before turning to her guest. "Did you enjoy the luncheon yesterday? I do so appreciate the opportunity to meet with the ladies the day after a ball."

"I do, as well," Jane agreed, deciding not to display the pasted on smile that her hostess struggled to maintain. "Although I admit to a bit of frustration at one of the articles you read from *The Tattler*."

The comment seemed to have Eugenia breathing a bit easier. "Oh, is that all?" she responded with a wave of her hand. At her visitor's raised eyebrow, she added, "I was afraid my niece had done something untoward, and you were here to render a report."

Jane blinked. "Did she, do you suppose?"

At that moment, Lady Jane Browning, youngest niece of Eugenia Pettigrew, appeared on the threshold and bobbed a curtsy. "Did I what, my lady?" the young woman asked, having heard Jane Fitzpatrick's query.

Jane gave the girl a nod and angled her head. "I was just

asking your aunt if you had done something to earn a mention in this week's *Tattler*."

Despite how the young woman paled at the comment, she managed to appear shocked by the countess' words. "Since I haven't yet read the newspaper, I'm not sure if I have been mentioned or not." She gave a nervous glance in her aunt's direction, as if she already knew she'd been caught and wondered how she would be punished.

Apparently it wasn't the first time Lady Jane had been caught doing something inappropriate.

"If you're referring to the mention of a *Lady J* seen kissing a man in the gardens..." the viscountess started with a wave of one hand.

"I am," Jane interrupted.

Eugenia stiffened. "I assure you, that particular Lady J is not *my* Jane," she said.

The countess regarded the viscountess for a moment before turning her attention to Jane. "I am not so concerned about *Lady J* as I am about whom she was seen kissing," she said in a quiet voice. She almost regretted having brought up the topic of the other party in question, but it was true that she really didn't care one whit if Lady Jane had kissed every other man in London.

As long as she hadn't kissed Andrew Burroughs.

"Lord Bellingham, you mean?" the younger Jane piped up in surprise.

The older Jane frowned. *Bellingham?* Although she had paid witness to a man who looked similar to Will Slater, Earl of Bellingham, take his leave of the ballroom at least three different times with young ladies in tow—one of those times with Lady Jane, in fact—she was rather surprised at the girl's response. Didn't she realize that by mentioning the man with whom she had been seen going into the gardens, she was making her impropriety known to her aunt?

And what would she think when she discovered that she

hadn't been kissing the Earl of Bellingham at all, but rather his bastard brother, Stephen Slater?

Eugenia allowed a 'huff '. "Why, just to take the air, I should think," she put in, motioning for her niece to come into the parlor. Jane did so, standing in front of a chair and waiting for her aunt to take a seat before she did so.

The blush that covered the younger Jane's face said otherwise. Knowing she had been caught—if not by her aunt, then by the woman who looked as if she were about to cry—she allowed a long sigh. "I admit, I was in the gardens with the Earl of Bellingham," Jane announced, her attention on their caller. "He was a perfect gentleman, however. Newly returned to these shores after eight years in service to His Majesty's Navy," she said with the kind of pride only a patriotic young lady could manage.

Lady Stoneleigh angled her head, relieved by the younger Jane's claim. "And Mr. *A. Burroughs?* What of him?" she asked in a quiet voice. Her attention was diverted to a maid who appeared in the parlor's doorway, wheeling an old-fashioned tea cart bearing a silver salver. A teapot and cups from the early-eighteenth century were arranged on the salver along with a sugar-pot and creamer.

Her aunt was quick to say, "I'll see to the tea," her clipped words sending the maid scurrying.

The younger Jane shifted in her chair, her face screwed up in concentration. "I do not believe I have ever met a man by that name," she answered after a moment. "I have heard the Burroughs name, of course, but only as it relates to the Duke of Ariley," she added, wanting the visitor to know she was familiar with the families in the aristocracy.

Meanwhile, Jane Fitzpatrick regarded the younger Jane with an expression that suggested immense relief. "Was Bellingham the only man with whom you toured the gardens?" she asked, her question sounding ever so innocent. "I ask only because I fear your reputation may be in jeopardy, given the report in *The Tattler*."

The comment had the desired effect, eliciting a gasp from Lady Pettigrew as well as a pair of rounded eyes on Jane Browning's face.

The younger Jane blinked. "Why, of course he was," she answered with a shrug, obviously relieved when her aunt placed a cup and saucer in Lady Stoneleigh's hands.

"If I remember correctly from yesterday, you prefer no milk or sugar?" Eugenia asked in a voice tinged with too much sweetness, her query made in the hopes she could divert the countess' line of questioning to something other than elicit visits to Lord Weatherstone's garden.

"You have it correct, of course," Jane acknowledged with a nod before turning her attention back to the younger Jane. "Tell me, was there any other 'Lady J' at last night's ball? That you know of, of course?" she asked before taking a sip of the tea. She managed to avoid grimacing at the flavor. *Goodness!* With all the tea shops in the town of London, couldn't Lady Pettigrew serve a proper cup of tea?

Jane Browning gave a nervous glance in her aunt's direction but considered the question for a moment. "Not that I am aware, my lady," she answered with a shake of her head.

The immense relief that settled over Lady Stoneleigh had her inhaling the steam that hovered over her teacup. Although the flavor was hideous, at least the scent was pleasant. "I do appreciate your candor, Lady Jane," she said with a nod. "Have you had an offer of marriage yet this season?"

The younger Jane seemed to relax, as if she knew the inquisition was over. "I have not, but then, I have not been anxious to receive such an offer."

Her response had both older women staring at her as if she had grown a second head. "Surely you jest," Eugenia responded with a stunned frown.

Lady Jane took a sip of the tea she had just been handed and grimaced. "I do not, actually. I think I should not marry until I am at least five-and-twenty," she said with a shrug. "And maybe not until I am even older. I understand some peasant girls don't marry until they are nearly thirty," she claimed with a nervous grin. "And they do so for *affection*."

Jane Fitzpatrick was sure Lady Pettigrew appeared about to faint at hearing her youngest niece's claim. "Thirty?" Eugenia repeated in a small voice.

The older Jane managed to suppress the grin she felt threatening to touch her lips. However would Lady Pettigrew manage her youngest niece if the gel remained underfoot for the next ten years?

"Jane!" Eugenia scolded the girl. "You cannot be serious."

The younger Jane allowed a shrug. "I think I would prefer the life of an independent woman," she said quietly. "I don't relish the idea of being married to a man who has a mistress but expects me to remain at home every night without company."

The Countess of Stoneleigh stilled herself, wondering how much Lady Jane knew of her situation. Did the girl's comment refer to her specifically? Or to her aunt? For Jane knew Lord Pettigrew had taken a mistress many years ago. A woman he had visited on a regular basis when the harlot was an employee of *The Elegant Courtesan*, a high-end brothel owned by the Earl of Norwick before he inherited the earldom. Rather profitable, *The Elegant Courtesan* featured a variety of ladies of the evening. One in particular had appealed to Lord Pettigrew so much, he had hired her as his exclusive mistress when David Fitzwilliam had been forced to close the brothel upon inheriting the Norwick earldom.

"Jane!" her aunt admonished her charge. "There will be no talking of *mistresses* in this household," she stated in a hoarse whisper.

"Oh, don't forbid her on my account, Lady Pettigrew," Lady Stoneleigh replied. "I am quite sure she's well aware of my late husband's employment of a mistress, as was the rest of the *ton*," she managed with an arched brow, her head held high as she made the comment. "*The Tattler* made mention of it in more than one issue."

She hadn't meant to make such a bold statement, but she thought perhaps the viscountess might see her own situation in a new light if others who had been in her shoes admitted their plight in the company of family members.

It wasn't as if they were the ones guilty of any wrongdoing. The men in their lives were the ones guilty of breaking their marriage vows!

Lady Pettigrew regarded her guest with barely contained fury. "Speaking of mistresses is wholly inappropriate, and I should prefer my niece not know of such... *matters*," she uttered in a hoarse whisper.

Lady Stoneleigh nodded. "Of course. Do forgive my impropriety. I merely thought she could avoid the heartache so prevalent among those who have to marry for a title rather than for love."

The younger Jane swallowed, rather relieved to hear the older Jane's candor. "I would like to marry for love, of course," Jane said quietly. "But the young men I have met at the entertainments so far this Season are not of my liking. Perhaps that will change as the Season progresses, but I do not hold much hope."

Lady Pettigrew allowed an audible sigh, her annoyance at Lady Stoneleigh's presence harder and harder to hide. "Really, Jane," she said after taking a long draught of her tea and then screwing her face into a grimace. "You must be open to *any* possibility. I have promised my brother I would see you *wed*."

The younger Jane allowed a nod. "And if I am married when I am thirty, you will still have kept your promise."

Eugenia Pettigrew angled her head, as if finally understanding her niece's point of view. "As long as you're amenable to taking in the rest of the entertainments for which we have accepted invitations, then so be it," she replied before draining her tea in a single gulp.

"And I would suggest you forget about the Earl of Bellingham as a possible beau," the elder Jane commented as she placed her tea cup and saucer on the low table in front of her chair. "I understand he has given his heart to another." She stood up. "Thank you for hosting me this morning, Lady Pettigrew." With that, she curtsied and took her leave of the Pettigrew mansion, a sigh of relief leaving her as she stepped into her town coach.

"The office of *The Tattler*," she said when the driver poked his head through the opening in the coach's ceiling. Although she was now confident Andrew Burroughs had done nothing untoward during the Weatherstone ball, she had a bone to pick with the editor of *The Tattler*.

Perhaps an entire skeleton's worth.

CHAPTER 26
AN UNEXPECTED
ENCOUNTER WITH AN EARL

In order to recover from the spectacle that is the annual Weatherstone Ball, our offices will be closed for new subscriptions the morning of Friday, May 8, 1818. ~ A mention at the bottom of the May 1, 1818 issue of *The Tattler*.

May 8, 1818, the office of Tattler Publishing

What an odd location for a newspaper, Jane thought as she regarded the front of the brick building that displayed the shingle for Tattler Publishing. Not a single window decorated the wall that faced Sackville Street, but one nondescript door, painted in scarlet red, could be found at the south corner. She wondered if she should knock, but decided as a place of business, there was probably a receptionist therein. Grasping the handle, she felt relief when it easily turned and the door opened. The odors of ink and rag assaulted her nostrils as she stepped into the small front office.

"Morning, miss," a pleasant voice sounded from somewhere to her left. "A tale to tell? I apologize, but we're not able to accept new subscriptions today."

Jane regarded the young man who had just stood up from

behind a rather cluttered desk. Although he wore a waistcoat, there was no topcoat in sight, nor a cravat, and his shirt sleeves were rolled up beyond his elbows as if he were a common laborer.

"Neither, actually," Jane replied, realizing too late that she could have claimed she came with news. Perhaps her chance of speaking with the editor would be bolstered if he thought she had some gossip to share. "I'm looking for Mr. Pepperidge. I understand he's the editor here."

The receptionist nodded. "I'll see if he's still here. Said something about having a meeting this afternoon."

When the man disappeared through a doorway behind his desk, Jane did a quick perusal of the tiny front office. The walls appeared recently papered, and framed covers of several issues of *The Tattler* hung in a symmetrical arrangement on one wall. A round table—Jane was fairly certain it was made by Chippendale —took up one corner and displayed an angled stack of the latest issue of the paper.

Her eyes immediately moved to the article claiming A. Burroughs was seen kissing Lady J in the gardens. She frowned as she began to read some of the other articles, rather stunned to discover most weren't salacious in nature at all, but rather factual accounts of what had taken place at Lord Weatherstone's ball. She was in the middle of reading the third article when the young man suddenly reappeared.

"Mr. Pepperidge will see you, miss, but he does have to leave in a few minutes for his meeting."

Jane acknowledged the comment with a nod, wondering if the editor always had a meeting when someone came to call on him. She followed the receptionist through the opening in the wall and past a large, black metal mechanical device—the printing press that created the despicable gossip sheet, she realized.

A rather tall man stood in a doorway at the other end of the room, a pair of spectacles perched on the end of his nose, under which a mustache hung. His dark brown hair, pulled back into a queue, was entirely at odds with his coloring. His clothing appeared recently pressed and of good quality, and his boots displayed a glossy sheen.

"Mr. Pepperidge, I presume?" Jane spoke before she was even halfway through the paper-littered press room.

The man, who appeared to be in his mid-thirties, gave a short bow. "I am," he admitted, reaching out with his right hand to shake hers. "Miss?"

"Vandermeer," she said, managing to provide her maiden name without blinking. She hadn't used it once since the day she married Michael Fitzpatrick, so it was a bit of a surprise when it tripped so easily off her tongue.

She dipped a quick curtsy even as her hand went to his for the handshake. Although she had the impression she had met the man before, she couldn't immediately place where it might have been. He no doubt attended events, or at least managed to get as close as he could in order to write about them, so it made sense she had seen him in passing.

"What is it I can do for you?" the editor asked as he waved her into his office, glancing back toward the entry to the press room as if he expected her to have someone else with her.

"Something rather simple," she replied as she stepped into the office. Jane wasn't sure what she expected to find, but it most certainly wasn't the beautiful oak desk and needlepoint-covered chairs in front of it, nor the Axminster carpet beneath it all. Although this desk was cluttered, it was certainly in better shape than the one in the lobby. Behind Mr. Pepperidge, a framed painting of a landscape hung in the center of the wall while bookshelves stuffed with bound books—Jane was sure she spotted a *Debrett's Peerage and Barontage* amid books about the European monarchies—stood floor to ceiling and filled the back wall. Despite the lack of windows on the front of the building, there was a single window in the wall adjacent to the door. "I wish to request that you print a retraction to one of your stories about Lord Weatherstone's ball," she stated as she took one of the needlepoint covered chairs.

Mr. Pepperidge angled his head to one side before seating himself in the leather-covered chair behind his desk. "My, I can't say as I've had such a request before," he responded, managing to keep the sarcasm from his voice. Upon seeing his visitor up close, he realized her identity. "Lady Stoneleigh," he added with a nod. She looked so much prettier dressed in blue than she did when wearing widow's weeds. Younger, too.

Jane schooled her features to remain as impassive as possible, thinking the editor must have had plenty of requests to retract stories in the past. Why, over the course of the past couple of months, the gossip rag had become well-known for printing fabricated tales. At least, that's what she'd heard from others when she paid calls. "Then I suppose this will be the first," she said with a straight face, not bothering to hide the sarcasm in her voice.

Mr. Pepperidge pulled a pad of paper to the middle of his desk and dipped his quill into an open ink pot. "What story is it you think needs a retraction, my lady?"

Straightening on the chair, Jane stated, "A. Burroughs was not kissing Lady J in the gardens during Lord Weatherstone's ball," she stated emphatically.

Resisting the urge to blink at Lady Stoneleigh's insistent words—he had been sure she was going to object to the mention of *her* being in attendance at the ball—he instead stared at her for a moment. "And you know this because..."

"She was kissing someone else at the time, but that's neither here nor there," Jane replied. "Mr. Burroughs was never *in* the gardens during the ball."

This time, Mr. Pepperidge blinked. "If she wasn't kissing Mr. Burroughs, then who was she kissing?"

Jane rolled her eyes. "As I said, it's neither here nor there whom she was kissing as she has no intention of marrying anyone," she stated, the words out of her mouth before she could censor them. Although, what harm could there be in admitting Jane Browning wanted to be an independent woman?

Mr. Pepperidge straightened in his chair, barely aware that the drop of ink on the tip of his quill had just plopped onto the paper below. Why, just yesterday, Lady Emelia had said something along the same lines. *Lady Jane Browning didn't wish to marry because she wanted to be an independent woman.*

At the time, he hadn't given much credence to Lady Emelia's claim, thinking she had simply made the statement as a lame attempt to fulfill that week's requirement for gossip. He knew she knew more, and it seemed as if she were almost about to provide more when he'd had to take his leave. Emelia's inability to share gossip prevented her from doing so, even under duress.

The young woman has my heart, he thought with a wan smile. He needed her in his life. He needed someone who wasn't about to regale him with every sordid tale told in a Mayfair parlor. He needed to be able to go home from the office and know that their dinners would be spent in quiet conversation about topics that truly mattered. Newsworthy topics, such as the latest inventions or the machinations of politics on the Continent, or the latest news from the United States. Or perhaps tales of what their children had done during the day.

Mr. Pepperidge had to tamp down the urge to simply get up and take his leave of the office right then and there and make his way to Aimsley House.

As soon as I can leave here, I'll pay a call on Lady Emelia and take her for a ride in the park, he decided. He didn't really have Lord Aimsley's permission to marry the young woman, though. The earl seemed reluctant to give it that day he had admitted to kissing Emelia in Lord Weatherstone's garden.

When the editor didn't provide a reply right away— indeed, Mr. Pepperidge appeared to be deep in thought—Jane finally allowed a sigh. "Why do you do it?"

The question brought the editor out of his reverie.

"Whatever do you mean?" he countered, not ever having heard the question before.

"This..." Jane waved a hand at his desk and then toward the wall behind her in an effort to indicate the press. "Gossip mongering?" she clarified. "'Tis very hurtful, you must know."

Mr. Pepperidge frowned and then gave his head a shake. He was halfway tempted to give her the same reasons he gave everyone else who asked the question.

If I didn't do it, someone else would.

And they might not do it as well, or they might be more mean-spirited in their approach, out to ruin perfectly good people. "Truth be told, I do it because it keeps me out of debt," he finally replied.

Jane blinked, rather stunned by the simple response. "And providing news that is true would not?" she countered.

The editor gave his head a shake. "True? What is the truth? Who makes that decision? How can we ever know what is true and what is false when we rarely hear both sides of the same story?"

Jane leaned back in her chair, needing its solidity to support her just then. No one had ever put forth those questions before, at least, not in Mayfair parlors.

"There are already newspapers that report on the news, my lady," Mr. Pepperidge continued. "I know I cannot begin to compete with them, nor would I wish to," he explained as he spread his hands along the edge of his desk closest to him. "However, if someone else besides me did this, you must know they might not be as light-handed with the gossip as I am."

"Light-handed?" Jane repeated, her voice a bit louder than she intended. "You print lies about people..."

"I print what I see. What I overhear. What is reported to me by those who were there when it happened or when it was said. It is never my intention to print something that is false."

Jane's breath left her body all at once. The man truly believed what he was saying, and yet... "And yet you reported that

Andrew Burroughs was kissing Lady Jane in the gardens," she accused. "As if you paid witness to it."

It was at that moment that Mr. Pepperidge realized Lady Stoneleigh's objection to the article wasn't due to Lady Jane and her reputation but rather Andrew Burroughs' reputation.

But why would a widow care about Andrew Burroughs' reputation? *And why did I think Andrew Burroughs was kissing Lady Jane?*

Mr. Pepperidge blinked. And blinked again when he realized just why it was that he thought the man kissing Lady Jane was Andrew Burroughs.

Lady Morganfield had pointed to him when he had asked as to the identity of the man dancing opposite them during the waltz. He was sure Adele Carlington knew who he meant. The man dancing with Lady Jane, a chit who couldn't possibly have a voucher to dance the waltz.

But what if she did not mean him? What if she thought he meant someone else?

"Does Mr. Burroughs bear a remarkable resemblance to the Earl of Bellingham, by any chance?" he asked, his eyebrows arched in a manner suggesting he had just figured out a rather difficult equation.

Jane's eyes widened. Although she hadn't seen Will Slater since his return to England—apparently, only a few in London had had that honor—she knew from talk in Lady Torrington's conservatory that the two brothers shared an uncanny resemblance to one another.

But Stephen Slater and Andrew Burroughs looked nothing alike.

"Not a bit," she replied with a shake of her head. "Although they are of a similar height, I suppose," she added as she angled her head. "Why do you ask, pray tell?"

Mr. Pepperidge tipped his head back for a moment and realized his confusion. Andrew Burroughs wasn't the man kissing Lady Jane in the gardens, which meant she was kissing the man who looked exactly like Will Slater, Earl of Bellingham.

Stephen Slater, the bastard brother.

Well, this would be an even better story if Lady Jane cared one whit about marrying, he thought with a bit of disappointment. Otherwise, Stephen Slater might be the one forced to marry the chit.

Mr. Pepperidge straightened in his chair, pinning his visitor with a glare at the same time his mustache decided to let go of its hold just below his nose. "Your concern isn't for Lady Jane's reputation but rather for Andrew Burroughs' reputation," he accused, about to demand further information as to why she would even care about the banker.

Was the widow involved with Mr. Burroughs?

He had half the article written in his head before he realized Jane was staring at him.

Jane blinked at the sight of Mr. Pepperidge's falling mustache. Blinked again when she took in the sight of the man without his mustache, imagining what he might look like without the ridiculous spectacles. Without the hideous dark brown wig pulled into a queue.

His features were suddenly far more familiar. Indeed, his identity was quite apparent. "Fennington?" she whispered in surprise. Fighting off the sense of vertigo that threatened to send her sideways and onto the floor beneath her chair, Jane stared at the editor. "Whatever are you doing?" she asked in alarm.

Felix Turnbridge, Earl of Fennington, stared at Lady Stoneleigh for a good ten seconds before one of his hands reached up to where his mustache should have been. "I don't know what you're talking about, my lady," he responded, his eyes catching sight of his fake mustache lying on the desk blotter. To an untrained eye, it might have been mistaken for a furry caterpillar. He quickly snagged the mustache between his thumb and forefinger and brought it back up to his lip. "My valet was a bit aggressive during my shave this morning," he said in his defense, reapplying the hair to his upper lip and holding it there with one finger.

Jane angled her head to one side as she regarded the earl with an arched eyebrow. "Is the Fennington earldom really in such dire straights that you have to engage in *trade*? In the trade of gossip, no less?" she asked, quickly assessing how she might use her new-found knowledge to get what she wanted—what she needed—from the editor.

Felix Turnbridge sighed. "It was," he acknowledged finally, realizing he could no longer hide his true identity from the widow. He sighed again. "I needed another source of funds, you see, and gossip seems to pay rather well."

The widow gave a sideways glance at what she could see of the office, just then realizing why the man had such costly accoutrements. Such a beautiful desk. Such beautiful carpeting. Such a well-stocked library. "Just how long have you been doing this, Lord Fennington?" she asked, ignoring his excuse.

"A few years," he acknowledged with a nod, realizing there was no fooling the widow. "I thought to sell the business once I had the debts paid and found a suitable wife," he added, realizing that when Lady Emelia accepted his offer of marriage, he really would need to put *The Tattler* on the market. He could probably earn enough from the sale so he and Emelia would live comfortably. He could even leave his heir with a solvent earldom. As for whom might be interested in buying the paper, though, he had no idea.

"It's about time you did," Jane murmured, one eyebrow arched up. "You're not getting any younger."

Felix felt the stab of her words but nodded. "As for secrets..."

"Yours will never get past my lips if you print that retraction," she interrupted.

His eyes widening in surprise, Felix regarded Jane for several seconds. "Why?"

The widow bit her lower lip, feeling ever so relieved to learn Andrew hadn't been kissing Lady Jane in the gardens— or anywhere else, for that matter. "I have the opportunity for a second chance in life," she responded, lifting her chin. "And I should like to enter into it without the hint of scandal hovering over the man who might be the center of that new life."

"Oh, that's good," Felix replied, a forefinger waving in the air. He quickly took the quill in hand and dipped it into the ink. He wrote in a furious hand, her words appearing as if by magic on the parchment in front of him before Jane quite knew what he was doing.

"What are you writing?" she demanded to know, alarm sounding in her voice.

"Your eloquent words, my lady. For the article I'm going to publish once you and Mr. Burroughs marry," he claimed without looking up from the parchment.

Jane's eyes widened. "But, I don't know that we're to be married," she countered, alarm still evident in her voice. "He hasn't proposed."

The editor lifted his head and regarded her a moment, his brows furrowing. "But of course you are," he argued. "You obviously love the man, or you wouldn't be so concerned about his reputation," he countered before returning his attention to writing out her words.

Jane gasped. *Love the man?*

Do I? She had been so angry and hurt when she had read the article, she hadn't had a chance to remember just how wonderful she had felt the prior morning, how positively euphoric she had felt when Andrew claimed he loved her.

She also remembered the doubt she had felt, too, but it had been doubt about herself. She believed Andrew's claim if only because he seemed so *certain* he loved her, despite the eighteen years that had passed since they had briefly courted.

"But that doesn't mean he feels enough affection for me to ask for my hand," she argued, not exactly sure she would even marry the man if he asked her.

After Lady Jane Browning's comments about choosing the

lifestyle of an independent woman—a life she was quite prepared to adopt before Andrew had reappeared the night before last—she had nearly convinced herself to make the necessary reservations for a ship to take her to the Continent. Make the arrangements necessary to live in Italy. She had practically been living the life of an independent woman all the years she was married to Michael Fitzpatrick, after all.

Felix frowned, his disappointment evident. "True," he finally acknowledged, his initial excitement fading as he set aside the quill. "But should he do so, I want the exclusive," he stated.

"What?" Her head shaking from side to side, Jane could hardly believe Lord Fennington's demand.

"Let me have the story. I promise to print it as you wish it to appear. No salaciousness. No scandal. Just a good, clean accounting of how you and the banker came to be betrothed and married." He paused a moment, his brows rising on his forehead. "You obviously have a history together," he whispered, as if he had just then realized there could be more to Jane and Andrew's story. "This didn't just happen overnight."

Jane blinked, about to argue that it had indeed just happened over a single night. But his suspicion that there was more to the story was certainly true, too.

For some reason, Andrew Burroughs could simply pick up where he had left off with her eighteen years ago. Despite having a wife and two—nay, three—children, Andrew had moved back to London and apparently decided to simply begin living the life he had thought he would be living eighteen years ago.

But can I? Jane wondered.

Oh, how different life would be with a loving man, she thought then. To wake up every morning with someone who cared for her, someone with whom to have breakfast every morning, dinner every night. To share a ride in the park during the fashionable hour. To sit with in the library whilst she read a book or had a cup of tea. To make love to before sleep took her for the night.

Oh, I think I do love him, she nearly murmured aloud.

Jane straightened in the chair, realizing the earl was regarding her with a quirked eyebrow. She angled her head to one side, wondering just why the Earl of Fennington would wish to write such a tale. Why he was so eager to print the story in his paper. *The Tattler* rarely featured clean stories, after all.

"Why?" she asked as she leaned forward.

Felix allowed a long sigh, one shoulder lifting. "*The Tattler* does on occasion feature real news, my lady," he claimed in a quiet voice. "And yours would be a tale of requited love, so unlike most of the sorry excuses for weddings we hear about so frequently." He rolled his eyes. "Or, perhaps it's because I am a hopeless romantic," he added. "Or because I, too, am about to be married, and I'm hoping it's with someone who feels affection for me." The words were out of his mouth before he could censor them, before he could change the inflection to make them sound more sarcastic and not so heart-felt.

Resisting the urge to giggle at his claim, Jane gave the man's words some thought. "You'll print the retraction?" she queried with an arched brow.

"I will, my lady," Felix replied with a firm nod.

Jane felt as if she were inviting a stranger into her life. "All right, Lord Fennington," she finally agreed. "I agree to let you print the story—if Mr. Burroughs and I do indeed decide to marry—but only if you print the retraction."

"It will appear in next Thursday's issue, I promise," he said, holding out his right hand. "Hopefully right next to the announcement of your upcoming nuptials." *And mine, too*, he thought.

Jane lifted her own gloved hand and shook his, hoping she wasn't making a deal with the devil. "And next to the announcement of your own nuptials, mayhap? I have noticed you escorting Lady Emelia on occasion," she countered.

Felix blinked, rather surprised she had paid witness to his

having spent time in Emelia's company on their rides in the park. "Perhaps," he replied with a nod, his manner sobering.

"Does the young man in the front office know who you really are?"

Felix gave a glance in the direction of the other office. "He does not, nor do I think he cares, at least as long as he receives his pay every month."

"So, why the disguise?" she asked. "The brown wig is hideous, you must know, and the mustache..." Jane allowed the sentence to trail off, not quite sure how to describe the facial hair that looked as if it had at one time been a furry caterpillar.

The editor allowed a chuckle as his picked up the mustache, a reminder that he had lost his favorite one during his last visit with Emelia in the park. He regarded it as if seeing it for the first time. "I have to keep some anonymity," he responded with a shrug. "We can't abide an earl working in trade, you must know."

Jane allowed a grin at the comment. What would the other lords think if they knew their peer was earning a living at printing gossip? Their gossip? "Have I made you late? Your clerk implied you had a meeting."

His eyes widening, Felix pulled out his chronometer and sighed. "If I leave now, I can make it to Parliament with a few minutes to spare," he said.

Nodding, Jane stood up. "Then I shall take my leave," she said as she curtsied.

The earl reached for her gloved hand and pulled it to his lips. "I do hope this all works out for you."

"And for you, my lord," Jane replied with one eyebrow arched up. With that, she took her leave of Tattler Publishing, light on her feet and feeling ever so ready for a ride in the park.

CHAPTER 27
WHEN A RIDE IN THE PARK IS NOT

e paid witness to Mr. A Burroughs kissing Lady J in the gardens behind Lord W's ballroom. How many is this, Lady J? Will you win the prize for most lips kissed in a single Season? An offer of marriage must be on someone's agenda this week. ~ An article in the May 7, 1818 issue of *The Tattler.*

ay 8, 1818, Lady Stoneleigh's residence

With a good deal of trepidation, Andrew Burroughs approached the townhouse in South Audley Street from which he had just left the day prior. A bouquet of red roses clutched in one gloved hand, he was about to lift the lion head knocker when the door opened.

"Good day, sir," the butler said as he opened the door wider and stepped aside. At no point did Simonton's expression indicate surprise at seeing the caller or the flowers he carried.

"Andrew Burroughs for Lady Stoneleigh," he said as he held out his calling card. He had half a mind to announcement himself as 'Lord Maximilian', but he rarely used the title. Besides, his card identified him as 'Andrew Burroughs'.

Simonton took it and gave a bow. "Lady Stoneleigh has asked

that you join her in the parlor," he intoned, turning and leading the way.

Giving a nervous glance behind him—he hadn't left the curricle in the hands of a stableboy or an urchin in need of some coin—Andrew followed the butler. He felt relief at seeing several vases overflowing with daisies decorating the hall table. Indeed, the mahogany table top was completely hidden from view, the daisies looking ever so like a white umbrella with yellow polka dots.

This is a good sign, he thought, thinking that if Jane had been upset with him, the daisies would have been redirected to the refuse heap out back.

When Simonton stepped aside and waved an arm into the parlor, Andrew gave him a nod. Nervous—he had expected to meet Jane in the hall and escort her directly to the curricle— Andrew now wondered if perhaps Jane had decided not to accept his offer of a ride.

With his free hand, he patted the pocket containing the ring he had purchased the day before. Instead of giving it to her after their ride, perhaps he should consider proposing right then and there!

He was about to give the thought some more consideration when he realized Jane was regarding him from the middle of the parlor. Dressed in a carriage gown—the blue was bright and set off her blonde hair and peaches and cream complexion to such good effect, he was forced to inhale sharply—Jane appeared every bit the countess she was, although perhaps younger than most widowed countesses.

"You're looking stunning, my lady," he murmured, remembering just then to bow.

Jane curtsied as she felt a blush color her face. "Thank you, Mr. Burroughs," she managed. "Won't you have a seat?"

A pang of disappointment shot through Andrew just then. Her use of his formal name sounded wrong to his ears. "I would rather..." He swallowed, holding out the roses to her. "These are for you, my lady. I fear there are no more daisies in Chiswick," he said.

Jane allowed a wan smile. "I cannot imagine why not," she murmured as she stepped forward to take the roses. Their gloved hands touched briefly, her eyes downcast as she took the bouquet. "They're beautiful. From Chiswick, as well?"

"Indeed," Andrew acknowledged with a nod. The florist no doubt thought him obsessed with flowers. He had warned her he might be back—hoped he would be back frequently— but he made sure to let her know he might not require further deliveries into the city.

The florist seemed rather relieved to hear it.

Jane glanced around the room, finally spying a crystal decanter that would have to work as a vase. "I fear there are no more vases in the house," she murmured as she threaded the stems of the roses into the small opening of the decanter.

Andrew angled his head, his eyes watching her every move, amazed when she moved the roses into a beautiful arrangement with a few deft touches of her gloved fingers. "I cannot imagine why not," he replied. After a moment, when Jane had finished with the roses and was leaning forward to take a sniff, Andrew stepped farther into the room.

"I swear on my life and those of my children that I did not kiss anyone other than you two nights ago," he announced.

Jane whirled around and regarded him with an arched eyebrow. "Of course you didn't," she replied.

Andrew's brows drew together. "Lord Torrington nearly challenged me to a duel over the matter," he said, even more nervous than he had been when he knocked on the front door. "I was able to convince him of my innocence in the matter— a case of mistaken identity, we finally figured out—but I'm afraid he was quite persistent with his intention to challenge me to a duel."

Blinking, Jane's expression changed to one of concern. "Oh?"

Goodness! What had Adele told her husband? And what had Andrew done to the man?

"He is my cousin, you see," he continued, moving his hands to clasp together behind his back. "So, I was forced to accept his challenge..."

"Oh, my God! Whatever did you do to him?" Jane asked in alarm, moving to stand directly in front of the banker. If something awful had happened to Milton Grandby, Adele would never forgive her!

"I made him a promise to make you a cousin by marriage, of course," he answered quickly. "He and my cousin, Gregory Grandby. They were both quite insistent, although I was rather surprised they would even want any more cousins given the number of us they already have," he added in an off-hand manner.

He reached into his waistcoat pocket and pulled out the velvet-covered box. "But they continued to insist, and once we figured we were all arguing on the same side, and since I am the youngest, they were wont to agree with me.

"Jane Vandermeer, will you do me the honor of becoming my wife?" he asked as he held out the box. Although he knew his hands shook, he hoped the gloves would hide his nervousness as he flipped the lid off the box and displayed the gold ring therein.

Jane stared in awe, first at Andrew and then at the ring he offered. "Oh, it's beautiful," she whispered as she peeled a glove off of one hand and placed a fingertip next to the sapphire. She stared up at Andrew, his eyes locking onto hers when she didn't answer right away. "Are you quite sure you wish to be married to a woman who would believe the ridiculous articles in a gossip rag?" she whispered.

Frowning, Andrew considered her words and wondered what he might have thought should the tables had been turned.

If there had been a mention of Lady Stoneleigh kissing someone in the gardens at Lord Weatherstone's mansion, what would I have done?

Why, he would have challenged the cur to a duel. He would

have punched the man across the jaw when delivering the challenge to meet him at Wimbledon Common. Pistols at dawn would have been too good for the rake.

"Considering what my reaction would have been, my lady, I cannot blame you one bit. In fact, it only convinces me that you must have some regard for me if the idea of me kissing another woman upsets you so," he whispered, his manner most serious. "I promise I shall never kiss another in the same way I kiss you," he murmured, his lips taking possession of hers just then.

Not expecting such a declaration—her late husband would never have been capable of such words—Jane allowed the kiss, reveling in the feel of his firm lips against her own, returning the kiss after only a moment of startled surprise. When she felt him pull away, Jane reluctantly let go of her hold on him. "And I shall never kiss another as I kiss you," she countered in a whisper.

"Well, except our children." Andrew said. "Although I would expect you to deliver your kisses only on their cheeks," he added with an arched brow.

Jane suppressed a giggle. "Only on their cheeks," she agreed as she plucked the ring from the velvet and held it between her thumb and forefinger. The thought of children had her happy and yet a brief melancholy followed when she remembered she probably couldn't have children.

Andrew removed a glove and took the ring from her grasp. He slid it onto her fourth finger, rather pleased at how well it fit. "I know I asked you for a ride in the park, my lady, but I was wondering if you might be amendable to a destination a bit farther away?" he queried, his bare hand covering hers.

Her eyes widening, Jane gave him a questioning glance when she was able to look away from the ring. "And where might that be?" she asked, a shiver of excitement leaving her nearly breathless.

"Our future home, my lady," he replied, barely able to contain his excitement.

Jane allowed a slow smile. "I look forward to it," she replied with a grin. When Andrew didn't immediately offer his arm and move to the door, she angled her head in question.

"Given the late hour, we may not be back before dark," he warned, hoping she wouldn't change her mind about going. "Or at all, if my lady would prefer..." He visibly swallowed. "Spending the night in her new bedchamber."

A shiver of excitement had Jane allowing a mischievous grin. "Why, Maximilian Andrew Burroughs. Are you intending to seduce me?" she teased as she pulled on her glove, frowning as she covered the sapphire with the kid leather.

Blinking, Andrew managed to appear rather shocked before his eyes darkened. "Only if you'll allow me the pleasure."

As they made their way to the vestibule, Jane approached the butler and stated, "Do let cook know I won't be home for dinner, and tell Nicole not to wait up for me."

Simonton blinked but managed a short bow. "Of course, my lady," he responded as he opened the front door.

Jane was quite sure she had never before seen her butler quite so discombobulated.

Meanwhile, Nicole watched her ladyship and her caller take their leave of the townhouse from where she stood at the top of the stairs, a sense of immense relief settling over her.

Just the hour before, the cook had read aloud the entire front page of *The Tattler*, three servants listening in rapt attention as she did so. Although there wasn't a single reference to anyone named 'Max', there were certainly several references to a 'Lady J'. Why, it seemed her ladyship had been quite the belle of the ball two nights ago!

"Good for you, milady," Nicole murmured from where she stood. "Good for you."

CHAPTER 28
A TOUR OF A FUTURE HOME

Rumor has it Merriweather Manor is nearly finished! Reports have us believing Sir W is behind the project, both in the design and the guineas. Workmen claim the interior is resplendent with odes to mythology and metallurgy (think marble statues in the alcoves, gilt on the walls, and silver in the butler's pantry). The exterior is certainly an improvement over what first appeared when Henry VIII married his fifth wife. Now we'll have to discover who will become the residents of this beautifully restored manor home. There must certainly be room enough in there for half the ton! ~ An article in the April 23, 1818 issue of *The Tattler.*

May 8, 1818, on the way to Merriweather Manor

Jane Vandermeer Fitzpatrick threaded her hand through Andrew Burrough's bent arm, enjoying how his firm hands on the ribbons had the lone Cleveland Bay pulling them along at an exhilarating clip. As they turned off Kingsbridge Road and onto the Great West Road, she nearly lost her bonnet as her own ribbons gave way. She giggled as Andrew slowed the horse to a canter, her gloved hand catching the ties before the hat was completely unseated from her head.

"I apologize, my lady," Andrew said above the noise of the curricle's wheels.

"Don't you dare, Max," she countered, retying the ribbons beneath her chin. She giggled as they hit a pothole and were momentarily airborne. "I haven't had this much fun in..." *My entire life,* she nearly said, just then realizing she had called him 'Max'. When they exchanged quick glances, he gave her a wink that had her grin widening to a brilliant smile.

Although she had thought the seven miles to Merriweather Manor might take an hour or more to negotiate, Andrew had them there in forty-five minutes. The late afternoon sun dipped behind puffy clouds as he pulled back on the reins and steered the horse to take a turn down a long driveway.

Wanting to see Jane's reaction to his childhood home, Andrew kept his attention on her face, rather satisfied to see her look of awe when the entire manor house came into view.

Halting the horse next to the fountain as he had done with his uncle's trotter the day before, Andrew quickly jumped down from the curricle and hurried to the other side, offering his hands to assist Jane.

She accepted his help, her eyes on the exterior of the manor house as she did so. "This is yours?" she whispered as she realized he had simply taken her by the waist and lowered her to the crushed granite below.

"Not entirely," he replied. "My uncle and I have been working on the plans for the restoration for some time, though," he explained as he offered his arm. "Several generations of Grandbys and Merriweathers and Burroughs were born here. It's large enough for all, although I wish it to be ours alone for as long as possible," he added before placing a kiss on her temple.

Jane gave him a long glance before returning her attention to the red brick manor. *Ours alone,* she thought, rather liking the words.

Although it was impossible to tell what might have come first—the west wing or the east wing—the bricks all looked nearly new. The hall between them was imposing and yet the greenery below and the charcoal slate roof above made it somehow welcoming. Except for where the drive led to the front doors, recently cut grass surrounded the building. A series of topiary trees, their shapes depicting perfectly formed spirals, lined the front entrance. The pump for the fountain in the center of the drive hadn't yet been primed, but she could imagine how the water would spout from its various figurines once it was working.

"Have you chosen your bedchamber yet?" she asked, finally tearing her gaze from the building to regard him.

Andrew lowered his gaze to hers. "Wherever you choose to spend the night is where I'll be," he countered with an arched brow. "Although I will warn you that there are not yet any servants on the grounds," he added in a quiet voice.

Jane allowed a smile. "Then we should claim our bedchamber before other family members do so," she replied. "And spend the night in order to reinforce our claim."

Rather stunned she would put voice to such a plan, Andrew nearly stopped in his tracks. "I do like how you think, my lady," he replied happily. "I have an apartment in mind," he said carefully. "But I will show you them all to discover if we are of a like mind." He was about to lead her to the front doors when he suddenly held up his free hand. Returning to the curricle, he pulled out a cloth-covered basket. He offered his free arm as he rejoined her, aiming another wink in her direction.

Jane suppressed the urge to giggle, practically running as they made their way into the house.

She wasn't expecting a curved staircase, nor the homage to Greek mythology on the ceiling. She wasn't expecting polished marble floors, nor the alcoves and carved wooden doors to studies and parlors and cloak rooms and a library with its own set of spiral stairs to the second level above. She wasn't expecting a breakfast parlor with a huge round table capable of seating ten. She did expect the dining room to be magnificent in size and seating and yet was still impressed. She wasn't expecting two long hallways with doors to a multitude of bedchambers.

She was expecting one of the bedchambers to make itself known as the master suite that she and Andrew would claim as their own. After opening more than a dozen doors along each hallway, she finally turned to Andrew in exasperation. "Have I missed one?" she asked quietly.

Andrew allowed a grin before he bussed her on the cheek. "Not exactly," he replied in a whisper. "We just haven't visited all of them yet. Come." He led her to the very end of the west hallway. "Although it's bright in the late afternoon, it's not the first bedchamber to be lit in the mornings," he said as he opened the door facing due west.

Jane stepped through and stopped in her tracks, marveling at the apartment before her. Unlike any of the other single-room bedchambers they had visited, this one featured a parlor in the front. Beneath the window overlooking the side garden, a rosewood escritoire was just one piece of an arrangement that included velvet-clad furnishings in deep blue. One carved door led to a master suite while another led to the mistress suite. Each bedchamber included dressers and huge beds with posters for canopies, although neither had been dressed with bed linens.

Between the two suites, a bathing chamber featured the latest in running water and a flushing toilet. The large copper tub, plumbed for water and drainage, took up an entire wall. A dressing room, with doors to connect both bedchambers, was adjacent to the bathing chamber.

"This one," Jane said after she had hurried into each of the rooms of the apartment. "Oh, can it be this one?"

Andrew could barely contain his chuckle at her excitement. "Partial to blue, are you?" he teased, noting how her carriage gown made her look as if she were already at home in the elegant surroundings. "I am," she acknowledged with a nod. After a pause, she added, "Did I choose the right one?"

Andrew smiled. "Since it was entirely up to you, then I suppose you did my lady," he replied with a grin. Before she had a chance to protest, his lips were on hers. Relief and yearning mixed to make for a tentative kiss that deepened only when Jane relaxed against the front of his body. His arms moved to embrace her as hers lifted to his shoulders, one hand making its way to the back of his neck.

When they finally ended the kiss, Jane sighed. "I was quite serious about spending the night," she murmured. "And now I'm quite sure you're having second thoughts about taking a wife who would put voice to such a scandalous..."

Andrew cut off her sentence when he recaptured her lips with his. "I am not," he whispered with a quick shake of his head. "I'm too old to be concerned with propriety," he added after he nipped her lips again. "Although, I suppose we'll have to locate some bed linens..." he started to say as he glanced around the room, wondering where he might find them.

"And food," Jane said with an arched eyebrow.

Andrew grinned. "I brought a picnic basket filled with everything we need for supper," he countered.

Impressed by his forethought, Jane angled her head. "I think I shall rather like being married to you," she commented.

Frowning, Andrew's head angled in the opposite direction from hers. "I would hope you will *adore* being married to me," he countered in a teasing voice.

As they made their way back down the staircase, Jane suddenly stopped her descent. At Andrew's look of concern, she sighed. "I spoke with Mr. Pepperidge today." Andrew didn't respond, but she could tell from his quizzical expression that he didn't recognize the name. "The editor of *The Tattler*."

Andrew rolled his eyes and continued his descent, Jane right beside him. "Did you threaten him with torture, or death, or to simply cancel your subscription?" he asked in a voice that tried but failed to tease.

Jane had to suppress a grin. "First of all, I don't have a

subscription to *The Tattler*. Second, I was there to request a retraction of the article that claimed you were kissing Lady Jane..."

Andrew stopped at the base of the stairs, turning so Jane was left on the first step and standing nearly nose to nose with him. He regarded her for a moment, his expression unreadable. "You didn't!"

Surprised at his response, Jane allowed a nod. "I did. Mr. Pepperidge is going to print it in next week's issue."

"In exchange for...?"

Jane frowned. "Whatever do you mean?"

"What did you have to give him to make him agree to print a retraction?"

The air seemed to go out of Jane all at once.

Oh, dear. She had agreed to let the man publish the story of how she and Andrew came to be betrothed and married, not believing it was a story that could be told anytime soon. She hadn't realized Andrew was going to propose that very day. "He would like to write and print an exclusive story about us."

Andrew frowned. "Us?"

Jane nodded. "He's a hopeless romantic at heart, and wishes to tell the story of how we came to be in love."

His eyes widening at this, Andrew couldn't decide if he should be incensed at the news or not, especially given that Jane had just admitted something very important. "And how, pray tell, does he know about *us*?"

Her eyes gave a sideways glance at the same time one shoulder lifted in a slight shrug. Then she remembered seeing Felix Turnbridge, Earl of Fennington, at Lord Weatherstone's ball. He had been waltzing with Lady Morganfield at the same time she and Andrew were dancing. "He said I wouldn't have requested a retraction of the news that sullied your reputation unless I felt affection for you. Which is true," she admitted. Leaning forward, she rested her forehead against his and closed her eyes. "And he saw us dancing together at Lord Weatherstone's ball. Did I do wrong?"

Deciding he rather liked being on the same level with Jane so that they could touch foreheads as they were doing, he allowed a sigh. He supposed any perceptive man would have noticed how much he adored Jane just by watching them as they danced, which had him wondering where Mr. Pepperidge might have been in the crowd.

But how did a gossip rag's editor snag an invitation to the Weatherstone ball?

"It sounds as if you did what you thought you had to do," he finally answered, one of his arms moving to wrap around her waist to pull her closer.

"I did, actually. I suppose this is where I'm supposed to tell you I love you," she murmured.

"That depends. Do you?"

Jane allowed a grin. "Oh, yes. Very much," she admitted before her grin disappeared and her lips suddenly pressed against his. She may have startled him with the move, but Andrew soon joined her in the kiss, wrapping his other arm around her shoulder to pull her entirely against the front of his frame. When the tip of his tongue separated her lips, he felt her entire body shiver beneath his hold. His tongue invaded her mouth, tangling with her tongue and tasting her teeth and lips. He delighted in her soft inhalations of breath, in her soft moans, in how her entire body thrummed against his. When he finally pulled his lips from hers, he left his forehead pressed against hers.

"How will we be sure Mr. Pepperidge keeps his word?" he whispered. "That he doesn't write something scandalous about us?" There was a hint of alarm in his voice.

Jane allowed a mischievous grin. "Why, that's the best part, my love. I know Mr. Pepperidge's true identity. He won't be publishing anything that puts us in a bad light for he knows if he does, I shall inform the *ton* as to whom he really is."

Andrew angled his head and finally allowed a small grin.

"I don't suppose you could share your knowledge with me?" he whispered, one eyebrow lifting. The cur had caused a good deal of trouble with his having mistaken a young rake's identity for Andrew's own.

Screwing up her face as she considered the question, she finally shook her head. "I don't suppose I could. Besides, I rather doubt you even know the lord."

The lord?

The man was a peer of the realm?

Why, of course he was! Else how would he have snagged an invitation to Lord Weatherstone's ball?

Someone was writing the gossip of the *ton* and printing it. And probably making damn good money at it.

Disappointed but not surprised Jane would keep a secret that had obviously come at a cost, Andrew sighed. "Let's indoctrinate the breakfast parlor, shall we, and have something to eat? Afterwards, I'll see to putting the horse into the stables, and then we can indoctrinate the..." He paused, a flush rising to color his throat and face.

"The bedchamber?" Jane finished for him, an eyebrow arching in question.

Andrew nodded, his thoughts of a gossip monger replaced with far more carnal thoughts.

Jane felt a sense of relief at the change in topic. She wanted desperately to tell him about the Earl of Fennington, but she had implied she would keep the man's secret. To do so, it would be easier if her mind was on something else.

Something else entirely.

CHAPTER 29

BREAKING IN A
BEDCHAMBER

We regret we were otherwise engaged and couldn't see to reporting on an ongoing story involving a widow and a widower. Are they merry? Or about to marry? See the next issue of The Tattler for details! ~ A note of apology in the May 14, 1818 issue of *The Tattler*.

May 8, 1818, back at Merriweather Manor

"I found them!" Jane called out happily, pulling a set of folded bed linens from the bottom of a walnut wardrobe. The scent of cedar wafted from the crisp, white linens as she tossed them onto the bed.

"As did I," Andrew said in confusion as he walked into the mistress suite carrying another pile of linens.

"For the bed in your room, no doubt," Jane said as she set about unfolding her stack.

"Oh," Andrew replied, the sound of disappointment evident in his voice.

Jane gave him a grin. "I'll help you if you help me..." She stopped when she noticed his crestfallen expression. "But we really only have to make up *one* of the beds. I should hope."

Andrew immediately brightened. He turned and went back to the master suite, dumping the linens onto the bed. He was back in the mistress suite just as a large swath of linen floated out from Jane's hands and settled onto the mattress. "You've done this before," he remarked, moving to the other side of the bed to straighten and tuck in the sides.

"As have you," Jane replied, impressed the man would know what to do when dressing a bed.

"Watched it being done, is more like it. I used to have a crush on one of the maids here when I was a young lad. Followed her from room to room and watched as she went about her duties, imagining how we might mess up the linens if she ever suggested a tumble."

Jane blinked, rather surprised to hear him put voice to such a story. "And did you ever? Tumble her?"

Andrew's eyes widened in alarm. "Never, my lady!" he claimed as he shook his head. "She had twenty years on me and was married to one of the footmen. Didn't find out that last bit until I'd followed her for an entire fortnight!"

Giggling, Jane was about to admonish him when she realized she was the age now that the maid would have been back then. "Have you always found older women attractive?"

Frowning, Andrew gave her question some consideration before finally saying, "No. Truth be told, you were the next woman for whom I felt affection," he said softly. "And I believe we are about the same age."

Jane stilled her body, one of the bed linens half unfolded as she regarded him. "No scullery maids, or Cyprians, or mistresses?" she countered, surprised by his claim.

Andrew shook his head. "No," his comment quite matter-of-fact.

Angling her head to one side, Jane thought back to when the two had met. The Countess of Norwick, David and Daniel Fitzwilliam's mother, Dorothea, had introduced them at her garden party. Although Jane had seen Maximilian Andrew

Burroughs at other *ton* events, she knew he wouldn't inherit a title—he was the third son of a duke. Still, the attraction was evident the moment he lifted her hand to his lips and kissed the back of it. He hadn't merely brushed his lips over her knuckles, but had actually kissed her fingers, the pillows of his lips leaving behind a hint of moisture that made her entire hand tingle. Why she wasn't wearing gloves at the time, she couldn't quite remember, but the man's kiss had left quite an impression.

"You felt affection for me at Lady Norwick's garden party?" Jane asked as she unfolded the other bed linen.

Andrew chuckled. "I felt affection for you long before we were finally introduced," he replied with a nod of his head, reaching out to take a corner of the bed linen from her.

Jane straightened. "How long?" Goodness, she hadn't had her come-out until the month before that garden party. When would he have had a chance to even *see* her before that day?

The banker sighed. "Since the day your father brought you into the Bank of England... to provide your signature for his accounts." He averted his eyes a moment, busying himself with pulling the bed linen into place over the bottom sheet.

Jane stared at him, trying to remember how old she was when her father informed her she was to accompany him to the bank. "I was... " She shook her head.

"Fifteen," Andrew finished for her. "I remember quite well because I quizzed my uncle about you for some time after you and your father took your leave of his office."

Her eyes wide, Jane regarded Andrew for several moments, finally moving to assist in pulling the bed linen into place. "I had no idea," she murmured.

She couldn't remember him even being *in* the bank that day, the day of her first visit to the Bank of England. She remembered her trembling hand threaded through her father's arm as he led her through the huge doors held open by a footman. The tap-tap of her father's Hessians as they made their way to Sir William's office. The smell of tobacco and leather assaulting her nostrils as they entered his office. The feel of the thick carpet beneath her feet as her father led her to a huge chair. And then meeting the venerable Sir William Burroughs, who turned out to be one of the nicest men she had ever had the pleasure of meeting.

He had settled himself back into his massive leather chair, his hands resting on his rounded belly, not unlike the way women who were expecting babe's held their hands over their middles.

Jane had signed her name on a number of documents placed before her, completely unaware of why she was signing her name. And then, less than ten minutes later, she was up and curtsying to the banker and her father was offering his arm, and they were taking their leave of the huge building in Threadneedle Street.

"Where were *you?*" Jane asked, her eyes finally clearing when she realized Andrew was staring at her.

Andrew was about to reply, "Right here, my lady," when he realized she was referring to that day at the bank. "I was there in my uncle's office."

Jane stared at him a moment. "Where?"

The banker lowered his head, not surprised she wouldn't have noticed him. "My desk was in another part of the office." He paused to pantomime where he would have been located with respect to his uncle's desk. "I would have been to your left and a bit behind you. I don't think you ever looked in my direction the entire time you were in my uncle's office, though," he said quietly, feigning offense.

Inhaling sharply, Jane shook her head. "I'm so sorry. I don't remember you. I was so…"

"Awestruck, yes," he finished for her. "Much like every other young lady who was ever ushered into Sir William's office."

"But you remembered me."

Andrew brightened. "God, yes. How could I not?" he countered before tucking his edge of the top sheet under the mattress. He angled his head. "I rather doubt this bed linen will require tucking in, my lady," he remarked, one eyebrow arching up suggestively. When Jane blushed—bless her heart!—he allowed a chuckle. "We'll simply pull it out, I'm quite sure," he whispered with a knowing grin.

Jane rolled her eyes. "I cannot quite believe this is happening. It's as if I've agreed to an illicit assignation..."

"You've done no such thing," he interrupted, hurrying around to the other side of the bed to take her into his arms. "We're... older. We're in love. We're to be married, and there is nothing for you to be ashamed of," he insisted.

The urgency in his voice had Jane reconsidering her words. "Tell me more about that day at the bank," she urged, wishing she had noticed him at his desk in the corner. It was hard to believe another two years had to pass before she was formally introduced to him.

Andrew moved to stand behind her and started to undo the buttons of her gown. "I was learning how to be an accomptant. My uncle told me of a young woman who was taking night classes in accounting so she could gain employment."

Jane nearly turned around in surprise, wondering what woman would expect to be hired as an accounting clerk. Andrew put his hands on her shoulders and turned her back around. "I know. I was shocked, as well, but Miss Emma Fitzsimmons wasn't about to be deterred from her plan."

"Fitzsimmons?" Jane repeated, instantly recognizing the name. Why, the Viscount Chamberlain was a Fitzsimmons. He worked in Whitehall, in the Foreign Office, but she didn't think he had a daughter.

"Back then, she was the sole owner of her late father's hat shop in Oxford Street," he explained, deftly undoing the buttons down the back of her gown.

"Fitzsimmons and Smith," Jane breathed. "I know the shop. I've purchased many a bonnet there." She half-turned, thinking he had finished undoing all the buttons.

Andrew nodded, briefly wondering just how many bonnets she had purchased.

Jane noticed his expression and sobered. "Not *that* many," she said in her own defense. "Six or... eight, perhaps."

Wiping the back of his hand over his forehead, Andrew let out a teasing, "Whew!" At Jane's widened eyes, he added, "I had a moment there where I thought perhaps I couldn't afford to take you as my wife," he claimed in mock despair.

"And if you couldn't afford me as your wife, you realized you couldn't afford me as your mistress, either." The words were out of her mouth before she could censor them, the tone teasing but the words striking too close to home.

Her home.

"Forgive me, I didn't mean that," she whispered.

Andrew arched a brow, wondering why she would put voice to the comment in the first place. Then he remembered learning her husband had only ever lived with his mistress. Only stayed in London when Parliament was in session, and then favored late nights at his club instead of spending them with his wife. "I would beg, borrow, and steal to have you any way I could get you," he claimed quietly.

Jane dipped her head, rather stunned by his words. After all these years, the man still wanted her.

Still felt affection for her.

She was about to follow the next train of thought but stopped herself. *No sense going there. Not when things are so perfect right now,* she figured. Perhaps she would never have to consider another alternative to that of spending the rest of her life with Andrew Burroughs. *Perhaps...* she shook herself out of her reverie.

What had they been talking about?

Bonnets.

Emma Fitzsimmons.

"Please, do go on with your story about Miss Fitzsimmons," she encouraged.

Curious as to where Jane had been just then—*were her thoughts of mistresses and absent husbands?*—Andrew realized perhaps it would be better to change the subject back to the reason he had pursued a career in banking.

He wanted her to understand why it was he sought an occupation. And he didn't want anything to ruin this evening. They might not have another night alone in the house. Another opportunity for him to convince Jane she wouldn't be making a mistake by marrying him. She might have accepted his ring, but he had the impression she had done so with a hint of reluctance, as if by doing so, she was derailing plans she had already set into motion.

"Well, I'm getting a bit ahead of myself here, but I will tell you the end of the story first. Miss Fitzsimmons did gain a position as an accomptant, you see. And in the process of proving to her employer she was an excellent accomptant, she managed to make the man fall in love with her." Andrew paused a moment, wondering if he should admit all the machinations that had gone into making that match when there might not have been any need for matchmaking. Even he didn't know how many others were involved in seeing to it Emma Fitzsimmons ended up married—those besides his uncle and Aunt Sophia.

Thomas Wellingham had probably fallen in love with Emma Fitzsimmons even before he hired her.

"Miss Fitzsimmons has been married to Mr. Wellingham, the owner of Wellingham Imports, for... fifteen, sixteen years now," he stated with a nod. "And she is still the lead accomptant at his company," he added as he resumed undoing all the buttons on the back of Jane's gown. He moved to undoing the fastenings that held up her petticoat. "Had she expressed an interest in becoming a banker, I do believe my uncle might have hired her over me."

Jane turned around, rather shocked by his claim. "The bank would never have allowed it," she countered as she moved to undo the mail coach knot in his cravat. She plucked his pin from the cravat, giving him an arched brow when she realized an emerald decorated one end of it.

"A gift from one of my sisters," he said with a shrug. "Claims it matches my eyes." This last was said with an impish grin as he blinked several times.

Jane had to agree as she held up the pin next to his face and glanced between his eyes and the jewel. "I do believe your eyes are bluer, though," she murmured.

Andrew chuckled. "How can they not be when we're surrounded by all this blue?" he countered, his hands spreading out to indicate the blue upholstered furnishings and drapes. "Yours certainly are."

A blush colored her face before Jane could set the cravat pin on the dresser, her loosened gown giving way from her torso as she returned to working on removing his cravat. "Now that you've told me the beginning and the end, is there more to your story about Miss Fitzsimmons?" she asked as she went about undoing the knot in the snowy white silk.

Andrew angled his head to one side in an effort to give her more room to work. "Indeed. You see, before the lady met and married Mr. Wellingham, my uncle was none too pleased with Miss Fitzsimmons. He wanted her to accept an offer of marriage. Thought her plan to work as an accomptant was ludicrous," he explained, watching her arms as she stood on tip-toe and unwound the white silk from around his neck.

"Perhaps she didn't think herself pretty enough to land a husband," Jane reasoned, moving her fingers to undo the ties that closed the top of his shirt.

"Oh, but she was," he insisted, immediately regretting the remark when he saw Jane's expression change.

Was that jealousy?

"Not as pretty as you, of course," he quickly added, "But she had been doing the books for her father's business for several years, and having sold the business to her late father's business partner, she decided she had to learn a trade in order to make her way in life."

Jane softened her stance, pulling the shirt tails from his

breeches a bit less aggressively than she would have if he hadn't qualified his assessment of Emma Fitzsimmons' appearance. "I suppose I can understand that," she murmured, wondering what she would have done if her father hadn't arranged a marriage for her, and if Andrew hadn't put forth his promise to ask for her hand.

Seamstress? She could sew, of course, but seamstresses made so little in the way of income.

Milliner? Better pay, but... the idea of making hats and bonnets for a living held no appeal. She rarely decorated her own, never pleased with how the silk flowers looked once she had finished sewing them into place.

Servant? She could make a bed, but there was so much more to keeping a house in working order.

Prostitute? The idea of unwashed men using her body for a moment of pleasure had her entire body shuddering in revulsion. She could barely abide Stoneleigh atop her, although that was usually because he was drunk and smelled of cheroots, his sour breath washing over her as he grunted and groaned on his way to his release.

Clerking? She rather liked adding numbers. She liked the logic, the rules of arithmetic always the same. She didn't always like the results, though, remembering there were times the allowance Stoneleigh provided barely covered her monthly expenses. Especially the months during the Seasons, when a new gown or a pair of slippers would have to wait until the next month, or she would exceed the limit he had set.

Knowing her fortunes would change at some point in her future, she had simply lived her life within the limits Stoneleigh imposed. She had something to look forward to the day he died, after all.

And then he had died.

Although she had expected to feel a sense of elation or relief or... *something*... to follow the news the courier delivered a year and three days ago, she had instead experienced only a sense of numbness.

It was several days before the feeling of sorrow hit her, forcing tears from the corners of her eyes. The sorrow hadn't been for the loss of Michael Fitzpatrick—how could she feel loss when she never felt anything for the man in the first place?—but rather for the children she never bore.

Would never bear, it seemed.

She had never once been pregnant from Stoneleigh's seed, but since he had fathered three boys with his mistress, she knew him capable.

If she were barren, as she suspected, Jane figured she would simply plan a future for herself as an independent woman. So Jane had set about creating a plan for her future, considering what she wanted to do and where she would do it.

She couldn't help but admire Lady Jane Browning's plan for her life, even if Society (and her father and aunt) probably wouldn't allow it. Or how Emma Fitzsimmons had reasoned she needed a position in order to make a legitimate living and then done what she needed to do in order to make it happen.

What Jane had planned couldn't be put into action right away —at least, not upon learning of Stoneleigh's death—not until she had completed a period of mourning. But then...

Jane swallowed, shaking the thought from her mind. Everything was different now. She hadn't planned for Andrew to reappear in her life. Hadn't planned for any man to simply appear and claim he wanted her to be his wife.

"Are you well?"

The words had Jane giving her head a quick shake. "I apologize. I was... woolgathering," she murmured.

"Certainly not from happy sheep," Andrew accused lightly, the back of one finger brushing against the side of her cheek. "If you're feeling jealous of my regard for Mrs. Wellingham, please know you needn't," he added, misinterpreting the sudden sadness that seemed to have settled on her.

Jane allowed a wan smile. "Your regard?" she repeated, the words sounding accusatory.

Andrew placed his hands over hers and brought them to his chest. "I owe her a great deal, it's true," he admitted. "You see, it was her insistence at wanting to make a living for herself—without having to count on a husband or the income from her father's hat shop—that had me realizing I should do the same." When Jane frowned at his words, he added, "I am the third son of a duke," he stated quietly. "I didn't want to live off of an allowance my entire life. Be at the mercy of my older brother for an income. My uncle didn't understand the concept as it applied to Mrs. Wellingham, but thank the gods he did when it came to me. He took me under his wing. Taught me what I needed to know to make a living on my own. As a result, I am not beholden to my brother or the dukedom for my living. And I have an occupation I enjoy immensely and make a good deal of blunt doing."

Nodding her understanding, Jane regarded Andrew for several moments. Perhaps she had nothing to worry about. Perhaps the intervening eighteen years really didn't matter. Perhaps he was the same man as he had been back then, even if she wasn't the same girl she was when they had parted all those years ago. "Your work, and your marriage, and your children—they really haven't changed you, have they?" she whispered in awe.

Andrew regarded her for a long time before he finally gave his head a shake. "I am the same man, Jane. Older, to be sure. Hopefully wiser." He paused a moment before his eyebrows arched. "Wealthier."

Jane allowed a grin at the relief she felt at hearing his words. Sliding her hands up inside his shirt, she delighted in how his body responded to her slight touch, in how his breath hitched when her thumbs brushed over his nipples. "You still haven't told me why you felt affection for me that day," she accused with an arched eyebrow.

Andrew frowned as she pushed his shirt over his head. Once he was free of the garment, he sighed. "You were... beautiful. Even in your fright, you..."

"Fright?" she countered in shock, wondering if she really did appear scared to death that first time she was ever in the Bank of England.

She had been apprehensive, of course. She had never been in the bank before. She had no idea how important the papers were that she signed. What she was agreeing to by signing them. How her life would change because of those simple signatures.

If I'd known, would I have signed them?

Would I have had a choice?

"You were scared to death, and yet, you were a model of grace as you signed all the documents my uncle shoved in front of you," Andrew said as he pushed Jane's gown down from her shoulders and completely off her body. He turned her around, plucking the ties of her corset and loosening each of them in turn.

"A model of grace?" she repeated, a hint of awe in her voice. She let out a sigh of relief as her corset gave way and she could breathe easier.

"Aye," Andrew replied, sliding his hands beneath the corset and pushing it down her body. "Despite your fright, you still managed to exude a sense of confidence..."

"I was scared to death!"

"... Perhaps that's why I thought you the perfect young woman."

"Perfect?" she repeated in surprise. *Christ! I sound like a parrot!*

"Aye. At least, *I* thought so," he replied as he pushed her petticoats to the floor. "I'll never forget that day. I fell in love with you," he added as he finished pulling her corset from her body, his lips moving to her nipples so he could suckle them through the fabric of her chemise.

Jane gasped, shocked at the sensations his lips created despite the translucent silk. The man had her nearly naked and completely at his mercy. "You're still half-dressed," she accused, frowning when she realized he still wore his breeches and boots. Her fingers moved to the placket of his breeches, undoing the fastenings as quickly as her fingers could do so.

"I rather like how you undress me, my lady," he murmured before capturing another nipple between his lips. "Leaves me wondering if I'll require the services of a valet."

Jane gasped when she pushed his breeches down past his hips, his smalls barely containing his engorged manhood as it sprang from his body. Her entire body shivered at the thought of what he had done to her with it only two nights ago. "*Why, though? Why did you fall in love with me?*" she asked again in a whisper, gasping as one of his hands moved to lift the chemise from her body, his palms skimming the sides of her body as he did so.

Andrew's lips captured a bare nipple as he continued to lift the chemise from her body, the silk slowly caressing her skin. He was in no hurry to remove the garment, delighting in her gasps and loving how her nipples hardened even more once they were exposed to his teeth and tongue. "I just did," he finally said, not quite sure why he had decided she was the one. The one he would take for rides in the park. The one he wanted as a mother for his children. The one he thought of every night before sleep took him to oblivion.

The one he would ask to marry him.

The two stared at one another for several seconds, their bare torsos pressed together. "I didn't *do* something...?" she whispered.

He shook his head. "You were just... *you.*" He sighed. "Sometimes, that is all there is, Jane. I fell in love, and I knew whenever I had the opportunity for an introduction, I would make the best of it." He paused to give her a kiss on the lips. "I thought I had, of course, but your father already had other plans for you," he explained with furrowed brows. *Something I would have known if I had read all of those papers that day.*

"An earl counts higher than a banker, of course," he added in a hoarse whisper.

"Even though you are the son of a duke," Jane replied in the same urgent whisper.

"Even though," he agreed with a nod.

Jane swallowed, feeling rather sad just then. "Did you know what those papers were all about? The ones that I signed that day?" she asked, her voice so quiet he could barely hear her.

"A few of them, of course," he acknowledged, giving up his hold on her so he could sit on the edge of the bed to remove his boots. "You were an only child. Niece of an earl. Distant cousin to the Earl of Everly. Your father had a small fortune, but he wanted it protected." *Especially from your future husband, whom you agreed to marry that day by simply signing that damned betrothal.*

Earl or not, Michael Fitzpatrick would not make a good steward for the Vandermeer fortune. Jane's father had known it even before he had made the arrangements for her to marry him. Why Richard Vandermeer thought it acceptable for his daughter to end up with the cur, though, was beyond his understanding.

Andrew regarded Jane for a moment, rather surprised she would allow him to stare at her as she stood nearly naked in the waning light from the room's only window.

Bess would never have allowed it. But he and Bess had never been more than fond of one another, never been more than friends. Even when she had allowed him to bed her, he knew she did so only out of a sense of marital duty. Despite his repeated attempts to make their relationship more than the arranged marriage it was, there was always the shadow of what Bess had suffered before their wedding.

Although she claimed to love her firstborn, Andrew always wondered if Henry was a constant reminder of how her life had been ruined because of one despicable man and one awful night.

Well, her firstborn was off at university now, bestowed with the Burroughs surname and, he hoped, still unaware of his true parentage. Henry was also rather protective of his younger brother and sister, a trait Andrew decided would be useful considering Sophia was due to have her come-out in a few years.

There was much to do between now and then. A house to finish, a wedding to arrange, and a life—two lives—to get back on track. In the meantime, he wanted nothing more than to spend one night alone with Jane.

Andrew allowed an expression of appreciation as he gazed at Jane. Nearly naked—she wore only her stockings— she continued to stare at him as if she were still trying to make a decision, her feet surrounded by the puddle of clothing he had removed from her body.

My very own Venus, he thought, imagining the clothes were an open clam shell.

My very own pearl.

Jane angled her head to one side, replaying Andrew's last words in her head. Rather surprised he knew anything about her father's fortune—Richard Vandermeer had been an investor in Worthington's early steam ships—Jane realized she really shouldn't have been. Andrew was a banker. He had been working in Sir William's office the day her father had placed almost all of his fortune—at least, all but her dowry—into an account in her name. *For the day you're left a widow,* he had said as he placed his hand on her shoulder. *Or for your children, should you precede your husband in death.*

Well, she was a widow with no children. *The money is mine to do with as I please.*

She hadn't yet touched the funds. For twelve months, she had deliberately avoided going to the Bank of England for fear she would clean out the account and simply disappear from London. *I could have gone to the Continent. To the United States. To India. To a cottage in Devonshire. To Italy.*

Jane stared at Andrew. "Is that why you wish to marry me? For my fortune?" she asked, her voice kept as impassive as possible. She had a thought to rail at him. To scream and accuse and feel as hurt as she had felt when she thought he had kissed another, but a part of her believed Andrew truly did love her, and not because of her fortune.

Jerking as if he'd been slapped, Andrew shook his head. "I am heir to one of my own," he answered simply, doing a poor job of hiding his hurt at her supposition. "Although I have spent a good deal of it on this house," he said with a roll of his eyes, "I have seen to it there is an inheritance for my three children when I die." He took a steadying breath. "My biggest fear this past year was of you leaving London. Using your inheritance to go somewhere... where I had no hope of finding you," he whispered, his breathing becoming more labored.

"And now? Are you having second thoughts?" Jane asked as she wrapped her arms over her bare breasts. *He knew about the papers.* Knew what she had agreed to, even if she didn't know at the time.

Andrew blinked and quickly shook his head. "God, no. Jesus, Jane. I'm trying to figure out how I'm going to get myself out of bed every day when all I'm going to want to do is spend them in bed with you," he replied in mock despair.

Relieved by his response, Jane slowly lowered her arms. "Oh," she murmured with a nod. "Well, all right then." Stepping out of the puddle of clothing at her feet, Jane moved to stand before him. Placing her hands on either side of his head, she regarded him for a long time before reaching up to settle a kiss on his forehead. "Then thank you for finding me when you did," she murmured. "I had half a mind to leave London the day after Lord Weatherstone's ball."

His arms were around her waist in an instant, his face pressed above one breast as he pulled her down onto the bed with him. She let out a squeak of surprise when he suddenly had her flat on her back, his body suspended over hers. "I would have found you," he vowed as he dipped his head to kiss her. "I would have brought you back and made you sign papers promising you would never leave me," he continued, his kisses continuing down the column of her throat.

"Papers?" Jane managed to reply before his lips once again captured hers, his chest lowering so the graying crisp curls tickled her breasts.

Lifting her knees to his hips, she shivered when she felt the length of his engorged manhood press against her quim, and shivered again as it slid along her honeyed folds. She broke the kiss when she felt the wet tip at her opening. When Andrew didn't move to enter her—Jane realized he seemed torn between claiming her or continuing his foreplay—she moved her hands to his buttocks and lifted her hips, guiding him into her until she could pull him hard against her.

Andrew let out a curse, the growl rumbling through his body before he could lift himself a bit. "A marriage certificate, of course," he managed to get out, the words forced out between gasps for air. "But first, I'm going to practice one of the Roman arts," he murmured between kisses to her jaw and the hollow of her throat. "To be sure you'll never go to Italy without me."

Roman arts?

Jane's eyes widened. Her entire body shivered despite not knowing exactly what he had in mind to do to her. She mew-led her disappointment as he pulled his manhood out of her, forcing her to let go of his hips as he moved down her body. He left soft kisses in his wake. He covered each breast with his mouth and worried her nipples with his tongue and teeth until she writhed beneath him. He continued to move down her body, kissing and nibbling, until his head was between her thighs.

Not exactly sure what he intended to do, Jane nearly shrieked when his hands slipped beneath her bottom and lifted her hips. When his lips kissed her most private place, she clutched the bed linens in an effort to anchor herself to the bed. When his tongue flicked across the swollen bud of her womanhood, Jane was sure she saw stars before her eyes. "Max," she murmured several times as the second, third, and forth flicks of his tongue had her chest rising from the mattress, her breaths coming in gasps as darts of pleasure shot through her lower body. A kind of tension built up within her, as if a spring were being wound tighter and tighter.

So when his lips captured the bud and suckled it, his tongue circling as if to wind the spring even tighter, she felt herself on the edge of sanity. Suddenly, the tight spring inside her body seemed to break and unwind in every direction, her entire body exploding into a release of pure pleasure, her vision filled with flashing lights, her cry of "Max!" filling the bedchamber and probably every room in the west hall. Her body shook and shivered and shook again when he flicked his tongue across her womanhood one last time.

Reveling in the sound of his nickname, Andrew pushed himself up from between her legs and drove his manhood into her slick haven, claiming her in one deep thrust that had her screaming his name again.

Gasping at how tight she gripped him, at how her body drew his manhood in even deeper, Andrew realized he wouldn't last long. A few more thrusts, and he was forced to allow his own release, the orgasm consuming his ability to hear or see or feel anything but pure pleasure and the sense of contentment that seemed to settle over him like a warm blanket once it was over.

He wasn't aware of how he ended up flat atop Jane's body, or how his head ended up next to hers on the only pillow they had managed to toss onto the bed.

When awareness finally found him again, Jane's fingers were sliding up and down one side of his body, tickling his ribs as her lips suckled the top of his shoulder. Her legs had lowered so they were no longer wrapped around his thighs, but his manhood was still tucked inside her warm folds.

"Are you all right?" she asked in a whisper that caressed his skin.

Andrew managed a chuckle that seemed to cause his entire body to vibrate. Although he thought to lift himself from her body, he felt boneless. "I apologize, my lady, but I do not think I can move," he whispered, despite one hand sliding up her arm so his hand could clasp her shoulder.

"Then don't," she murmured, her eyes half-closed. She took a deep breath and let it out slowly, watching as his body lifted slightly and then lowered in turn.

"I'm crushing you," he countered.

"And keeping me warm."

In a move she wasn't quite sure how he managed, Andrew flipped over so Jane found herself atop him. In another move, the bed linen wafted over the top of her and settled onto her back.

"So glad I didn't tuck that side in," he murmured before he closed his eyes and drifted in and out of consciousness.

CHAPTER 30
AN EARL UNVEILS HIMSELF

hen did we know it was time to reveal our identity? At some point, one realizes they shouldn't have been hiding in the first place. The results, of course, are unknown to me at this time. ~ The editor's final article in the May 14, 1818 issue of *The Tattler.*

ay 14, 1818, the last day of scheduled meetings

Felix Turnbridge regarded his image in the looking glass, rather startled to see how old he appeared. He rarely gave a thought as to how others saw him, but now he knew exactly what they must be thinking.

He's old.

Old and without a wife. Without an heir.

Flipping the glass so that it no longer reflected his image, Felix sighed. *I'm not even thirty,* he thought with derision, rather shocked when he realized he would soon be thirty.

Or was he already? And about to be one-and-thirty? He shook his head, aware if he gave his age another moment of thought, he would have a headache.

The problem with taking a wife at this stage was finding one willing to marry him, he supposed.

Well, finding a willing woman probably wasn't that difficult given there were dozens of available young ladies that had made their debuts not more than a few months ago, most of whom would be more than happy to accept the suit of an earl.

But young women who were well under twenty years of age were of no interest to him.

He wanted one who was a bit more mature. A bit more worldly. One who could do him proud when it came to entertaining. When it came to overseeing his household.

When it came to sharing his bed.

He had one in mind, of course. Had for nearly two months. One he would welcome with open arms and an open...

Felix shook his head. Now was not the time to be considering how he might *feel* about a particular woman. Not when he knew how much she must have come to despise him. Hate him, even.

If he approached her as Felix Turnbridge, Earl of Fennington, rather than his alter ego, Mr. Frederick Pepperidge, he knew she would figure out fairly quickly that he was the one who had made her life rather uncomfortable these past two months. And she would do so despite his repeated attempts to court her. Despite his attempts to make her realize just how much he wanted her.

How much he liked her.

Loved her.

Felix shook his head again, wondering from where that last thought had come. He really was fond of her, of course. How could he not be? She could have divulged all manner of awful information about her fellow aristocrats. She could have saved herself weeks of meetings with him had she just given him more in the way of juicy morsels. Morsels that would have released her from his blackmail. Released her from the made-up prison he had created in an effort to keep her close.

Instead, she had only provided the least damning information, the least hurtful and least scandalous news during their weekly meetings. And what had seemed rather juicy had been about aristocrats he had never heard of, members of the *ton* whose identities were completely unknown to most Londoners.

From where had that information come? Some of it was identical to what The Gossip Goddess had sent to him. *Was she The Gossip Goddess?* He shook his head.

She *had* spent four years in Switzerland. Perhaps she was merely familiar with a different set of the *haute ton*.

Still, her gossip hadn't been the least bit damning.

To know there was a woman out there—an earl's daughter, no less—who wasn't driven by petty jealousy to embarrass her fellow aristocrats was somehow a relief. To know there was someone who wasn't a gossip, wasn't a bully—even when given the chance to be so anonymously—gave him hope that not all in the *ton* were vicious.

Why, the regard she showed for her peers was enough to make him fall in love with her.

He dared a glance at the long pasteboard box that had been delivered only a few moments ago. The florist had assembled a collection of bright red hot-house roses and had arranged them with greenery in a white tissue wrapper. When he removed the lid to verify they were indeed red roses, the scent had wafted over him like a soft caress, much like her scent did whilst they sat on the bench in Hyde Park. Like it had that very first time he had approached her in Lord Weatherstone's gardens.

Ah, Lord Weatherstone. The man had to know that by growing a myriad of hedgerows and beautiful plants and flowers, by commissioning a fountain and importing all manner of statuary, by displaying one of the best renditions of Cupid, the end result would be a magical environment in which to fall in love.

How could he not? Lord Weatherstone had probably proposed to his own wife in those very gardens!

Well, today Felix would join Lady Emelia on the bench in Hyde Park as he had done every week for the past seven weeks, but he would not be wearing his usual disguise. No awful wig and bulbous nose and mustache and gold-rimmed spectacles. Nor would his manner of dress suggest he was anything other than an earl. He had a new top hat from Fitzsimmons and Smith, one with a crown that wasn't quite as tall as the one Mr. Pepperidge sported. His valet had polished his Hessians so they practically reflected his image. Nankeen breeches were perfectly cuffed below the knee, and his pocket watch hung from a chain pinned to his pale gold embroidered waistcoat pocket. The deep green topcoat, made of superfine and tailored to perfection by Jeffrey Garth, had been delivered only moments before the roses.

Daring a glance at the mantle clock, Felix realized he had been woolgathering for far too long. Having dismissed his valet after the man had finished shaving him, Felix pulled on his top coat and glanced out his window to find a stableboy had already pulled Juno and his phaeton around to the front curb.

Lifting the box of roses in one arm and then his cane in the other, Felix made his way down the stairs and out to the equipage, feeling as if he was either entering his next stage of life or walking to his death. For at that moment, they both felt the same.

Emelia sighed as she regarded the park bench. Still damp from the early morning fog, it wasn't exactly inviting. She pulled her handkerchief from her reticule and wiped the slats before taking a seat. *The last time*, she thought with relief. Today would be the last time she would ever sit on this bench. Even if she was given a chance to do so in the future, she rather doubted she would ever voluntarily sit here again.

The crunch of boots on crushed granite had her eyes lifting. The well-dressed gentleman who approached carried a long box in one arm and dangled a cane from the other hand. Everything he wore suggested he followed the dictates of current fashion, dictates made by some commoner named Beau Brummel, if the rumors were to be believed.

Emelia tore her gaze away when she realized she was almost staring at the man as he walked toward her.

Feeling a bit alarmed—no one had ever walked by the bench during her other meetings with Mr. Pepperidge—she forced herself to simply nod in his direction and act as if she was merely enjoying a morning in the park. But when he stopped and bowed before her, Emelia was forced to look up. She was also forced to put out her arms when the man offered her the pasteboard box.

"What...?"

"Good morning, Lady Emelia," Felix said as he removed his hat and bowed again. "I've a message from Mr. Pepperidge. You have completed your task, and your assistance is no longer required."

Emelia stared at Felix Turnbridge, Earl of Fennington, at once stunned at how handsome and at how perfectly perfect he seemed. She was quite sure she had never seen him like this before, though. Certainly not in the daytime. Certainly not when he fetched her for their weekly rides in the park.

But she realized he looked ever so much like the man in her sketch pad.

"Please. Do open it," he encouraged her, indicating the box with a nod. He moved to take the seat next to her, much like Mr. Pepperidge would do.

Emelia blinked before lowering her gaze to the box. She pulled off the lid with one hand as she held the box in the crook of her arm, gasping when the arrangement of bright red roses appeared in their tissue and blanket of greenery. "Oh!" she managed to get out, inhaling deeply when she smelled the heavenly scent. "They're beautiful," she whispered, turning her attention to the man who sat next to her.

Felix was regarding her with a look of uncertainty, as if he had something to say but wasn't sure if he should. Emelia recognized the look immediately. Recognized it because it was the look Mr. Pepperidge had given her the last time they had met, just before he took his leave of her. As if he regretted having to leave her side.

The look she had captured in the image she had drawn in her sketch pad.

"Felix Turnbridge," the man said, removing this hat and setting it off to his right at the end of the bench. He turned his body on the bench slightly, so he was angled in her direction.

"The Earl of Fennington," Emelia said quietly. "Or do you prefer Mr. Pepperidge?" she asked, attempting to keep her voice as impassive as possible.

At that moment, she wasn't sure if she was incensed with the man or relieved he was finally revealing his true identity.

The man visibly swallowed, the motion of his Adam's apple apparent beneath his cravat. "Damnation," Felix muttered under his breath. "Fennington, actually. I rather hoped you wouldn't recognize me so quickly," he managed to get out then. "Give me a chance to explain before you have the opportunity to either slap me across the face or..." He stopped then, realizing she looked as if she really was going to slap him. Or mayhap punch him as she had done to the man at Warwick's when he had attempted to kiss one of her classmates. She had left the bounder with a broken nose and a shiner that lasted several weeks. "Go ahead then. I deserve it, I know," he said with a nod, lifting his face so she would have a clear target for her open hand. Or closed fist.

For a moment, he thought his perfectly straight nose was about to be realigned.

Emelia stared at him for a moment, the urge to slap him replaced with a feeling of pity for the man. He seemed so sorrowful, as if he knew very well that what he had done was wrong and wondered how he was going to make it right.

Lifting one gloved hand to his cheek—she had to suppress a grin when she saw him wince and nearly close his eyes in anticipation of the hit—she merely lay it against his clean shaven face and then reached up to kiss him on his other cheek.

Although he barely moved, she felt him give a start at the unexpected gesture. Pulling her hand away, she was about to return it to the edge of the box when his gloved hand caught it and lifted it to his lips. He stared at her before swallowing. "Thank you," he murmured, kissing her knuckles.

"Oh, no. You don't get off that easily, my lord. You owe me an explanation," she replied with an arched eyebrow, her voice sounding as reasonable as she could make it. She still had a mind to wallop the man, perhaps with a fist to his perfect, never-been-broken nose, but then he would bleed all over his snowy white cravat and beautifully embroidered waistcoat, and, well, that wouldn't really be fair to his poor valet.

Nor would it do his nose any good.

She rather liked his nose just the way it was.

"I do," he agreed with a nod. "I hardly know where to start..."

"At the beginning, of course," she interrupted, noticing just then her hand was still held in his and pressed against his chest, her fingertips grazing the bottom folds of his cravat. A diamond-tipped cravat pin winked in the early morning light.

Felix blinked at her words, realizing how reasonable they sounded. "All right, then," he said with a nod, not giving up his hold on her hand. He took a deep breath and held it for a moment before letting it out. "I used to look forward to attending the entertainments of the *ton*. The balls, with all the beautiful gowns and jewels and lit candles. Soirées. House parties, where we would engage in card games and spend the evenings dancing and playing charades," he said in a quiet voice.

"Used to?" Emelia repeated, noting how the recollection did not seem to bring him any joy.

He nodded. "I soon discovered that my fellow aristocrats seemed to take perverse pleasure in the foibles and unfortunate circumstances of others. They did so in the form of gossip. Sometimes in the most cruel way," he explained quietly. "And almost always at the expense of someone who didn't deserve it."

Emelia regarded him with a look of confusion. "And yet, *you* are the publisher of *The Tattler*," she countered, wondering how he could find fault with others who started gossip when his news sheet printed it so all of London could read about it.

Holding up a hand, as if to halt her comment, Felix gave her a nod. "I started *The Tattler* for two reasons. I needed an income. Because of my father's excessive gambling, I inherited an earldom deep in debt. I also saw the publication as a means to spread gossip about those who were the worst purveyors of it," he added with a nod. "And I made sure that the other gossip— the stuff that wasn't really so awful or, most importantly, wasn't true at all—was given short shrift or proven impossible."

Frowning, Emelia considered his words. It was true the most vicious of the news wasn't always so very newsworthy. That some of the gossip wasn't really gossip at all but rather tidbits of information anyone could obtain from simply paying a call and being invited into a Mayfair parlor for tea.

Some of it was downright amusing.

Foibles, indeed.

But nothing that truly did harm to anyone who didn't deserve it. "And being kissed in Lord Weatherstone's gardens is... somehow *awful*?" she countered.

Mr. Pepperidge had threatened her with printing an article about *her*. Printing a mention of her being in the gardens at Lord Weatherstone's garden party—with Lord Fennington— him, no less—kissing. A mention of how the earl had escorted her around a hedgerow, and without so much as a *may I kiss you?* or a *would you do me the honor of a kiss?*, he had simply lifted her chin with one gloved hand and kissed her senseless. Kissed her until her insides had melted and her reason had left her. Kissed her until she would have done anything he asked.

Kissed her until she would have responded with a "Yes," to an offer of marriage or to an offer of bedding her, her ability to make a decision having left her brain long before her ability to say, "No," to being kissed in the first place.

"You were the one who kissed me!" she added just then, realizing how scandalous it would have seemed to anyone who saw the two of them hidden behind the hedgerow.

She'd been so stunned, so shocked, she could do nothing more than allow the kiss. It had been so very pleasant, the sensation of excitement coursing through her body in an instant, her pulse racing at the thought that Felix Turnbridge, he of the dark blonde hair, blue-blue eyes, and never been-broken-nose that made him far more handsome than he any right to be, had decided she was worthy of a kiss.

She could only imagine what it might have been like to have been kissed in those same hedgerows in total darkness. To not know it was Lord Fennington who kissed her. Even in the daylight of the garden party, she had allowed her eyelids to fall in an effort to concentrate on what his lips were doing so that she might follow suit.

His height was all the more apparent as he had kept his hand along her jawline to hold her head at an angle as he continued to kiss her, continued to slide his lips over hers and suckle them gently, to nip her lower lip and then take her lips again at a slightly different angle, only pulling away when the kiss was complete.

And then he had the audacity to apologize.

I am not a rake.

She hadn't seen his expression as they returned to the party. Didn't know if his face was as flushed as she knew her own to be. But his scent had enveloped her, filling her nostrils with a most delightful combination of spice and amber. The warm scent she smelled now. Well, the scent that wasn't being drowned out by the lovely roses that rested in the pasteboard box that lay across her lap.

"Yours was my first kiss," she whispered, turning to stare at him. "Only kiss. But... but *why?*" she asked, one brow furrowing in confusion.

Felix blinked, rather surprised by the question. "How did you figure out I was Mr. Pepperidge?"

"Your cologne," Emelia replied simply. "And from your face without the awful mustache. I did a drawing of you," she added as she indicated her sketch pad. She opened the pad to the page with the drawing, the fake mustache still stuck in place.

"Oh," he replied, his breaths becoming shorter. Labored. "Damn," he added under his breath. *Well, at least my favorite fake mustache wasn't completely lost.* Seeing it on the drawing made him realize just how hideous he looked wearing it, though.

"You didn't answer my question," she accused.

"I was overcome by your loveliness."

Emelia made a sound not unlike a snort. "Is that what you tell all the chits you kiss during your assignations?" she countered.

Felix straightened, a hurt expression displaying as he shook his head. "You are lovely. And I have never before kissed a woman quite like..."

"I am old enough to know that cannot be!"

Rather surprised at her response, he furrowed his brows. "How old are you?" At her quelling glance, he added, "I only ask because I fear you and others will accuse me of cradle robbing. I am actually younger than I look. Not quite thirty."

Emelia sighed, remembering he was the same age as her oldest brother, Adam. "I am three-and-twenty. My brother, Alister, has been married to Julia for... for two years, and she's the same age as me!"

Well, at least I guessed right, he thought. "He's a groom in her father's stables," Felix countered, knowing Alister was really in charge of the Harrington House stables, but that still made him a groom. "Besides, it's not as if you've been available for courting. You've been off at school in Switzerland," he countered.

"Yes, but I haven't had so much as a single offer... ever!" Emelia finished, obviously a bit incensed.

Felix held up a finger. "About that," he said quickly. He paused though and allowed a long sigh. He couldn't exactly ask for her hand on the same bench he had used to gather information for his publication. She would probably deny him on that basis alone.

Bad karma and all.

"Would you come with me on a ride in Park Lane? We could walk there, but..."

"I've no chaperone," she replied with a shake of her head.

The earl angled his head, realizing she spoke the truth. "I shan't do anything untoward, I promise," he replied as he stood up from the bench and turned to assist her by putting the lid back on the box of roses and taking the box from her. He offered her his other hand.

"But what if we're seen?" she asked as she allowed him to lead her away from the bench and toward the carriageway beyond the hedgerow.

"I rather doubt there will be a mention of it in *The Tattler*," he responded with a shrug.

Emelia blinked, realizing he had a point. "Where are we going?" she asked as his phaeton and horse came into view. The gray mare tossed her head at the sound of their voices, and she knickered softly.

"To the... to the scene of the crime, so to speak," the earl replied. He placed the box of roses on the back of the phaeton and turned to lift her onto the bench, ignoring her startled gasp when she was forced to place her hands on his shoulders when she was airborne. A moment later, she was seated on the high-perch phaeton and staring down at Felix.

A glimpse of her stockinged ankle had Felix stilling his movements.

Jesus!

He might not make it to his thirtieth birthday if he couldn't get himself under control.

He had a brief glimpse of Mark Comber, Earl of Aimsley,

meeting him at Wimbledon Common, a dueling pistol aimed in his direction.

"What is it?" Emelia asked when she realized he was staring at her foot. She adjusted her position on the bench seat and made sure to shake out her skirts so they covered her half-booted feet.

"Just as I imagined, you have a lovely ankle," he said as he bounded up to take the seat next to her on the bench. Juno, tossing her head again, lurched forward even before Felix had the reins secure in his hands. "And Juno is more anxious than me," he added as the horse was off at a quick trot toward the gates.

Not ever having ridden on a phaeton, Emelia struggled to hang onto something—anything—to keep her from flying off the bench. The anything turned out to be Felix, whose arm was suddenly offered for hers to wrap around. Gingerly, she did so, reminding herself there wouldn't be an article in *The Tattler* about this. About how close her thigh was to his on the bench. About how there was no chaperone—not that there was room for anyone else on the conveyance. They had only ever ridden in a curricle on their weekly rides in the park, where there was plenty of room for her maid. The phaeton was barely large enough for two people!

"This is rather invigorating," Emelia managed to get out as Juno took the turn onto Park Lane, nearly galloping as she made her way.

"Yes," Felix replied with a nod, his own breaths coming faster as he considered what he was about to do. "Yes, it is. I do hope you'll be amenable to what I have to say," he managed before the mare was once again under his control and racing down Park Lane. "I wanted to speak with you the very same day I kissed you in the gardens, but your father wouldn't allow it."

At the mention of her father, Emelia gasped and turned to stare at the earl. "Why ever not?"

Felix managed a shrug as he handled the ribbons. "He

wanted to be sure I had given it a great deal of thought, I suppose," he answered. "Which I did. Now I expect he'll make you do the same."

Frowning, Emelia wondered at the man's words. In just a few minutes, she would learn whatever had him driving them far too fast down Park Lane.

CHAPTER 31
A SLEEPY HOUSEHOLD
COMES ALIVE

Circumstances find us once again having to apologize for not learning more about our widow, Lady S, and widower, Mr. A. Burroughs. Seems they have taken their leave of London and perhaps of their minds. Bedlam, anyone? ~ An article in the May 14, 1818 issue of *The Tattler*.

May 14, 1818 at Merriweather Manor

Bird song had Jane's eyes opening to the sight of her fingers resting in salt and pepper curls. Blinking, she realized her head was nestled into the small of Andrew's shoulder. One of her legs was between his, and her entire torso was pressed against the side of his body. The crisp curls on his chest were dimly lit from the only window in the room, their position changing as his chest rose and fell with his even breathing.

Listening intently, Jane was sure she heard voices, although she couldn't be sure if their owners were inside the house or somewhere outside. A horse whinnied. The wheels of a dray cart squealed in protest.

When Andrew's breathing changed, Jane gave a start as she felt his manhood lengthen and harden against her hip. She moved her hand down through his gray curls, her fingers seeking to stroke the velvety softness.

The thought of how it had felt deep inside her just hours ago had her insides turning molten, her core throbbing in response. The way Andrew had claimed her—there could be no other word to use to describe how he had thrust himself into her—had her so aroused, she wanted nothing more than to relive the experience, although more slowly given the early morning hour.

Remembering his reaction to what she had done only a week ago—*had it really only been a week?*—she pushed herself up onto one elbow. Her gaze raked up and down Andrew's body as her fingers continued stroking the length of him. Although his eyes were still closed, an expression of contentment appeared as he allowed an audible sigh.

Moving the leg that was between his so it was on the other side of his body, Jane climbed atop his body, straddling him. His manhood—hard and wet at its tip—seemed to know its mate was near as she lifted her hips and rubbed her warm, wet folds along the length of him.

At the sound of Andrew's groan—his eyes were still closed, but he seemed to be enjoying a rather erotic dream— Jane guided his manhood inside her and slowly, very slowly, lowered herself onto the length of him. Her breath hitched several times as she opened herself to the welcome intruder, lifting and lowering a bit more until he was completely seated inside her.

Leaning over his body, her breasts barely touching the crisp curls on his chest, she splayed her hands into the mattress on either side of Andrew's body. She was about to lift her hips to pull off of him when his hands grasped her hips and held her in place.

"Do you realize I was dreaming of you doing this?" he murmured, a huge grin lighting his face. "This very moment?"

"Because you wanted me to be doing this?"

Andrew blinked away sleep and grinned. "Aye."

Jane gave a slight shrug. "Dreams do come true, I suppose," she whispered, a lock of hair falling to cover part of her face.

Using a hand to push away the blond curls, Andrew lifted his head and leaned forward to kiss her. "They do, indeed, my lady," he murmured, settling back onto the bed. Using the palms of his hands, he pushed her up so she was sitting upright as his knees bent behind her. "Especially if you put your hands on my thighs."

Her eyes widening at his suggestion, Jane gasped as she did what he suggested and felt him move inside her. Although she could barely move her hips, Andrew pushed up against her, surprising her with his upward thrust. "Dreams really do come true," he repeated as he lifted her hips with his hands and then pulled them down to meet his next upward thrust.

Her back pressed against his thighs, Jane was about to agree but found she couldn't put voice to her words. Closed eyes meant she missed the move that had Andrew using his thumb to press against the space where their two bodies merged, the pressure and slight circular motion setting off a series of skittering orgasms that built to a crescendo of tension and a cataclysmic release so sudden, Jane could barely breathe. Pleasure beyond her imagination took hold, forcing her back to arch against his thighs before her boneless body fell forward onto Andrew.

One last thrust had him stunned. His own release, beyond his ability to stop, started just as he caught Jane's falling body. He barely had her settled atop him when his seed spilled into her, his groan so loud he was sure the birds heard him and stopped their incessant singing.

He felt more than heard Jane's burble of laughter, forcing a smile to his face even before the last vestiges of his pleasure had begun to subside.

"I do believe we shall have the very best marriage," he whispered as he stroked her back, his forefinger tracing the bumps of her spine, first up one side and then down the other. "For the rest of our lives, but then, I believed that eighteen years ago."

Jane lifted her head and regarded Andrew for a moment, the lock of blonde hair once again covering one of her eyes. "Are you to be the master of this house?" she asked in a whisper, once again aware of the sounds down below. Goodness, how long had they slept?

"I am. And you its mistress, I should hope. Our children shall be the first to occupy the nursery..."

"Children?" Jane countered in alarm.

From the sound of her voice, Andrew realized he had to tread lightly. They hadn't yet discussed children, but he hadn't seen to using a French letter the nights he had spent with her, either. Just because Jane hadn't borne a Stoneleigh heir didn't have him concerned in the least, though. From what his uncle had told him, Michael Fitzpatrick was rarely in the same house with his wife. "Should we be blessed with any," he added with an arched brow.

Jane relaxed atop him again, although the smile didn't return to her lips. "You would welcome more?" she asked in a small voice.

"Of course," he replied, his fingers working their way to the sides of her ribs.

"And if I cannot... have children?"

Andrew managed a shrug. "I am father to three, two of them my own flesh and blood," he replied quietly. "So I will not be disappointed if I do not father another." After a moment, he added, "But do not be surprised if in nine months, you are round with my child and about to give birth."

Jane allowed a grin, once again relaxing atop his body. "I rather doubt it will take nine months for me to know I am about to give birth," she replied, her eyelids heavy. In a moment or two, she was sound asleep.

Beneath her, Andrew closed his eyes and allowed sleep to take him once again, oblivious to the racket of movers and dray carts and horses down below.

CHAPTER 32
AN EARL SPIES AN EARL ON
A MISSION

First, we would recommend you not drive in Park Lane in a phaeton at full gallop. ~ The new editor's first article in the May 21, 1818 issue of *The Tattler*.

ay 14, 1818, Aimsley House
Following a rather satisfying meal in the breakfast parlor with his countess, Mark Comber, Earl of Aimsley, escorted Patience to her salon at the back of the house and bussed her on the cheek. A tea tray had already been delivered, curls of steam rising from the pot.

"Where is our daughter, do you suppose?" he asked, realizing she should have been in the breakfast parlor with them. Given her absence, the two of them had enjoyed a rather quiet breakfast where Patience fed him bits of bacon while he kissed her between bites. They had never done anything like it before, and he found himself hoping his daughter would be skipping breakfast more often in the future.

Then he remembered it was a Thursday. Their daughter hadn't been at breakfast on a Thursday morning in two months.

Patience settled into her favorite upholstered chair and gave a sigh. "She left early this morning for one of her early morning walks in the park," she replied. "I think she's contemplating what to do next," she added with an arched brow.

Although Patience had always thought her only daughter would be married long before she turned twenty, Emelia had other plans. The girl could have continued school at Warwick's Grammar and Finishing School in London, as most of the daughters of the aristocracy did in their teens, but Emelia had insisted she be allowed to attend finishing school elsewhere. Having grown up with brothers, she had become a bit of a tomboy. Realizing she had no hope of surviving life with other young women raised to be perfect copies of their mothers, Emelia figured she had better take her leave of London and attend a school where she wouldn't be recognized as the sister of Adam and Alistair Comber.

Four years in Geneva had afforded her an education as well as an appreciation for how others outside of the *ton* lived. It did not, however, provide a string of suitors interested in making her a married woman, although Patience wondered if Emelia would have been open to such offers. Now that she was back in London, most thought her too old to make a suitable match.

Although not particularly beautiful, Emelia was still pleasing to the eye, carrying herself with the confidence of a woman who had lived on the Continent and exuding a happy character that attracted young matrons to her at her first few *ton* events.

That is, until just after Lord Weatherstone's garden party. Suddenly, Emelia seemed withdrawn. Nervous. Unhappy, almost.

Patience had nearly asked her about what might have happened to bring on such a change in her countenance, but then she remembered the letter from Mr. Pepperidge. The blackmail. Of course her daughter would turn sullen given the demands of the publisher of *The Tattler*. Today would be the last day of her scheduled meetings with Mr. Pepperidge, though. The last day of supplying gossip that was either untrue or so insipid, it wouldn't garner anyone's attention.

"I don't expect there's really anything to worry about," the earl commented, thinking just then he might have to give his daughter her dowry and send her out in the world to be a spinster if a certain someone didn't exercise his option to ask for her hand. It had been eight weeks since the Weatherstone's garden party.

Patience gave her husband a slight shake of her head. "I suppose not. You may get a visit from an interested party any day now, though," she said with a bit more hope than she felt. After all, Emelia was riding in the park with Lord Fennington every week. Even if the girl didn't seem to believe he was courting her, who knew if he was or wasn't?

Perhaps he was considering her for matrimony.

"As long as she doesn't do something to warrant a mention in that damned *Tattler* rag," Mark replied with an arched brow as he took his leave of the salon and headed to his study.

Patience was about to assure him that Emelia was incapable of doing any such thing and then thought better of it.

She knew from Mr. Pepperidge's letter that Emelia had done something. She had kissed Lord Fennington in Lord Weatherstone's gardens.

Patience couldn't help but smile at the thought.

About to take a seat at his massive oak desk, Lord Aimsley paused and instead glanced out the window facing Park Lane. The early morning fog had lifted and the sun shined brightly, so it should have been no surprise to see a red phaeton racing down the street, the gray mare pulling it nearly at a full gallop. Mark Comber was surprised, though, when he realized a woman he was fairly sure was his daughter was seated on the high-perch bench and holding onto the Earl of Fennington.

Holding on as if her very life depended on it.

But then, it probably did given how fast the Percheron was running.

Thinking the earl was merely giving Emelia a ride back to Aimsley House, Mark moved to his desk, took a seat, and got to work on an open ledger.

CHAPTER 33
A PROPOSAL GOES AWRY

Returning to the scene of the crime is not recommended, dear reader. ~ The new editor's first article in May 21, 1818 issue of *The Tattler*.

Meanwhile...

When the red phaeton was nearly in front of Lord Weatherstone's mansion, Felix Turnbridge struggled to slow down the headstrong Juno as they pulled up to the curb. He was down from the phaeton in two steps, offering Emelia assistance in another five, and feeling ever so relieved when she allowed him to simply lift her down from the phaeton by placing his hands on either side of her waist.

Holding out his arm, he forced himself to walk slowly as he led her to the front door of the residence, a butler opening the door even before they had gone up the front steps and past the Ionic columns flanking the door.

"We're in need of the gardens," Felix said, pulling a calling card from his waistcoat pocket.

Obviously having heard the same plea in the past, the butler simply stepped aside and allowed them in. "This way," he said as he led them to a set of glass doors at the back of the ballroom. "The fountain is down and to your right," he added as he opened the doors.

"Thank you," Felix said with a nod as he led Emelia through the doors and down the flagged terraces. He slowed his steps as the heady fragrance of late spring flowers filled his nostrils. "Do you remember where you were when I kissed you here?" he asked as they passed by several hedgerows, the tall shrubs making up a faux maze through the back half of the gardens.

Emelia glanced about, surprised at how different the gardens looked in the morning light. "Here, I think," she said as she led them between two hedgerows.

"And the last time you were in these gardens?" he asked, knowing she had been here during Lord Weatherstone's ball despite her claim that she spent the entire evening in the ballroom.

She allowed a shrug. "Here, as well. I was watching Lady Jane, and then Lady Lucida, and then Lady Victoria as they were being kissed by Lord Bellingham," she said as she pointed to an opening in the branches.

The earl's eyes widened at hearing the list of women Stephen Slater had kissed that night during the ball. "It wasn't the Earl of Bellingham, you know," Felix said with a hint of amusement.

Emelia gave him a quelling glance. "I know that now. It was his brother, Stephen," she agreed, remembering the comments about how the two Slater boys looked so much alike they could trade places—and apparently had for a time.

Her cousin, Victoria, was now married to the bastard of the Marquess of Devonville. Apparently, three times was the charm when it came to kissing.

"Aye. The bastard," Felix murmured, a slight grin lighting his face. He lowered his forehead to hers and took a deep breath, willing himself to calm down and consider what he was about to do.

"Are you about to propose marriage?" Emelia asked.

Felix blinked. "Well, I was about to, yes," he admitted carefully. "Why did you think we came back here?"

Emelia had to suppress a giggle. "I thought you were wont to steal a kiss again..." Her comment was cut off as his lips captured hers in the same kiss he had bestowed on her that day of the garden party.

The same sensation of excitement had her entire body arching up against his, the same tendrils of pleasure had her pulse racing. This time, though, Felix had his hands at her waist, as if he had to hold onto her for balance.

When his lips pulled away, it was because he had to take a breath—take a breath and then kiss her again before finally pulling away to take one of her hands in his. "Will you do me the honor of being my wife? Of having my children, and of being my countess?" he asked before kissing her knuckles.

Emelia stilled herself for a moment, her thoughts about the earl rather scattered. He could certainly kiss well, she considered, which had to count for something in a relationship that entailed the need to produce an heir. He would probably be a generous lover in their marriage bed, seeing to her pleasure before he took his own.

Although she wasn't really supposed to know of such things, she was three-and-twenty. The whispers and titters of matrons younger than she had her well-versed in what happened in a marriage bed.

On the other hand, though, the man had blackmailed her. Had tricked her into sharing bits of gossip. Had made her life a rather uncomfortable one these past two months.

Was he really the one she wanted to spend the rest of her life with?

"You never told me *why* you blackmailed me," she finally answered.

Felix blinked. And blinked again as he straightened. "I wanted you to have a reason to meet with me," he replied simply. "My way of courting you without your knowing it. And I suppose I wanted to be sure you weren't like the others."

Emelia shook her head. "Whatever do you mean?"

Sighing, Felix realized he wasn't explaining himself very well. "I cannot abide a malicious gossiper," he stated. "I had to be sure you weren't like the rest of the gossips," he added quickly. "And you aren't. You don't even know *how* to gossip. And I don't think you want to know. You'd be incapable of it as you always seem to see the best in your peers."

Taking a step back, so that she was nearly pressed against the back wall of the gardens, Emelia shook her head. "I'm afraid I don't see the best in you right now, though, my lord," she murmured.

Felix swallowed. "Wh... what?" The word came out sounding a bit strangled, and his expression was once again the one he displayed the week before, when he had left her on the park bench.

"You *blackmailed* me. You've made these past two months nearly intolerable. Two months that should have been enjoyable because I haven't been in London in an age, and all because you were *testing* me?" she half-questioned, her ire increasing with each point she made.

Felix shook his head. "It wasn't like that," he countered. "I... I grew fond of you. I found myself looking forward to our meetings..."

"Oh, did you now? You looked *forward* to them whilst I *dreaded* them," she replied, tears collecting in the corners of her eyes. "How dare you?" she whispered.

Before Felix quite knew what was happening, Emelia slipped through the slight opening in the hedgerow. Stunned at her sudden disappearance and realizing he couldn't begin to fit through the same opening, Felix exited the hedgerow maze the way they had gone in, looking left and right as he did so. "Emelia!" he called out. *Oh, damn it all to hell. I've gone and made a cake of this*, he realized as he headed toward the fountain, hoping he would find her there.

But Emelia wasn't by the fountain. Nor was she near the statue of Cupid, nor under the apple tree. Thinking he might find her behind another hedgerow, Felix made his way along every one, glancing this way and that, but to no avail.

Emelia was gone.

Crestfallen, the earl made his way back to the house, the butler opening the French doors before he reached them.

When the butler seemed concerned at only seeing Felix, the earl regarded him for a moment. "I take it Lady Emelia already left?" he half-asked.

The butler shook his head. "She has not come through these doors, my lord," he replied. When his gaze shifted sideways, Felix frowned.

"Is there another way out of the gardens?"

Nodding, the butler said, "There is a door to the alley, at the very back of the gardens." He didn't admit there was also a gate at the front, figuring no one but the gardener ever used it.

Felix sighed, feeling ever the fool. "She's gone then," he murmured.

The butler gave a shrug. "But probably not far, my lord."

About to take his leave of Lord Weatherstone's house through the front door—he remembered he hadn't hobbled Juno and feared she and his phaeton might be long gone by now—he paused when he realized what the butler had said.

"Whatever do you mean?" he asked.

Straightening to his full five-foot, six-inch height, the butler said, "The Aimsley residence is just two doors down, my lord," he said as he pointed south.

Felix nodded and thanked the man, deciding he would pay a call on the Earl of Aimsley.

Something I should have done first, he thought to himself.

CHAPTER 34
IF ONLY, IF EVERY

hen is a comedy not? When someone needs a drink. And if it spills? Although crying over spilt milk only makes the mess larger, we do recommend an occasional cry. It soothes the soul and bothers the male persuasion like nothing else.~ The new editor's first article in the May 21, 1818 issue of *The Tattler.*

few minutes later...

Patience Waterford Comber, Countess of Aimsley, was enjoying a cup of tea in her salon overlooking the back gardens when a sudden movement there caught her eye. Startled, she set aside her cup and saucer, wondering what—or who— had entered the modest garden from the alley. Not yet ten o' clock in the morning, she rather doubted a thief would attempt entry into the house at this hour of the day.

Hurrying to stand before the window, she pulled back the sheers to see her daughter leaning against the back gate. Obviously in distress, Emelia held one arm across her middle and one hand over her face as she slowly slid down the gate into a heap of muslin and superfine.

Running from the salon—there was no door to the backyard

from the room—Patience rushed through the hall and into the conservatory, passing her husband's study on the way.

Startled when he realized someone had rushed past the open door of his study, the Earl of Aimsley stood up and was about to look out when his butler appeared.

"My lord, the Earl of Fennington is paying a call. Should I let him know you're in residence?" Hummel asked as he held out a calling card. The earl took it, his brows furrowing as he studied the words on the card.

"Yes," he murmured, glancing around the threshold. "I suppose he's brought Lady Emelia home."

The butler blinked before giving his head a quick shake. "Lady Emelia is not with the earl, my lord."

It was the Earl of Aimsley's turn to blink. "Who was that... running by just now?" he asked, thinking it might have been Lady Emelia, hoping she wouldn't be caught in the company of the Earl of Fennington.

Hummel blinked again. "I'm sure I don't know what you mean, my lord. I've just come from the vestibule."

The earl nodded, deciding he would allow the butler a bit of leeway. Emelia was Hummel's favorite, and the man was no doubt protecting the young woman. "Leave him in the vestibule for a few minutes. I need to check on the females of the household," he ordered and turned to be sure there was a decanter of brandy on the console behind his desk.

Christ! It's not even noon, and I need a drink!

Lady Aimsley hurried to join her daughter at the back gate of the grounds of Aimsley House and lowered herself to the ground next to Emelia. "What is it, Emmy?" she asked, her short breaths a testament to just how quickly she had made her exit from the manor house.

Emelia whimpered in response. "I've made a cake of it, Mother," she replied with a sniffle, a hanky finally appearing from her pocket.

"Did Fenn propose?" Patience asked in a quiet whisper.

Emelia regarded her mother with an arched eyebrow. How did her mother know someone had proposed? "The Earl of Fennington."

Patience considered the answer for a moment and then angled her head. "Felix Turnbridge." Her expression didn't give away her thoughts of her oldest son's best friend. Of how she had hoped for this day ever since she knew just how honorable the man could be.

Well, except for the fact that he had kissed her daughter in Lord Weatherstone's garden and was doing it where London's favorite gossip monger could see.

Emelia allowed a nod. "The very same," she acknowledged sadly.

The countess allowed her back to lean against the fence, her shoulders sagging in the process. "I knew he was in the market for a wife. I'm rather impressed he set his cap on you," she murmured absently. "He's..." She shook her head. "Nearly thirty? Or older, perhaps?" she guessed. At least he wasn't in his mid-thirties. There were any number of aristocrats married to girls half their age! "If he has spoken to your father, I am not aware of it."

Patience wondered how Aimsley would react to the news. Either he would be delighted to have their last child settled and out of the house, or he would bellow and bawl about losing his only daughter to the clutches of a poor man.

But Lord Fennington was an earl. Certainly that accounted for something.

Emelia deserved to be a countess. She had attended the very best finishing school in Geneva, and she excelled at everything important when it came to being a young lady in the aristocracy. Elocution, dancing, needlework, painting. Well, the painting could use a bit of work, but she was certainly an accomplished artist when it came to drawing portraits. Why, Emelia could draw anyone's likeness with her charcoals or a pencil.

"I know something about Lord Fennington, you see," Emelia

managed between sniffles. "I wasn't sure at first, but I discovered it quite by accident and shall never forgive him for what he's done. For what he's doing."

Alarm bells ringing in her head, Patience stared at her daughter. "Whatever is Lord Fennington doing?" she asked in a hoarse whisper.

Emelia was about to answer when her father appeared in front of them, his large frame towering over them and his expression one of confusion.

"I can see something is amiss, and since I just paid witness to a runaway phaeton with you barely on board, I can only imagine the worst," he warned in a low voice, his attention directed on his daughter. "Both of you. In my study, right now." He lowered himself a bit and offered a hand to Patience. She took it and allowed him to pull her up. He followed with his other hand, Emelia giving a mournful sigh before she took it and allowed him to lift her to her feet and beyond.

When her feet were back on terra firma, Emelia dared a glance in his direction and realized he wasn't truly angry. Probably just curious. After all, when had the earl ever discovered his wife and daughter on the ground at the back fence?

"Should I be expecting a visit from Fennington?" he asked before they made it to the back door of the townhouse, not adding that the earl was already waiting for him in the vestibule. He had a mind to leave the man waiting for him for the rest of the day.

Emelia shook her head. "I rather doubt it, Father," she replied. "I did not accept his proposal."

"That's interesting news."

The words had Emelia turning her head to regard her father as they stepped through the back door. "It is?"

Aimsley paused to allow his wife to come alongside him and he offered his arm as they headed down the hallway to his study. "Of course. You two have obviously been courting in secret in addition to your once-a-week rides in the park. A situation I am not at all happy to learn," he warned.

"But, we haven't been," Emelia argued. "I am as shocked by his proposal as Mother is," she added when she caught his brief look of disbelief. Her brows furrowed. "Has he asked your permission to marry me?" she asked, thinking perhaps the earl had skipped the courting stage and simply made arrangements directly with her father.

"He did." Aimsley paused, deciding not to put voice to another thought until he had the two females ensconced in the study where their discussion couldn't be overheard by any servants. Word of Fennington's runaway phaeton would be circulating in Mayfair parlors soon enough. No need to have Park Lane residences learning of the unseemly display on this day.

Closing the study door behind her, Emelia approached her father's desk and took the seat opposite it.

"What do you think you're doing, young lady?" Aimsley asked in a gruff voice.

Emelia straightened in the chair, wondering if she had misunderstood his orders. "I thought you wanted to learn what this is all about," she ventured. "It's a bit of a tale."

Aimsley and his wife exchanged quick glances. "I'll order tea," Patience said with a nod to her husband, moving to the door to summon a footman.

Mark Comber returned the nod and offered his arm to his daughter. "Perhaps it would be better if we discussed this in more comfortable furnishings," he suggested, indicating the divan and overstuffed chairs near the fireplace. At Emelia's look of surprise, he added, "It's not an inquisition, Emmy."

Emelia blinked. "It's not?"

Aimsley gave his daughter a quelling glance. "Of course not. Can you help it if you've been the unwilling victim of a gossip monger?"

Patience and Emelia both gasped. "How did you know?" Emelia asked in a whisper. "I told no one of the arrangement."

The earl waited for the two women to move to the end of the study before he allowed a sigh. "Just because you didn't see fit to taking a footman with you on your morning walks in the park does not mean that a footman wasn't nearby," he countered, waiting for the women to sit down before he took a seat in a wingback chair.

"You had me followed?"

Aimsley allowed another sigh. "You're my daughter. You're my only daughter. So, yes, I had you followed," he replied. "I have to admit to a bit of shock at learning the identity of the man you were meeting with." At the sound of the door opening, he straightened and gave a stern look, a warning, perhaps, that they needed to cease their conversation until the butler had finished placing the tea tray and an assortment of plates of biscuits and cakes on the low table in front of the countess.

Patience took the teapot before the butler could and thanked him. "I shall do the honors," she said with an elegantly arched eyebrow.

Knowing when he had been dismissed, Hummel quickly took his leave of the study.

Waiting for the 'snick' of the latch indicating the door was closed, Patience turned her attention from pouring tea and directed it to her daughter. "I know where you were going on those morning walks," she stated with a sigh. "I read Mr. Pepperidge's letter," she admitted. Then she realized nearly as quickly that her husband had already learned the identity of whomever Emelia had been meeting with in the park.

"A park bench on the east side, not too far from the carriage drive on this side of Hyde Park," Emelia said quickly.

"To meet... whom did you think you would be meeting?" he asked with an arched brow.

At this, Emelia lowered her eyes. "Mr. Pepperidge, the editor of *The Tattler*."

Patience bit her lower lip, realizing she should have told her husband about the letter and about the blackmail.

"The one and only," Mark replied with a roll of his eyes. "Which begs the question. Why?"

Emelia took the tea her mother offered and stared into the steaming cup. Her reflection, wavering in the swirling liquid, seemed as perplexed as she felt just then. How could she have been so bamboozled?

"I was kissed by Lord Fennington while we were in Lord Weatherstone's garden." She ignored her mother's attempt at a gasp—apparently to make it sound as if she didn't already know —and her father's roll of his eyes to continue the sordid tale. "Mr. Pepperidge claimed to have paid witness to it, or someone reported to him that they had seen the kiss, and I was given the ultimatum to either provide gossip I heard whilst paying calls— for eight weeks—or else the report of the kiss would be printed in *The Tattler*."

There.

Once she put voice to the situation, it didn't seem nearly as sordid as she had thought for the past two months. But from the look on her father's face, she may as well have promised her firstborn babe to the editor of *The Tattler*.

Perhaps she already had.

I may be giving birth to said baby, she realized. That is, if she ended up having to accept the earl's offer of marriage. She didn't yet know how her father would weigh in on the situation.

"What aren't you telling us?" Patience whispered as she leaned forward.

Emelia's eyes widened. "I don't know what you mean," she replied before she realized her mother probably did realize there was just a bit more to the sordid tale. Before she could say anything, though, her father heaved a sigh.

"I gave Fenn permission to court you one day a week for eight weeks," he claimed. "Now, have you managed to discover a way to spend *additional* time in the earl's company?" he asked, one dark eyebrow arching up with his query.

Emelia sank into her chair, her tea in danger of spilling. "Just at evening entertainments. I certainly didn't realize he was *courting* me," she argued. At the look of confusion on her mother's face, she dared a glance at her father. "So, *you* knew he was courting me?" she half-questioned.

The Earl of Aimsley cleared his throat, knowing his wife's attention was on him. "He made mention of an interest in you," he admitted. "Said he thought you would make a suitable countess..." At Emelia's shake of her head and the tears that suddenly streamed down her face, he stopped and frowned. "What, pray tell, did Fennington *do* to you besides kiss you in the gardens?" he asked, his voice gruff.

A sob shook Emelia before she answered. "He blackmailed me," she claimed. "He made me tell him gossip..."

Although she had started to give her mother an explanation at the back gate, it was at that moment that Patience Comber realized what her daughter had been trying to tell her. "The editor of *The Tattler* is the Earl of Fennington?" the countess half-asked as her eyes widened in sudden understanding. "The *rogue!*"

Emelia nodded. "I didn't know at first, of course. In fact, it wasn't until his mustache fell off last week, and I did a drawing of him without the awful wig and fake nose he was wearing that I realized he could be Lord Fennington. When he showed up today for our last meeting, he wasn't even in disguise as Mr. Pepperidge. He confirmed everything before we left the park and rode off to Lord Weatherstone's house. That's where he proposed..."

"Proposed?" her father repeated. He seemed to think on this bit of information for a moment "Well, I suppose he *did* ask my permission for your hand that afternoon after he kissed you," he murmured, although he didn't seem too concerned about the situation, either.

"He admitted to kissing our daughter?" Patience asked in alarm. "Why... why didn't you say something?"

The earl gave a shrug. "I gave him permission to court our daughter for eight weeks. I told him he could see her *once* a week. I didn't want him rushing into anything he might regret, so I thought I would give him an out. Apparently, once a week wasn't enough, so he took advantage in the guise of his alter ego to spend more time with Emelia."

Although the explanation seemed innocent enough, Patience Comber wasn't the least bit happy to learn that Felix Turnbridge had an alter ego in Mr. Pepperidge, editor of *The Tattler*. "That despicable man!" she shouted, coming to her feet.

Forced to rise when his wife did, Mark rolled his eyes again. "Come now, Patience. So the man publishes a gossip rag. He probably makes a *fortune* on it. What harm does a bit of...?"

Now, Mark Comber, Earl of Aimsley, was well aware he had married a Waterford girl, a daughter from a family that could boast members of strong will and stronger convictions. A family that was known for standing up for what was right and treading on what was wrong in Society. So he really should have known she wouldn't take his comment as lightly as he intended it. Instead, her arm flew through the air so the palm of her hand intersected his cheek at just the right angle in order to remind him of the fact. And to send a series of bright stars dancing in front of his blinking eyes.

"Mother!" Emelia gasped as her hands went to her mouth. For a moment, she felt sorry for her father, but fear of his reprisal had her more worried about her mother.

"Gossip, I'll have you know, is the single most destructive force in the *ton*," Patience stated between gritted teeth. "It has sent perfectly behaved young ladies into awful marriages. It forced Lady Brougham to leave London. It kept Lord Thorncastle from considering the only love of his life to be his wife— for over ten years—and it cost my sister her marriage. It nearly cost *you* your younger son." She was about to go on, but her husband had gathered her into his arms and pulled her head against his shoulder.

Emelia wondered if he was truly consoling her or just making sure she couldn't hit him again. There was a bright red mark where her mother's hand had landed on his cheek. Apparently, her mother had taken lessons from her sons in how to hit. Either that, or she had been a tomboy in her youth, too.

"I wish to apologize, my lady," he whispered hoarsely. "As one who does not believe anything unless I have either been there to see it for myself or was the one doing it, I had no idea others would believe such twaddle, especially from the pages of a rag claiming to be a news sheet." He paused a moment and regarded his daughter from the corner of his eye. "As for our daughter, I suppose we need to think on her situation..." Even before he could finish his thought, he could feel his wife stiffen in his arms.

"She is not marrying Lord Fennington," Patience stated firmly.

"Not for the time being, anyway," he agreed with a nod. When his wife pulled away to regard him, obviously shocked by his words, he added, "Perhaps we should hear *her* thoughts on the matter."

Emelia gave a squeak. "Whatever do you mean?"

After seeing to seating Patience on the divan, the earl settled back into his wingback chair and sighed. "Come now. You wanted to marry the man not eight weeks ago..."

"When I thought he was an honorable man," she interrupted.

"Until you discovered he was someone else in *addition* to being the Earl of Fennington."

Emelia blinked as she considered her father's words. "True, but I certainly don't wish to marry him *now*," she claimed. "He blackmailed me!"

"Because he wanted an excuse to see you more often. He wanted you to be the first person he spent time with on Thursday mornings. And he discovered how much he enjoyed his time with you," Mark said quietly. "I believe his comment was something like, 'I had no idea how pleasant a morning could be until such time as I had the privilege of spending mornings with your daughter. She hasn't a mean bone in her body and only sees the best in her peers.'

"He's quite in love with you, Emmy."

Emelia stared at her father for a long time, well aware that her mother was giving him the same look of disbelief as she was doing at that very moment. "You gave him permission to marry me, didn't you?" she accused, her voice quavering.

Mark nodded and then bobbed his head from side to side. "Not exactly, but I didn't forbid him from doing so. To be fair, I didn't realize he was using your supposed knowledge of gossip as an excuse to meet with you. I merely thought you were meeting him in the park because you felt affection for him."

Emelia's eyes were as wide as they could be at hearing her father's comments. "I despise Mr. Pepperidge!" she retorted, her head shaking in disbelief.

"How do you feel about Felix Turnbridge?"

The earl's daughter held her breath a moment before letting it go. Panic seemed to grip her. Had the Earl of Fennington promised something in return for her hand in marriage? Had he turned down her dowry? Or had her father promised...? She blinked and forced herself to stop breathing so quickly. If she wasn't careful, she would faint, and she never fainted. Ever! "He's the same man."

"And yet, you must feel some affection for Fenn," her father countered gently. "You rode with him in the park every week for the past eight weeks. I saw the way you looked at him," he said in a quieter voice. "Until five minutes ago, your mother wanted him as another son," he added, his expression daring Patience to counter his claim.

Emelia was well aware of how her mother seemed to sink into the divan just then, her face reddening in embarrassment. She had been the one to introduce them, not ten minutes before the damning kiss had sent everything into motion. "She did before she learned more about his character," she agreed. Her eyes widened as she turned her attention on her mother. "How did *you* know about the blackmail?" she asked.

Her mother's sigh might have been audible through the entire house if the door to the study had been open. "I read the letter Mr. Pepperidge sent you," she admitted. "I saw the look on your face when you were reading it in the salon, and I knew it held what must have been awful news, so when you went up to get dressed to go for your first ride with Fenn, I... I read it." She paused a moment, not at all surprised by the look of hurt on Emelia's face. "I immediately called together my friends, and we devised a way to put Mr. Pepperidge in his place."

Aimsley straightened in his chair. "You were the one who provided the ridiculous gossip," he accused in a quiet voice.

Patience nodded. "The Gossip Goddess. She's really five of us..." Her brow furrowed. "How do *you* know about the ridiculous gossip?" she queried. "I thought you said you didn't read *The Tattler*," she countered.

Mark Comber adjusted his position in his chair, obviously embarrassed at having been caught in a lie. "I... I heard the other lords making light of it whilst in the robing room," he replied. "For over a month, they've been making jokes about non-existent members of the aristocracy," he added with a shrug. "The Gossip Goddess is quite popular, it seems. You have quite the following."

Patience stared at her husband, stunned by his words. "Oh," she murmured. Her face brightened after a moment. "Well, I suppose this is good news."

Emelia gasped. "I was the messenger of it."

Her mother nodded. "We sent it in by post, as well, just to back up what you were telling Mr. Pepperidge. So your gossip would seem more believable to him. I know you're not capable of gossiping. "

A knock at the study door had the three of them inhaling sharply. "Come!" Aimsley called out, deciding there was nothing more to be discussed. Whether or not Emelia ended up married to the Earl of Fennington depended on the two of them.

As for his opinion on the matter, he found he really didn't have one at the moment. That is, until Hummel opened the door and announced that the Earl of Fennington was still in the vestibule.

Now, this should be interesting, he thought before helping his wife to her feet and then turning to his daughter and offering her a hand as well. "I'll hear what he has to say. In the meantime, you two make yourselves scarce." He bussed Patience on the cheek and led them to the study door. Turning his attention to Hummel, he said, "Give me a minute and then bring him here."

"What will you...?" Emelia started to ask.

"Off with you," he replied, pushing her toward the door. "I'll see to the rogue."

Emelia screwed her face into a determined scowl. "I want to be present when you do."

Aimsley sighed and rolled his eyes for probably the twelfth time that day. "So you can pay witness to me challenge him to a duel?" he countered.

Her eyes wide in shock, Emelia shook her head. "Father, no!"

The earl took a deep breath and held it for a moment, making sure his face reddened enough to make him appear angry. "Will you promise to marry Fennington?"

Staring at her father in horror, Emelia gulped.

CHAPTER 35
THE OFFENDING EARL
MAKES AN APPEARANCE

ow, dear reader, they claim love is deaf and dumb. We believe it is stupid, too. At least, it seems to make some people do stupid things, and always with the understanding that they will be forgiven their foible. ~ The new editor's first article in May 21, 1818 issue of *The Tattler.*

moment later...
When he was sure the butler was headed to the front door and his wife was ensconced in her salon, Aimsley ducked back into his study. Rather than taking a seat behind the massive oak desk, he instead leaned against the front of it, his arms crossed and one knee bent so a booted toe rested in the Aubusson carpeting. When the butler appeared in the doorway with Lord Fennington in tow and stepped aside, Aimsley angled his head to one side.

Felix Turnbridge stopped just past the threshold, barely aware of how the butler seemed to slink away from behind him. He allowed an audible sigh and a deep nod. "I suppose you're entitled to put a fist in my face," he said quietly. "Heaven knows, I deserve it."

Aimsley blinked, surprised by the other earl's comment.

The man had the gist of it, it seemed.

"I had a mind to," he admitted. "And I might still do it. But I suppose I should ask you what the hell is going on?" He uncrossed his arms and stood up on both feet, his frame straightening to a height that nearly matched that of Lord Fennington's.

Felix dared a glance behind him, aware the door was still open. He wondered how many servants might be lurking about, hoping to eavesdrop on two earls about to tussle over Lady Emelia Comber. He reached out and pulled the door hard enough so it swung and clicked shut on its own. "I've become rather enamored with your daughter," he finally stated, his chin thrust out as he made the claim. He knew he had startled the other earl with his candor when Aimsley's eyebrows both lifted in unison. "I very much want to make her my wife, but I have... I believe I have angered her." His head drooped as he made the admission.

"Disappointed her, is more like it," Aimsley countered with a sigh. He waved toward the chairs near the fireplace.

Felix shook his head. "I wondered if I might have the opportunity to press my case with her. She deserves an explanation, you see—"

"She deserves a better man than you," the older earl countered with a roll of his eyes. He was suddenly aware of just how hurt the other man was, though. "But if she'll agree to meet with you, then you have my permission," he stated. He paused a moment. "First, though, tell me why an earl, of all people, would own a gossip rag. And go about in a disgusting disguise to gather gossip? Surely you must have others who could do the dirty work for you?" he half-asked with a good deal of annoyance.

Felix sighed again. "The disguise was a bit much, I agree, but it was necessary as I wished to spend more time with Lady Emelia. I was already at the agreed upon limit as Lord

Fennington, but by making her agree to meet with me as Mr. Pepperidge, I was granted another half-hour or so of her time and attention every week. I cannot tell you how blessed I felt, nor how ashamed I am at having pretended to blackmail her in order to get that precious time with her."

Aimsley stared at Felix, his head barely shaking as he listened to the explanation. "Oh, my God, you do love her," he whispered as realization dawned.

"I do," Felix agreed, nodding twice. "I fear I may have made too many cakes of this to ever gain admittance to her kitchen again, so to speak, but with your permission, I should like to try. I owe her a thousand apologies. And an explanation, I suppose. I tried earlier, but..."

The other earl frowned at the mention of too many cakes and hoped his daughter's kitchen hadn't been literally visited by Fennington. His daughter's kitchen had better be in pristine condition! Why, if there was a bun in the oven...

Aimsley shook his head, realizing Fennington meant the words metaphorically. He finally nodded and was about to reply when he remembered there was someone else in the study. Someone besides Lord Fennington.

He glanced toward the fireplace, aware that his chair—the one he had been sitting in during his conversation with his wife and Emelia, the one that was usually angled toward the fireplace —had been turned so it faced the wall. Although he wasn't positive anyone was sitting in it, he was fairly sure it was occupied. "I believe you've had her undivided attention ever since you entered this room," Aimsley murmured as he stepped away from the desk and moved toward the fireplace. There, in his favorite wingback chair, was Emelia holding a damp hanky to her nose. A few tears were apparent on her cheeks, but she was no longer crying. And her attention was decidedly not on him but on something in her mind's eye. That is, until he cleared his throat.

"I used to think having a daughter would be easy," he stated when she lifted her red-rimmed eyes to meet his. "Your mother only ever cried when someone died. Or that one time when Lady Pettigrew wore the very same gown as she did to some garden party..."

"It was the queen's garden party!" Emelia whispered hoarsely, a brow furrowing at her father's odd comment. "And mother wore it much better. She had the figure for it," she stated firmly.

Her father frowned, not at all expecting a comeback such as that from his daughter. "Nevertheless, I have paid witness to your tears twice in one day. Seeing you upset like this makes me want to put a fist into the face of the one who has caused them."

Emelia straightened in the chair. "Oh, no. Please don't," she answered with a quick shake of her head. "And these tears are merely leftover from when you last saw me only a few minutes ago," she argued. She lowered the hanky and angled her head, a move that copied what he did many a night at the dinner table.

For some reason, the familiar gesture had the earl allowing a grin. "I'll give you two ten minutes, and not an hour more," he teased.

Emelia's eyes widened at the odd comment. "You're going to leave me alone with him?" she whispered in alarm.

Her father shrugged. "You've spent far longer than that with him whilst in the park, young lady. Just promise me you won't kill the man. I don't think your mother could abide the scandal, even if she was the one who would report it to *The Tattler*."

Blinking, Emelia took a moment to realize her father was teasing her.

At least, she hoped he was.

She had no intention of killing Lord Fennington. Maiming him, yes. Or giving him a piece of her mind so that his ears would burn for a week, yes. "Assure Mother I shall avoid a scandalous act," she said, her voice a bit louder.

Realizing she wanted to be on her feet—Lord Fennington was tall enough and certainly didn't need to be towering over her as she listened to his apologies—Emelia stood up from the chair. She smoothed her skirts and wiped away the remaining tears from her face before coming out from behind the chair.

Barely aware of her father taking his leave of the study— her attention was entirely on Felix Turnbridge—Emelia dared a breath and dipped a curtsy when he gave a deep bow. She had barely straightened before he was suddenly right in front of her, his hands having captured one of hers to raise it to his lips to kiss the back of it.

Lingering far longer than he had a right, Felix continued to hold her hand to his lips. When he finally straightened, he left his head bent so his forehead nearly touched hers. "Please, forgive me, Lady Emelia. Forgive my ruse. I never intended for you to feel threatened by my words..."

"But I did," Emelia countered.

"I know that now, of course," Felix agreed. "I know you would never tell secrets. It's not in your nature to be a gossip."

"And yet, you are."

Felix inhaled sharply. "It's true, I publish *The Tattler*. I do so because..." He paused, not sure if he wanted to admit just how desperate he had been for funds when he had the idea to profit from what he thought was harmless gossip.

"Because?" Emelia prompted him. The scents of amber cologne and citrus laundry soap washed over her, enveloping her in a familiar comfort. She wanted nothing more than to simply allow herself to fall against him, to allow his arms to pull her close, to rest her head in the small of his shoulder and pretend nothing untoward had happened.

But it had.

Felix Turnbridge was the publisher of *The Tattler*. He was Mr. Pepperidge, her blackmailer. He was everything she loved and despised all in one package.

"I wanted to be able to support a wife and family," Felix finally admitted.

Emelia frowned. "But, you're an earl," she retorted.

Felix nodded. "I was a very poor earl. Thanks to his excessive gambling, my father left the estate in a disaster of debt, I'm afraid. I sold every unentailed property to help cover the debts, but I still found myself owing thousands of pounds to bill collectors. To gaming hells. I discovered my father had spread his debt far and wide, you see."

Shaking her head, Emelia wondered how that could be. Felix was always impeccably dressed. His townhouse appeared, at least from the outside, to be one of the premiere properties in Bruton Street. He drove a sporty phaeton. He owned a matched set of greys that must have cost a fortune at Tattersall's as well as a Percheron that was his prized possession. "No one would believe you are poor," she argued.

Angling his head to one side, Felix sighed. He had never thought to speak of money to a woman before, but now it seemed necessary. Essential. "Because I am no longer poor, my lady. Thanks to what I've made from the weekly sales of *The Tattler*, I have restored the Fennington earldom to its former state of glory. I have bought back the furnishings I had to sell, the lands adjacent to Fennington Park in Gloucester, the property in London. My bank account is once again flush and able to cover the monthly bills and afford me the opportunity to court a woman with the intention of marrying her, and all because people are willing to pay for gossip."

Emelia couldn't help but flinch at that last bit. "Will you continue to profit from gossip, my lord?" she asked in a quiet voice. "After you are wed?"

Inhaling sharply, Felix considered her question. "That depends, my lady."

Furrowing her brows, Emelia shook her head. "On... on what?"

Felix sighed. He really didn't wish to answer the question, but realized she would learn the truth if he didn't provide it first. "On the dowry of the woman I marry."

Emelia gasped and nearly stepped back, but one of his arms

had moved to the back of her waist and kept her close. "Surely your earldom brings you some income, I should think," she countered.

"A bit. Enough to cover the expenses to repair cottages for the farmers and to pay the servants. To buy seed and cover pensions for those who have retired from service to the earldom. But that is all."

Emelia swallowed. The Aimsley earldom must have been far more profitable for her father. She never heard him bemoan his financial state. There had been the one time when he complained about having to set aside the funds for her dowry, but he had made the comment in jest.

At least, she thought he had made it in jest. Was fifty thousand pounds a lot of money?

For a man to rely on his wife's dowry to provide financial support for the rest of their lives meant he had no other means of income. An aristocrat wasn't exactly allowed to work. No wonder Lord Fennington had worn a disguise when he was Mr. Pepperidge. The *ton* would have a field day when they learned Felix Turnbridge was Mr. Pepperidge!

If they learned he was Mr. Pepperidge.

"How is it you're able to hide your avocation from the *ton*, my lord?" Emelia asked in a quiet voice, not the least bit bothered by how his free hand came up to cup the side of her face. By how his lips seemed to hover just inches from her own.

"A very poor disguise, it seems," he murmured.

"Mr. Pepperidge is not a very handsome man," she agreed.

"But the Earl of Fennington? What do you think of him, my lady?" he whispered.

"Oh, Lord Fennington is a very handsome man, my lord," Emelia replied quietly, wondering if she should simply stand up on tip-toe and kiss the man. God knew she wanted to.

Even if he was Mr. Pepperidge.

Eeewww.

"For that, I think I should bestow a kiss on her ladyship,"

Felix murmured, his arms moving to pull her against the front of his body. From her manner, he realized she must have forgiven him. Must have understood his reasons for having become Mr. Pepperidge.

Perhaps talk of money was necessary when gaining a woman's trust. A woman's agreement to marry him.

"Not unless that kiss includes a marriage proposal."

The two moved apart as if a strong wind had blown them away from one another, although Emelia held onto one of Felix's hands as if to ground herself.

Mark Comber stood in the doorway of his study, his head angled to one side as he regarded his daughter and the Earl of Fennington. "I gave you ten minutes..."

"You said an *hour*," Emelia argued, her free hand moving to rest on a hip to indicate her annoyance.

One of Aimsley's bushy eyebrows ascended to nearly his hairline. "For that, young lady, I may *force* you to marry Fennington," he warned. "Especially now that I have your Mother convinced. I do hope you understand how difficult that was to accomplish."

Emelia dared a glance at Felix. "He hasn't yet offered, Father," she replied, one of her own eyebrows arching up in a counter warning.

The earl's eyes widened, and he gave a short bow. "Carry on," he sighed as he quickly took his leave of the study. Before he had closed the door, Emelia realized her mother was also out in the hall.

Faith! Was the entire household listening at the door to the study?

Emelia turned to regard Felix, her eyes hooded. "He had a point," she whispered.

"A kiss first," Felix replied, pulling her into his arms and covering her lips with his own.

Emelia was about to protest, but what good would it do? She wanted the kiss as much or more than he did. A kiss that matched the one he had bestowed on her in Lord Weatherstone's garden. The one that had launched all the events of the last eight weeks into motion. The one that had her imagining how she might spend her days and nights in Felix Turnbridge's company. Imagining a life as a countess of a poor earldom, but one with tenant farmers who were content and pensioners who could afford their retirements. Imagining an heir and a spare and daughters to keep them in their place.

When Felix finally ended the kiss, mostly because he needed to breathe and partly because he needed to propose before they were interrupted again, he allowed a wan smile when he watched as Emelia slowly opened her eyes.

"Yes, I will marry you," she said with a nod.

Felix sighed. Spared from having to form another verbal proposal of marriage—he had asked her in Lord Weatherstone's garden only the hour before—he simply nodded. "Thank you," he replied.

Before the two could give up their holds on one another, the door to the study burst open and Patience Comber stepped in. "Well?" she said, her eyes wide and bouncing back and forth between Felix and her daughter.

"We are to marry," Felix replied with a nod.

And with a good deal of relief.

CHAPTER 36
A GOSSIP RAG BECOMES THE TALK OF THE TOWN

ay 15, 1818, in the offices of The Tattler

Patience Comber entered the back office of *The Tattler* and regarded the fine furnishings and the carpet. She admired the bookshelf and its collection of reference books, rather glad she had negotiated to have them included in her purchase. She took note of the inkwell and the pens at the top of the blotter. She studied the seal for correspondence, deciding it would do. She took a seat in the large leather chair, rather liking how balanced it seemed. But her favorite item had to be the nameplate that the sign painter had mounted on the office door only moments ago.

The Gossip Goddess.

The countess had never thought to run a gossip rag. At least, not before her daughter had married the editor. The terms of the marriage between Lady Emelia and the Earl of Fennington required that Felix Turnbridge, AKA Mr. Frederick Pepperidge, divest himself of the newspaper. Who better to buy it than one of the women who had been supplying him with false gossip for nearly two months?

Oh, she wouldn't be doing this venture by herself, of course. Before she worked out the terms of the deal with her husband's help, she had assurances from several other ladies of the *ton* that she would have help in the endeavor. Help with news worthy to print. Real news of the *ton*.

No fake aristocrats. No false or made up reports.

She also made it clear there was to be no malice in what was printed. No deliberate attempts to make certain someone was blackballed at White's or given the cut direct unless they earned it of their own volition.

"Are you moved in?"

Patience turned to find her husband surveying her new domain. "There was nothing to move in," she replied as she approached him. She placed a kiss on his cheek as he took her hand in his, intending to lift it to his lips. "It's all here," she added with a wave of her free hand.

Mark Comber gave a nod of appreciation. "Christ, that desk is as large as mine," he murmured. "Are you sure we can't get you something a bit more... petite?"

His countess aimed an elegantly arched eyebrow in his direction. "I rather like this desk, and all the other furnishings, truth be told. I think I'll be keeping everything just the way it is."

The earl nodded. "I spoke with your pressman. He's amenable to continue to work here. I may have offered him a bit more blunt to see to it he does. No use having a newspaper if you don't have someone to print the damn thing," he commented.

"Can I afford to give him a raise?" Patience asked in alarm.

Suppressing the urge to laugh at her, Aimsley angled his head to one side. "My darling, your charities are going to find their coffers quite full in a matter of months," he replied. "I have to give Fenn a good deal of credit for coming up with a way to pay off his father's debts so expediently. Turns out our daughter didn't marry a pauper after all, and as long as Fenn doesn't gamble away her dowry, they should be set for life."

Patience gave her husband another peck on the cheek.

"Thank you."

The earl's brows ascended. "For what?"

"For knowing better than the rest of us." At Aimsley's continued look of confusion, she added, "You gave him the benefit of the doubt. You knew Fenn loved our daughter..."

"Because he told me he did," he replied. "Well, I don't think he used the word *love* exactly, but a man knows when another is smitten. He was smitten."

Patience kissed him again, this time on the lips.

"What was that for?" he asked in a whisper.

"For agreeing to buy this business so that our daughter could marry him."

He nodded and glanced back at the desk, its smooth surface completely free of the stacks of letters that had arrived in the past couple of weeks. Patience had placed them in organized piles on the credenza behind the desk in an effort to provide some order to the chaos she had inherited upon the purchase of *The Tattler*.

"What is it?" Patience asked as she followed his gaze to the desk.

Aimsley arched a mischievous eyebrow and kicked the office door shut. "I think it's time we create some gossip of our own," he remarked, moving Patience until the back of her thighs were up against the edge of the desk. She gave a yelp as he lifted her bottom onto the desktop and then fumbled with the fastenings of his breeches.

Her eyes wide, Patience had to place her hands behind her and straighten her arms to keep from falling backwards. "You mean, something like, *The Gossip Goddess tumbled on her own desktop by a rogue. See page 6?*"

"Rogue?" Aimsley repeated. He paused to give that some consideration and then quickly reached down to pull up her skirts and petticoats. "I was thinking something like, 'highwayman' or 'Rake of London'."

Never having seen her husband lower his breeches in broad

daylight, Patience had to suppress a cry of surprise at seeing his tumescence emerge fully erect.

"What about 'Earl of Erection'?" she offered, one eyebrow arching up to waggle a bit. *Faith!* He was certainly ready for a tumble!

"Oh, that's good," he replied as he stepped forward and impaled her in one thrust, his hands bunching her skirts against her belly. His face ended up pressed between her breasts, his breaths shallow as her legs wrapped around his back. Still supported on her arms, Patience allowed her head to fall back as her husband had his way with her, one of his thumbs working its magic against her ripening womanhood as his thrusts deepened and quickened in rhythm. The thought of a particular broadsword came to mind somewhere in the middle of a thrust, and Patience inhaled sharply.

Perhaps because of her sudden intake of breath, the earl growled. That sound and how his body stiffened in anticipation had Patience wrapping her arms around his shoulders. She held on as the welcome waves of pleasure coursed through her body. "Aimsley," she managed to whisper before she felt his body spasm and the wash of warmth fill her lower body.

The earl inhaled sharply and held on for a minute more before wrapping his arms around her waist. "I haven't done anything this scandalous since I tumbled you in Lord Weatherstone's library," he whispered hoarsely.

Patience couldn't help but giggle. "That was ages ago," she replied, her breaths still short.

"The night Emelia was conceived," he murmured before taking a deep breath.

But Patience gasped at the comment. "You think so?"

Her husband nodded. "I do. Which is why I thought it rather fitting she ended up being ruined on the same property. She's in good company."

Patience kissed him on the cheek. "I hardly think being kissed in Lord Weatherstone's gardens counts as ruination, especially when no one actually saw them," she countered. "But it is fitting." She sighed.

Aimsley took another deep breath. "Well, now that we've indoctrinated your desk, I suppose I should let you get to it," he said, refastening his breeches.

His wife allowed a sigh of disappointment. "We could indoctrinate the carpet. I had it cleaned only yesterday," she countered.

Mark Comber stared at his countess for several seconds, a shocked look on his face. "Oh, my. If we're not careful you're going to cause as much gossip as you see fit to print!"

Patience allowed a teasing grin. "Well, I *am* The Gossip Goddess," she replied happily. "And you are the Earl of..."

Aimsley placed a finger over her lips. "Will be. Later," he whispered, not about to let her put voice to his new moniker. Replacing his finger with his lips, he kissed her as he put her skirts and petticoats to rights.

"I had better get an exclusive," she whispered when he finally ended the kiss and pulled away.

"You always do, my goddess. You always do."

CHAPTER 37
A WEDDING NIGHT WITH A WANTON WIFE

Three months later

"May we do that again?" Emelia whispered once she was aware Felix no longer breathed so deeply. He had her held against his body so she was nearly atop him, her head resting on his chest.

She hardly knew the whereabouts of the rest of her body. The man had seen to it nearly every inch of her was either kissed, or licked, or touched, or rubbed, or suckled until she could hardly breathe. Every part of her seemed to tingle, or vibrate, or hum, or buzz.

Her mother had warned her it might be so. She had also cautioned that it might not be so pleasurable, which had her wondering if her father still did this with her mother.

She quickly shook the thought from her mind, concentrating instead on the burble of laughter that she felt beneath her ear. Lifting her head, she found Felix regarding her with a huge grin. His heavy-lidded eyes betrayed the short nap he had taken following their earlier lovemaking.

"Do you mean right now or... in general?" he asked in a hoarse whisper.

Emelia smoothed a hand over his bare chest, the pads of her

fingers barely touching his skin. "Both?" she ventured, gasping when she felt his manhood harden against her belly.

Well, she supposed she had her answer.

Felix's arms tightened around her waist, one thumb moving to caress the side of her bare breast. He grinned again when she reacted, her soft inhalation of breath a sign she wasn't numb from his earlier ministrations. "You're not too sore?" he murmured as his hand slid down to her hip. He reveled in how her skin reacted, how it heated at his touch, at how it shivered beneath his fingertips. He cupped the globe of her bottom, smoothing his palm over the soft flesh and then reaching out with a finger to stroke the damp space between the tops of her thighs. At her sudden jerk and yelp of surprise, he tightened his hold on her waist. "Are you sure?"

Emelia nodded against his chest, and then let out another cry of surprise when she was suddenly on her back and he seemed to hover over the top of her. His lips captured hers in a teasing kiss, one where his lips were barely there and then they were off exploring her jaw, her earlobe, the side of her neck and then back to her lips.

Her hands smoothed down the sides of his body, her fingers on an expedition to discover the places that had him gasping, had his body shivering or shaking. She was aware of how the tip of his manhood sought her most private place, the velvety rod hard as it slid along her honeyed folds. She had a mind to reach down and help it to its destination, her core throbbing in anticipation.

"Patience," he murmured between kisses. "I have a couple of nipples yet to kiss," he whispered as he held one breast in his palm. "You have such a delectable body, it will take some time to..."

"Hurry," Emelia whispered, her questing hand reaching down to discover the balls pressed against her quim. A finger circled the taut flesh, causing Felix to jerk in reflex.

How did she know to do that? When she did it again, this time continuing despite his body's reaction, he growled. He was about to admonish her when he realized just how ripe and ready her body was for his manhood. Giving her nipple a quick suckle that had her chest rising from the bed, Felix lifted himself over her. "Wrap your legs around my hips," he whispered as he guided one of her thighs with his hand while he held himself up on the other elbow.

"Hurry!" she whispered again once her other leg was around his thigh.

"At your service, my lady," he managed before he entered her, aware of how her ankles had interlocked each other behind the small of his back.

The thought of those shapely ankles had his breaths coming faster. He had caught sight of one of them as he had lifted her onto his phaeton, although at the time, it had been covered in a silk stocking. Now both were bare, as was the rest of her body.

Her nightrail had long ago been stripped from her, his hands smoothing it up and over her body as his lips kissed her from her ankles to her neck. Once it was over her head, he had continued his kisses and strokes and all manner of pleasuring her. Meanwhile, her arms were trapped above her head, encased in the fine lawn sleeves, making it impossible for her hands to deter him from his mission.

At least, for a few minutes.

Once his tongue had dipped between her thighs to find her womanhood and stroke it two or three times, she had finished pulling the nightrail from her arms and used her fingernails to stroke his scalp. The memory of it had his entire body shivering in response.

Now he wondered how he would hold on, how he would delay his ecstasy given her behavior. Her anxious demand had him almost too excited. He would have pushed into her more slowly in deference to her first night as his wife, but her hands had taken hold of his buttocks and pulled him into her—hard. Her wet haven, as tight as it had been the first time he had taken her earlier that night, seemed to undulate around his cock. He groaned in response as she gasped his name.

Gently! he forced himself to think, although nothing about what she was doing would suggest a gently bred young lady.

He kissed her then, his lips sliding over hers in a series of short, sweet kisses. "Demure, you are not, my sweeting," he murmured, pulling himself out of her an inch or so.

She shook her head. "Should I be? Now, I mean? Because I thought..."

He kissed her again, swallowing her words. When he pulled away, he pushed into her again. "No, not in our marriage bed," he managed to get out before he readied himself for another thrust. "You can be as undemure as you like."

When she pushed against him as hard as he pushed into her, Felix nearly let out a curse. "Am I doing this right?" she whispered.

Leaning down to kiss her one last time, he murmured, "Oh, yes." Another thrust, and then another and stars appeared before his eyes. Emelia, her head thrown back into the pillow so her neck was completely exposed, cried out his name as her hands gripped the sides of his body. When he was completely spent, the spasms of pleasure having subsided to occasional tickles and twitches, Felix slowly lowered himself until his head settled onto the pillow next to hers.

He was barely aware of her hands moving to his hips, of her lips leaving a kiss on his shoulder, of her contented sigh as she allowed sleep to take her. But he heard her murmur, "I love you," before he, too, drifted off to sleep.

EPILOGUE

ear Readers, it seems it's past time we introduce ourselves as the new editor of The Tattler. The former editor, Mr. Pepperidge, has taken a wife and finds he wishes to spend more time at home than in the office. Fear not, however, for our services were secured for your gossip enjoyment long ago, and we have simply picked up where he left off. In the meantime, he promised you a story about a certain widow and widower who, after marriages to others, rekindled their romance from nearly twenty years ago. We're sorry to report we still haven't been able to secure an exclusive for you, but we can report a certain widowed countess is about to give birth to her first baby. Lord M is said to be 'over the moon'. We have to wonder just how many of those rooms at Merriweather Manor are set aside for his future brood. ~ The new editor's article in the February 18, 1819 issue of The Tattler.

*F*ebruary 20, 1819, Merriweather Manor

"I swear, I was never this nervous when Bess was giving birth," Andrew claimed as he paced in front of the desk in the study in Merriweather Manor. He sobered suddenly. "God rest her soul."

Older cousins Milton and Gregory Grandby exchanged

knowing glances. "If it's any consolation, I'm always nervous when Christiana is in labor. Ten times, so far," Gregory replied, hoping his words might help his younger cousin. "Although to be fair, it was really only nine times since there was a set of twins in there somewhere."

"So far?" the Earl of Torrington repeated, refilling his glass of port. "Do you expect you'll be having *more?*"

Gregory shook his head. "Not really, but French letters aren't exactly easy to come by these days," he replied in a hoarse whisper. He held out his own empty glass and the earl saw to filling it.

"When will we know?" The new patriarch of Merriweather Manor stopped in his tracks and stared at his older cousins. "Will someone come down? Or do I...?"

Grandby had to suppress the urge to laugh out loud at Andrew. "My countess will let us know. Or Mrs. Grandby will come down," he added, motioning toward Gregory to indicate his wife, Christiana, was with Jane, too. "You really need to relax a bit, Max, or you're going to hyperventilate and faint."

"My money is on him fainting," Gregory said with a grin.

"And who is the midwife? She looked rather familiar. Tell me, how can that be?" Andrew pressed, ignoring Gregory's comment.

Gregory sighed. "She's familiar because you met her when you came for dinner at Woodscastle last May. Mrs. Wellingham. She delivered all of my children..."

Andrew whirled around and stared at his cousin. "Mrs. Wellingham? As in... *Emma Fitzsimmons?*" He blinked. And blinked again. "The accomptant?"

The woman who inspired me to work in trade is delivering my baby?

He shook his head several times. "An *accomptant* is delivering my baby?"

This last was asked in a voice so filled with disbelief, the other two men in the study were forced to lean backwards in their chairs before they exchanged quick glances. "Aye," they both answered in unison.

"Where is the midwife?"

Gregory found he had to raise a hand to his mouth in order to hide his sudden humor. *Am I this bad when Christiana is about to give birth?* He glanced over at his older cousin, whose own twins were now nearly eighteen months old. How had the earl behaved when he discovered his wife was about to give birth?

The tip-tap of slippers on the marble in the great hall outside the door brought all three men to their feet. Adele Grandby poked her head around the edge of the half-opened door before she stepped in completely. "You all look as if you're about to have *coronaries*," she accused with a grin as she brought a blanket-wrapped bundle to Andrew. "Max, meet your new son," she announced as she placed the babe into his arms.

Andrew's eyes widened as he took in the sight of the wrinkled, red face that poked out from inside the blanket. A shock of dark hair, still wet from its rinse in warm water, was apparent. "How is she? How's Jane?"

Angling her head to one side, Adele sighed. "She's fine. Tired, of course. Sleeping for now."

"Can I see her?" he asked as his cousins were suddenly on either side of him, staring down at the bundle he held.

"He's as ugly as George was," Grandby remarked, immediately regretting the comment when Adele gave him a quelling glance and a hushed, "Milton!"

"They're all ugly until the second or third day," Gregory chimed in, moving to take the bundle from Andrew. "I've got him. You go see your wife."

Nodding, Andrew took one last look at his new son before managing a bow in Adele's direction. He took his leave of the study and took the stairs two at a time as he rushed to Jane's bedchamber at the end of the west hall.

"Is she all right?" he managed to get out as he burst into the apartment.

Mrs. Emma Wellingham regarded him from the threshold to Jane's bedchamber as she dried her hands on a bath linen. She managed a curtsy and a quick glance at her patient before turning back to him. "She's fine, Mr. Burroughs," she whispered. "Still sleeping, in fact. I take it you've met your son? He has quite a pair of lungs on him, and he's a good six pounds."

Andrew struggled to catch his breath. "I... I have. He does? Is?" He stopped to realize he hadn't even thought of how heavy the babe was. Hadn't even been that concerned about the boy, in fact. His only worry had been about Jane. "Thank you," he added as he took another breath. He stepped forward before stopping again, as if he were torn about hurrying in to see his wife or continuing his conversation with the midwife. "I have to admit, I was a bit concerned when my cousin said you were the midwife," he whispered hoarsely.

"Oh?" Emma responded, her hands dropping to her sides, the damp linen clutched in one of them. Rather tall already, the woman seemed to add another two inches to her height as she straightened, as if she were expecting to have to do battle with the man.

He held up a staying hand. "You were my inspiration for choosing to go into trade, you see, as a clerk at the bank. Imagine my shock to learn... you had other skills, as well."

Emma's eyes widened, and then she relaxed and allowed a wan smile. Although she had met the man when he had come to Woodscastle for dinner—back before he married Jane Vandermeer Fitzpatrick—most of the evening's conversation had to do with the renovations on Merriweather Manor. Woodscastle, the home she and her husband shared with Gregory and Christiana Grandby, wasn't far from the manor and had undergone similar renovations when Gregory married her husband's sister. "I fear I proved quite vexing to your uncle," Emma commented quietly. "He was determined to play matchmaker. Succeeded finally, although I often wonder if he was disappointed in my choice of husband."

The banker frowned. "He was not, I assure you," Andrew said, his head shaking from side to side.

Emma allowed a grin, deciding Sir William couldn't have been all that disappointed. Thomas Wellingham had built his father's business into a profitable enterprise. "And while I don't deliver babies as a matter of course, I've attended to my sister-in-law. She has given birth to ten of them over the years."

Andrew nodded. "Still, it's rather fortuitous you were available. And so close. I know I must have seemed rather panicked when you arrived, and it's only because... I was," he admitted sheepishly as one thumb scratched his eyebrow. "We were in the middle of eating dinner. Thank the gods Grandby's wife knew of you. She just happened to be here with the earl." He paused a moment to take another breath. "I apologize for my curt behavior earlier. It's not as if I haven't been through this before—I have three older children—and yet..."

Emma had to suppress the urge to giggle at the memory of Andrew Burroughs as he grabbed her hand in the vestibule and nearly carried her up the curved staircase and down the long hallway to his apartment. She lifted her free hand to cover her mouth. "And yet, it never seems to get easier, does it?"

The man sighed. "No, it does not," he agreed. "I take it you must have learned midwifery from someone a long time ago."

Emma nodded. "I did my charity work at Mrs. Dawes' Home for Unwed Mothers whilst I was a student at Warwick's," she replied. Having attended the finishing school carried far more clout now than it did back in the days she was a student there. Although she never cared for the classes—or rather, the cost of the tuition to attend the boarding school— she had shared a room with Christiana Wellingham and probably would never have met her husband if she hadn't.

"Ah! My daughter, Sophia, is there now," Andrew claimed, his face brightening.

Emma allowed a larger grin and dared a glance back into the bedchamber. When she returned her attention to the banker, she gave him a nod. "Mrs. Burroughs is awake if you'd like to see her now."

The words weren't even finished being spoken before Andrew was making his way into Jane's bedchamber and to her side.

"Were you surprised?" he murmured as he lifted a hip onto the edge of the bed and leaned over to kiss Jane on her forehead. He took one of her hands in his and kissed the back of it.

"That we have a boy?" she whispered. Her blonde curls were damp around her face, but otherwise she looked as if she had just awakened for the day.

"That you were pregnant with my child," he countered in a teasing tone. "I distinctly remember telling you about nine months ago that you couldn't be surprised if you found yourself about to deliver a baby nine months from then."

Jane attempted to sit up but collapsed back onto the pillows behind her. "Yes, you did," she replied with a roll of her eyes. "Now, pray tell, what have you done with him?"

Andrew's eyes widened. "Oh! Oh, my. I left him in the study with Gregory and Grandby!" he said in alarm. "Knowing them, he'll have already downed his first scotch and smoked his first cheroot!"

Although she might have found his words amusing, Jane's attention was on Andrew's cousin, Gregory. The older man stood on the threshold with a bundle resting against his shoulder, its bottom held up with one large hand, looking as if he had done the very same hundreds of times in the past.

As the father of ten, he probably had, she realized.

"I assure you, my lady, neither event has occurred," the older Grandby cousin stated, but he couldn't help but display a huge grin at Andrew's claim. "Yet."

He moved into the room when Jane waved him in, her arms held out so she could take the baby. "Congratulations. You have a Burroughs boy. He'll be tall. He'll be loud. And he'll be handsome," he announced as he gave up his hold on the babe. "Almost makes me want another."

"Thank you," Jane murmured, her attention on the baby. "I'm so sorry about interrupting dinner as I did. Such a shock, to be eating and then..." She allowed the sentence to trail off, remembering how comical it must have been for her guests when Andrew insisted on carrying her up to her room.

"No need to apologize," Gregory replied. "But I should find my wife and be heading home. Thomas will wonder what's become of Emma. Good night, and thank you for dinner." He gave a bow before moving to shake hands with Andrew.

"Let Grandby know I'll be down to see them off," Andrew murmured.

"No need," Gregory said. "They took their leave a few minutes ago. We all ate the dessert course in the study, and Adele was anxious to get home to her own babies. You've got her thinking of having another, by the way," he added before he gave a short bow and took his leave of Merriweather Manor.

Andrew turned to gaze at his wife. "See what we've done, my lady?" he murmured.

Jane grinned. "Indeed. In more ways than one." She glanced down at the bundle in her arms. "And better late than never."

EXCERPT

Read on for an excerpt from
Book 2 in The Widows of the Aristocracy
The Enigma of a Widow (aka The Enigma of a Spy)

June 17, 1816

Lydia regarded the south side of the British Museum, rather surprised to find there wasn't already a line of people in queue for the Monday morning's ten o'clock opening. Montagu House, the building purchased by the Board of Trustees of the museum to house its collections, featured a series of steps leading up to a portico and a set of double doors.

"On a lovely day such as this, the museum is never very crowded, my lady."

Turning to find the driver of her coach-and-four standing at the curb, Lydia nodded. The clear blue sky was dotted with white puffy clouds. The air actually held a hint of warmth, unlike the other spring days that had come before. With no rain in sight—a rare occurrence this particular year—most Londoners who weren't laboring at their jobs would be spending the beautiful day out-of-doors. "Then I shall have the place all to myself," Lydia responded with a grin.

The thought of viewing artwork created more than a millennia ago excited her. That someone had the skills to cut and carve marble into such detailed works of art meant the ancestors of humanity weren't the barbaric creatures she had been warned of whilst still in the schoolroom in Merriweather Manor.

For every Spartan, there had been an Athenian, after all.

Viewing statues of mostly naked men would have been nearly impossible if there were too many others with her in the Gallery. On a day such as this, she had the room to herself.

She didn't exactly *study* the statues, but surreptitiously surveyed them as she slowly walked around each one. She found them intriguing. Men nowadays weren't so very different from those of two- or three-thousand years ago, she decided, although she only had experience with the two from current times. Perhaps the Greeks were more beautiful. Youthful, mayhap. Or perhaps they only depicted younger subjects because it was difficult to carve wrinkles into marble.

The reclining man before her was definitely youthful, his body barely muscled, his face relaxed as if he were sleeping. She could almost feel his soft breaths as he lay there, one arm raised above his head and angled so its hand was atop his curly hair whilst the other was bent with its hand resting beneath his chin. He wasn't entirely naked but wore a cape tossed over one shoulder, and the folds of a skirt were strewn about his midsection. His feet sported sandals with leather ties wrapped about his thick ankles.

Awareness of another's presence in the gallery had the hairs on the back of her neck reacting.

The sensation of a soft breath wafted over her shoulder again, this time bearing the slightest hint of sandalwood and spice cologne. Stiffening where she stood, Lydia realized someone was standing directly behind and to her left. A man, no doubt, given the scent of his cologne. She was about to put voice to a complaint, but he put voice to a most audacious claim before she had a chance.

"I've been told I look exactly like him," the male voice whispered, almost in her ear.

Lydia carefully stepped to the right and turned slightly, amazed to see that, yes, the intruder did indeed look exactly like Adonis. Or *Endymion sleeping on Mount Latmos,* if one remembered the label mounted next to the block of marble. He was also impeccably dressed in a superfine navy topcoat, an elaborately embroidered waistcoat in red and gold, and buckskin breeches that, at the moment, left absolutely nothing to the imagination as far as his muscular thighs and the bit of anatomy that was located just above them. A quick glance at his tasseled boots, and Lydia was sure she could see her reflection. One of his gloved hands was pressed onto the top of a cane handle decorated in ornately-patterned silver plate while the other held what appeared to be a sketch pad.

"You do, in fact," she murmured, her gaze darting back and forth between the statue and his living twin. "Are you related, perhaps?" she asked with an arched eyebrow.

"My mother must have thought so. She named me Adonis," he replied with an equally arched eyebrow.

Lydia turned completely to face the man, taking a step back when she realized just how close he had been standing. "Did she now?" she replied, not exactly sure how to respond to such an odd claim.

Now that she could see his entire face—he really did look like the youth depicted in the statue—she realized he was older. At least ten years older than the Adonis carved in the statue. The planes of his face were sharper, perhaps, and a slight scar ruined his otherwise perfect face just below his right cheekbone. If he had ever attended any *ton* events, she couldn't remember having seen him at them. Probably because he would have been surrounded by debutantes hoping to gain a dance—or his hand in marriage.

The man was positively beautiful.

"It's been my downfall, actually. Whoever takes a gentleman

seriously when his name is that of history's most beautiful man?"

Not exactly sure how she was supposed to respond to such a rhetorical question, Lydia merely replied with, "Who, indeed?"

His brows furrowed. "You, I hope."

Lydia blinked and then quickly glanced around, wondering if anyone was paying heed to their conversation. If a gossip should spy them speaking to one another as they were, she could only imagine the stories that might be heard in parlors up and down Park Lane. "I'm quite sure we've never been introduced," she whispered hoarsely, and then moved to the next statue. Another one from Greece, which meant the man was naked. *Why did the Greeks depict their heroes naked when the Romans carved them with their clothes on?* she wondered, realizing her cheeks were probably bright red. Of course her attention went directly to the statue's genitals. At least they were on the small side, and not carved in too much detail.

She wondered if the man who claimed his name was Adonis would follow her, hoping on the one hand he would not, and then, on the other, hoping he would.

What's wrong with me? she quickly admonished herself.

He was no doubt a bounder, a rake, perhaps, accosting ladies as they viewed scantily clad statues of beautiful men. But there was something about him that suggested he was a bit lost. Lonely. His manner of speech suggested he was a gentleman. He was certainly dressed as a man of leisure, and yet...

She whirled around, realizing he *had* followed her. He was once again directly in front of her, closer than was proper, close enough that their foreheads would touch should either one of them lean forward very much. The scent of his cologne wafted over her even as his eyes closed. She watched as he inhaled deeply.

"Your perfume is positively intoxicating," he whispered before slowly reopening his eyes.

Once again, Lydia had no idea how to respond to such a

comment. No one had ever put voice to such a claim before—at least, not quite like this. The chemist who had created the perfume for her at Floris merely said it was appropriate for a widow of means. *Orange blossom combined with a hint of spice,* he said, never divulging what spice he had added to make the subtle fragrance. At least, she had thought it subtle. Adonis' claim that it was intoxicating had her wondering if she was giving off more spice than she intended.

Lifting her eyes to meet his, Lydia was startled by how he stared at her. "I really don't think it appropriate for you to say such a thing," she stammered, wondering if she should give the chemist a tip when she next paid a visit to Floris.

"Why ever not?" he countered, a look of hurt crossing his face. "I thought honesty was always best..." He rolled his eyes before allowing a sigh. "You are right, of course. I forget sometimes." His eyes darted to the side and then refocused on her, as if he were trying to decide what to say next.

Lydia blinked again, wondering if perhaps the man was a simpleton. He spoke well, and yet his conversation was wholly inappropriate. A quick look around assured her no one was watching them, at least. His next words had her on edge, though.

ABOUT THE AUTHOR

A self-described nerd and lover of science, Linda Rae spent many years as a published technical writer specializing in 3D graphics workstations, software and 3D animation (her movie credits include SHREK and SHREK 2). An interest in genealogy led to years of research on the Regency era and a desire to write fiction based in that time.

A fan of action-adventure movies, she can frequently be found at the local cinema. Although she no longer has any tropical fish, she does follow the San Jose Sharks. A member of Novelists, Inc. and frequent speaker at book conventions, she makes her home in Cody, Wyoming.

For more information:
www.lindaraesande.com
Sign up for Linda Rae's newsletter:
Regency Romance with a Twist

www.ingramcontent.com/pod-product-compliance
Lightning Source LLC
Chambersburg PA
CBHW031215120726
47905CB00002B/339